MASTERS OF

SCIENCE FICTION

Volume 2

JEROME BIXBY:
"ONE WAY STREET" and other stories

ARMCHAIR FICTION & MUSIC
PO Box 4369, Medford, Oregon 97504

For more information about Armchair Books and products, visit our website at…

www.armchairfiction.com

Or email us at…

armchairfiction@yahoo.com

SHE LOOKED ABOUT THE SAME...

...space-black hair, blue eyes, a little too light, much too shrewd. Passionate mouth, the rest of her built to match. She had on a pink traveling outfit, drastically cut back...

—from "Nightride and Sunrise."

ABOUT JEROME BIXBY...

Not just an exceptional short story writer, Jerome Bixby was also editor of the pulp magazine favorite, "Planet Stories," from 1950 to 1951. In the 1960's he added screenwriting to his list of achievements. "It's a Good Life" was used in the original "Twilight Zone" series. He also wrote four "Star Trek" episodes and it was his distinct imagination that initiated the "mirror universe" concept. This eclectic collection is a wonderful example of Bixby's wide range creativity.

TABLE OF CONTENTS

SMALL WAR 5

LABORATORY 20

CAN SUCH BEAUTY BE? 46

THE HOLES AROUND MARS 62

WHERE THERE'S HOPE 84

AND ALL FOR ONE 92

GOOD DOG 108

NIGHTRIDE AND SUNRISE 116

THE SECOND SHIP 146

THE BAD LIFE 153

ZEN 188

MIRROR, MIRROR 198

HALFWAY TO HELL 209

ANGELS IN THE JETS 237

BATTLE OF THE BELLS 253

ONE WAY STREET 271

THE SLIZZERS 297

THE MONSTERS 309

Small War

People have endured numerous irrational and suicidal cultures, because someone was able to say, "Aw, t'ell with it!" at just the right time...

OBVIOUSLY he agreed with me that it was the thing to do—absolutely the only thing. Looking back across the years to that cold, snow-blowing day on the iceball, this simple fact is my greatest consolation whenever I begin to think of all the wonderful things Earth may have lost as a result of my action. All we might have learned—

But he concurred.

I suppose he must wonder sometimes too, if he's still alive. It happened so quickly, so spontaneously—almost before we knew what we were doing. I suppose he must sit by the fireside as I do—if he has fires on his planet—and speculate on all he may have lost to that planet in one moment of decision: a cure for some dread disease; some technological gimmick to fill a slot; some valuable sociological concept...who knows? All these are things I wonder about, surely, and more.

But it was the thing to do; I did it, and he did it, and all without one single word being exchanged—though naturally we couldn't have discussed the matter even if we'd felt a need to, not knowing each other's tongues.

Don't think it wasn't painful, though. It was the hardest thing I've ever done in my life; it was agony. But I'm glad I did, and I don't give a damn what you think about it.

As for now, I see no harm in telling the tale. I'm too old to be hurt by censure. I've loafed on my pension for forty years now, and done all the reading and bad landscape-painting and deep-sea fishing I ever wished to; and now the doctors say I haven't much time left. So I'm going to tell what happened one hundred and eighty-five years ago on the iceball, and one of my great-great-great-grandchildren—who is a newsman—will see that it gets around. Then you who are reading this will probably curse me for a fool or even a traitor—so here and now I extend my own very heartiest curses to those who will curse me. The devil with you all—I did what I thought was wisest, and I'd do it again.

> People have endured numerous irrational and suicidal cultures, because someone was able to say, "Aw, t'ell with it!" at just the right time . . .

For a moment, the two figures just stood and stared...

SMALL WAR

by Jerome Bixby
(illustrated by Milton Luros)

And so would he, I'll bet.

I was young, then—seventy-six, healthy, tough. The year was 2419. I was a Starman—one of those vital, restless, maladjusted specimens they sift out of the mainstream of college grads, and mold, train, strip of 51% of their humanity, give a colonel's rank and send out to explore the Galaxy in sixty-foot multi-C-drive ships.

On May 12, 2419—I'd never forget that date, even if I didn't have microfilms of my old ship's logs; though you can be damned sure the logs don't contain this story—on May 12 I was in Messier 13, prowling through a clump of unnamed stars I had bypassed in my examination of the likelies (F and G stuff, mostly). I was looking for intelligent life; for worlds that could be profitably colonized; for any and all offbeat data to be added to our growing understanding of the physical universe. I was biologist, physicist, chemist, anthropologist, psychologist all wrapped up in one six-foot-four hard-muscled, hard-brained bundle. I'd trained for forty years, and been on the job only fifteen—and maybe that's why I did what I did: I was also young enough to be idealistic.

THE NEEDLE withdrew from my arm; I came out of hypnosleep right in the middle of my favorite symphony. Sourly, I looked out my port to see what kind of sun had prompted my ship to wake me up.

Red dwarf—an old, sullen devil. A glance at a dial told me there were six planets, two of them gas-giants, another a crisp cinder hustling around within four million miles of the sun. They were out, naturally. The other three—

I pushed the button marked LAND, ate some cold roast beef left over from my last waking—too damn lazy to set the autocook half the time—and held out my arm for the hypo again: we were on planetary drive now, and it'd be several days before we made planetfall: might as well rest. Besides,

Mozart interruptus is enough to drive a man mad.

My ship chose the iceball to land on first: high albedo. It wasn't all iceball, of course—one of those one-revolution to one-year affairs. The twilight zone was -90^0, and that's where my ship set down, true to its tapes.

The needle again. I came up out of sleep, still tasting the roast beef, and got my first look out the port at this unnamed planet of an unnamed sun where I was to commit one of the most unthinkable acts in the history of mankind.

Cold and white; ice-cliffs; forty-foot drifts; leaden skies; scudding clouds, with that dying sun riding an ice-blue horizon like a far dusty garnet.

My ship had already run off a tape on the planet. The atmosphere was high on helium, but it would do. I ate again, took a shower and rubdown, got my heavy coldsuit from the suit-locker. Adjusted the mask—not an oxygen-mask, just protection against the cold—and checked my guns.

I paused in the airlock, in the flank of the ship. It was the damnedest most unlikely planet I'd ever seen. Unlikely in the sense that here was a cloud that probably *could* support life— air and soil readings were all right, and the temperature wasn't too extreme—but it just didn't feel right. It had the dead, or never-even-lived, look; I'd seen a thousand that hit me that way, and never been wrong. I decided to give it an hour: if I didn't spot a shrub or a critter by then, the hell with it; the next one out had looked better, anyway.

I dropped out of the airlock. My A. G. unit floated me down twelve feet to the snow. I lit lightly, and started off in my cautious A. G. walk—if I hadn't had the unit at my belt, I'd have nailed myself into the bedrock: it was a small planet, but dense—lots of pull. Another argument against my finding anything interesting.

I stopped on a ridge about a mile away and made sure my ship was sending. It was: *dit-dit-dit*. I went on, and lost sight of it in minutes. The ridge gave onto a long ice-slope, which several mile's farther on crumpled up into a welter of vein-blue canyons. It was snowing lightly, and the wind was frisking up—hard gusts that swayed me. I looked off in the direction it was blowing from, and saw a white wall about twenty miles off, churning massively, reaching up into the gray sky. Snow-storm. A big one—probably it had been wandering around and around the cold side ever since the planet shook down—the weather phenomena of these one-spin one-year jobs are fascinating.

The white wall came nearer. I crunched along, ignoring it. My coldsuit was a home, if need be; plenty of food-capsules, a water-maker, disposal apparatus, central heating, a face-shield I could draw up if hard particles came along. If the seeing got too bad, I'd simply boost my A. G. to .1% and use my proton-pistols as reactors and home to the ship on the beam.

So I ignored the snowstorm and, pretty soon it was all around whistling and roaring. Small snow; hard flakes. I kept going. I kept my eyes on the dials of my box—it would tell me if any kind of life, from ninety-foot monsters to a single bacterium, was within a dozen yards of me.

They didn't let out a flicker.

Dutifully I trudged along, my A. G. hoisting me ankle-deep in the snow. I'd always hated snow, and still do, preferring tropical climates and warm worlds. The small red sun appeared through the snow, then winked out again like a rat's eye. It hadn't moved from its spot on the horizon. It might move ten seconds of arc in a year, I thought—the planet was steady on.

Half an hour; not a flicker of life. I pointed the muzzle of the box right, left, down, up, probing with the tight-beam for anything that might be outside the field. Nothing anywhere.

I started back, intending to give the other side of the

planet a fast brush and then head for the next one. Farther out, but a brisk spinner. Warm.

NOW I'D BETTER fill you in on a few things. I don't know how well you studied your history-books—but I've noticed that even the history-books my grandchildren bring around tend to underplay the organized idiocy that prevailed on Earth before 2031.

You remember 2031; that's the year we finally built the edifice, proudly, on the stinking ashes of a dozen world conflicts. We dedicated it, and we stood around looking up with admiring faces as if it were something we'd just dreamed up, instead of something we should've had brains enough to do centuries ago.

Well, by God, we *had* to, by that time. It was One World or Bust—with every nation on the planet possessing an alphabet of weapons capable of doing the busting. Italy's proton-cannon, for instance—the grandpa of the deadly sidearms I wore right now. Or America's cobalt bomb. Or Russia's mysterious ray that they could bounce off the Heaviside with 100-square-mile accuracy. Or little Latvia, who surprised everyone in 2014 by suddenly thumbing her nose at the rest of us from the moon.

None of us would *use* our godawful weapons, of course. Goodness, no; we'd fight our wars like civilized people, with plain old tanks and rifles, or even with fists, rather than with—

Nuclear bombs or missiles or deadly rays. Or bacteria. Or ugly, unbelievable gases. Perish the thought!

Now, however, about our little disagreement—

Go out, my friend, and get into a fight with a guy. Get damn good and mad, and see that he gets plenty mad, too; then, if you're both packing guns...

Fists, hell.

So we revised the world and brought out a new edition, to the accompaniment of anguished bleats from the classicists. Morons yawped of national integrity, as if Earth were still divisible; idiots spoke doubtfully of limited war to achieve honorable ends, and maniacs shouted *war* to achieve all they desired.

And everyone with a grain of sense cried peace—for peace was at last unalterably equated with survival of *you*, not just of ten others guys.

Men who had spent millions constructing inside-of-mountain retreats with thirty-foot walls came forward and threw their weight around—because thirteen nations had a pint size missile that could vaporize mountains.

The peace was designed. With an eye to "country-states' rights"—that is, interior affairs were left alone, within reason. Scarcely anything was changed, in fact, except that the first country-state to go for its gun would simply cease to exist. By covenant.

So simple. Hardly anyone wants to die; scare a selfish man enough, and he'll outrun jaguars in changing his tactics. Scare a fool, and he'll follow.

Nice, peaceful world. It lasted for a few centuries.

Then the deep-seated aggressive drives which had always hounded Earthmen again demanded more dramatic release than the simple, successful living of a life; and, as always, misfits and psychopaths in the top echelons leaped to direct that release.

The common man was propagandized, indoctrinated, made pitifully enthusiastic. He was ready for action anyway by that time, having been unable to wallop hell out of strawmen for too long a time. *Lebensraum* was needed; and certain resources; and pre facto security against possible aggression.

Join the Navy and see the Solar System.

Unified Earth began its centuries-long brawl with its neighboring worlds. It conquered and conquered again. Easily. Five times, to be exact—the sum of Sol's intelligent life-forms to be subjugated. In fact races were easily awed or spanked into submission; older and wiser races stared in stupefaction as the sky rained maniacs.

I wonder if perhaps someday that drive will die out, weeded by Time from the mass-unconscious, or will at least express itself on saner levels: if the frantic need men feel to reassure themselves of their greatness—if not of their very existence—by carving their initials across the Milky Way will vanish?

At any rate, we took Mars, and its quiet brown people. Venus, and its artistically brilliant amphibians. Ganymede. Titan. Callisto.

Then we tried for the stars.

We're still trying. No luck yet, that anyone *knows* about.

I WAS THINKING of all the above as I crunched through the snow of the iceball toward my waiting ship.

Oh, I'd been indoctrinated, all right, in case you're wondering. I was a good soldier. *Terra Uber alles*. Earth, the master, the missionary, the clod of Destiny.

But, as I've said, I was young enough to be idealistic.

Actually, I hadn't been conscious of being a rebel during my training-period and my first few years in space. But five years now—five years out in the star-clouds, all by myself, only my own thoughts for company, save for an occasional jaunt back to Sol for a breather...it was a lot like waiting for zero-hour on an old-time battlefield, I guess: in all that loneliness you get near yourself, and you begin to wonder: *why?*

I crunched along, glancing at the dials on my box now and then, and wondering: *why?*

In Des Moines, we manufacture a deodorant powder for Venusians, prescribed by law, in order that they may avoid offending Earthmen.

I crunched along.

The little Martian villages have vanished. Ugly and unsanitary. Shining steel towns, now.

Snow under my feet, and silent dials.

Ganymedians now function on a twenty-four hour day. They seem to have trouble adjusting to this schedule, possibly due to the fact that they evolved on the planet.

Snow. Motionless needles on dials. Red sun through the thinning storm, throwing a bloody glow against the ice-ridges ahead of me.

Of course, there are practical considerations. Mars' mineral wealth. Venus' undersea store of radioactives. Titan's value as a laboratory and observatory. And I must say that Earth administers her Empire capably.

Don't all tyrannies? At first, at least? Build beautiful roads?

The pitfall will come…and the devil with you all, once again. *I* won't be around to see it. Mars, with its barbed tentacles not yet raised; the knife-edged teeth of Venus; the sharp little hoves of Ganymede…don't you think we're due to get our lumps? Don't you think there are undergrounds? Don't you think they're learning? Don't you think they *hate*?

What *fools* we are…we should have gone as friends…

I see, looking at the above, that I have allowed my emotions to get the better of me. But really, when I think of the dilly I put over on the iceball planet, I choke up inside— that ambivalent sort of feeling, where you want to howl with laughter and at the same time are half-strangled…maybe by fear? Fear of punishment? Or by regret, or feelings of guilt, as if you were recalling a delightful but scurrilous seduction?

I don't know. In a way, what I did was criminal. It was

the deliberate scuttling of a great moment, the rape of a stream of thought and effort that had been building toward that moment, motivated by scientific curiosity and now by imperialism, for many centuries. It was a pigeonholing of history. But history repeats itself—and at least *my* hands are clean. Let the far future take care of itself.

I was crunching along, rather boredly, when the dials on my box went crazy.

I STOPPED in my tracks and peered ahead of me, instantly tense, prepared for anything, my proton-pistol ready, clicked on, humming. All I could see was rushing, swirling snow—the thick tail end of the storm was on me.

I was about halfway back to my ship by now...ahead of me, as I recalled, lay a wide, shallow gully, then the long ice slope, then the high blue ridge beyond which lay the ship.

Slowly I swept the muzzle of the box in an arc before me. As it went to the right, the needles slammed hard into position.

The hair along the back of my neck stiffened; life was coming toward me, Monster?

Mouse?

Mountainous?

Miniscule?

I took a reading, and almost dropped the box. I blinked in utter, appalled disbelief.

I read the dials again, with utmost care, checking the figures against the tables in my mind, number by symbol, number by symbol. It was impossible.

The dials said that the life I had detected was human.

I checked the little dial on the side of the box, to see if the damned thing had slipped a cog and was registering *me*. It wasn't—my personal jitters were screened out, as always.

I took a step forward in the blinding snow, pistol aimed at

the spot the dials indicated. At that moment the snows parted, and I saw a far-off figure on the other side of the gully.

He wore a coldsuit; he carried a gun, and a box—which he was reading as I'd read mine.

The snows closed down again, leaving me standing there flat-footed, jaw hanging behind my mask, thinking, *Well, I'll be utterly damned!*...and trying to imagine, while the dizzying impossibility of the moment was still strong in me, the mathematical chances of one Starman like myself running into another Starman working the same corner of the Galaxy.

The chance was vanishingly small, but Fate had turned a microscope on it and turned it up in all its fantastic improbability. Thousands upon thousands of stars in Messier 13. Lord knows how many planets, and how many square miles of terrain on those planets.

Out of this infinitude of places to be, he and I had wound up on the same square acre at the same minute. The same *century* would have been unbelievable enough!

They'll never believe this, I thought. *Not even when we both report it. They'll think it's a rib...*

Another hole in the snow. I waved at the approaching figure. The snows closed in, opened up again, streaming past him—the fall was getting thicker.

He waved back.

I shouted, against the wind, "Hi!"

He shouted back, but I couldn't make out his words.

We each stepped off our respective sides of the gully at the same time, our A. G.s floating us down the white slopes as we sought to get to each other and shake hands and pound backs and say, *Lord, it just can't have happened! I'm AG-1279-13-A...who're you?*

The snow again. Rushing whiteness. When they swept aside, we were within twenty feet of each other.

I think the sense of *wrongness* hit us both at about the same instant. I stopped. He stopped. Suddenly there was an iciness along my back that this gray snowball of a world couldn't account for.

The gestalt *Terran Starman* crumbled. It was the biggest shock of my life, I guess. I can hope for no other moment more stunning, more thrilling, more shot through with mystery and import.

He was an alien. A star alien. So, of course, was I.

HIS COLDSUIT...there were small differences. The cut wasn't quite the same. It was bulkier—or else he was. The fabric was not brown, like mine, but grayish. His box was not of steel but of some dull yellowish metal, and bore a short aerial or antenna—different principle, evidently. His gun was an alien whirl in his hand.

We stood there for about five seconds, each a bird and a snake. His eyes, long and goldish and slanting upward, were as wide and startled as mine were.

Then we did an absolutely preposterous thing. There we were, two highly intelligent beings, star travelers, representing two civilizations which were quite obviously scouting the galaxy (I didn't think for one moment that he was a native of the iceball...the suit, the box, the A. G. unit)...moreover, two civilizations which were similar if not virtually identical in many areas.

Know what we did?

As if our strings had been cut simultaneously, we dropped flat on the snow and became almost invisible to each other. I squalled. I think he did, too. I was trembling violently. My eyes were bugging. I recall that I was sticking my tongue out till it pressed the fabric inside my mask, as if to reject the whole thing.

I was on one side of a low, flat snowdune. He was on the

other side of it.

There we lay.

The snow pushed across the top of the gully, an almost horizontal white-rushing wall above us—the storm was lashing its tail; the wind screamed, and so did my mind. And his, I'll bet.

Representatives of two space-conquering peoples, we lay and practically wet our pants.

A minute passed. I was thinking: *A humanoid...a humanoid! In a coldsuit! Carrying a box, like me! Oh, no...I must have been seeing things! Some kind of mirage...*

Another minute.

Hell, yes, I must've been seeing things.

I poked my head up.

He had gotten the same idea at the same time. We widened our eyes at each other and ducked again.

...He *was* there; and I was. Together we were an impossibility. It wasn't much help to run over in my mind all the arguments against the likelihood of duplication of human form in even the *same* environment, much less in that of some distant alien world...Good Lord, the complex of factors! And it did no good to wonder at the mathematical probability of our encountering each other in this manner—

It had happened. And it was stupefying. It was totally unexpected and unpredicted. I had run across all sorts of lower life-forms in my explorations, and had thought myself blasé...but to stumble over an alien who was practically a mirror-image...

All right, so I'm belaboring the point; you're probably just as shocked as I was. Well, I'm going to shock you a damsight more.

In fact, I can almost cut my story short. It's not really a story, anyway—I'm just telling you what happened. Straight reporting. Take it or leave it.

We lay there, and I began to feel pretty silly. Snow was in my face. I shifted, snorted, felt still sillier. And after a while I got an idea. I would try to show the alien that I was inclined to be friendly.

I LIFTED my proton-pistol, pointing its conical barrel at the rushing, boiling clouds of snow that swept across the top of the gully. Pointing it thus, I raised it above the level of the snowdune that separated us.

I held it there, hoping he wouldn't blow my hand off.

After a moment, I raised my head too. Again we widened our eyes at each other. He'd been staring at my pistol.

He blinked and ducked down again. Turning over on my back, I aimed the pistol at a snowbank some sixty feet from me and pulled the trigger. The bank hissed into white vapor, with a red flash.

Three seconds later, a snowbank on the alien's side of our dune hissed into vapor, with a green flash.

So far, so good, I couldn't help grinning. He was fast on the uptake.

Now came the important part.

I held the pistol up again, looking over the top of the dune. I waited until the top of his head, then his long slanting bright-gold eyes came up.

I tossed my pistol onto the white dune between us; and waited.

His strange whirl of a pistol followed a moment later, came to rest close to mine.

We looked at each other, eyes across the whiteness.

I let out a long shivery breath and stood up. He did too. We mounted our respective sides of the dune, light on our A. G.s, and walked toward each other.

I held out my hand, wondering if the gesture would mean anything to him. He gave me a strong handclasp.

Maybe the most important thing that happened that gray, white-rushing day on the iceball was the fact that I laughed aloud when I saw his *other* whirl-gun clasped to his belt. And that he laughed when he saw the twin to my proton-pistol holstered at *my* belt.

But it isn't important *now*. Nobody will know how important it really is, as far as I'm concerned, for a thousand years—or however long it does take us to come into contact with his race again, whatever it is and wherever they're from.

We stood there. Two worlds. Shaking hands. With those guns at our belts.

And that's pretty much the way things stand now, one hundred years later. Real politic...and a shame...and a danger...

You say the above isn't true? Well, of course it isn't; we didn't let it happen. But it's what might have been.

Our eyes narrowed, and I lost my grin behind my mask. His eyes became speculative gold flames. We were trained, observant men. And equally thoughtful ones, evidently. We read each other in those few seconds. We read our similarities, our identities—in dress, in weapons, in purpose, even in the look in our eyes. We read each other's worlds. Sometimes I wonder if he, at least, did it telepathically.

Then I released his hand, stooped to pick up my gun, and passed by him on the way to my ship. I looked back once. He was looking back, too. Then the snow.

Laboratory

Trying to keep a supercolossal laboratory invisible when two curious aliens are poking around can be a trying affair for even the most brilliant of minds...

GOP'S THOUGHTS had the bluish-purple tint of abject apology: "They're landing, Master."

Pud looked up from the tiny *thig*-field he had been shaping in his tentacles. "Of course they are," he thought-snapped. "You practically invited them down, didn't you? If you'd only kept a few eyes on the Detector, instead of day-dreaming—"

"I'm sorry," Gop said unhappily. "I wasn't day-dreaming, I was observing the magnificent skill and finesse with which you shaped the *thig*. After all, this system is so isolated. No one ever came along before...I just supposed no one ever *would*—"

"A Scientist isn't supposed to suppose! Until he's proven wrong, he's supposed to *know!*" Thirty of Pud's eyes glowered upward at the tiny alien spaceship, only ninety or so miles above the surface of the laboratory-planet and lowering rapidly. The rest of Pud's eyes—more than a hundred of them, set haphazardly in his various-sized heads like *gurf*-seeds on rolls—scoured every inch of the planet's visible surface, to make certain that no sign of the Vegans' presence on the planet, from the tiniest experiment to the gigantic servo-mechanical eating pits, was left operating or visible.

Irritatedly he squelched out of existence a *yim*-field that had taken three weeks of laborious psycho-induction to develop. His psycho-kineticut stripped it of cohesion, and its faint whine-and-crackle vanished.

"I told you to deactivate all our experiments," he snapped at Gop. "Don't you understand Vegan?"

LABORATORY

By
JEROME
BIXBY

First published in "If, Worlds of Science Fiction" December issue, 1955

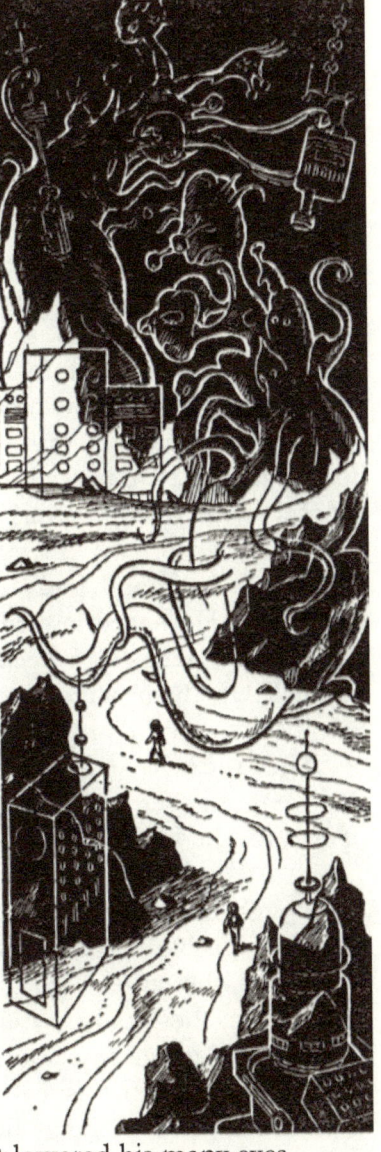

Illustrated by
Ed Emshwiller

Abashed, the Junior Scientist lowered his many eyes.

"I—I'm sorry," Gop said humbly. "I thought the *yim* might wait until the creatures landed, Master...perhaps their auditory apparatus would not have been sufficient to reveal its presence to them, in which case the field would not have had to be—"

"All right, all right," Pud grunted. "I appreciate your point...but, dripping mouthfuls, you know that *any* risk of detection is too great. You know the regulations on Contact!"

"Yes, Master."

"Speaking of which, part of your seventh head is showing."

The Junior Scientist included the head in the personal invisibility field, which he himself was broadcasting.

"Of all the suns in this sector," Pud thought, eyeing the little spaceship, "and of all the planets around this particular sun, they have to choose this one to land on. Chew!"

Gop flushed. A member of the Transverse Colon Revivalists, he found Pud's constant atheistic swearing very disturbing. He sighed inwardly. Usually at least one of Pud's heads could manage to keep its sense of humor, but right now all of them were like proton-storms. The Senior Scientist was on the verge of one of his totalitantrums.

"They must have sighted flashes from our experiments," Pud went on, "before you decided you could spare just *one* set of eyes for the Detector!"

Though both Vegans were invisible to other eyes, they remained visible to each other because their eyes were adjusted to the wavelength of their invisibility fields. By the same token, they could see all their invisible experiments—a vast litter of gadgets, gismos, gargantuan gimmicks, shining tools, huge and infinitesimal instruments, stacks of supplies, and various types of energy fields, the latter all frozen in mid-activity like smudges on a pane of glass. The sandy ground was the floor of the Vegans' laboratory; small hills and outcroppings of rock were their chairs and workbenches. Like a spaceship junkyard, or an enormous open-air machinery warehouse, the laboratory stretched away from the two Scientists in every direction to the planetoid's near horizon.

Pud intensified the general invisibility field to the last notch, and the invisible experiments became even more invisible.

The *thig*-field was a nameless-colored whorl of energy in the Senior Scientist's tentacles. In his concern for the other experiments, he had forgotten to deactivate it. It grew eagerly to the size of a back yard, then of a baseball diamond, then of a traffic oval, and one shimmering edge of it touched his body, which he had not insulated. Energy crackled. Pud jumped forty feet into the air, swearing, and slapped the field into non-existence between two tentacles.

His body, big as an apartment house, floated slowly downward in the laboratory-planet's light gravity.

The tiny alien spaceship touched the ground just as he did. The rocket flare flickered and died.

The ship sat on its fins, about thirty feet—Vegan feet— away. In its shining side, a few Vegan inches above the still smoking rocket tubes, was a small black hole.

"Master, look!" Gop thought. "Their ship is damaged...perhaps that's why they landed!" And he started to extend a tentative extra-sensory probe through the hole.

Pud lashed out with a probe of his own, knocking Gop's aside before it could enter the hole. "Nincompoop! ...don't go esprobing until we know if they're sensitive to it or not! Can't you remember the regulations on Contact for just one *minute*?"

The tiny spaceship sat silently, while its occupants evidently studied the lay of the land. Small turrets halfway up its sides twitched this way and that, pointing popgun armament.

Pud inspected the weapons extrasensorily, and thought an amused snort: the things tossed a simple hydrogen-helium pellet for a short distance.

Gop, nursing a walloping headache as a result of Pud's rough counterprobe, thought sourly to himself: "I try to save the *yim*...that's wrong. He forgets to deactivate the *thig*...that's all right. I esprobe...that's wrong. He esprobes...that's all right."

At last: "They're getting out," Gop observed.

A tiny airlock had opened in the side of the ship. A metal ladder poked out, swung down, settled against the ground.

The aliens—two of them—appeared; looked down, looked up, looked to the right and to the left. Then they came warily down the ladder.

For a few minutes the giant Vegans watched the creatures wander about. One of them approached one of Pud's tails. Irritatedly Pud lifted it out of the way. The little creature snooped on, unaware that twenty tons of invisible silicoid flesh hung over its head. Pud curled the tail close to him, and did likewise with all his other tails.

"You'd better do the same," he advised Gop, his thought-tone peevish.

Silently, Gop drew in his tails. One unwise move, he knew, and the Senior Scientist would start thinking in roars.

One of Gop's tails scraped slightly against a huge boulder. The scales made a tractor-on-gravel sound.

Pud thought in roars.

The tiny creature had stopped and was turning its helmeted head this way and that, as if trying to see where the sound had come from. It had drawn a weapon of some sort from a holster at its belt—another thermonuclear popgun.

The creature turned and came back toward the Vegans, heading for his ship. Pud lifted his tail again. The creature passed under it, reached the ship, joined its partner.

"I HEARD it too, Johnny," Helen Gorman said nervously. "A loud scraping noise—"

"It seemed to come from right behind me," Johnny Gorman said. "Damn near scared me off the planet...I thought it was a rockslide. Or the biggest critter in creation, sneaking up on me. I couldn't see anything, though, could you?"

"No."

Johnny stood there, blaster in hand, looking around, eyes sharp behind his faceplate. He saw nothing but flat, grayish-red ground, a scattering of stone outcroppings large and small; nothing but the star-clouded black of space above the near horizon, and the small sun of the system riding a low hillock like a beacon.

"Blue light," he said thoughtfully. "Green light. Red and purple lights. And a mess of crazy colors we never saw before. Whatever those flashes were, honey, they looked artificial to me..."

Helen frowned. "We were pretty far off-world when we saw them, Johnny. Maybe they were aurorae—or reflections from mineral pockets. Or magnetic phenomena of some kind...that could be why the ship didn't handle right during landing—"

Johnny studied the upside-down dials on the protruding chest-board of his spacesuit.

"No neon in the atmosphere," he said. "Darned little argon, or any other inert gas. The only large mineral deposits within fifty miles are straight down. And this clod's about as magnetic as an onion." He gave the surrounding bleak terrain another narrow-eyed scrutiny. "I suppose it *could* have been some kind of aurora, though...it's gone now, and there isn't a sign of anything that could have produced such a rumpus." He looked around again, then sighed and finally holstered his blaster. "Guess I'm the worrying type, hon. Nothing alive around here."

"I wonder what that sound was."

"Probably a rock falling. This area's been undisturbed for God knows how many million years...the jolt of our landing just shook things up a little." He grinned, a little sheepishly, "As for the landing...I was so scared after that meteor hit us, it's a wonder I didn't nail the ship halfway into the planet, instead of just jolting us up."

Helen looked up at the three-foot hole in the side of the ship.

Johnny followed her gaze, and grunted. "We'd better get to work." He turned to the ladder that led up to the airlock. "I'll rig the compressor to charge the spare oxytanks...we'll have to delouse this air of ammonia, but otherwise it's fine. Look, honey, I won't need any help; why don't you get busy on a PC?"

Helen nodded, still staring up at the meteor-hole. "You know," she said slowly, "it wouldn't happen again this way in a million years, Johnny. Thank God, this clod was here...we ought to name it Lifesaver."

"Yeah, sure," Johnny said ironically. "It'll save our lives. Only thing is, it got us into this mess in the first place!"

He started up the ladder, using only his arms, legs trailing.

Helen got down on hands and knees and began poking around for the two dozen or so samples needed for Standard Planetary Classification. Bits of rock, air, vegetable growth, dust—the dust was very important. All went into vac-containers at her belt.

Then suddenly she said, "O-o-o- *oof!*" and reared back on her knees and clapped both hands to her helmet. Her eyes squeezed shut behind her faceplate, then opened wide and frightened.

By the time her hands reached her helmet, Johnny had his blaster out and was floating toward the ground, looking around for something to shoot at. His boots touched, and two long light-gravity steps brought him to her side.

Pud had been leaning over the tiny spaceship, one of his faces only feet above the little creatures.

Gop's thought came: "What are they?"

"Fanged if I know. Bipeds…never saw such little ones." Pud adjusted several eyes to a certain wavelength and studied the creatures through their spacesuits. He gave Gop a thought-nod: "Mammals. Bi-sexual. They're probably mates."

"It's a miracle they didn't land right in the middle of one of our experiments."

That brought back Pud's ill temper. "Miracle! Didn't you see me give this cosmic kiddycar of theirs a couple of psychokineticlouts so they'd land where they did?" The Senior Scientist glared around at their thousand-and-one experiments, and then down at the little spaceship, smaller than the smallest of them, squatting on toy fins. He curled a tentacle, as if wishing he could swat it.

Gop knew, however, that despite Pud's irritation at having his work interrupted, he was just a little intrigued by the aliens. No matter how insignificant they were they were animate life of some intelligence, and Pud must be wondering about them.

Gop thought it might be a good idea to dwell on that, in order to keep Pud from getting his heads in an uproar again.

"Can you get into their thoughts?" he inquired.

"I haven't tried. I don't think I could keep my potential down to their level."

"Wonder where they're from?"

"Who cares?" Pud snorted. "I just wish they'd go away."

Gop noted, though, that Pud's heads were lowering closer over the creatures.

"They're nowhere near acceptable Contact level, are they?" Gop said, after a moment.

"From their appearance, I'd say they're even beneath classification. Reaction motor in their ship. Primitive weapons. Protective garments...they can't even adjust physically to hostile environments!"

A minute passed.

Pud said, "Mm. Well. I think I *will* see what I can read...just to have something to talk about at the Scientists' Club."

He sent out a tentative probe...a little one...just enough to register in one of his brains the total conscious content of one of the little creature's minds. He was afraid to go deeper, after the subconscious, though actually that was far more important. But deep probing would probably be felt for what it was, while conscious probing was just a little painful.

The creature popped erect in its squatting position, and clapped its upper extremities to its head.

The other one, which had been scrambling up the ladder to the ship's airlock, drew its popgun and joined the first.

"They're from someplace called Earth," Pud said. "In the V-LM- 12Xva Sector of this Galaxy, as nearly as I can make out. They're an Exploration Team, sent out by their planet to gather data on the nature of the physical universe." He paused to consult the third memory bank of his fifth brain, where he had impressed the content of the creature's mind. "They've had space travel for about two hundred of their years. I translate that as about eleven of ours." He consulted again. "Highly materialistic, Externally focused, Very limited sensorium. An infant race, chasing everything that moves, round and round through their little three-dimensional universe. They've a long way to go."

"What are they doing here?"

"Hm." Pud consulted again. "A routine exploration flight brought them to this system…and an almost unbelievable coincidence has served to delay them here. They dropped their meteor-screens for just a moment—at just the wrong moment. A large meteor came along, entered the ship, and destroyed both their atmosphere-manufacturing equipment and the large pressure tank of atmosphere which they kept as reserve in case the equipment should fail." He paused. "Mixture of hydrogen and oxygen…they can't live without it. At any rate, the ship was evacuated, and they barely had time to get into the…mm, spacesuits, they call them…which they now wear. The accident left them with no atmosphere whatever, except the small amount in the tanks of those suits. That will be exhausted in a short time…I gather that if this planet hadn't been here, they'd have been goners. As it stands, they plan to charge their spare suit-tanks, which weren't harmed, with the air of this planet, and then return to their Earth, subsisting on the tanked air, by hyperspatial drive…" Again Pud paused. "Hm. Well, now! I'd overlooked that. So they have hyperspatial drive, at least…and after only two hundred years of space travel! Hm. Perhaps they *are* worth a closer look…"

Pud lowered his heads over the two little aliens, who were moving warily, popguns drawn, away from the ship.

"Pud," Gop said nervously.

"What?"

"One of them is crawling toward the time-warp."

"Well, don't tell *me* about it…lift the warp out of the way!"

Gop extended a tentacle, first reconstituting it on the seventh atomic sublevel so he wouldn't get it blown off, and gently picked up the time-warp. It looked like a blue-violet frozen haze in his grasp. He set it down on the other side of the spaceship, anchoring it again to *now* so it wouldn't go flapping off along the time-continuum.

"So they *didn't* land because they saw flashes from our experiments," he said a little triumphantly.

One of Pud's heads turned and gave the junior Scientist an acid look, while the others continued to observe the aliens.

"They lowered their meteor-screens," he said nastily, "thus bringing about this entire bother, because they wanted to get a better look at the flashes."

Gop was silent, but he thought acidly: "That's what you say—you won't let *me* esprobe, and when you do, you manage to prove it's all my fault."

JOHNNY GORMAN had just said to Helen, "I want to chip a few samples off that outcropping over there...come on, hon."

He started toward the ridge of gray-black rock. Helen followed on his heels.

"As-pir-in," she said, deliberately falsetto, and her helmet-valet fed her another pill with a sip of water.

"Then we'll go back and stick inside the ship until the tanks are charged," Johnny went on, a little grimly. "I think we're just edgy. Planets don't give people headaches...and there's nothing alive within a million miles of this dustball." He hefted his blaster, which he had adjusted to Wide-Field. "But just in case..."

"Pud," Gop said, still more nervously.

"Yes, I see, you idiot! Lift the *tharn*-field out of their way...I'll take care of the space-warp generator!"

The giant Vegans, for all their bulk, moved soundlessly and at great speed until they were between the aliens and the stone outcropping toward which they appeared to be heading. Gop extended a tentacle, curled it at an odd angle, and picked up the shimmering *tharn*-field, which was the Vegans' reservoir of Basic Universal Energy. Set in any energy matrix, *tharn* became that energy; added to any existing energy, *tharn* augmented it to any desired potential. Thus it was extremely valuable to their experiments…and very risky stuff to handle, as well.

Gingerly, Gop set the *tharn* down beyond the outcropping. At the same time he picked up several instruments that lay nearby—an electron-wrench, a *snurling*-iron, a *plotz*-meter, several pencil-rays. He placed them on the ground beside the *tharn*.

Pud had curled twelve tentacles around the space-warp generator—it was as big as a city block, and heavy, even in light gravity. He puffed a thought at Gop: "Give me a tentacle."

Gop helped his Master place the generator safely on the other side of the ridge.

Johnny Gorman banged off a handful of rock, and shoved it into the vac-container at his belt.

"Okay, hon," he said. "Let's go."

They stood one more moment atop the ridge, looking out over the barren, rusty-gray plain that the ridge had until now concealed from their gaze.

"Looks just as dead as the rest," Johnny observed. "I guess we were just jumpy over nothing." He turned to start down the slope. "Come on."

In three long light-gravity steps he had reached the bottom, and turned to steady Helen.

She wasn't there.

She had tripped and tumbled off the other side of the ridge. He could hear her screaming.

"*Putrefied proteins!*" Pud roared. "Help me get it out of the *tharn!*"

31

The two Vegans leaned over the ridge. While Gop forced the writhing folds of the *tharn*-field apart with two reconstituted tentacles, Pud reached in, plucked the little alien out and set it upright.

It immediately scrabbled up the side of the ridge as fast as it could and joined its mate, which had bounded up the other side.

"Now look at what you've done!" Pud raged. "What about the rules on Contact! The Examiners will get this out of us when we report on our Projects...mountains of bites, we've *revealed* ourselves!"

"Not really, Master," Gop said, rushing his thoughts. "All the creature will know is that it tumbled into the field, and then was somehow ejected by it...a trick of gravity, perhaps...a magnetic vortex...it won't know what really happened—"

"That—field—was—supposed—to—be—turned—*off*," Pud said, every one of his faces green with rage.

"I—"

"You are a stupid, clumsy, fewheaded piece of provender!"

Gop flushed clear down to his tails. "I'm sorry," he said. "I can't think of everything at once! I must have accidentally activated the *tharn* when I moved it. I'm *sorry*!"

Pud clapped a tentacle to his prime forehead. "What next!" he moaned.

"Oh, Johnny, Johnny," Helen sobbed. "I tripped when I started to turn around, and fell down the other side, and all of a sudden...it was horrible...I thought I was going *crazy*—"

Johnny Gorman had his arms tight around her. Behind her back, his blaster was pointed straight down the far slope of the ridge, ready to atomize anything that moved.

"What, honey?" he said. "What happened? I didn't see

anything near you...what happened?"

"It was like I was in a hurricane...I couldn't see anything, but something seemed to be whirling around me, something as big as the universe...and it seemed to be whirling *inside* me too! I felt—it felt like... Johnny, I was *crossed!*"

"Crossed?" He shook her gently. "What do you mean, you were crossed?"

"It felt like my right side was my left side, and my heart was beating backwards, and my eyes were looking at each other, and I was just twisted all downside up outside and inside out upside, and...Johnny," she wailed, "I *am* going crazy!"

"Oh, no, you're not," he said grimly. "You're going back to the ship! I don't know what gives with this creepy clod, but I know we're not moving an inch outside the ship until we blast off! *Come on!*"

"They're crawling back toward their ship, Pud...*look out*, they're heading for the dimensional-warp!"

Pud extended a tentacle ninety feet and slapped the dimensional-warp out of the path of the scurrying creatures.

The warp bounced silently on the rocky ground, caromed like a fireball from boulder to boulder, encountered stray radiation from the *tharn*-field that still glowed invisibly on the other side of the ridge, and became activated; it emitted concentric spheres of nameless-colored energy, and a vast snapping and crackling.

"*There*," Gop thought triumphantly at Pud. "That's just what I did with the *tharn*-field...I guess nobody is above accidents, eh?"

Pud thought pure vitamins at his Junior Scientist. "You idiot, I didn't accidentally turn on the warp! You left the *tharn* on, and *it* triggered the warp! *Why didn't you deactivate the* tharn?"

"Why didn't *you*?" Gop shot back. "You were there too!"

Pud lashed a tentacle over the outcropping, and the *tharn-field* became inactive. Then he looked around, and every eye in his prime head popped. "Look out, the dimensional-warp is spreading…it's lost its cohesion…oh, digestion, they're in *that* now!"

Johnny and Helen Gorman were in a universe of blazing stars and nebulae that whirled like cosmic carousels; of gas clouds that seethed in giant turbulence…it was the universe of creation, or a universe in its death-throes.

"*Johnny…*"

"*Helen…*"

The boiling universe exploded away from them in soundless radiation, in all directions…in *five* directions, their subconscious minds told them…it vanished into nothingness, a nothingness that surrounded them like white blindness, and then suddenly it was restored again, roiling, churning, flashing with the bright eyes of novae, shot with the sinuous streamers of rushing gas clouds, pulsing with the heartbeats of winking variables…

And suddenly they were tumbling head over heels along the rocky ground of the little planetoid again.

"*Johnny…*"

"*Helen…*"

"At least we got them out of *that*," Pud puffed. "The sub-temporal field, Gop…help me lift it…hurry!"

"Master, *all* our experiments are activated! The *tharn* radiated enough to activate *everything*!"

"*Help me lift the sub-temporal field!*"

"Master, it's too late…they're *in* it!"

A million miles above their heads was the vast sweep of All Time, like a rushing, glassy, upside-down river…they tumbled through a chaos where Time, twice in each beat of their hearts, bounced back and forth between creation and entropy, and took them with it…Time was a torrent beneath whose surface they were yanked back and forth from Beyond the End to Before the Beginning like guppies on a deep-sea line; a torrent whose banks were dark eternity, and whose waters were the slippery substance of years…

"Johnny…"

"Helen…"

Pud deactivated the sub-temporal field with a lash of a tentacle, and the two little aliens rolled from it like dice from a cup, gasping and wailing. Immediately they started running again toward their ship, dodging between the faint flickers of red, blue, green, scarlet and nameless-colored light that marked the location of those experiments which, now activated and releasing their fantastic energies, defied even the invisibility fields that still surrounded them.

The aliens brushed against another experimental field, and it twisted itself in one millionth of a second into a fifth-dimensional topological monstrosity that would take weeks to untangle—if it didn't explode first, for it bulged dangerously at the seams.

Pud hastily back-tentacled the field into an interdimensional-vortex, where, if it did explode, it would disrupt an uninhabited universe so far down on the scale of subspaces that nobody would get hurt.

Then the Senior Scientist gathered ten tons of machinery in a tentacle and hoisted it while the creatures ran beneath. Gop was psychokineticarrying five energyfields toward the sidelines, with another dozen or so wrapped in his tentacles. Pud silently dumped his load of machinery and reached for something else in the creatures' path.

But the creatures scurried erratically, stopping, dashing off in this direction, skidding to a halt as they saw something else to terrify them, and then dashing off in that direction just as the Vegans had dealt with an obstacle to their progress in *this* direction.

"Pud! ...one of them fell through the intraspatial-doorway to the other side of the planet!"

"Well, for the love of swallowing, reach through and *get* it! If those beasts see it, they'll tear it to pieces!"

HELEN GORMAN faced something that was a cross between a tomcat and an eggplant on stilts. It looked hungry. It bounded toward her in forty-foot lopes.

"Johnny...*Johnny, where are you...*"

Helen fainted.

Several other garage-sized beasts converged on her, all looking as hungry as the first. In reality, they weren't hungry—their food consisted of stone, primarily, while they also drew sustenance from cosmic radiation. But they liked to tear things to pieces. They were native to the planetoid; the Vegan Scientists had gathered them up and shoved them through the intraspatial-doorway to this side of the planet, where they wouldn't be underfoot all the time. It was a one-way doorway, through which Pud or Gop would occasionally reach to pluck one of the beasts back for use in experimentation.

Now, just as the beasts reached Helen Gorman, one of Gop's tentacles came through the doorway, followed by one of his smaller heads. The Junior Scientist picked up Helen, and hastily extruded another tentacle from the first to bat aside one of the beasts that leaped after her.

The part of the tentacle bearing Helen Gorman swished back through the doorway. The head and the rest of the tentacle followed.

The beasts commenced fighting among themselves, which was what they did most of the time anyway.

Gop, however, in his haste, had forgotten to repolarize the molecules of his body while retreating through the doorway…and the moment he cleared the doorway on the other side of the planet, the doorway reversed—still one-way, but now the *other way*.

And eventually one of the beasts, attracted by all the flickering and flashing and frantic scrabbling visible through the doorway, abandoned the fun of the fight and leaped, like a ten-ton gopher, through the opening.

The others followed, naturally. They always chased and tore apart the first one to cut and run.

Gop had just set Helen Gorman on the ground, and Johnny Gorman, seeing her apparently materialize from thin air and float downward, had just started to stagger toward her, when the ten-ton gopher began to vivisect one of Pud's tails. The animal hadn't seen the tail, of course—pit was invisible. But it had stumbled over it, and been intrigued.

Pud leaped ninety feet into the air, roaring. Roaring out loud, not thought-roaring. And roaring with a dozen gigantic throats. The sound thundered and rolled and crashed and echoed from the low hills around.

The beast fell off Pud's tail, bounced, looked around, and made for Johnny Gorman as the only visible moving object.

Johnny's eyes were still bugging from the gargantuan roar he had just heard. He saw the beast and dodged frantically, just as Gop's invisible tentacle shot out to bowl the beast over.

In dodging, Johnny tumbled into another energy-field.

…He stood on his own face, saw before his eyes the hairy mole on the back of his neck, and threw a gray-and-red inside-out hand before his eyes in complete terror. Then Pud nudged him gently out of the field, and before Johnny's eyes, in an instantaneous and unfathomable convolution, the hand became normal again.

About that time the rest of the beasts emerged from the intraspatial-doorway. While some of them continued the fight that had begun on the other side of the planet, others started for Johnny Gorman and for Helen, who was now sitting up weakly and shaking her head.

A beast resembling a steam-shovel on spider's legs rammed full-tilt into a force-field. The field bounced fifty feet and merged with another field in silent but cataclysmic embrace, producing a sub-field, which converted one tenth of one percent of all water within a hundred foot radius to alcohol.

The effect on Johnny and Helen was instantaneous...they became drunk as hoot-owls. Their eyes bleared and refused to focus. Their jaws sagged. Johnny stumbled, and sat down hard. He and Helen stared dolefully at each other through their faceplates.

Pud gave up every last hope of avoiding Contact.

He picked up Johnny with one tentacle and Helen with another and set them down on top of their spaceship, where there was just enough reasonably flat surface on the ship's snub nose to hold them.

The beasts were chasing one another around and around through the wreckage of the laboratory. They romped and trampled over delicate machines, sent heavier equipment spinning to smash against boulders; they ran head-on into sizzling energy-fields and, head-off, kept running.

Pud grabbed up an armful of beasts, raced to the doorway, reversed it and poured them through. He grabbed up more beasts, threw them after. Gop was busily engaged in the same task. Some of the beasts began fighting among themselves even as the Vegans held them—Gop jumped as one tore six cubic yards of flesh from a tentacle. He healed the tentacle immediately, then hardened it and all his other tentacles to the consistency of pig iron. He held back that particular beast from the lot. When the others had been tossed through, he hauled back his tentacle, wound up, and pegged the offending beast with all his might. It streaked through the doorway like a projectile, legs and eyestalks rigid.

Pud plucked a machine from the two-foot claws of the very last beast, and tossed the beast through. Then he examined the machine—it was beyond repair. He slammed that through the doorway too.

In ten seconds, the two Vegan Scientists had slapped and mauled all their rioting experiments into inaction.

Silence descended over the battleground. Silence, more nerve-shattering than the noise had been.

PUD LOOKED around at the remains of the laboratory, every face forest-green with rage.

Machines lay broken, tilted, flickering, whining, wheezing, like the bodies of the wounded. Delicate instruments were smashed to bits. The involuted field that Pud had flung through the vortex had evidently burst, as he had feared—for the vortex had vanished. So, probably, had the universe the field had burst in. The two fields that had interlocked were ruined, each having contaminated the other beyond use. Other energy-fields, having absorbed an excess of energy from the *tharn*, were bloated monstrosities or burned-out husks.

It would take weeks to get the place straightened up...even longer to replace the smashed equipment and restore the ruined fields.

Many experiments in which time had been a factor would take months—and in some cases years—to duplicate.

All that was bad enough.

But worst of all...the little aliens had been Contacted.

Like it or not, the aliens knew that something was very much up on this planetoid.

Like it or not, they'd report that, and more of their kind would come scurrying back to investigate.

Pud groaned, and studied the little creatures, who sat huddled together on the nose of the ship.

"Well," he thought sourly to Gop, "here we are."

"I—yes, Master."

"Do you think that from now on you'll watch the Detector?"

"Oh, yes, Master—I will."

"And do you think it matters a Chew now if you do or not? Now that we've *revealed* ourselves?"

"I—I—"

"We have a choice," Pud said acidly. "We can destroy these little aliens, so they can't report what they've seen. That's out, of course. Or we can move our laboratory to another system...a formidable job, and Food knows whether we'd ever find another planet so suited to our needs. And even if we *did* do that, and they found nothing when they returned here; they'd still know we were around somewhere."

"They wouldn't know that *we're* around, Master."

"They'd know *something* is around...don't mince words with me, you idiot. You know that they've seen enough to draw the very conclusions we don't want them to draw. You know how vital it is that no race under Contact-level status know of the existence of other intelligent races...particularly races far in advance of it. Such knowledge can alter the entire course of their development."

"Yes, Master."

"So what are we to do, eh? Here we are. And there—" Pud motioned with a tentacle at the little aliens—"they are. As you can see, we must reveal ourselves to still a greater extent...they can't even get into their ship to leave the planet without our help!"

Gop was silent.

"Also—" Pud sent a brief extrasensory probe at the aliens, and both of them clutched at their helmeted heads—"their problem of air supply is critical. There is very little left in their suit-tanks, and the time required for their machines to refine air from this planet's atmosphere has been wasted in—in—the *entertainment* so recently concluded. At this moment they are resigned to death. Naturally, we must help them." He paused. "Well, my brilliant, capable, young Junior Nincompoop? Any ideas on how we can help them, and still keep our Scientists' status when the Examiners get the story of this mess out of us?"

"Yes, Master."

"I thought not." Pud continued his frowning scrutiny of the aliens for a moment. Then he looked up, his faces blank. "Eh? You do?"

"Yes, Master."

"Well, great gobs of gulosity, *what?*"

"Master, do you recall the time experiment that you wanted to try a few years ago? Do you recall that the idea appealed to you very much, but that you wanted an intelligent subject for it, so we could determine results by observing rational reactions?"

"I recall it, all right. My brave young Junior Scientist declined to be the subject...though Food knows you're hardly intelligent enough to qualify anyway. Yes, I remember...but what's that got to do with—"

Pud paused. The jaws of his secondary heads, which were more given to emotion, dropped. Then slowly his faces brightened, and his many eyes began to glow.

"Ah," he thought softly.

"You see, Master?"

"I do indeed."

"If it works, we'll have no more problem. The Examiners will be pleased at our ingenuity. The aliens will no longer—"

"I see, I *see*...all right, let's try it!"

Pud reached down and picked one of the aliens off the nose of the ship. It slumped in his grasp immediately. The other alien began firing its popgun frantically at the seemingly empty air through which its mate mysteriously rose.

The thermonuclear bolts tickled Pud's hide. He sighed and relaxed his personal invisibility field and became visible. That didn't matter now.

The alien stared upward. Its face whitened. It dropped its popgun and fell over backward, slid gently off the ship's nose and started a slow light-gravity fall toward the ground.

Pud caught it, and said, "I thought that might happen. Evidently they lose consciousness rather easily at unaccustomed sights. A provincial trait."

He slid the aliens gently into the airlock of their ship.

The Vegans waited for the aliens to regain consciousness.

Eventually one did. Immediately, it dragged the other back from the lock, into the body of the ship. A moment later the lock closed.

"Now hold the ship," Pud told Gop, "while I form the field."

Flame flickered from the ship's lower end. It rose a few inches off the ground. Gop placed a tentacle on its nose and forced it down again. He waited, while the ship throbbed and wobbled beneath the tentacle.

Now, for the first time, Gop himself esprobed the aliens. He sent a gentle probe into one of their minds—and blinked at the turmoil of terror and helplessness he found there.

Faced with death at the hands of "giant monsters," the aliens preferred to take off and "die cleanly" in space from asphyxiation, or even by a mutual self-destruction pact that would provide less discomfort.

Gop withdrew his probe, wondering that any intelligent creature could become sufficiently panicky to overlook the fact that if the "monsters" had wanted to kill them, they would be a dozen times dead already.

Pud had shaped a time-field of the type necessary to do the job. It was a pale-green haze in his tentacles.

He released the field and, under his direction, it leaped to surround the spaceship, clinging to it like a soft cloak. As the Vegans watched, it seemed to melt into the metal and become a part of it—the whole ship glowed a soft, luminescent green.

"Let it go," Pud said.

Gop removed his tentacle.

The ship rose on its flicker of flame—rose past the Vegans' enormous legs and tails, past their gigantic be-tentacled bodies, past their many necks and faces, rose over their heads.

Gop sneezed as the flame brushed a face.

And Pud began shaping a psychokinetic bolt in his prime brain. For this purpose he marshaled the resources of all his other brains as well, and every head except his prime one assumed an idiot stare.

He said, "Now!" and loosed the bolt as a tight-beam, aimed at the ship and invested with ninety-two separate and carefully calculated phase-motions.

The ship froze, fifty miles over their heads. The flicker from its rocket tubes became a steady, motionless glow.

Pud said, "Now," again, and altered a number of the phase-motions once, twice, three times, in an intricate pattern.

The ship vanished.

As one, the many heads of the Vegan Scientists turned to stare at the point in the sky where they had first sighted the ship.

There it was, coasting past the laboratory-planet, tubes

lifeless; coasting on the velocity that had brought it from the last star it had visited.

There it was, just as it had been before the tiny aliens had sighted the flickerings that had caused them to relax their meteor-screens.

There it was, sent back in time to before all the day's frantic happenings had happened.

Pud and Gop esprobed the distant aliens...and then looked at each other in complete satisfaction.

"Fine!" Pud said. "They don't remember a thing...not a single alimentary thing!" He looked around them, at the shambles of the laboratory. "It's a pity the experiment couldn't repair all this as well...is everything turned off?"

"Everything, Master."

"No experiments operating, you nincompoop? No flashes?"

"None, Master."

"Then they should have no reason to land, you idiot."

"You know," Pud said, "in a way it was rather a fortunate thing that they landed. It enabled me to perform a very interesting experiment. We have demonstrated that a crea-ture returned through time along the third *flud*-subcontinuum will not retain memory of the process, or of what transpired between a particular point in time and one's circular return to it. I'm glad you stimulated me to think of it. Best idea I ever had."

Pud turned his attention to the ruins of the laboratory. He moved off, half his heads agonizing over the destruction caused by today's encounter, the other half glowing at its satisfactory conclusion.

Gop sighed, and esprobed the little aliens for the last time...a final check, to make certain that they remembered nothing.

"Johnny, how about that little planet down there...to the left?"

"Let's drop the meteor-screens for a better look."

Hastily, Gop reached out and tapped the meteor aside.

"Heck, that planet looks like a dud, all right...but it's two days to the next one...and I've got a terrific headache!"

"Funny...I've got one too."

"Well, what say we land and stretch our—"

By that time Gop had hastily withdrawn his headache-causing probe. He stared anxiously upward.

After a moment, he said, "They're landing, Master."

Can Such Beauty Be?

The trick, you see, is to find work for the Devil's idle hands!

ON March 11, 1929, while tottering barefoot over a vast expanse of white-hot coals in everlasting efforts to reach a sparkling stream of clear, cold water that really wasn't there, the damned soul of Mrs. Elbert M. Trumbull abruptly stiffened in its tracks and turned its eyes upward. A look of wonder and expectation replaced that of hopeless suffering. The soul emitted a sound that unmistakably smacked of glee, and shot upward, seeming to dwindle in size rather more than could be accounted for by its rapid ascent to, and through, the roof of Hell.

The demon who reported the matter to His Illustrious Foulness was understandably incoherent. Damned souls simply did not fly away through the roof of Hell. They stayed, and screamed, and suffered endlessly. The thing was without precedent—and Hell was in a bad way if this set one now.

HIS Illustrious Foulness blew his stack. He swore and stamped and kicked his bronze throne. He committed the reporting demon, and all those fiends and demons who had been on duty at the Area of Torment in question, to six months in solitary, with only holy water to drink and a Bible for recreation. They left, wailing.

Then he put in a call to Heaven.

"Just what," he roared, the instant the connection was made, "is going on up there? One of my souls just escaped, and the circumstances reek of reincarnation! It was observed to shrink to babysize, just as it flew through the roof. Damn it all, you know it's strictly against policy for any of my souls to be reincarnated!"

The cherubim at the Heavenly Switchboard put his call through to the Recording Angel, who claimed no knowledge of the matter. The Devil's strong language soon caused the Angel to hang up in a huff, after first informing His Illustrious Foulness that no slightest attempt would conceivably ever be made by anyone in Heaven to have reincarnated any soul from the nether realm; that such lost souls scarcely qualified for the honor, and that in any case no one named Mrs. Elbert M. Trumbull was or ever had been scheduled for it; that the Devil had blessed well better look around for another explanation.

Grumbling, the Devil ordered a triple-check on the incident, which revealed nothing. The soul had simply vanished—perhaps Earthward, to resume mortal form, though, on the basis of the evidence, reincarnation seemed not to be the answer. At any rate, there was no possibility of tracing the soul.

If it *had* been reincarnated, then it was quite beyond grasp till the incarnation was over; while if the Recording Angel had been leveling and the soul had not been reincarnated, then not even God knew where it could be, and certainly the Devil could not bother scouring the Universe for it.

Snarling, he took the obvious step of rendering Hell even more escape-proof than it had been—by doubling the guards and turning up the fires along the boundaries—and tried to forget the whole thing.

MONTHS passed. The offending demons and fiends were released from solitary, with time off for bad behavior. They returned to their guard duties, which you may be sure they performed with utmost care, wanting no more of that holy water. They were seen to swizzle extraordinary amounts of lava during the next few weeks, as if wishing to rid themselves of a good taste.

Years passed. Souls came and sorrowfully entered into eternal torment. Demons howled, and thrust red-hot pitchforks at *derrieres*. Fires flamed, and sulphur stank.

The Devil sat his throne and ruled his realm with magnificent cruelty, and amused himself offhours by researching a project that had interested him for some centuries—that of traveling through Time.

In the back of his infernal mind was the notion of someday returning to the Original Battleground, forearmed with hindsight as it were, licking the pants off the Heavenly Hosts and pulling a switch on history.

On July 2, 1953, something happened that had not happened for a Hell of a long time: a mortal drew the right sort of star, inside the right sort of circle, with the right sort of chalk, and said the right sort of gobbledegook.

His Illustrious Foulness was plucked like a guppy from the middle of an important ways-and-means conference and whisked up to the mortal plane to consult there with some brave mortal who evidently had reason to barter its soul.

NIGHTTIME, fog, a glistening London street. Big Ben struck eleven.

"Good Heavens," a young man's voice said, "Can such beauty be?"

The yellow glow of the streetlight, made hazy by the fog, showed that she was indeed beautiful. Also, hardly of the highest intellectual caliber. Her eyes, as she turned them in the direction of the young man, had all the depth and animation of a wax-work Elizabeth's.

"Was you addressin' me, guvnor?" she said.

"Indeed I was... Please forgive me, miss—I know it's not proper, but I spoke without thinking, Oh, I *do* beg your pardon, but you are the loveliest woman I have ever seen. Rome, Cairo, Vienna, Paris—never have I seen such exquisite beauty!"

Her beautiful face broke into a beautiful smile, a discouragingly suspicious smile, an encouragingly stupid smile. "Ga'rn. You toffs 're all alike, comin' around with your fancy talk and tryin' to get a girl to forget her good ways. Ga'rn, or I'll yell f'r a bobby."

The young man, whose name was Peter Trumbull—of the Boston and Long Island Trumbulls, filthy rich—said, "Oh, no, I beg of you. Don't do that. I have no intention of bothering you, really, I'll go on, as you wish, in just a moment. I assure you that I am not the sort of man who goes around at night accosting strange young ladies...especially young ladies of such obvious breeding and respectability as yourself, if I may say so."

The stupid, beautiful smile.

"Well-l-l, now, I guess you may, at that. Now, off with you, or—"

"Oh, but first let me *really* look at you. Please—one full picture of your loveliness to take away with me into the night. Come here, child—here below the streetlight."

TAKING her elbows, Peter Trumbull steered her into the illumination. He peered into her face, noted the full and wonderfully formed lips, the skin smooth as new cream, the blue eyes with their luscious tones of gray and green, the soft yellow hair upon which trembled tiny beads of moisture caught from the fog. With practiced eye he analyzed the expression on her face right down to the last millimetrical nuance. It was pleased, it was flattered—and still wary. And without a doubt she hadn't a brain in her head. Not much will power, either. She had come along readily enough to stand under the light. Without being obvious about it, he dropped his eyes, and saw a bosom so full and shapely, even under her rather shabby coat, as to curl his fingers into iron hooks.

Now he closed his eyes, as if transported by the vision of her beauty. Apparently drawn by magnets more potent than any mortal male could resist, his hands touched her cheeks, pressed tenderly.

"My Heavens," he whispered, and with his eyes still shut, swayed a little. "You're ten times lovelier than I thought. You remind me of my dear old mother—none was lovelier than she—though I've only seen her portraits, poor thing, she departed this world as I entered. Oh, would *I* could paint a portrait—were a painter, a sculptor, even a photographer. Seized with inspiration as I am at this divine moment, I would take you to my flat and—"

"Now, guvnor," she said, cheeks moving like satin beneath his thrilled fingertips. "I can still 'oller for that bobby, you know—"

"Oh, no. I would *paint* you, my child, and, as I said, seized with inspiration as I am, I'm sure it would be one of the masterpieces of all time!"

At last she simpered. *About time*, he thought.

"Well, now, be that as it may, guvnor, I really oughter go—"

"JUST another moment," he said, pressing the cheeks lightly and noting with satisfaction that she stayed…these dumb ones were usually good hypnotics. "Alas, my dear, I am *not* an artist, though God knows my father saw to it that I had enough instruction to make me a dozen. I am only—" he spread his hands eloquently, brought them back instantly to her cheeks—"only a man. A lonely man, in this strange land, on this strange street—a man who in this brief moment has been swept, nay, borne aloft! into an enchanted fairyland, where the fog and the dark are no more, before the shining sun of your loveliness."

The smile again.

A moment's silence.

"You're American, ain't you? You talk like one."

She'd ventured a word! *She'll give*, he thought.

"Yes," he said. "Over on a short stay, and now that I've seen you...an unforgettable one."

Her name, she told him over tea and cakes in a joint off the Circus, was Mary Dingle. He told her that it was a beautiful name, as singularly beautiful as its owner. The smile. She lived southside, but had been born in Liverpool. *How* had Liverpool allowed such a fair flower to escape? The smile. She worked in a shoe factory. *What!* Not an actress, a showgirl...at the very least a model? The smile.

When they got to the door of his flat, she hung back a little, the smile now uncertain, eyes a little glazed by his flow of flattery.

But she simply *must* come in and meet Sis. It would be dreadfully disappointing for Sis to hear all about such an interesting and exciting person and never get to meet her. The smile.

Sis wasn't home, naturally. Naturally...Sis didn't exist.

Wouldn't Mary wait to meet Sis? ...Sis must have just stepped out for a second.

Well—I—I...s'pose so.

A drink in the meantime?

Another?

Another?

Let's relax on the couch.

Another?

Oh, come, let's do the bottle.

YOU really remind me most amazingly of my mother....how beautiful she was. How beautiful *you* are. Poor dear mother, marrying senile old father. Must've been

after his money, you know. Really a wonder he ever manufactured me, at his age. Don't you think it must be frightful
to be senile?

He had to explain what senile meant, as he'd hoped he
might. This he did in a roundabout fashion, beginning with
youth and its clean and wholesome glories of the flesh, so
stifled by meaningless mores, and ending with senility and all
one had lost in that abysmal and inevitable state, and how
short life was, really, and live while you may.

Well, guvnor...I wouldn't rightly know if it was awful or
not. I s'pose it...I mean, I've 'ad no experience in such...I
mean... S'pose I oughter go, maybe I could meet your sister
some other...

One more moment, then...

Let me drink one last sip of your beauty. You have such
beautiful hair... Let me touch it... And those sweet little
shell-like ears... You know, this really isn't like me at all, but
I—I'm tempted to—I *will*—I can't stop myself—I'll *nibble*
that ear!

She trembled like a twig in a gale, and then like a twig in a
hurricane, and objected for a second to progressively more
wondrous enterprises he undertook, and then Peter Trumbull
achieved his heart's desire.

What strategem to adopt afterwards? Obviously, the Oh-
God-what-have-I-done, can-you-forgive-me one. He wept.
Soon, she had stopped her own weeping and was consoling
him. He moaned he was sorry. How could he have done it?
That's all right, she said: you didn't mean any 'arm, it just 'ap-
pened, that's all.

When she left, it was considerably elevated by her efforts
to pull him through the emotional crisis he had brought upon
himself by so impetuously abusing her, and with all the vague
feelings of tenderness and understanding and Acceptance of
Fate that a girl like her feels when a man like him has worked

his wiles, and with the promise that they would meet to-morrow in the park.

Not on your sweet life, Peter Trumbull thought as he went to sleep with a happy little smile: *tomorrow I'm on the boat and on my way back to good old Boston, and so long, Mary.*

WHEN Peter didn't meet her in the park the next day, or the day after that, Mary Dingle went to his flat and was informed of his departure to America. Feeling quite wronged, but not too desperately unhappy (Granny had worried about men) she went about her business.

Several months later, the encounter was compounded by discovery of her interesting condition.

What was a poor girl to do? Her salary was barely enough to keep her roofed and fed, with a pound a week going off to Granny in Liverpool. So it was hardly possible to fly to America in pursuit of the father-to-be. Besides, thinking it all over, even her limited powers of calculation were sufficient to tell her that Peter Trumbull was just the type to brush her off should she appear at his doorstep with a bundle.

Oh, the dog, she thought, the dirty dog. 'E's done me proper, and now 'e's gone so I can't get 'im to do me right.

Now Mary Dingle was, in more than one respect, an unusual girl. Her beauty, for one thing. For another, she was extremely determined; though never about much of anything you or I would think important. And, within the framework of her small array of knowledge and limited mental prowess, she was resourceful. The few data that managed to seep through the stony barriers which fate had placed about her brain were used with fair sense and often with shrewdness.

Probably the most unusual thing about her was that she had managed to include an interest in the occult.

Granny was solely responsible for this. Granny was a mysterious old woman—a little potty, if the truth be known—and the tales she had told Mary as a child had stuck. Tales of leprechauns, of druids, of vampires and werewolves and a demon or two, and the lot of them sworn to be true— indeed, to be personal experiences—and perhaps they were, who can say?

Granny had had books, also old and mysterious, and she had often read to Mary from them, and when Mary had come to London the books had come with her, as Granny was getting too old to read, and getting religion, besides. Now it was Mary's custom to peruse them and think upon their revelations, particularly on weekends, on the supposition that they contained a great deal that one should know about life. They were among her earliest recollections, you see, and so little had been added to those subsequently, that few distinctions had been drawn between fact and fancy to make anything at all appear unlikely.

WE almost always take recourse to the familiar. So, as Mary Dingle's interesting condition developed—and her concern as to her fate—she thought to appeal to the occult powers to help her out.

Half-measures wouldn't do. Mary decided to enlist the aid of the Devil himself. Books came out, and the ritual was gotten down pat, and the plan of coercion was formulated.

Mary drew the right sort of star, in the right sort of circle, with the right sort of chalk, and said the right sort of gobbledegook.

The Devil appeared, a sheaf of smoking asbestos paper in one hand. Without looking up, he read on: "—and it is therefore evident that stricter measures must be taken with the souls on Level B-1956399, if discipline is to be—"

He paused, startled, sniffed the air, looked up and saw Mary Dingle cringing back against the bureau. His glowing eyes widened. He snorted sulphurous smoke. He looked down and saw the starred circle.

"Well, by the heartwarming screams of a flayed thing," he said, scowling. "Called me right up, didn't you, child? That took nerve!"

"Y-y-yes, guvnor."

"H'm, London, I suppose." His eye narrowed, and two beams of bright, hard, red light struck out and passed through Mary's own eyes and seemed to scrape the back of her skull.

She closed her eyes. "Don't you try nothin' funny, now, guvnor. I've read about your tricks, and you won't get anywhere."

The Devil sighed, a sound like a file on glass. "All right, child. I'm hooked, fair and square. What can I do for you?"

She told him about Peter Trumbull and her interesting condition.

THE Devil smiled slyly. "Ah," he said, "I see no reason to help you, child. You've nothing to offer me. You cannot barter your soul, for your sin has made it mine already!" And he laughed a very cruel laugh, and lashed his tail.

"I know that," Mary said. "But I'll give you a reason, right enough, all right. You're in that circle, guvnor, and there you stay until you 'elp me! I can keep you there as long as I like!"

The Devil's jaw dropped. "You wouldn't!"

"I would."

"It's never been done!"

"I'll do it."

The Devil studied her closely for a moment, frowning. "Yes, indeed, I suppose you could. But it wouldn't help you at all with your problem, would it? And I assure you that your entire lifetime, even if you chose to spend it beside this circle in which you have trapped me, would be no more than a flickering instant to me."

"Oh, I know that too. But I'll just bet you wouldn't like

waitin', even my lifetime. You've got too much to do. I've read 'ow busy you are, and things in 'ell would be in a fine state if you was to take fifty years off. Besides, I wouldn't just sit 'ere. Don't you think it! I'd borrow some money and rent this 'ole 'ouse and charge *admission*—'ow would you like *that* guvnor?"

The Devil considered, rubbing his jaw with his tail. "H'm. It's an ingenious threat," he said at last. "No, I shouldn't like that at all. It would be humiliating beyond endurance. Then, too, I'd be driven out of my mind by people trying to destroy me—technological age, and all that." He scowled at Mary, and she retreated a step. "All right! What do you want?"

"Peter Trumbull, I want 'im back, so 'e can do right by me."

"That's all?"

"That's all."

"YOU'RE really rather fortunate, you know," the Devil mused. "Your immortal soul is already mine, or will be when you die; yet here you are in a position to bargain with me for anything you wish to have during your mortal existence. Unusual, to say the least."

"I only want Peter Trumbull. I *got* to 'ave him. I'm a respectable girl, and 'e's done me proper, and now I got to 'ave 'im. Get 'im back for me...or *'ere you'll stay*."

"H'm," said His Illustrious Foulness. He closed his eyes and was silent a moment. He seemed somehow in communication. Then he smiled evilly, "I'm afraid that's quite impossible. Your Peter Trumbull fell overboard from the ship that was taking him back to America. He's been in Hell for some months now."

"Oh," Mary wailed. "That's gone and done it! Now my poor baby will be born without no father, and I'll be the disgrace of my family, and I'll walk the rest of my life 'angin' my 'ead, and—" She paused and narrowed her beautiful eyes at the Devil. "Now, look 'ere, you just *do* somethin'—You got powers. You do somethin' about this, guvnor, or I'll—"

"But it's impossible," the Devil snapped. "What can I do? Peter Trumbull is dead. No one returns from Hell. And I have important business to attend to. If you'll please release me, I'll be gone."

Mary Dingle sat down on the edge of the bed and folded her arms. "Do somethin'!"

"But—"

"Oh, I know 'ow to persuade you, all right." Mary picked up the Bible she'd put on the bed and started to read. The Devil shuddered and shrank back until his tail touched a portion of the starred circle. There was a flash, and a snapcrackle, and he yelped in pain.

"Do somethin'," Mary said, "—'And after these things I 'eard a great voice of much people in 'eaven, sayin' 'Alleluja; Salvation, and glory, and 'onor, and power, unto the Lord our God'—do somethin', guvnor, or you'll be mighty sorry."

THE Devil gnashed his teeth, and sparks flew. "Oh, I'll enjoy the moment I get my hands on you! I'll develop several horrible punishments that till now I've only contemplated!"

"Be that as it may, you do somethin' right now about Peter, or else! I guess my soul is lost anyway, so I want to live a fine old life while I got it. Peter Trumbull's rich, and that don't 'urt any!"

"But I tell you, it's utterly impossible to return a soul from Hell! Only once has a soul escaped, and the incident is still a complete mys—" The Devil was suddenly very still for a moment. His jaw dropped. "Trumbull? *Trumbull?*" He spat flaming sulphur, which fell to the carpet and commenced to eat a hole. "TRUMBULL is the young man's name?"

"Peter Trumbull," she said calmly. "I want to 'ave Peter

Trumbull…and 'is money."

The Devil stared at her with his malevolent and crafty expression and said slowly, "Ah, now I begin to understand something that happened quite some time ago. Yes, indeed, I *do* understand." He looked up at the ceiling and began to grin a fiendish grin.

"Don't you try nothin' funny, now, guvnor," Mary said nervously.

"Oh, no. Not at *all*. I wouldn't *think* of it. Why, I'm going to grant your wish, child. It's absolutely necessary that I do, for many reasons, some of which you wouldn't understand."

"Best reason is I've got you 'ere, ain't it? Now you get busy—"

"Oh, yes, that's a good one. A very good one. But a better one is that, in a sense, I've *already* done it. So now I must *do* it. Ah, yes, I must have done—or must do now—what I'm about to do—because I once did."

Mary bit her lovely lip.

"Since what happened," the Devil went on, "*did* happen, I must now *make* it happen. Badness sakes, I just hope no word of this seeps up to my Brother—it might alert him to the fact that I'm meddling with Time. *Now*—" he stretched up to his full height and flapped his tail about so menacingly that Mary flipped backwards across the bed with a muffled scream—"you want to have Peter Trumbull?"

"Y-yes."

"And you want the Trumbull millions?"

"Y-yes."

Whisht!

MARY DINGLE, unremembering, found herself in bed in a big, lovely home on Long Island, in America. Here she had lived for two years (she thought). Ever since '24, when

58

she'd married old Trumbull for his dough (she thought).

Her loving, doddering husband, Elbert M. Trumbull, was just phoning his private physicians, looking pleased and proud. This was the day! This would show those idiots who'd diagnosed false pregnancy! He'd show them, by God, that a Trumbull was good to the very end! He'd given his lovely young wife a child (he thought), and labor was commencing.

Actually, all these thoughts, and many, many more, had been instantaneously implanted in their minds by His Illustrious Foulness, in the brief instant he'd spent on Long Island before returning to Hell. Actually, Mary Dingle had just appeared out of thin air in the palatial home of old Trumbull, the bachelor, and he'd been flabbergasted before the Devil fixed things up.

Actually, they weren't married. Actually, no doctors had examined her, or diagnosed her condition one way or the other. Actually, the entire complex situation as it appeared to its protagonists had been fabricated by the Devil and implanted in Mary's mind, and in old Elbert's, and in the doctors', and in the minds of everyone even remotely connected with Elbert and his lovely young "wife." So no one was ever the wiser.

All the paraphernalia necessary to Mary's role in the quasi-situation—clothing, toilet articles, the marriage certificate, her own birth certificate, even a portrait or two by the very best artists...just about everything that accumulates as a person lives a life—had been created and put in their proper places by His Illustrious Foulness. So, in an unreal sense, the situation was real; and that seems good enough for most people anyway.

Thus, for a few hours, "Mrs. Elbert M. Trumbull" enjoyed the Trumbull wealth. Small good it did her, though. And later that day, as she had so fervently wished, she had Peter Trumbull. He weighed six pounds, seven ounces. Then, from complications, she died. Old Elbert wept and mourned, and Mary Dingle, by reason of her peculiar sins, went to Hell faster and with more of a pratfall at the end of the trip than anyone in the memory of the receiving demon.

The Devil, quite naturally, never achieved his desire to practice advanced punishments upon her. For the date of her arrival was January 27, 1926, and she was just another soul, and His Illustrious Foulness would have no notion for some time hence that she was anything at all out of the ordinary.

So three years passed, and Mary's damned soul vanished with a gleeful sound to be born in Liverpool, and the Devil swore and puzzled, and Mary grew up, went to London, walked a foggy street and met Peter Trumbull, shortly after which the Devil was himself summoned to London, where, as you have read, he recognized the Time circuit for what it must be, and chuckling with fiendish mirth sent Mary back to bear her own lover-to-be, who was twenty-seven years later to become his own father, and so on around and around.

AFTER leaving Long Island and returning to 1953, the Devil mused on his way back to Hell. Obviously there was nothing to be done about Mary Dingle, short of going back though Time again and multiplying her torments during her three-year stay. And doing so wasn't worth the risk, for it might, in some way, warn the Heavenly Hosts that he was fooling around with Time and might be planning, as he certainly was, eventually to return after centuries of preparation and start the great battle all over again and this time win it. Enough risk had been taken already, though it had been quite necessary: the girl had had him on the spot, and moreover, the wheels of Time had obviously demanded that he move as he had to account for the hitherto inexplicable disappearance of the soul of Mrs. Elbert M. Trumbull.

MARY DINGLE all things considered, got off damned

easy, to put it literally. It goes to show that while no one bests the Devil, some may get the better of him. Three years in Hell is hardly enough to discourage even the smallest of sins. And though Mary certainly hadn't very much time to enjoy her life as Mrs. Trumbull, she had lived a fairly pleasant if abbreviated life as plain Mary Dingle, or would, and besides, she'd never really wanted much out of life, or wouldn't. So we will leave her going around and around in Time, and it is better not to puzzle on that.

For the next six hundred years the Devil took pains to see that Peter Trumbull got the very worst Hell had to offer, thus trying to work off a part of his irritation at the whole affair. However, Peter was one of the most unrepentant and unregenerate scoundrels ever to enter the place, and at last, in a moment of utter fury before which discretion fled, the Devil informed him that he was his own father (expecting the news to shatter the man, in accordance with prevailing Earthly notions on such matters). Far from being shattered, or even fazed, Peter laughed long and loud, and spread the story around so that eventually it reached the ears of a small and unobtrusive demon who, beneath false horns and tail, was in reality a spy from Above.

So at the end of those six hundred years, when at last the Devil felt equipped to sally into the past and do battle with his Brother, the Heavenly Hosts were forewarned, and succeeded in ambushing him and stranding him in a parallel time continuum, where he probably wanders still.

...And soon Satan will return to be thus trapped, and Hell should go to pot without his rulership, and the world should be a pretty wonderful place without his dastardly influence, and...

Good Heavens! Can such beauty be?

The Holes around Mars

Science said it could not be, but there it was. And whoosh—look out—here it is again!

SPACESHIP crews should be selected on the basis of their non-irritating qualities as individuals. No chronic complainers, no hypochondriacs, no bugs on cleanliness—particularly no one-man parties. I speak from bitter experience.

Because on the first expedition to Mars, Hugh Allenby damned near drove us nuts with his puns. We finally got so we just ignored them.

But no one can ignore that classic last one—it's written right into the annals of astronomy, and it's there to stay.

Allenby, in command of the expedition, was first to set foot outside the ship. As he stepped down from the airlock of the *Mars I*, he placed that foot on a convenient rock, caught the toe of his weighted boot in a hole in the rock, wrenched his ankle and smote the ground with his pants.

Sitting there, eyes pained behind the transparent shield of his oxygen mask, he stared at the rock.

IT was about five feet high. Ordinary granite—no special shape—and several inches below its summit, running straight through it in a northeasterly direction, was a neat round four-inch hole.

"I'm *upset* by the *hole* thing," he grunted.

The rest of us scrambled out of the ship and gathered around his plump form. Only one or two of us winced at his miserable double pun.

"Break anything, Hugh?" asked Burton, our pilot, kneeling beside him.

"Get out of my way, Burton," said Allenby. "You're

obstructing my view."

Burton blinked. A man constructed of long bones and caution, he angled out of the way, looking around to see what he was obstructing view *of*.

He saw the rock and the round hole through it. He stood very still, staring. So did the rest of us.

"Well, I'll be damned," said Janus, our photographer. "A hole."

"In a rock," added Gonzales, our botanist.

"Round," said Randolph, our biologist.

"An *artifact*," finished Allenby softly.

Burton helped him to his feet. Silently we gathered around the rock.

Janus bent down and put an eye to one end of the hole. I bent down and looked through the other end. We squinted at each other.

As mineralogist, I was expected to opinionate. "Not drilled," I said slowly. "Not chipped. Not melted. Certainly not eroded."

I heard a rasping sound by my ear and straightened. Burton was scratching a thumbnail along the rim of the hole. "Weathered," he said. "Plenty old. But I'll bet it's a perfect circle, if we measure."

Janus was already fiddling with his camera, testing the cooperation of the tiny distant sun with a light-meter.

"Let us see *weather* it is or not," Allenby said.

BURTON brought out a steel tape-measure. The hole was four and three-eighths inches across. It was perfectly circular and about sixteen inches long. And four feet above the ground.

"But why?" said Randolph. "Why should anyone bore a four-inch tunnel through a rock way out in the middle of the desert?"

"Religious symbol," said Janus. He looked around, one hand on his gun. "We'd better keep an I eye out—maybe we've landed on sacred ground or something."

"A totem *hole*, perhaps," Allenby suggested.

"Oh, I don't know," Randolph said to Janus, not Allenby. As I've mentioned, we always ignored Allenby's puns. "Note the lack of ornamentation. Not at all typical of religious articles."

"On Earth," Gonzales reminded him. "Besides, it might be utilitarian, not symbolic."

"Utilitarian, how?" asked Janus.

"An altar for snakes," Burton said dryly.

"Well," said Allenby, "you can't deny that it has its *holy* aspects."

"Get your hand away, will you, Peters?" asked Janus.

I did. When Janus's camera had clicked, I bent again and peered through the hole. "It sights on that low ridge over

there," I said. "Maybe it's some kind of surveying setup. I'm going to take a look."

"Careful," warned Janus. "Remember, it may be sacred."

As I walked away, I heard Allenby say, "Take same scrapings from the inside of the hole, Gonzales. We might be able to determine if anything is kept in it..."

One of the stumpy, purplish, barrel-type cacti on the ridge had a long vertical bite out of it...as if someone had carefully carved out a narrow U-shaped section from the top down, finishing the bottom of the U in a neat semicircle. It was as flat and cleancut as the inside surface of a horseshoe magnet.

I hollered. The others came running. I pointed.

"Oh, my God!" said Allenby. "Another one."

The pulp of the cactus in and around the U-hole was dried and dead-looking.

Silently Burton used his tape-measure. The hole measured four and three-eighths inches across. It was eleven inches deep. The semicircular bottom was about a foot above the ground.

"This ridge," I said, "is about three feet higher than where we landed the ship. I bet the hole in the rock and the hole in this cactus are on the same level."

GONZALES said slowly, "This was not done all at once. It is a result of periodic attacks. Look here and here. These overlapping depressions along the outer edges of the hole—" he pointed— "on this side of the cactus. They are the signs of repeated impact. And the scallop effect on *this* side, where whatever made the hole emerged. There are juices still oozing—not at the point of impact, where the plant is desiccated, but below, where the shock was transmitted—"

A distant shout turned us around. Burton was at the rock, beside the ship. He was bending down, his eye to the far side of the mysterious hole.

He looked for another second, then straightened and came toward us at a lope.

"They line up," he said when he reached us. "The bottom of the hole in the cactus is right in the middle when you sight through the hole in the rock."

"As if somebody came around and whacked the cactus regularly," Janus said, looking around warily.

"To keep the line of sight through the holes clear?" I wondered. "Why not just remove the cactus?"

"Religious," Janus explained.

The gauntlet he had discarded lay ignored on the ground, in the shadow of the cactus. We went on past the ridge toward an outcropping of rock about a hundred yards farther on. We walked silently, each of us wondering if what we half-expected would really be there.

It was. In one of the tall, weathered spires in the outcropping, some ten feet below its peak and four feet above the ground, was a round four-inch hole.

Allenby sat down on a rock, nursing his ankle, and remarked that anybody who believed this crazy business was really happening must have holes in the rocks in his head.

Burton put his eye to the hole and whistled, "Sixty feet long if it's an inch," he said. "The other end's just a pinpoint. But you can see it. The damn thing's perfectly straight."

I looked back the way we had come. The cactus stood on the ridge, with its U-shaped bite, and beyond was the ship, and beside it the perforated rock.

"If we surveyed," I said, "I bet the holes would all line up right to the last millimeter."

"But," Randolph complained, "why would anybody go out and bore holes in things all along a line through the desert?"

"Religious," Janus muttered. "It doesn't *have* to make sense."

WE stood there by the outcropping and looked out along the wide, red desert beyond. It stretched flatly for miles from this point, south toward Mars' equator–dead sandy wastes, crisscrossed by the 'canals,' which we had observed while landing to be great straggly patches of vegetation, probably strung along underground waterflows.

BLONG - G - G - G -...st - st - st -...

We jumped half out of our skins. Ozone bit at our nostrils. Our hair stirred in the electrical uproar.

"L-look," Janus chattered, lowering his smoking gun.

About forty feet to our left, a small rabbity creature poked its head from behind a rock and stared at us in utter horror.

Janus raised his gun again.

"Don't bother," said Allenby tiredly, "I don't think it intends to attack."

"But—"

"I'm sure it isn't a Martian with religious convictions."

Janus wet his lips and looked a little shamefaced, "I guess I'm kind of taut."

"That's what I *taut*," said Allenby.

The creature darted from behind its rock and, looking at us over its shoulder, employed six legs to make small but very fast tracks.

We turned our attention again to the desert. Far out, black against Mars' azure horizon, was a line of low hills.

"Shall we go look?" asked Burton, eyes gleaming at the mystery.

Janus hefted his gun nervously. It was still crackling faintly from the discharge, "I say let's get back to the ship!"

Allenby sighed. "My leg hurts." He studied the hills. "Give me the field-glasses."

Randolph handed them over. Allenby put them to the shield of his mask and adjusted them.

After a moment he sighed again, "There's a hole. On a plane surface that catches the Sun. A lousy damned round little impossible hole."

"Those hills," Burton observed, "must be thousands of feet thick."

THE argument lasted all the way back to the ship.

Janus, holding out for his belief that the whole thing was of religious origin, kept looking around for Martians as if he expected them to pour screaming from the hills.

Burton came up with the suggestion that perhaps the holes had been made by a disintegrator-ray.

"It's possible," Allenby admitted. "This might have been the scene of some great battle—"

"With only one such weapon?" I objected.

Allenby swore as he stumbled. "What do you mean?"

"I haven't seen any other lines of holes—only the one. In a battle, the whole joint should be cut up."

That was good for a few moments silent thought. Then Allenby said, "It might have been brought out by one side as a last resort. Sort of an ace in the hole."

I resisted the temptation to mutiny. "But would even one such weapon, in battle, make only one line of holes? Wouldn't it be played in an arc against the enemy? You know it would."

"Well—"

"Wouldn't it cut slices out of the landscape, instead of boring holes? And wouldn't it sway or vibrate enough to make the holes miles away from it something less than perfect circles?"

"It could have been very firmly mounted."

"Hugh, does that sound like a practical weapon to you?"

Two seconds of silence. "On the other hand," he said, "instead of a war, the whole thing might have been designed to frighten some primitive race—or even some kind of beast—the *hole* out of here. A demonstration—"

"Religious," Janus grumbled, still looking around.

We walked on, passing the cactus on the low ridge.

"Interesting," said Gonzales. "The evidence that whatever causes the phenomenon has happened again and again. I'm afraid that the war theory—"

"Oh, my God!" gasped Burton.

We stared at him.

"The ship," he whispered. "It's right in line with the holes! If whatever made them is still in operation..."

"Run!" yelled Allenby, and we ran like fiends.

WE got the ship into the air, out of line with the holes to what we fervently hoped was safety, and then we realized we were admitting our fear that the mysterious hole-maker might still be lurking around.

Well, the evidence was all for it, as Gonzales had reminded

us—that cactus had been oozing.

We cruised at twenty thousand feet and thought it over.

Janus, whose only training was in photography, said, "Some kind of omnivorous animal? Or bird? Eats rocks and everything?"

"I will not totally discount the notion of such an animal," Randolph said. "But I will resist to the death the suggestion that it forages—with geometric precision."

After a while, Allenby said, "Land, Burton. By that 'canal.' Lots of plant life-fauna, too. We'll do a little collecting."

Burton set us down featherlight at the very edge of the sprawling flat expanse of vegetation, commenting that the scene reminded him of his native Texas pear-flats.

We wandered in the chilly air, each of us except Burton pursuing his specialty. Randolph relentlessly stalked another of the rabbity creatures. Gonzales was carefully digging up plants and stowing them in jars. Janus was busy with his cameras, recording every aspect of Mars transferable to film. Allenby walked around, helping anybody who needed it. An astronomer, he'd done half his work on the way to Mars and would do the other half on the return trip. Burton lounged in the Sun, his back against a ship's fin, and played chess with Allenby, who was calling out his moves in a bull roar. I grubbed for rocks.

My search took me farther and farther away from the others—all I could find around the 'canal' was gravel, and I wanted to chip at some big stuff. I walked toward a long rise a half-mile or so away, beyond which rose an enticing array of house-sized boulders.

As I moved out of earshot, I heard Randolph snarl, "Burton, *will* you stop yelling, 'Kt to B-2 and check?' Every time you open your yap, this critter takes off on me."

Then I saw the groove.

IT started right where the ground began to rise—a thin, shallow, curve-bottomed groove in the dirt at my feet, about half an inch across, running off straight toward higher ground.

With my eyes glued to it, I walked. The ground slowly rose. The groove deepened, widened—now it was about three inches across, about one and a half deep.

I walked on, holding my breath. Four inches wide. Two inches deep.

The ground rose some more. Four and three-eighths inches wide. I didn't have to measure it—I *knew*.

Now, as the ground rose, the edges of the groove began to curve inward over the groove. They touched. No more groove.

The ground had risen, the groove had stayed level and gone underground.

Except that now it wasn't a groove. It was a round tunnel. A hole.

A few paces farther on, I thumped the ground with my heel where the hole ought to be. The dirt crumbled, and there was the little dark tunnel, running straight in both directions.

I walked on, the ground falling away gradually again. The entire process was repeated in reverse. A hairline appeared in the dirt—widened—became lips that drew slowly apart to reveal the neat straight four-inch groove—which shrank as slowly to a shallow line of the ground—and vanished.

I looked ahead of me. There was one low ridge of ground between me and the enormous boulders. A neat four-inch semicircle was bitten out of the very top of the ridge. In the housesized boulder directly beyond was a four-inch hole.

ALLENBY winced and called the others when I came back and reported.

"The mystery *deepens*," he told them. He turned to me, "Lead on, Peters. You're temporary *drill* leader."

Thank God he didn't say *Fall in*.

The holes went straight through the nest of boulders— there'd be a hole in one and, ten or twenty feet farther on in the next boulder, another hole. And then another, and another—right through the nest in a line. About thirty holes in all.

Burton, standing by the boulder I'd first seen, flashed his flashlight into the hole. Randolph, clear on the other side of the jumbled nest, eye to hole, saw it.

Straight as a string!

The ground sloped away on the far side of the nest—no holes were visible in that direction—just miles of desert. So, after we'd stared at the holes for a while and they didn't go away, we headed back for the canal.

"Is there any possibility," asked Janus, as we walked, "that it could be a natural phenomenon?"

"There are no straight lines in nature," Randolph said, a little shortly. "That goes for a bunch of circles in a straight line. And for perfect circles, too."

"A planet is a circle," objected Janus.

"An oblate spheroid," Allenby corrected.

"A planet's orbit—"

"An ellipse."

Janus walked a few steps, frowning. Then, he said, "I remember reading that there is something darned near a perfect circle in nature." He paused a moment. "Potholes." And he looked at me, as mineralogist, to corroborate.

"What kind of potholes?" I asked cautiously. "Do you mean where part of a limestone deposit has dissol—"

"No. I once read that when a glacier passes over a hard rock that's lying on some softer rock, it grinds the hard rock down into the softer, and both of them sort of wear down to fit together, and it all ends up with a round hole in the soft rock."

"Probably neither stone," I told Janus, "would be homogenous. The softer parts would abrade faster in the soft stone. The end result wouldn't be a perfect circle."

Janus's face fell.

"Now," I said, "would anyone care to define this term 'perfect circle' we're throwing around so blithely? Because such holes as Janus describes are often pretty damned round."

Randolph said, "Well..."

"It is settled, then," Gonzales said, a little sarcastically. "Your discussion, gentlemen, has established that the long, horizontal holes we have found were caused by glacial action."

"Oh, no," Janus argued seriously. "I once read that Mars never had any glaciers."

All of us shuddered.

HALF an hour later, we spotted more holes, about a mile down the 'canal,' still on a line, marching along the desert, through cacti, rocks, hills, even through one edge of the low vegetation of the 'canal' for thirty feet or so. It was the damnedest thing to bend down and look straight through all that curling, twisting growth...a round tunnel from either end.

We followed the holes for about a mile, to the rim of an enormous saucer like valley that sank gradually before us until, miles away, it was thousands of feet deep. We stared out across it, wondering about the other side.

Allenby said determinedly, "We'll burrow to the *bottom* of these holes, once and for all. Back to the ship, men!"

We hiked back, climbed in and took off.

At an altitude of fifty feet, Burton lined the nose of the

ship on the most recent line of holes and we flew out over the valley.

On the other side was a range of hefty hills. The holes went through them. Straight through. We would approach one hill—Burton would manipulate the front viewscreen until we spotted the hole—we would pass over the hill and spot the other end of the hole in the rear screen.

One hole was two hundred and eighty miles long.

Four hours later, we were halfway around Mars.

Randolph was sitting by a side port, chin on one hand, his eyes unbelieving. "All around the planet," he kept repeating. "All around the planet..."

"Halfway at least," Allenby mused. "And we can assume that it continues in a straight line, through anything and everything that gets in its way..." He gazed out the front port at the uneven blue-green haze of a 'canal' off to our left. "For the love of Heaven, why?"

Then Allenby fell down. We all did.

Burton had suddenly slapped at the control board, and the ship braked and sank like a plugged duck. At the last second, Burton propped up the nose with a short burst, the ten-foot wheels hit desert sand and in five hundred yards we had jounced to a stop.

Allenby got up from the floor. "Why did you do that?" he asked Burton politely, nursing a bruised elbow.

Burton's nose was almost touching the front port. "Look!" he said, and pointed.

About two miles away, the Martian village looked like a handful of yellow marbles flung on the desert.

WE checked our guns. We put on our oxygen-masks. We checked our guns again. We got out of the ship and made damned sure the airlock was locked.

An hour later, we crawled inch by painstaking inch up a

high sand dune and poked our heads over the top.

The Martians were runts—the tallest of them less than five feet tall—and skinny as a pencil. Dried-up and brown, they wore loincloths of woven fiber.

They stood among the dusty-looking inverted-bowl buildings of their village, and every one of them was looking straight up at us with unblinking brown eyes.

The six safeties of our six guns clicked off like a rattle of dice. The Martians stood there and gawped.

"Probably a highly developed sense of hearing in this thin atmosphere," Allenby murmured. "Heard us coming."

"They thought that landing of Burton's was an earthquake," Randolph grumbled sourly.

"Marsquake," corrected Janus. One look at the village's scrawny occupants seemed to have convinced him that his life was in no danger.

Holding the Martians covered, we examined the village from atop the thirty-foot dune.

The domelike buildings were constructed of something that looked like adobe. No windows—probably built with sandstorms in mind. The doors were about halfway up the sloping sides, and from each door a stone ramp wound down around the house to the ground—again with sandstorms in mind, no doubt, so drifting dunes wouldn't block the entrances.

The center of the village was a wide street, a long sandy area some thirty feet wide. On either side of it, the houses were scattered at random, as if each Martian had simply hunted for a comfortable place to sit and then built a house around it.

"Look," whispered Randolph.

One Martian had stepped from a group situated on the far side of the street from us. He started to cross the street, his round brown eyes on us, his small bare feet plodding sand,

and we saw that in addition to a loincloth he wore jewelry—a hammered metal ring, a bracelet on one skinny ankle. The Sun caught a copperish gleam on his bald narrow head, and we saw a band of metal there, just above where his eyebrows should have been.

"The super-chief," Allenby murmured, "*Oh, shaman me!*"

As the bejeweled Martian approached the center of the street, he glanced briefly at the ground at his feet. Then he raised his head, stepped with dignity across the exact center of the street and came on toward us, passing the dusty-looking buildings of his realm and the dusty-looking groups of his subjects.

He reached the slope of the dune we lay on, paused—and raised small hands over his head, palms toward us.

"I think," Allenby said, "that an anthropologist would give odds on that gesture meaning peace."

He stood up, holstered his gun—without buttoning the flap—and raised his own hands over his head. We all did.

THE Martian language consisted of squeaks.

We made friendly noises, the chief squeaked and pretty soon we were the center of a group of wide-eyed Martians, none of whom made a sound. Evidently no one dared peep while the chief spoke—very likely the most articulate Martians simply squeaked themselves into the job. Allenby, of course, said they just *squeaked* by.

He was going through the business of drawing concentric circles in the sand, pointing at the third orbit away from the Sun and thumping his chest. The crowd around us kept growing as more Martians emerged from the dome buildings to see what was going on. Down the winding ramps of the buildings on our side of the wide, sandy street they came— and from the buildings on the other side of the street, plodding through the sand, blinking brown eyes at us, not making a sound.

Allenby pointed at the third orbit and thumped his chest. The chief squeaked and thumped his own chest and pointed at the copperish band around his head. Then he pointed at Allenby.

"I seem to have conveyed to him," Allenby said dryly, "the fact that I'm chief of our party: Well, let's try again."

He started over on the orbits. He didn't seem to be getting anyplace, so the rest of us watched the Martians instead. A last handful was straggling across the wide street.

"Curious," said Gonzales. "Note what happens when they reach the center of the street."

Each Martian, upon reaching the center of the street, glanced at his feet—just for a moment—without even breaking stride. And then came on.

"What can they be looking at?" Gonzales wondered.

"The chief did it too," Burton mused. "Remember when he first came toward us?"

We all stared intently at the middle of the street. We saw absolutely nothing but sand.

The Martians milled around us and watched Allenby and his orbits. A Martian child appeared from between two buildings across the street. On six-inch legs, it started across, got halfway, glanced downward—and came on.

"I don't get it," Burton said. "What in hell are they looking at?"

The child reached the crowd and squeaked a thin, high note.

A number of things happened at once.

SEVERAL members of the group around us glanced down, and along the edge of the crowd nearest the center of the street there was a mild stir as individuals drifted off to either side. Quite casually—nothing at all urgent about it.

They just moved concertedly to get farther away from the center of the street, not taking their interested gaze off us for one second in the process.

Even the chief glanced up from Allenby's concentric circles at the child's squeak. And Randolph, who had been fidgeting uncomfortably and paying very little attention to our conversation, decided that he must answer Nature's call. He moved off into the dunes surrounding the village. Or rather, he started to move.

The moment he set off across the wide street, the little Martian chief was in front of him, brown eyes wide, hands out before him as if to thrust Randolph back.

Again six safeties clicked. The Martians didn't even blink at the sudden appearance of our guns. Probably the only weapon they recognized was a club, or maybe a rock.

"What can the matter be?" Randolph said.

He took another step forward. The chief squeaked and stood his ground. Randolph had to stop or bump into him, Randolph stopped.

The chief squeaked, looking right into the bore of Randolph's gun.

"Hold still," Allenby told Randolph, "till we know what's up."

Allenby made an interrogative sound at the chief. The chief squeaked and pointed at the ground. We looked. He was pointing at his shadow.

Randolph stirred uncomfortably.

"Hold still," Allenby warned him, and again he made the questioning sound.

The chief pointed up the street. Then he pointed down the street. He bent to touch his shadow, thumping it with thin fingers. Then he pointed at the wall of a house nearby.

We all looked.

Straight lines had been painted on the curved brick-colored wall, up and down and across, to form many small squares about four inches across. In each square was a bit of squiggly writing, in blackish paint, and a small wooden peg jutting out from the wall.

Burton said, "Looks like a damn crossword puzzle."

"Look," said Janus. "In the lower right corner—a metal ring hanging from one of the pegs."

AND that was all we saw on the wall. Hundreds of squares with figures in them—a small peg set in each—and a ring hanging on one of the pegs.

"You know what?" Allenby said slowly. "I think it's a calendar! Just a second—thirty squares wide by twenty-two high—that's six hundred and sixty. And that bottom line has twenty-six—twenty-*seven* squares. Six hundred and eighty-seven squares in all. That's how many days there are in the Martian year!"

He looked thoughtfully at the metal ring. "I'll bet that ring is hanging from the peg in the square that represents *today*. They must move it along every day, to keep track…"

"What's a calendar got to do with my crossing the street?" Randolph asked in a pained tone.

He started to take another step. The chief squeaked as if it were a matter of desperate concern that he makes us understand. Randolph stopped again and swore impatiently.

Allenby made his questioning sound again.

The chief pointed emphatically at his shadow, then at the communal calendar—and we could see now that he was pointing at the metal ring.

Burton said slowly, "I think he's trying to tell us that this is *today*. And such-and-such a *time* of day. I bet he's using his shadow as a sundial."

"Perhaps," Allenby granted.

Randolph said, "If this monkey doesn't let me go in

another minute—"

The chief squeaked, eyes concerned.

"Stand still," Allenby ordered. "He's trying to warn you of some danger."

The chief pointed down the street again and, instead of squealing, revealed that there was another sound at his command. He said, "Whooooooosh!"

We all stared at the end of the street.

NOTHING! Just the wide avenue between the houses, and the high sand dune down at the end of it, from which we had first looked upon the village.

The chief described a large circle with one hand, sweeping the hand above his head, down to his knees, up again, as fast as he could. He pursed his monkeylips and said, "Whooooooosh!" And made the circle again.

A Martian emerged from the door in the side of a house across the avenue and blinked at the Sun, as if he had just awakened. Then he saw what was going on below and blinked again, this time in interest. He made his way down around the winding lamp and started to cross the street.

About halfway, he paused, eyed the calendar on the house wall, glanced at his shadow. Then he got down on his hands and knees and *crawled* across the middle of the street. Once past the middle, he rose, walked the rest of the way to join one of the groups and calmly stared at us along with the rest of them.

"They're all crazy," Randolph said disgustedly. "I'm going to cross that street!"

"Shut up. So it's a certain time of a certain day," Allenby mused, "And from the way the chief is acting, he's afraid for you to cross the street. And that other one just *crawled*. By God, do you know what this might tie in with?"

We were silent for a moment. Then Gonzales said, "Of

course!"

And Burton said, "The *holes!*"

"Exactly," said Allenby. "Maybe whatever made—or makes—the holes comes right down the center of the street here. Maybe that's why they built the village this way—to make room for—"

"For what?" Randolph asked unhappily, shifting his feet.

"I don't know," Allenby said. He looked thoughtfully at the chief. "That circular motion he made—could he have been describing something that went around and around the planet? Something like—oh, no!" Allenby's eyes glazed. "I wouldn't believe it in a million years."

His gaze went to the far end of the street, to the high sand dune that rose there. The chief seemed to be waiting for something to happen.

"I'm going to crawl," Randolph stated. He got to his hands and knees and began to creep across the center of the avenue.

The chief let him go.

The sand dune at the end of the street suddenly erupted. A forty-foot spout of dust shot straight out from the sloping side, as if a bullet had emerged. Powdered sand hazed the air, yellowed it almost the full length of the avenue. Grains of sand stung the skin and rattled minutely on the houses.

WhoooSSSHHHHH!

Randolph dropped flat on his belly. He didn't have to continue his trip. He had made other arrangements.

THAT night in the ship, while we all sat around, still shaking our heads every once in a while, Allenby talked with Earth. He sat there, wearing the headphones, trying to make himself understood above the godawful static.

"...an exceedingly small body," he repeated wearily to his unbelieving audience, "about four inches in diameter. It travels at a mean distance of four feet above the surface of the planet, at a velocity yet to be calculated. Its unique nature results in many hitherto unobserved—I might say even unimagined—phenomena." He stared blankly in front of him for a moment, then delivered the understatement of his life. "The discovery may necessitate a re-examination of many of our basic postulates in the physical sciences."

The headphones squawked.

Patiently, Allenby assured Earth that he was entirely serious, and reiterated the results of his observations. I suppose that he, an astronomer, was twice as flabbergasted as the rest of us. On the other hand, perhaps he was better equipped to adjust to the evidence.

"Evidently," he said, "when the body was formed, it traveled at such fantastic velocity as to enable it to—" his voice was almost a whisper—"to punch holes in things."

The headphones squawked.

"In rocks," Allenby said, "in mountains, in anything that got in its way. And now the holes form a large portion of its fixed orbit."

Squawk.

"Its mass must be on the order of—"

Squawk.

"—process of making the holes slowed it, so that now it travels just fast enough—"

Squawk.

"—maintain its orbit and penetrate occasional objects such as—"

Squawk.

"—and sand dunes—"

Squawk.

"My God, I *know* it's a mathematical monstrosity," Allenby snarled. "*I* didn't put it there!"

Squawk.

Allenby was silent for a moment. Then he said slowly, "A name?"

Squawk.

"H'm," said Allenby. "Well, well." He appeared to brighten just a little. "So it's up to me, as leader of the expedition, to name it?"

Squawk.

"Well, well," he said.

That chop-licking tone was in his voice. We'd heard it all too often before. We shuddered, waiting.

"Inasmuch as Mars' outermost moon is called Deimos, and the next Phobos," he said, "I think I shall name the third moon of Mars—*Bottomos.*"

Where There's Hope

The women had made up their minds, and nothing—repeat, nothing—could change them. But something had to give...

IF YOU called me here to tell me to have a child," Mary Pornsen said, "You can just forget about it. We girls have made up our minds."

Hugh Farrel, Chief Medical Officer of the Exodus VII, sighed and leaned back in his chair. He looked at Mary's husband. "And you, Ralph," he said. "How do you feel?"

Ralph Pornsen looked at Mary uncomfortably, started to speak and then hesitated.

Hugh Farrel sighed again and closed his eyes. It was that way with all the boys. The wives had the whip hand. If the husbands put up an argument, they'd simply get turned down flat: no sex at all, children or otherwise. The threat, Farrel thought wryly, made the boys softer than watered putty. His own wife, Alice, was one of the ringleaders of the "no babies" movement, and since he had openly declared warfare on the idea, she wouldn't even let him kiss her goodnight. (For fear of losing her determination, Farrel liked to think.)

He opened his eyes again to look past the Pornsens, out of the curving port of his office-lab in the Exodus VII's flank, at the scene outside the ship.

At the edge of the clearing he could see Danny Stern and his crew, tiny beneath the cavernous sunbeam-shot overhang of giant leaves. Danny was standing up at the controls of the 'dozer, waving his arms. His crew was struggling to get a log set so he could shove it into place with the 'dozer. They were repairing a break in the barricade—the place where one of New Earth's giant saurians had come stamping and whistling through last night to kill three colonists before it could be blasted out of existence.

It was difficult. Damned difficult. A brand-new world here, all ready to receive the refugees from dying Earth. Or rather, all ready to be *made* ready, which was the task ahead of the Exodus VII's personnel.

An Earth-like world. Green, warm, fertile—and crawling, leaping, hooting and snarling with ferocious beasts of every variety. Farrel could certainly see the women's point in banding together and refusing to produce children. Something inside a woman keeps her from wanting to bring life into peril—at least, when the peril seems temporary, and security is both remembered and anticipated.

Pornsen said, "I guess I feel just about like Mary does. I—I don't see any reason for having a kid until we get this place ironed out and safe to live in."

"That's going to take time, Ralph." Farrel clasped his hands in front of him and delivered the speech he had delivered so often in the past few weeks. "Ten or twelve years before we really get set up here. We've got to build from the ground up, you know. We'll have to find and mine our metals. Build our machines to build shops to build more machines. There'll be resources that we *won't* find, and we'll have to learn what this planet has to offer in their stead. Colonizing New Earth isn't simply a matter of landing and throwing together a shining city. I only wish it were.

"Six weeks ago we landed. We haven't yet dared to venture more than a mile from this spot. We've cut down trees and built the barricade and our houses. After protecting ourselves we have to eat. We've planted gardens. We've produced test-tube calves and piglets. The calves are doing fine, but the piglets are dying one by one. We've got to find out why.

"It's going to be a long, long time before we have even a minimum of security, much less luxury. Longer than you think... So much longer that waiting until the security arrives before having children is out of the question. There are critters out there—" he nodded toward the port and the busy clearing beyond— "that we haven't been able to kill. We've thrown everything we have at them, and they come back for more. We'll have to find out what *will* kill them—how they differ from those we *are* able to kill. We are six hundred people and a spaceship, Ralph. We have techniques. That's *all*. Everything else we've got to dig up out of this planet. We'll need people, Mary; we'll need the children. We're counting on them. They're vital to the plans we've made."

Mary Pornsen said, "Damn the plans. I won't have one. Not now. You've just done a nice job of describing all my reasons. And all the other girls feel the same way."

SHE LOOKED out the window at the 'dozer and crew. Danny Stern was still waving his arms; the log was almost in place. "George and May Wright were killed last night. So was Farelli. If George and May had had a child, the monster would have trampled it too—it went right through their cabin like cardboard. It isn't fair to bring a baby into—"

Farrel said, "Fair, Mary? Maybe it isn't fair *not* to have one. *Not* to bring it into being and give it a chance. Life's always a gamble—"

"*It* doesn't exist," Mary said. She smiled. "Don't try circumlocution on me, Doc. I'm not religious. I don't believe that spermatazoa and an ovum, if not allowed to cuddle up together, add up to murder."

"That isn't what I meant—"

"You were getting around to it—which means you've run out of good arguments."

"No. I've a few left." Farrel looked at the two stubborn faces: Mary's, pleasant and pretty, but set as steel; Ralph's, uncomfortable, thoughtful, but mirroring his definite willingness to follow his wife's lead.

Farrel cleared his throat. "You know how important it is that this colony be established? You know that, don't you? In twenty years or so the ships will start arriving. Hundreds of them. Because we sent a message back to Earth saying we'd found a habitable planet. Thousands of people from Earth, coming here to the new world we're supposed to get busy and carve out for them. We were selected for that task—first of judging the right planet, then of working it over. Engineers, chemists, agronomists, all of us—we're the task force. We've got to do the job. We've got to test, plant, breed, rebalance, create. There'll be a lot of trial and error. We've got to work out a way of life, so the thousands who will follow can be introduced safely and painlessly into the—well, into the organism. And we'll need new blood for the jobs ahead. We'll need young people—"

Mary said, "A few years one way or the other won't matter much, Doc. Five or six years from now this place will be a lot safer. Then we women will start producing. But not now."

"It won't work that way," Farrel said. "We're none of us kids any longer. I'm fifty-five. Ralph, you're forty-three. I realize that I must be getting old to think of you as young. Mary, you're thirty-seven. We took a long time getting here. Fourteen years. We left an Earth that's dying of radioactive poisoning, and we all got a mild dose of that. The radiation we absorbed in space, little as it was, didn't help any. And that sun up there—" again he nodded at the port—"isn't any help either. Periodically it throws off some pretty damned funny stuff.

"Frankly, we're worried. We don't know whether or not we can have children. Or *normal* children. We've got to find out. If our genes have been bollixed up, we've got to find out why and how and get to work on it immediately. It may be unpleasant. It may be heartbreaking. But those who will come here in twenty years will have absorbed much more of

Earth's radioactivity than we did, and an equal amount of the space stuff, and this sun will be waiting for them… We'll have to know what we can do for them."

"I'm not a walking laboratory, Doc," Mary said.

"I'm afraid you are, Mary. All of you are."

Mary set her lips and stared out the port.

"It's got to be done, Mary."

She didn't answer.

"It's going to be done."

"Choose someone else," she said.

"That's what they all say."

She said, "I guess this is one thing you doctors and psychologists didn't figure on, Doc."

"Not at first," Farrel said. "But we've given it some thought."

MacGuire had installed the button convenient to Farrel's right hand, just below the level of the desktop. Farrel pressed it, Ralph and Mary Pornsen slumped in their chairs. The door opened, and Doctor John J. MacGuire and Ted Harris, the Exodus VII's chief psychologist, came in.

WHEN it was over, and the after-play had been allowed to run its course, Farrel told the Pornsens to go into the next room and shower. They came back soon, looking refreshed. Farrel ordered them to get back into their clothes. Under the power of the hypnotic drug, which their chairs had injected into them at the touch of the button, they did so. Then he told them to sit down in the chairs again.

MacGuire and Harris had gathered up their equipment, piling it on top of the operating table.

MacGuire smiled. "I'll bet that's the best-monitored, most hygienic sex act ever committed. I think I've about got the space radiations effect licked."

Farrel nodded. "If anything goes wrong, it certainly won't

be our fault. But let's face it—the chances are a thousand to one that something *will* go wrong. We'll just have to wait. And work." He looked at the Pornsens. "They're very much in love, aren't they? And she was receptive to the suggestion—beneath it all, she was burning to have a child, just like the others."

MacGuire wheeled out the operating table, with its load of serums, pressure-hypos and jury-rigged thingamabobs that he was testing on alternate couples. Ted Harris stopped at the door a moment. He said, "I think the suggestions I planted will turn the trick when they find out she's pregnant. They'll come through okay—won't even be too angry."

Farrel sighed. They'd been over it in detail several times, of course, but apparently Harris needed the reassurance as much as he did. He said: "Sure. Now scram so I can go back into my act."

Harris closed the door. Farrel sat down at his desk and studied the pair before him. They looked back contentedly, holding hands, their eyes dull.

Farrel said, "How do you feel?"

Ralph Pornsen said, "I feel fine."

Mary Pornsen said, "Oh, I feel *wonderful!*"

Deliberately Farrel pressed another button below his desktop.

The dull eyes cleared instantly.

"Oh, you've given it some thought, Doc?" Mary said sweetly. "And what have you decided?"

"You'll see," Farrel said. "Eventually."

He rose. "That's all for now, kids. I'd like to see you again in one month—for a routine checkup."

Mary nodded and got up. "You'll still have to wait, Doc. Why not admit you're licked?"

Ralph got up too, and looked puzzled.

"Wow," he said. "I'm tired."

"Perhaps just coming here," Farrel said, "discharged some of the tension you've been carrying around."

The Pornsens left.

Farrel brought out some papers from his desk and studied them. Then, from the file drawer, he selected the record of Hugh and Alice Farrel. Alice would be at the perfect time of her menstrual cycle tomorrow...

Farrel flipped his communicator.

"MacGuire," he said. "Tomorrow it's me."

MacGuire chuckled. Farrel could have kicked him. He put his chin in his hands and stared out the port. Danny Stern had the log in place in the barricade. The bulldozer was moving on to a new task. His momentary doubt stilled, Farrel went back to work.

TWENTY-ONE years later, when the ships from Earth began arriving, the log had been replaced by a stone monument erected to the memory of the Exodus VII, which had been cut apart for its valuable steel. Around the monument was a park, and on three sides of the park was a shining town—not really large enough to be called a city—of plastic and stone, for New Earth had no iron ore, only zinc and a little copper. This was often cause for regret.

Still it was a pretty good world. The monster problem had been licked by high-voltage cannon. Now in their third generation since the landing, the monsters kept their distance. And things grew—things good to eat.

And even without steel, the graceful, smoothly-functioning town looked impressive—quite a thing to have been built by a handful of beings with two arms and two legs each.

It hadn't been, entirely. But nobody thought much about that any more. Even the newcomers got used to it. Things change.

—And All for One

Shipwreck! Not a new tale, but the oldest of all. But this was a spaceship wreck on the most desolate world in the void— and it was four hungry survivors, "one for all—

THE drift-winds of Mars brought winter suddenly to Al-cronah-haut. The small red sun was made smaller and more red by scudding clouds; the surface of the Great Canal sank to a few crusting inches, and the pumps of the water merchants worked overtime to stock their tanks against the coming bleak months.

At the lower end of Boulevard B27, beyond the ugly work-village of Kam and squatting on a sandstone bluff overlooking the skeletal litter of the Akron freight locks, was the Outer-Worlds Explorers' Club, Chapter XIV, a flat, redrock building, guilty of the randomness of native architecture, and connected to an observatory a little distance away by an unkempt garden pathway of *kanl* and *linla.*

Inside, this night, a young Martian shivered and got up to put another log on the fire. It flamed high, and sent the chilly shadows scooting back into the corners of the room to sway angrily against the dark paneling and glassed-in book-and-curiocases that mounted to the high, timbered ceiling.

Facing his companion, Rof Unain hiked up his tunic to warm his lower midsection, "I suppose," he said, "that Mars' winter is a picnic compared to that of Tethys, Mr. Millikan?"

The fat, gray-haired man closed his book—one of many he had written—and stretched his outmoded grav-boots toward the fire. As the Club's most distinguished member on Mars, and its oldest one besides, Miles Millikan possessed for his use the big chair directly before the fireplace. He shifted in it now and sighed, raised his eyebrows at the young man. "You would like to hear the story, perhaps –" his voice was dry, and a little amused "—while we wait for our steaks?"

"I would indeed!" Rof Unain nodded eagerly, "I've read about it, of course—when I was a kid—but I'd be honored to hear it first hand…"

Outside, the whining wind threw heavy *schluffs* of snow against the leaded windows, and played cold music on the singing sculptures in the garden. The fat man's pale eyes stared into the fire, as if seeking in its leaping redness an image with which to begin his tale. The log fire was an anachronism—and the members of this club were, for the most part, anachronisms too. There was an atomic furnace in the cellar, but the old men preferred to stalk the halls and trophy rooms and shiver their dynamic memories of Pluto and Ganymede and the icy oceans of Neptune, then to retire to the clubroom and warm themselves before carbon flames as they had long ago on those rugged worlds.

Millikan said slowly: "It was two, maybe three hundred miles off-world that the Drive backlashed. God knows why—and maybe Caddo knows why too, wherever he is: he went with the Drive. Four of us—*the* four—were up in Control.

"Greenberg said, 'The hell with old Ringsy—I'll try to world us on Tethys…'"

The spaceship came thundering down through the snow, her starboard tubes fused into a seething, white-hot tumor. She flicked a mountain top, sheeting off snow, seeming to ride a moment on a bridge of white fluff that dropped back and down into a sparkling haze.

Another mountain top miraculously avoided; another, miles further, notched deeply into its soft white shoulder.

Then, hissing and screaming like a cat, the ship struck glancingly on a long ice slope, bounced, took the air for another six miles and smashed down again. She began to

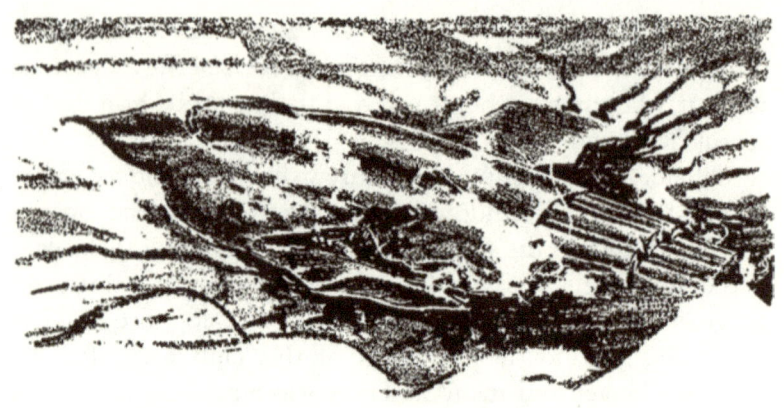

Shipwreck! Not a new tale, but the oldest of all. But this was a spaceship wreck on the most desolate world in the void — and it was four hungry survivors, "one for all —

—AND ALL FOR ONE

By JEROME BIXBY

roll—rather, to cartwheel—end over end, on and on, to vanish over the lip of a ravine. A thud, the trembling of an avalanche, then a muffled roar as the tanks blew infernally beneath settling tons of ice and snow. A green flare, and some foul smoke that dissipated quickly in the thin air, and the *I. S. Angel* had made angels of sixty-three men.

The other four—there had been sixty-seven in the crew— lay in the snow—*in* the snow, not on it—each unconscious at the bottom of the little tunnel his flying entrance had created. Each wore an alumalloy bulger, with gadget belt and hotsy that had been turned on before the crash. And each—since the *Angel* had cracked up at 10:31 p. m. shiptime, and after hours of tension and activity preparatory to the intended landing upon Saturn—was carried off into an exhausted

"There she is! We won't starve to death anyhow. But we've got to act fast . . . she's freezing in fast! Once that ice locks her in, we're done!"

slumber at the end of his stunned insensibility.

Tethys' grey nightwind came shrieking across the icy plateau, darkening the racing snow that lifted and fled level before it. Snow-devils danced from pockets and crevices to be whipped and shredded and their flaky atoms sucked into the striding storm. White hours passed; and Millikan, Chief Correlator, was the first to awake. His voice came out hoarsely:

"McNutt? Greenberg? Lacy?— McNutt? Greenberg?—"

At last he remembered to pull his arm up out of the arm of the bulger and switch on his talky. He fumbled at the inner control-board, "McNutt? Lacy? Greenberg?—"

He heard breathing sounds—he held his breath and heard them still, "Hey Nutsy—Greenberg—who's alive?"

He heard a groan, and a stifled *Hot damn*!

"Hello there! Lacy? Hello—"

"Millikan! Is that you, chief?"

"Yeah. Looks like we made it—"

The young but competent voice of Lacy, Astrogator, scraped out of his earphones. "Where's *Angel?*"

"Don't know—probably screwed herself up against a mountain. Where're you?"

"I hate to say it," came the drawling answer, "but I think it's a grave."

"Me too. We're down in the snow—"

"Uh! How far down?"

"Let's make like moles and see—" Millikan began to squirm around, kicking his legs and arms until he had enlarged a space that permitted him to turn over. Lying on his stomach, he pointed upward and flashed his wristlight, "Lacy—"

"Yeah, dammit—"

"I'm just a couple feet. I think we hit a hard surface, broke through and went in a little way. There's a blizzard up there—it's corking us in. Better try to climb—"

"And don't make too much fuss doing it," a new voice growled, "or you'll cave in your tunnel. I just did."

Millikan grinned in the darkness of his helmet. "Hi, Greenboig. That's me, you and Lacy. Now if McNutt only made it we can play Asteroids."

"Asteroids hell! I'll boot you in yours—get me outa here!"

"Lacy, I think Greenberg wants some help—how much does he owe you last counting?"

"Eighty sol-credits, but let it slide. I can spare it, and him too."

While Greenberg gave them a boiling in three languages, all non-terrestrial, Millikan and Lacy went worm-like up their tunnels. Always the feeling that below was nothing but white

quicksand—maybe hundreds of feet down. Swim! Fly up
and out of the brittle cotton—struggle up, slide down—damn
the stuff! is this the way up?—or *sideways?*

Poke a hand up, fingers clawed, and Lacy, standing on the
surface, grabs and yanks. Out of the snow with a crunch and
a stagger—and into a blinding, white-clotted inferno. They
bumped their face-plates together. "Lacy, I kiss you—"

"Miles baby, your eyes—that soft, curly—"

"Yeah," said Greenberg sourly into their earphones. "I
vote for polygamy. I'm virile too—come and get me!"

They found him under the crust, several feet away from
the entrance of his tunnel. "I can feel you stamping—" his
voice was oddly tight,"—you're right over me!"

Millikan and Lacy pounded through the hard, milky
surface, and dug out the fluff beneath. Metal clicked on
metal, and soon Greenberg, Pilot, sat in the snow, his thin
face twisted behind his face-plate. "Surprise—" he hissed,
"I'm surprised! I got a broken arm and didn't even know it!"

Leaving him nursing and cursing, the other two went to
search for McNutt. They found his tunnel several dozen feet
away and squatted beside it. Lacy adjusted his proton-buster
to light heat and aimed it at the opening: "I'll melt him out—
"

Millikan knocked the ray aside. "You'll ice him in, you
mean! Wait."

The wind screamed and flooded against them, forcing
them to resist it at an angle, pushing great churning walls and
spirals of snow across the plateau, whose horizon could not
be seen, nor the sky above it, through the thick motion.

Millikan put his talky at full volume and spoke loudly:
"McNutt! Hey Nutsy—wake up!"

"Mmm?" A yawn. "That you, chief?"

"Yeah, and Greenberg and Lacy. Give a wiggle." Then,
as an aside to Lacy: "That's why he's such a lousy medico—

he slept his way through college."

Lacy grinned. "How'd he graduate?"

"The Dean was a female."

This brought a vulgar noise from McNutt, who finally shoved head and shoulders out of the tunnel and was hoisted to his feet. His heavy, pink features were loose and astounded. "You mean we're still alive?"

"This look like Heaven?" came a snarl from Greenberg.

"And since when do spacemen go there?" McNutt gazed about him wide-eyed. "Bejabbers, I think this's the other place, all right!"

The three men rejoined Greenberg and huddled together, warm in their bulgers, only dimly visible to one another through the leaping snow. They rocked on their hips as the sucking wind piled white buttresses against their hunched forms, then stripped them down, whisked them away into the shrouded greyness.

"What happened? We got tossed right out of the damned ship, that's what!" Millikan flashed excellent teeth in a grin. "Remember? I saw you guys go streaking—then I went. What luck! She started to pinwheel, Control split like a herring, and here we are!"

"Where's that?" said McNutt dubiously.

"Yeah; which way do we walk?"

Lacy added. "Anybody know?"

They took out their compasses; they switched on their suit lights and thumbed out charts from the clips by the inner control-boards. High above, for a moment, the whiteness parted and, startlingly, the tiger's eye of Saturn stared down at the four of them. Her rings seemed to writhe in the snow, then she faded and the color was gone.

Millikan studied the Tethys chart, adjusted his all-world compass after the specific vagaries listed there. Finally he said: "We're right smack on *12*F, *22* northern. There's an I. P. Station on this clod—look at *2*N across .6 southern. That ex is where we head for—"

Lacy whistled softly. "About forty Earth days, if you count ten miles a day!"

"And forty nights," growled McNutt, "and not an Ark in sight—or even a flexible Flyer—

Tiny ground-swells of snow rippled toward them, lapping at their ankles, spraying up to tap on their helmets like rats' claws.

"Check your bulgers," said Millikan, "Anybody got any concentrates?" He searched his own cubbies, found no edibles; and "None here," rasped into his earphones, and "Empty—we didn't have any time—" and, succinctly from McNutt: "Nah, hell!"

Millikan wiped his face-plate inside and out, steam and snow. His lips were tight. "We'd better locate *Angel.*"

They walked along the level sweep, tracing the *Angel's* hopping course by the huge, dented-in patches of ice where her searing rump had mashed the surface for a split-second melt. They came to the ravine, and grouped at its edge to stare down. Finger-sized in the distance, pointing rudely at the boiling clouds of whiteness that raged across the abyss, was the dead *Angel*, standing slant-wise in a pool of steam and stained water, her exploded engine room flaring out in jagged petals. The debris of the snowslide had melted from over her, had made a metal island of her.

Millikan hopped down goat-like from the ice-drowned crags of the rim, skipping across crevices, plowing through sleek, fresh snow slopes, shorn by the avalanche. Tethys' light gravity socked his feet gently into the crusted bottom.

McNutt and Lacy followed more slowly, helping the agonized Greenberg over the rough spots. After a backward glance, Millikan waded out into the pool. He stopped halfway.

"Here's Jack," he said into his talky. A dead face looked up at him from the bottom of the pool, and for some reason he bent to lift up the body, but the body wasn't there. Not even all of the head.

Chest-high in the already clotting water Millikan made his way to the port side and found the airlock sprung open. He pulled himself up and in, and stumbled along the dark, crazily twisted corridor toward the store room.

By the time he came out again Greenberg had fainted and McNutt had joined suits with him and was bending through the belly lock of his bulger to work over the unconscious man. Expertly he set and bound the broken arm and checked Greenberg's oxygen, turning it a little higher. Then he closed the inner lips of the other suit, straightened back into his own and closed its inner lips, separated the bulgers and closed the outer lips of both.

Millikan came crunching up to them. "We don't eat," he said. "Everything's ashes."

Lacy cursed softly, and McNutt drew his thick brows together. "Forty days on water," he growled, "Well, it's been done. At least we have water—the whole damned world's water!"

Millikan checked his filter dial. "Oxy, too. Plenty outside."

"We—" Lacy swallowed "—won't the Smithsonian start up a search for us?"

"Sure. But where on which moon do you think they'll start, kid?"

They sat there for a while, but Greenberg, looking more than ever like a skull, didn't regain consciousness. Finally Millikan said : "Let's get going. We'll take turns dragging him…"

Every hour they changed positions, the leader going back to the rear of the single-file to pull Greenberg along and the rest moving up a place. Only the first man kept his eyes open, wary of the sheer, treacherous cutbanks and gaping crevices that appeared wide beneath his probing feet; the others followed blindly, the hand of each on the gadget belt of the man preceding.

The snowball that was Tethys raced around its ringed parent, and under its sleek white shell four bellies shrank, four faces gaunted. Like the undead they stumbled through the days—like the dead they slept at night. On the third day Greenberg was able to keep his feet, and they made better progress.

And on the eighth day they saw the "white monkeys."

"Up there! *Look—behind that bank!*" Millikan, at the rear, pointed as he shouted, and the others turned in slow motion. Lacy raised his proton-buster and snapped a shot at the scurrying form. It faded into the blurred whiteness, and he ran, staggering a little, to the spot and found it empty. He came back slowly.

"Everybody carry your gun," said Millikan, and got his out, "We'll eat the next one."

The racing snow gave another red-yellow glimpse of Saturn above them—their daily glimpse, caused by some freak of clashing gravities.

"Golly, I'd like to be up there in Pilka right now... I've got a little female there with everything!" McNutt raised his eyes for a second, looked down again as he tripped and nearly fell.

"Dames yet!" said Greenberg acidly. "And with tentacles. What would you do with her in your condition?"

McNutt grinned weakly, "You guys don't really know me."

"I bet. The System birth rate'll sure take a dive if you drop out here, Nutsy. Mass suicides, too—all the dames jumping out of windows huh?"

White turned to gray as night came soaking through the eternal snow, and Lacy's eyes began to hurt. He moved to the rear, giving the lead to McNutt.

"There's another one!" Millikan brought up his gun and fired three fast shots. "Hell! you can't hit 'em—you can hardly see 'em in—*there!*—"

A furry, round-eyed head poked around the edge of a snowdune, jerked back in time to avoid a silent, sweeping quartet of rays. McNutt hunched his huge shoulders in his bulger and licked his lips. "I ate monkey once," he said, "in Sumatra. Wasn't bad. Come on out, you little *sutzes!* come and get it!" His red eyes searched the surrounding white death.

Lacy sat down abruptly, "How many more days, Miles?"

"The rate we're going, about thirty." The others sat down too, forming a circle, and chipped and scrubbed at their crisply iced faceplates. "How's the arm?"

"Okay." Greenberg was silent for a moment. Then, wearily: "Why in God's name do they build the store room right next to the engine pit?"

Millikan grunted, voicing a shrug. "To save space which saves money—maybe to cut down on the population. It's a Eugenicist plot. You crash, the Drive goes br-r-r-t! and you starve to death."

"I thought McNutt was going to cut down the population."

"Like hell," rumbled McNutt. "I'm not dying out here—"

"None of us are," Millikan broke in. "Come on now—up! We'll rest later. Slow and easy. We'll make it."

Next day they came, like bulgered skeletons, to the edge of the plateau, and saw below a land of tortured, ice-drenched ridges that sheered far down to merge shapelessly into a welter of vein-blue canyons. The snow was less heavy here, and the wind, broken and diverted, less powerful.

"We'd better knock off and sleep here. The climb down—" Millikan wheeled, sent his ray cutting out into the snow, "Damn you!—I almost got that one!"

He squinted through his face-plate, then spoke sharply: "Greenberg, winged or no you're still our best shot. Come on—let's get one of those damned things!"

The two men faded back onto the curtained plateau, and McNutt and Lacy sat in the lee of a snowdune, shifting forward now and then as it threatened to creep over them. They waited, eyes bright and red, for the glad shout in their earphones that would mean food had been gotten. And it came; it filled their helmets and brought them to their feet.

"Lacy—Nutsy! I got one! It walked right into the blast!"

Then they heard Greenbergs voice: "Where? Where, Miles?"

"Over this way—hell, where are you?—oh, I see you. Where's the monkey?—This way. Help me lug it! Man, what a break this—*Greenberg watch out*—that crevice—" They heard a gasp, then a scream from Greenberg—"Mi-iles!—" Then Millikan's dull voice: "He fell. Greenberg fell into a hole. It all caved in on him—"

Minutes later Millikan came back. Lacy and McNutt stood rigid as robots by the snowdune. Silently they cut up the big chunk of skinned white meat, broiled the pieces in their bulgers' cookers. It had a sweet, sickish veal taste.

"I couldn't get to him in time—" Millikan's voice was an unsteady grating sound. "He hung on to the edge of the hole and looked at me. And I couldn't get there in time. He looked at me…"

The monkey meat lasted them seven days, during which they followed their compasses and worked their way deep down into the ridge and ravine country. Then came four more foodless days, and their steps slowed and faltered.

They found a stone idol, cruel and ugly, and about it some tumbled ruins of what might once have been a sort of temple; and, crouched in this scant shelter, they stared up at the tormented snow that lashed horizontally, like a ceiling, across the ice-glassed canyon rim.

Lacy got up suddenly, and said: "Mary, I think it might snow."

He took off his leather jacket, put it in the belly hatch of his bulger and, after closing the inner lips, opened the outer ones and took out the garment. He draped it gently over the idol. Then he turned briskly, strode to a fallen column, rapped on it.

"Some service, please. Ah there, I'd like a box of aspirin—" He paused to listen, pursed his lips. "Two credits? Tch. Well, I guess inflation can't last forever." He picked up some snow and dropped it on the column. "This will pay for it, won't it? Very well then, ask the manager—although I'm sure it'll be all right."

He leaned on the column, whistled a few bars. His eyes traveled the length of the column, and he strained his ears to hear a distant conversation.

The wind shrieked over the top of the canyon.

He straightened and smiled; his eyes came slowly front again. "I was sure it would be. Thanks, no need to wrap it—"

He returned to the idol, put a handful of snow in its mouth, waited for a while and then pressed his metalled hand to its forehead. "Ah, that's better. Now you've got to rest and relax, dear—cold's nothing to fool with."

He went back to the column, rapped again, "Two tickets please, front balcony center."

Then he sat beside the idol, his eyes fastened raptly on the frozen, featureless ice slope opposite him. The night came across the far plateau and into the canyons, and the deep snows with it; whipping, twisting masses of whiteness that were caught by the jagged walls and flung roaring to the canyon floor to break in foamy explosions and spread like water. From their concealment behind a crumbling altar Millikan and McNutt watched the two mounds become smaller and smaller; and at last, when day came, there was only a snowdune, sparkling and clean and very smooth.

"I suppose we'd better dig him out," said Millikan. He and McNutt got to their feet and went to the spot where Lacy sat beneath the snow. His figure didn't move as they kicked the snow away from about it, and McNutt tapped the silent helmet and it rang like a broken bell. Lacy exploded up and began to fight them.

"Where's Mary?" he shouted, and sent McNutt tumbling back into a drift.

"She's gone on ahead, Lacy!" Millikan held his arms. "She's waiting for us at the I. P. Station—"

Lacy butted him in the chest and ran staggering down the canyon. He vanished, but his voice came strongly into their earphones: "Mary! Mary—you'll catch pneumonia! Don't you want my shirt, dear? Mary—"

McNutt sat in the snow, only his bulgered torso showing. "Let him go. He'll find a rock and call it Mary and die happy."

"Can't do that. Wait here—I'll get him."

McNutt waited. In his earphones he heard Millikan calling, and Lacy's unabated shouts and babblings. Minutes passed. Then he heard a grunt, and there were no more shouts and babblings. "What happened?" he asked.

"Don't know," came Millikan's reply. "I think he fell and busted his talky. Lacy! *Lacy!*—ah, I can't see anything but snow. Lacy! L-l—wait! –there he is! Lacy! Lacy?—*holy hell, it's a monkey*! E-easy now—oh Lord—hah!—hahaha—I got him, Nutsy! I got the white stinker!—"

And then, much later: "Nutsy—I think Lacy's gone. I can't go on looking for him any further or I'll end up lost myself."

Millikan came back, gasping for breath his face yellow and tight. They broiled part of the monkey meat and ate it, packing the rest, as they had before, into their cubbies.

Thirty six days after the death of the *Angel*, her two survivors topped a low rise and saw a level, white-blown plain before them. Millikan clapped his hands. "Last lap!" he cried jubilantly. "Smooth going, now!"

McNutt stood silently, eyes and mouth troubled. Then: "Yeah. You know, I've been thinking, Miles. It's funny that Greenberg didn't yell after he fell in that hole. The gravity here isn't enough to squash a man."

"Probably knocked out."

"He might still be alive then," mused the big man. "Lacy, too. Maybe a searching party could locate them!"

Millikan's smile had stiffened over his teeth. "Yeah," he said evenly, "I guess one could."

"And we could guide them, couldn't we?"

"Count me in!"

McNutt said heavily: "Let's get going, chief." He stood aside. "After you."

They walked a little way out onto the plain, silently.

Millikan shouted: "There's a monkey!—"

McNutt whirled convulsively, his gun already out, peering into the thick-hung whiteness. "Where? Where? —I don't see—*damn you, Miles...*"

"...it was horrible," said old Millikan. "I saw McNutt from sheer weakness go spinning down into that bottomless crevice. God! his screams —" he cut a piece of fat from his steak, putting it carefully on his salad plate. He shook his head and went on: "And so close to the I. P. Station and safety, too. I got there by nightfall of the next day."

Rof Unain sipped his brandy and pouted as he tasted it deep in his throat. The clubroom was shadowed again; the logs in the fireplace had burned down to tired coals. "It's a remarkable story," he said, "and a bitter one—a most sardonic one. Why were McNutt and Lacy and Greenberg spared by a miracle from death in the crash, only to die horribly on the way out?"

Millikan shrugged plump shoulders. "Who knows?—it's very much like a dream now. Thirty years is a long time."

They stared into the fireplace.

"I think," said Unain, "that my first act as a member of this club will be to propose a toast to those who didn't make it."

"Agreed."

They lifted their glasses and drank.

After a short silence, the young Martian said: "Strange, though, that McNutt should fold like that. I mean, I've seen his photographs—big strapping man—when I was a kid, of course. It was pretty much of a story, that crack-up—I remember—"

"Yes." Millikan stifled a belch. "More than you realize."

"I imagine so. You have to live something like that to— they were never found, were they?"

"No. I led the searching party myself."

"Shame—crying shame." Unain choked a little as he swallowed too much brandy. "It still puzzles me, though— McNutt *was* a big man, wasn't he? I should think he'd have outlasted you all—"

Millikan cut his steak deftly, ousting a strip of gristle. He pondered for a moment, his face reminiscent. "No," he said, "you're wrong there. He wasn't really what you'd call muscular. Big he was, but soft—mostly fat."

The Good Dog

Mr. Bixby is an impeccant gentleman with a heart only slightly smaller than left field at Yankee Stadium. As a dedicated defender of the underdog, his stories carry a strong message of equality for all—even if he has to go to Hell to prove his point...

ONCE, long ago, the Devil built a bridge—in the twinkling of an eye a bridge of seasoned wood and greystone appeared over a stream in the center of a small village which shall here be nameless, for both village and bridge are gone, and what's past is past.

The Devil built the bridge with the proviso that the soul of the first being to pass over it should belong to him. To this the townspeople agreed—for they had a plan.

The poet Longfellow has recorded what followed:

"At length the bridge being all completed,
The Abbot, standing at its head,
Threw across it a loaf of bread,
Which a hungry dog sprang after,
And the rocks reechoed with the peals of laughter
To see the Devil thus defeated."

Longfellow does not go on to describe with what earth-shaking snarls the Devil greeted this stratagem. Nor does he record the wails of the unoffending dog as the Devil pounced upon it ere it had even sniffed the bread which had lured it to its doom, and wrested its soul brutally from its galvanized body and disappeared Hellwards in a puff of rotten smoke. The bridge had been gotten, the Devil had been done, and that was enough for the townspeople, and evidently, for Longfellow as well.

But this seems rather an anthropocentric view to take of

the matter. What of the *dog*?

Some of you will object that animals have no souls. Let me assure you that they do. Regard if you will the faithful watchdog, the mother tiger defending her young, monkeys at their clever play, swallows in migration slowing for a cripple, the limpid eye of the fawn, the dog mourning at his master's grave or, *probatum est*, finding his way with mystic determination to his master's side across miles upon miles of unknown terrain; regard the mother bird feeding her young, the mating minuet of the peacock who in the East symbolizes immortality, the community spirit of an ant-city—regard all these, and tell me animals have no souls: and I will tell you that we had better define our terms.

But let's have no debate—the dog had a soul, and the Devil made off with it, albeit with exceeding lack of enthusiasm.

The dog's lineage is as uncertain as is certain the fact that it was a very good dog. It was frankly a mutt. At the time of its demise it was six years and odd months old; and never in its life had it bitten anyone, or bayed with sleep-destroying vigor in the early morning hours, or chewed or torn up any possession of the villagers', or stolen one particle of food. It was known as a friendly dog: mothers had trusted it to romp with their children. Assuredly it had chased cats; but this scarcely figures as a canine sin, and besides it had killed none of them. Far from blood-lust, its sole emotion at such times was regret that it could not climb trees and continue the sport.

Children wept at the scene of its sacrifice, while adults admired the bridge, and the episode proved to be one of the basics of many later and interesting neuroses.

A brief description will suffice: medium size, white with brown spots, one floppy ear and a tail that had been broken by the wheel of a farmer's cart as the dog had slept by the roadside. Of these characteristics the dog in dying suffered the loss only of its coloration: its soul was uniformly grey.

Upon reaching Hell, the struggling, howling, thoroughly outraged dog-soul under his arm, the Devil paused at the great bronze doors of his Castle, faced in the general direction of midwestern Gehenna, released the soul and, before it could fall to the smoking flagstones, swung one cloven foot and punted it away with every ounce of his fury and indignation.

Yowling, legs and tail rigid, the soul rose up, up, up, to disappear into the red-flickering haze that surrounded the Castle. The superhuman impetus of the kick traveled it in fantastic flight like some Spartan dog of Diana, high above the landscapes of Hell. Gradually the flight leveled, rounded downward, faster and faster, thick stinking air whistling louder and louder past the dog-soul's flapping ears, ruffling its grey soul-fur, bringing tears to its horrified eyes; faster and faster descending toward the ugly terrain that waited below. Its soul-hackles rose at the sight of coiling, unquenchable flames, of vast red-shot towers of smoke like dragons' breath; it curled its lips at the sight of spraying torrents of lava and blinding lakes of molten brass and iron; it gritted its teeth at the sight of jagged cliffs and dizzy black mountains and abysmal valleys from which rose the crack of whips, the clatter of demoniacal hooves, the cacophonous screeching of the damned.

It began to howl.

Far below, a demon looked up, pricking his ears. "What in Hell was *that?*"

Another demon wrenched his pitchfork from the buttocks of a prostrate soul. He squinted upwards. "Don't know...it's the Damnedest sound *I* ever heard. Maybe the Chief is trying out some new method of tormen—"

"Look out," said the first demon. "Something's falling toward us... *duck*!"

The dog-soul came turning and twisting down to splash deep into a pool of lava. Droplets like liquid rubies flew in every direction, some of them lighting on the soul-skin of the prostrate human soul, who whined shrilly, and others on the skins of the demons, which twitched in pleasure.

The dog-soul surfaced and swam about in the pool, lips drawn back, ears flattened, nose pointing upward, head straining forward, eyes wide. He dog-paddled. He barked his many misgivings.

The demons approached the pool cautiously. One, whose name was Zut, poked his pitchfork at the swimming soul. "What is it?"

The other demon, whose name was Pud, dropped to his knees, thrust his arm into the pool, fished around, got a good grip on the dog-soul, yanked it out. The dog-soul snarled and shook itself, eyeing the demons with utter distrust.

"I think it's a dog," said Pud, rubbing the lava into his arm.

"A dog?" said Zut doubtfully. "In Hell?"

"That's what it looks like. I wonder what on Earth he did?"

They leaned on their pitchforks, regarding the dog. The dog squatted, staring back at them warily. Some silent moments passed. When the demons made no hostile move, nor any move at all, the dog began to lick at the lava on his fur, worrying hardening bits with his teeth, keeping one eye always on the pair who stood watching.

Stinging smoke curled along at ground-level, like the ghosts of snakes. The prostrate human soul took advantage of his tormentors' preoccupation, and crawled away, inch by inch, and soon was lost to view in the red-flickering smoke.

Pud said, "They just never learn, do they? That Damned

fool thinks he can give us the slip."

Zut said, "Yetzer will get him."

From nearby in the smoke came a blood-curdling shriek. The sucking sound of a pitchfork being withdrawn from fatty tissue. The dog pricked its ears.

Pud grinned evilly. "Yetzer got him."

They looked at the dog; finally Zut said, "Well?"

"Well, what?"

"How do you torment a dog?"

"H'm."

"I've heard they bite."

The dog stood up, reassured by the relative peace and quiet after that walloping kick and his resultant vast flight. He gave his tail a tentative wag, eyeing the demons somewhat more warmly.

"Watch out," Pud said.

The demons moved back a pace. The dog followed, frisking a little. The demons clutched their pitchforks in front of them and retreated another step. The dog halted and squatted, tongue lolling, eyes now merry.

When the dog stopped, the demons stopped.

"You know," Zut said finally. "I think it wants to be friendly."

Pud scowled, "Watch your language."

"Well, *look* at it."

They studied it. It looked back at them, panting, eyes sparkling, tail thumping the ground and sending up little whirls of black ashes.

"You may be right," Pud said, "Go find out."

After a moment he said, "Well, go *on*. You can see he wants to be friendly."

"Why don't *you* go, then?"

"I'll see that he doesn't get away."

Zut skinned back his lips, revealing three-inch fangs.

"That's right," Pud said encouragingly. "Ours are bigger than his. Besides, there are two of us."

"Then let's *both* go," Zut said. He gave Pud a shove. "Follow me."

Together, pitchforks ready, they advanced toward the dog.

Playfully the dog bounded away into the smoke.

A moment later he bounded back, straight toward them, eyes gleaming redly, barking at the top of his lungs, grinning a dog grin.

The demons yowled and started to run. Pud tripped over his pitchfork. Zut tripped over Pud. They tumbled to the ground one this way and one that; dropping their pitchforks in order to protect themselves at close quarters.

The dog came over and sniffed at Pud's ear. Pud moaned. The dog dropped to his belly with a grunt. He licked the ear.

Pud flushed a dead white.

"You see?" said Zut, looking on in awe. "He *does* want to be friendly."

Slowly Pud's hand went toward the pitchfork beside him.

"Careful," Zut cautioned.

"I don't care," Pud said in a low, tight voice. "It's too much Bless me, I—I feel *unclean*...to *think* that a damned soul would try to be friendly! I only hope nobody *saw*—"

"Courage," Zut whispered.

Pud's hand groped for the handle of the pitchfork, found it closed on it.

He said a silent sacrilege. He leaped to his feet, raised the pitch fork high:

"Your damnation begins!" he roared.

The tines of the pitchfork swished down, entered the dog's hindquarters, traveled through the length of his body as through vapor, emerged from the very point of his nose. No agonized howl. No agonized leap. He only blinked.

Pud looked astounded. He tried again. This time the dog leaped at the shining tines as they emerged from his chest, and seemed disappointed when his jaws failed to close on solid substance. He barked playfully.

Pud spat vitriol and tested the tines on the ball of a long-clawed thumb. "Now what do you make of *that?*"

Zut had rolled over and was sitting up, looking thoughtful.

"He doesn't feel a thing," Pud said sourly. "I don't get it."

Zut pursed his lips. "C'mere, boy," he said, masking his revulsion, "Nice dog."

Tail wagging, the dog went to him.

Pud shuddered and looked around uncomfortably. "Now *you're* displaying what almost amounts to—to friendship!"

"Well, I'm not enjoying it!" Zut snapped. "I just want him to hold still, so I can find out something." He led the dog over to the pool of red-glowing lava into which it had originally plunged. The dog eyed the pool doubtfully and pulled back a little.

"What are you doing?" Pud asked.

"Well, it just occurred to me that he didn't wail and scream when he fell in here. He didn't seem to suffer at all. And now he doesn't feel our pitchforks."

"So?"

"So maybe he isn't—well, I know it sounds crazy, but— maybe he isn't *damned!*"

Kneeling beside the dog, he thrust one of its paws into the pool of lava. Interested, Pud came over to watch.

The dog stood there, paw in lava. He whined in friendly, puzzled fashion. Zut released the paw. The dog commenced licking off the lava.

Pud passed the tines of his pitchfork through the dog's abdomen and shrugged, "I guess he isn't, all right."

"What is *this?*" roared the superior demon, glaring at the stern-wagging soul they had brought in.

They told him.

"What is *this?*" roared the Chief Demon, glaring at the stern-wagging soul.

They told him.

"What is *this?*" roared the Fiend in Charge of Torment, glaring.

They told him.

"I know what this is," the Devil sighed. "In fact, I've been expecting it to show up. First time I've lost my temper in centuries. Hand it over...I've already made the necessary arrangements."

"Well, *hello*, boy," said Saint Peter. "They told me you'd be showing up. Come on, now...no, not *that* way—not so close to the edge. *This* way...through the gates. You missed out on that bread, but there's a Heavenly steak waiting..."

Nightride and Sunrise

Spacemen call it "the Spectre": what it really is, nobody knows—but long before Death comes aboard, you know he's coming.

TUESDAY 3:15 P. M., SHIPTIME

I CAME out of it fast—I always do. After twelve years of constant use, *inertite* doesn't leave much of a bang in its hangover. Even at that, though, my head felt like a baked potato; I waited until it settled down. Then I opened my eyes and blinked myself alive.

By my bunk, the port was writhing with colors: a thousand rainbows in combat, laced by the unnamed star-colors that are the coronet of hyperspace.

My gimmick—the autohypo, that is—came out of the wall again, scanned for me with its radar pinwheel, and made a determined pass at my arm. I dodged the needle, swung my feet off the bunk and into my sandals on the floor, yawning. The gimmick considered these movements, decided that I was awake, ergo its job done, and went back into its cubby and turned itself off.

I got up and reached at the dial-studded wallboard over my desk, pressing the button that activated every slamband in the *Starling*. A hundred needles spat *restorite* into a hundred wrists. A hundred people jerked and twitched up out of their drugged sleep, crew and passengers alike—I could tell because I could watch their metabolic processes scurrying toward normal on the wallboard dials—and most of them would immediately start to feel sicker than a goat in free fall.

I collected my kit, checked on myself in the mirror—my imagination saw another grey hair or two—and went out to ease the sufferings of the brood.

Fletcher's eternal post-switch nausea I squelched as usual

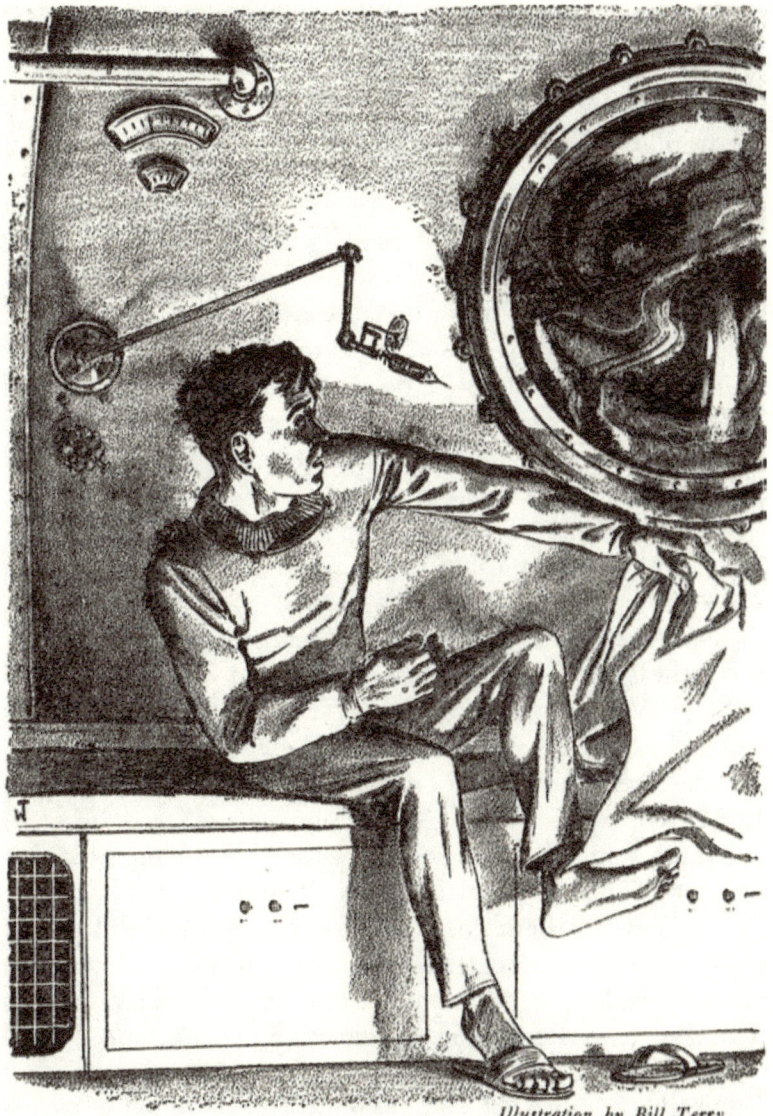

Illustration by Bill Terry

with a piece of peppermint candy. His illness was largely psychosomatic, and I dreaded the day I'd have to report that Fletch was becoming too neurotic for hyperspace piloting. A good man, a fine one: but the responsibility was getting him—just as it gets them all. He grinned at me, and said: "Whatever this is, darling, it's wonderful stuff!" He sucked on the peppermint. I agreed with him. The human mind is also wonderful stuff.

I went the rounds of the operations rooms, handing out pills and taking pulses and peering into pupils. No more *restorite* needed here; these guys were all old-timers like myself.

In astrogation I came upon a green-faced kid.

"Hello," I said, "you're new this trip."

He started to salute—I do wear a colonel's stripe, God knows why, I certainly don't rank the captain—and I had to "at ease" him. His pupils were dilated, his pulse blurred and banging with tachycardia.

"You'd better go off duty far a while, son," I told him. "Go down to your cabin and read, maybe take a radiogen bath."

The clear call of Duty or Death, the old Academy foolishness, stiffened his back. He smiled and said, "I'm all right, sir," and avoided my needle. Beneath that smile he felt like hell. I knew it, and he knew I knew it, so I didn't argue. I said, "Well, this'll do for the time being," and gave him a stiff emetic.

Fletch grinned; I'd pulled the same trick on him, his first trip out. "That'll do it nicely, honey," he said.

Our new assistant cosmographer thanked me and turned back to his chart desk, where he began to hunch lower and lower. Finally, after less than a minute, he excused himself with a reproachful look in my direction that told me I was a bum doctor.

"And so, Fletch," I said, "it goes. If you're going to live by *inertite*, you've got to respect it." I snapped shut my kit and headed for the door. "Any odd stops this trip?"

He shook his blond head. "Straight through to Goran III,

no specials."

I DESCENDED the spiral stairwell, past my quarters, down to the passenger level. The green-and-chrome roundabout corridor was significantly deserted. I studied the physiograph card slotted on the door of the first cabin, then buzzed for a view just to make sure. The guy inside flashed me right away; he was an old hand at hyperspacing, sure enough—he was reading comfortably, gave me a wave.

Sometimes they try to fake it, but you get so you can spot them. Out here, a doctor has to be a Jekyll and six benevolent Hydes: physician and surgeon, physiologist and psychiatrist, chemist and ecologist, father confessor and general factotum. He has to be brave and resourceful (that's what the travelogues say) and more than a *bissel meshugeh* (that's what I say).

At cabin *32* I needed it. When I buzzed, the viewer took a long, one-way look at me. The suspicious type. Then a woman's voice said:

"Come in, Petey dear."

My shoulders twitched. It ran down my arms to my hands. I pushed open the door and said, "Hello, Nyra."

She looked about the same: space-black hair, blue eyes, a little too light, much too shrewd. Passionate mouth, the rest of her built to match. She had on a pink traveling outfit, drastically cut back. I saw that she still dressed, at thirty, like a hopeful nineteen.

"Hello, Petey," she said. "Long time we don't see each other. Someone told me you were on one of these ships; I didn't know it was this one."

"Or you'd have taken another."

"I'm sure I wouldn't have cared much either way." She showed her sharp little teeth that used to shiver me through. Now I thought they looked like the incisors of a young dog.

A very young man came unsteadily out of the bathroom, wiping his face with a towel. I looked at him with pity, and, since I'm human, a touch of academic jealousy. Nyra pasted herself onto his arm. "My husband, Larry Stone," she said smugly. "Larry, this is Doctor Peter Miles, a very old friend."

His hand was dry and warm, and I thought he seemed like a nice sort; tall and wide, probably a bearcat of a lover. Trust Nyra to pick them. She'd never stopped picking—even during our marriage.

"A very old friend," Nyra repeated, with just enough overtones to stiffen Larry's big hand in mine. His eyes flickered behind his smile, and I thought, *Tough, kid—you're on your way out. Do you know yet that she's tired of you? Want a membership card?*

I went through the motions of tending them. Nyra, like my customer in the first cabin, was used to the inertia drug. But Stone was walking in circles, and how that boy hated to admit it! I finally got a sedative and some *restorite* into him, and all of a sudden he was asleep.

Then, before I could escape gracefully, Nyra had turned on the heat—with nothing more interesting in mind than to see how uncomfortable she could make me. She kept herself between me and the door, her eyes mocking me. I sparred with her, but I'd never been able to beat her at that game, and I couldn't raise my voice in purple prose because Larry's drug-ridden sleep was disturbed and precarious.

At last I did something I'd wanted to do for a long time. I grabbed her and pulled her against me. She came right along, looking cool, helpless and a little outraged. I could read in the brightness of her eyes that she had about had her fun, and was ready to yell and sic her husky Larry on me.

I played it that way. I bent as if to kiss her—she would let it go that far, just for kicks—and at the last moment I clamped my hands hard around her throat.

Her yell bumped against her closed windpipe and went back down again in a hell of a hurry. Her eyes were so wide that I could see the edges of the red membrane that lined the inside of her eyelids. Then I talked to her, in a low, rotten voice.

I went all the way to the end of the nasty speech I'd so often dreamed of whispering into that pink, almost-transparent ear. Then I repeated parts of it I thought would bear repeating. Then I left.

I would have slammed the door, if a sliding spaceship door could be slammed.

THREE more cabins—two more headaches and a poor devil who wouldn't come out of his bathroom; I left him a pill on his bed—and I got another shock.

The voice that said, "Wait a minute," was pure, clean honey—golden tan, shining and sweet. I knew it well; and when she flashed me, I recognized her from many video viewings.

It was Merlin Gale. I was afraid of staring when I went in, but I didn't; I gawped. Her hair was black, like Nyra's; but whereas Nyra was strictly boudoir, Merlin Gale was sunlight and out-of-doors. Her eyes were a smoky autumn and her skin tea-rose. If I had ever thought that she was only a product of the pretty-poison greens and blues and leads that get painted on video faces to make them look acceptably inhuman to the ike, I knew better now.

I looked around for a husband. I didn't see one. Nor any sign of one.

"I'm," I said, "the ship's husband. I mean, the houseboat's physician. Oh hell, my name is Peter Miles and I'm a doctor and how do you feel?"

She was sitting cross-legged on the bed, amid a litter of magazines from the *Starling's* library. "Doctor?" she murmured. "And so nice looking too, in a stuffy sort of way...all that distinguished gray hair, and you're not over forty at most!"

I dropped my kit on my foot. "Thirty-eight," I said faintly. "The gray is hereditary."

"I feel awful," she went on cheerfully. "I'm glad you came. I've been toying with the idea of opening my port and ending it all."

"The port won't open," I said, "and you *look* wonderful."

I picked up the kit, fumbled out a capsule, saw that it was a cathartic, and felt around for the right tin. It evaded me with studied perversity; I finally had to take my eyes back into my own head and use them to search the kit.

My confusion kept her smile alive. "Are you always so distracted, doctor?"

"Nothing rattles me but perfection," I replied gallantly. I was rather proud of that reply, and my pride carried me right on into plain foolishness: "But please don't think me impulsive, Miss Gale. I've loved you for years." Which was the truth, of course; bachelor spacemen can hardly survive without some *Wunschmädchen* to carry them to and fro across the barren light-years. I had found mine—and here she was.

She leaned back, hugging her knees, and studied me with open interest. "I believe you," she said. "And I think I like it. You're the only interesting person I've seen aboard this coffin. What do you do when you're *not* rattled?"

I finally found the right tin of capsules. "I doctor," I said. "But if you get any more candid with me, you'll have to take over. I've had a rough day." I made vague motions in her direction with the capsules. "Uh—you said you weren't feeling well—"

She laughed and put out a warm hand. I sat down beside her on the bed, for the simple reason that I couldn't have stood up a second longer. "No pills," she said. "My dad and

I used to space this galaxy from Sol to Magellen—*inertite's* old stuff to me."

"But you said—"

"I was bored. Reduced to reading those horrors you're sitting on. But you've cured that already, Doctor Pete."

She was grinning like an imp. No woman was going to work faster than Peter Miles. I gathered together my animal magnetism, which had been without a keeper for a long time. I said, "Dinner at six?"

"Six-thirty," she amended. "I'm doing a ship's broadcast. Jackson talked me into it, and I've got about two hours to dream up an act."

"Jackson?" I said bitterly.

"My agent. He's a dear. He has seven children and they all look like him—that is, rather like a rabbit. I don't know how he does it!" She gave me that wonderful smile that was the end of roaming, and walked me to the door. "Out now," she said. "Where do we meet?"

I told her—dining salon, third level bow, ask any steward—and left in a daze.

BACK in my own cabin, I began to set out and check the needles for Goran III. This time, when we sidestepped *out* of hyperspace, the passengers wouldn't wake up for quite a while. Not, in fact, until I had pumped them full of antitoxins.

I glanced at my schedule: 27 hours, a little over, to Goran—six more hours in hyperspace, the remainder on planetary drive. Then what? I was thinking about Merlin Gale, of course, but when I discovered that I'd been working on the Aldebaran VII needles I pulled my moonstruck self together and got down to business.

The job done, I strolled up to Control. Fletch was slouched in his big swivel-seat, staring out at the rushing varihued blur of hyperspace, I didn't have to read his thoughts to know them—I'd heard them all, often before, in the deliria of pilots a good deal farther gone than Fletch:

A hundred people—a hundred lives—got to world them—two light-years every second—what happens if—my God, maybe the—if I've made a mistake somewhere—

I dropped a hand on his shoulder, "Thinking about home, Fletch?"

"Yeah—in a way, lover-boy." He looked up at me. "This hyperspace run is freaky, isn't it?"

"All situations are freaky," I said. Standing beside him, I studied his blink-time against my own pulse-rate. "The reason people never learn anything from history is that most 'future' events break totally with the past. If you can't develop an attitude of total acceptance toward whatever the future might bring, you're in for a continuous series of nasty shocks."

Underneath this cushion of chatter I was watching him as closely as I dared. The flight wasn't over, but already it was clear that Fletch was through. I'd have to report him out—and I hated like blazes to do it. When we got to Goran, he would go through a company conditioner. He wouldn't know what it was, though; it would look like a runabout, or a small office or a video booth. But when he came out he wouldn't want to hit space any more. He'd want to go back to Earth and buy a farm, maybe raise a family. The company would supply the farm.

I was still gabbing. "After all, why should the hyperspace run be any freakier than anything else?"

He rubbed a hand across his mouth, stretching the lips, "I—can't make words out of it." He was blinking steadily, but at unnaturally long intervals now. With each blink his pupils got bigger. "There's something wrong out there, baby. No stars—lotta colors—ever try to figure out what hyperspace is like, actually?"

"No Fletch. I've been told that it isn't really like anything, that it's a mathematical fiction. That's good enough for my poor brains. But if the colors bother you, why look at them?"

"They come through my eyelids—I sit here—with a hundred people under my tail—drowning in rainbows—I—I think just think what if I *didn't* then *maybe* and all those *people* and—" He was on his feet, and I hit him with the hypo on my ring—under the guise of clapping him on the shoulder. He'd think he'd passed out of his own accord; essential, or he'd smell the conditioner coming.

There's a fast turnover on hyperspace pilots. Hard come, easy go.

Ingres and von Bietz helped me lug him to his quarters. We laid him out on his bunk. He was smiling a little.

"It's a wonder," von Bietz said slowly, "that this didn't show up during his pre-flight screening."

My own eyes were on Fletch, I'd seen older and tougher men pull the same thing. The job was basically intolerable, and that was that; but it wouldn't do for an answer to Beetsy's implied question.

"There's a late pregnancy in cabin 18," I said shortly. "God knows how *she* got an okay for hyperspacing. But that's the way they run this line. Them as don't like it can hire out to the Mars ore run, I guess. Barring that, suppose we drop it about Fletch; he'll have it tough enough from now on."

They stood by silently while I wrote an explanatory note to Captain Stanard. I gave it to Ingres and he left for the bridge; he was up for senior pilot now that Fletch had folded.

I checked Fletch once more—he'd come out of it in roughly three hours, and then there'd be a nasty hour or so. Then Beetsy and I walked back to Control, without words, and looked at the colors.

AN hour later, the pregnancy in 18 set about clinching my point to Beetsy. The *inertite* had hit her, but good. A flustered steward called me down, and I found her in the last stage of labor. I want to go on record as saying that modern obstetrics are harder on the doctor than on the mother; she was smiling and making with ship's gossip while I sweated like a Gany on Venus. And devil take the thick-thumbed execs who won't give a space-medico trained help; they must think a high salary buys them a sorcerer. A breech delivery is a bad do for one man.

At last I spanked, and there was a healthy blatting. I left mother and infant, the one radiant and cooing, the other making like a prune wired for sound, under the wing of one of the salon waitresses; one who had been through being a new mother several times. Seeing the maroon salon-uniform reminded me of my date with Merlin Gale. I looked at my watch and swore. After eight already. I damned near spaced it to her cabin; she was there, smiling.

"Boy or girl?" she asked immediately.

"Girl—" I sighed with relief. "To be named Petrina, after me, poor accursed infant... I'm glad you knew. I'm terribly sorry, it was black of me not to let you know."

"A nice young lieutenant called me from the control room. He said you'd left swearing like mad, damns and blasts and the blankety-blank desk-chair spacers, so I expected you to forget."

Thank Heaven I'd done some male boasting to Ingres...but maybe Merlin would rather I hadn't? Or was it apparent that I had? Maybe it had been just as well...I was one sadly confused medico.

"Tomorrow night, then?" I said, tentatively.

"Same time, same place."

I said, "Same people—" and our gazes locked. Then, as I

turned to leave, she put her hand on my arm.

"I've met a lot of heels, Peter," she said. I knew what she meant. The Bachelor Girl of the Telewaves was famous for skinning wolves alive.

"Out here a guy doesn't get much chance to practice that stuff," I said shakily. "Or it could be I'm too old."

"Oh!" She smiled slightly. "Not that!"

I moved in.

"Now *git*, Doctor Pete," she went on hastily. "I have a thought or two to think before tomorrow night." And I found myself outside the door, with it closing on me, and she was still smiling to draw out the sting.

I took my excess nervous energy back to my quarters and used it to recheck the Goran needles. I don't keep a diary, or I'm sure I would have filled it with bad poems. At my age!

I was still checking when Stanard buzzed me.

"Petey," he said. Only the one word, but all of a sudden there was a menacing rub to the air. You globe-lubbers wouldn't know the feeling. But a spaceman knows it too well.

"What's up, Captain?"

"We don't know." His big face was all red angles in the screen, tight and watchful. "I've checked the master board and everything is dokey. But something's gone foul, I can smell it from here."

"So can I."

"Come on up to the bridge, then. Maybe we don't know what it is till it breaks, but we'd better hold a caucus."

He didn't mean Fletch, of that I was sure. The Spectre—go on, laugh—was in the hull. Stanard was already thinking of throwing everybody on inert at once, though the colors of Goran wouldn't separate out from the warring rainbows for another two hours; he would call a caucus for no other reason.

As I passed Nyra's door, I heard quarrel sounds.

I looked to the lifeshells and checked my bulger. The caucus would find nothing wrong; we would smoke and toss it around and end up nowhere; but the Spectre would remain, and would pay off in red. The spaceman's Spectre is honest: it makes no promises it can't overfulfill.

I'd remember this trip—if I was able to get off at the end of it.

*   *   *

TUESDAY, 10:48 P. M., SHIPTIME
FLICK.

My port was hung with salted velvet. We were out of limbo; the universe was back in space. My little monster zoomed hastily for its niche.

Everything was—normal. There was a yellow dwarf visible off to starboard—my side of the ship. That was Goran, with its family of six and no grandchildren; an Edge-system, with the outpost stars of the Milky Way curtaining half its heavens, and the rest an unimaginable black, sequined with far-between glows that were not stars but galaxies. I thought how glad Fletch would be to see it. It was all in all a lovely sight, and in the clear monochromatic light the Spectre seemed to evaporate. I gathered my needles and a leather case of capsules and ascended to Control, picturing a honeymoon on a world without a moon, but (forgive me) with the honey.

Ingres came out easily, and set about touching up his course, bouncing the ship a mite this way and that to get the feel of the board. He kept sneaking glances outport at Goran, obviously satisfied with the precision of his first personally-organized heave-ho out of hyperspace.

Beetsy, on the other hand, simply wouldn't wake up—it happens that way sometimes, and can frighten the hell out of a young medico the first time—so we let him sleep it off in his chair. His snoring was sinful.

Our junior cosmographer glared at me—the story of my perfidy had evidently reached him—but submitted to my supplementary dose of *restorite*. His pallor vanished almost at once, and his eyes began to sparkle. A grin started in them and spread to his lips; I threw it back at him, and that was that.

I took the kid along with me on my rounds to familiarize him with the routine. He had had nothing but standard spaceman's first-aid training, but he made a good helper, handing me the correct needles as I called their colors. We made the rounds of the gang in Operations, pumping serums, vaccines, toxoids and antibodies wholesale into them and rebalancing their hormone systems to resist—or, rather, accommodate—conditions on Goran III. Then, as we left each cubby, I gave each man his shot of *restorite* and we escaped before he became sentient. For an hour they'd all feel like absolute hell, and it was better that they be left alone with their misery.

My blase friend in the first cabin was up already and playing himself a quiet game of Asteroids. Evidently he was somewhat *inertite*-resistant after so many years and had snapped out of it by himself. I asked him, and got the right answer: traveling salesman. I don't think I've ever seen a tougher specimen; not even our immunizing routine bothered him. It's a pity all of them aren't like that. I'd have an easier job—if I had one at all.

Larry Stone was sprawled on the bed, but Nyra wasn't around. Went walkabout, no doubt, in defiance of the alarms, and got dropped somewhere 'tweendecks or on the promenade. Her hard luck; I could trust *inertite* to keep her pinned indefinitely. Wonderful stuff, *inertite*; does things to your atoms. At least I think it's atoms.

We hit Jackson, Merlin's rabbity agent—the noise that had refused to out come of its bathroom—who proved to be somewhat of a problem; he was sex-hormone sensitive and I had to run a titration on his blood-serum to determine what fraction of the usual shot he could take without going into aliphatic shock. The kid watched with interest, until just before the *restorite* shot, when I sent him on to Merlin's cabin to bare and bind her arm. Then I stuck the rabbit for the last time, got an appropriate squeak, and ducked out the door.

At that instant I heard the kid scream. I've spaced a long time, and heard ship's hulls ring with terror before. I ran.

He was leaning against the wall, doubled up, with his arms folded across his stomach. That time he didn't have me to blame for it. I closed my eyes so hard they clicked, then looked again. It was still there. It was stupefying—the ultimate nightmare of every hyperspace medico.

Red, red, red, all over the place. Some blobs of white and gray, some things that looked like flattened ropes, some things like chips and splinters of stone. Everything that goes to make up a human being, spread out for inspection—literally painted on walls, floor, even some on the ceiling on the far side. Smeared by a hard-striding giant. Mad red mural of instant, violent extermination.

A red mural that no one could ever identify as Merlin Gale.

I WENT quietly insane, I told the kid to call Stanard down here fast, and he moved off, crabwise. I began to cry. I ran my finger along the doorjamb; it came away wet and I closed my fist on it and shook it at the air and at God.

Stanard came, his face a baby pink—the pallor of shock bleaching out his spaceburn. He'd seen all this before, in the old days, but it's a thing to which nobody can become callused. A corpse is one thing—but this profane wash of human stuffs...

He looked at the cabin number. "Miss Gale?" he said. He knew it was. His mouth tucked in at the corners: his eyes were bleak holes, nightbound craters on the surface of his skull. "What happened, Petey?"

"I don't know, Cap, I don't know—"

He put a hand on my arm. "Pull yourself together, man. You've seen—"

I shook it off. "Get out!" I screamed in a whisper. "For God's sake get out!"

He didn't get out. But then he understood.

There wasn't much to look at except the garish fact. I picked up the slamband that lay in the swamp. I looked at it. Then I wrapped my handkerchief about it.

Stanard looked at my face, and what he saw jolted him back a step. "Petey," he said in a heavy voice. "Will you let me say that accidents do happen? You were saying the same thing to Fletch a while back, if Fletch's babbling means anything."

My voice, thread-thin, began to tear words out of my brain. "No accident. Look here, Cap."

Almost jealously I showed him the slamband. The *inertite* needle had been broken off. When I had pressed my button, the needle hadn't touched her skin. When I had pressed my button, Merlin may have been laughing, thinking of me, waiting for the weight of the *inertite* I would send her to depress her bed. When I had—

I heard my voice again, scrambled, jagged, cold, like crushed ice. "I'm going to kill whoever did this, Cap. Hear me; I'm going to kill him."

The door opened and there was Tam, the ship's detective. His pale eyes photographed the room, the captain's face, mine. "I get around," he said. "It's my job. I saw you and Miss Gale a while ago, Petey. So—I'm sorry."

And he was. Tam is all right. "See anything else, Tam?" I said.

"Nothing but Fletch. Making like tomcat in the stairwell with that itch from *32*. His privilege, I suppose. Why?"

I showed him the slamband. He took one look, then looked back to the all-over death that flowered out from the dent in the wall. "A killing, is it?"

"And I want the killer, Tam," I said. "Give him to me when you get him, Tam."

The pale eyes warmed a little, but he said: "I can't do that, Petey. And I'll need that slamband."

"You can't have it until I've worked on it."

A cleanup detail was already standing outside the door, shifting its feet. It had to be done—a spaceship is no place for an infection to start. But when I saw the plastibags and the flamers I began to lose my mind again, to tremble and make jerky movements. *Leave it all alone,* I wanted to shout at them—*don't put Merlin in those things—don't touch her—don't sear her to ashes and gas...*

"You'd better turn it over," Stanard said, softly, but with iron edging his voice. "Petey, I hate to do this. But there's a letter in my hands that puts this whole business in a damned odd light. I think you'd best cooperate with Tam. Or else I'll—issue the necessary orders, Petey."

I stared at him. What he said made no sense. I knew only that I wouldn't surrender that slamband, orders or no orders. I was essential to the life of the ship; there was no possible substitute or pinch-hitter for me on board. I began to back through the door.

"I'll try it my way first," I said. "This is flesh and blood and that's my field; Cap my field, Tam, doctors are detectives too in a way, don't you forget that, stay away from me until

I'm through. Stay away from my quarters."

"You're doing yourself a bad turn, Petey," Stanard said.

"It's been done," I said. "I've had it. You'll get your slamband. But you'll wait for it. You'll have to."

I said, "Goodnight, gentlemen," in a voice as ironical as you please, but I ran my nose into the door on the way out. I was blind with scalding tears.

I could hear someone else weeping hoarsely as I passed Nyra's door. She was always good at that. And that *she* should still live…

IN my cabin, I became sick as the kid had been. A doctor shouldn't, but any lover would.

Finally I took out the slamband and examined it, through a fog that kept gathering in my eyes and rolling down my cheeks. At last I had to go into my bathroom and plunge my face into ice water. I was really blind when I stood up—you can see that I was something less than a doctor right then, or I would have known what a shock I was giving my optic nerves—but the moments during which I had to wait inside the basin waiting for my sight to return were good for me.

When I came back into the cabin proper, I had no tears left. My cheeks and my fingers and my heart were icy.

The black stellon slamband was intact, save for the needle. I cleansed it carefully, making sure that I was not obliterating possible fingerprints, handling it as I had before, with cloth, gently. The strap was set to the last notch. I tried to remember: had Merlin worn it on her wrist, or on her upper arm? I couldn't remember having seen it on her at all. Probably, then, she'd worn it on her leg, just above the knee. The set of the strap confirmed that, more or less.

The needle had been snapped cleanly, not filed or dogged over or jammed. To do that, the killer had had to dismantle the pistons, for both needles hung well back in their grooves and would come out normally only in response to the buttons in my cabin. The killer, then, had a working knowledge of slambands—which eliminated the average traveler, who was told that tampering with the bands would result in an explosion.

I had scraped the bits of flesh and fine limb hair from the band before washing it. I examined these now. It is impossible to describe the detachment with which I did this. All humanity in me was far aspace; there was only an educated beast crouching at my desk.

But I found nothing. No who; no why; no when or where. Nothing but how, and that had been evident from the moment I had first picked up the slamband from the bloody jelly.

After two hours I re-wrapped the slamband, put it in a cylinder, and tubed it down to Tam's lab. He screened me a second later.

"Thanks for being so careful, Petey," he said quietly. "I'll do my best with—what you've left me." He was reaching toward equipment even as his screen faded.

My eyes burned. I'd smoked myself into a stupor, I lay down on my bunk. Stanard and Tam had been kind and decent, and I'd done no more than waste time. Now that Tam had the band...

I closed my eyes over my thoughts. Had Merlin mentioned knowing anyone on the ship? Only Jackson—no, surely not Jackson. But who then? —my thoughts returned to the rabbity man.

Then to the slamband.

Merlin...

A weak light was playing over my closed eyes. Goran III, inflating in my port. We would land in a few hours. I would get up and make my final round, to see how my shots had taken. Then we'd go out; I would show Merlin the alabaster towers, the chattering native section, the shielded and un-approachable continent where the beings from Goran IV, in exile, held themselves aloof from all the rest of the galaxy. I would kiss her and we would be married.

Sleeping is practice for death. That night I became an expert.

*　　*　　*

WEDNESDAY, 11:22 A. M., SHIPTIME

I BEGAN the final round that morning like a robot interne; the sleep hadn't helped. I moved automatically, doing what I had to do, avoiding thinking about that moment to come when I would have to pass Merlin's cabin without stopping, and listen to the silence welling out of it.

Ingres and Beetsy both seemed to be under considerable strain. I felt a sort of repressed, uneasy sympathy; neither of them would meet my eyes for more than a moment at a time, and they submitted to my tests with no chitchat other than a few monosyllabic platitudes. At another time I might have been more sensitive to it, and hence more curious, but now it barely reached me. I was numbly glad not to have to talk.

My oldtimer told me briefly that he was all right, just running the usual post-shot fever. How was I? The brief question from him touched me more than a thousand effusions from someone else would have—but I could not afford to have any emotions now. I said stiffly that I was all right and went on.

Mother was convinced that baby was going to die. I assured her that it was only post-shot fever. She didn't believe me. I didn't care.

Before I reached Nyra's cabin my nostrils began to twitch. I smelled something damned familiar—as familiar and as characteristic as the odor of cinnamon or citrus oil or vinegar. But half my brains were out of circuit with grief. I couldn't place it, though I tried without much interest.

It was very powerful right in front of Nyra's cabin. I buzzed long and loud. When the door slid back the odor came rolling out in great waves.

Larry Stone stood in the partly open door, blocking the way. His face was damp, and his big shoulders hunched when he saw me, I said expressionlessly, "Hello, Stone. Did you find Nyra?"

"Find—Nyra?"

"That's what I said, I hadn't the time nor the spirit to go scouring the decks for her after what happened. Did you find her, or is she still sprawled in some bunk in the crew's quarters?"

It was brutal, but what could I care then for the puppy's feelings? Curiously, he took no offence—perhaps he had learned a few things about Nyra. He said, "Yes. Sorry. I found her. She's all right."

"Better let me check her. She shouldn't be under *inertite* this long. Take only a moment."

"She—I believe she's out strolling the deck someplace, I gave her the *restorite* shot myself." He turned slightly to wave at some apparatus on the cabin desk. "I knew how things were with you, Doctor Miles. I felt I shouldn't bother you, and I've had considerable experience in physical chemistry."

That was the odor. I said, "She's just coming out of it now?"

"Yes, but she seems all right. I'd appreciate it if you waited to check on her, She's—"

"I know how she is," I told him. I could just see Nyra, awakening reluctantly at noon after a long night, part of which she had spent in the wrong bed. But there was nothing I could do about that. "I'll have to check, Larry, if you please. It's my responsibility, and the line's. Besides, I've seen some bad things happen, even in experienced hands; you'll understand that I can't trust a physical chemist to be a doctor too."

He didn't move. "I can assure you—"

"I can't take your assurance." My patience was beginning to evaporate.

He moved then, just enough to get himself more firmly in the way. "I've paid for privacy," he said coldly. "I'm sure I can demand it from the captain."

"Fine," I said, reaching for the buttons beside the door. "I'll buzz the captain right now." While I was at it, I buzzed Tam, too. Even the wolverine that was eating out my heart hadn't been able to prevent me from noticing certain things. One of them was the odor, which was that of *restorite* in the second, *not* the third and final stage of its distillation. If Nyra had been shot full of that stuff, she was dead; if she hadn't, then she was still under wherever she was, which was certainly not strolling the deck. And if she was still under, then it had not been Nyra I had heard crying last night; it had been *Larry Stone*—perhaps after he had killed her with his shot of under-prepared *restorite*? Or after he had been deserted for some crewman for the night?

In an incredibly short time I was able to introduce Larry to Captain Standard and to Tam and—for some reason—to Ingres. Sullenly Larry stood back to let us in. The Cap's face was a mask of iron; Tam studied us alternately, first me, then Larry, then me again.

On the desk an atoburner flamed under a squat tripod, and a retort dripped clear liquid into a test-tube.

Nyra was nowhere in the cabin.

STONE sat down on the edge of the bed, looking like a cornered animal, head down, eyes gleaming up.

"So she went strolling," I said. "The dead go strolling. Or else she's here, still alive, but invisible."

His lips started to tremble; he pressed them together and stared at the floor. Tam's face took on a professional hardness. He said, "Where's your wife, sonny?"

"I don't know."

"Then why are you distilling *restorite* for her?"

"She has to be on board ship somewhere," he said. "I wanted to get her back in here before she was found. I was ashamed—is that so strange? If she doesn't care which bed she sleeps in any more, I do. I wanted to get off-ship with her without my horns showing to everybody on board. But I haven't been able to find her. Why haven't *you* found her? It's your responsibility."

It was, too. Larry's explanation was hard to listen to, but it held water.

That is, it held water to me. But Stanard's face did not alter, and Tam kept looking at me now and then with that inexplicable searching expression. The Cap said:

"Mr. Stone, I'm not entirely satisfied. For one thing, there's a letter in my possession—"

That letter! I hadn't thought of it again until now. I still didn't understand it.

But Larry Stone did. He seemed to melt. He slumped forward and retched slightly, his face in his hands. "That letter," he moaned. "You've read it. Oh, my God, why should Nyra write such a letter? She told me about it—she read it to me—she *laughed*!"

"I've read it," Stanard said. "So you can understand that, because of the letter, I have to regard our failure to find her here as very serious."

He swung on me. "Just in case you're ignorant of all this, Petey—and I hope to God that you are—Mrs. Stone sent me the letter yesterday, after we were a few hours out. It was rather incoherent, but in essence it said that she feared a violent death at the hands of her husband. However, she didn't say which husband she meant—and we have two of them on board—"

"Oh," I said. It seemed funny to me. I had already lost my life. I had nothing left me that any human force could threaten. But now I understood why Ingres was here. The Cap had expected, if things turned out for the worst all the way around, that he would have to take both of us—Larry and me—into custody.

"I think I know where Nyra is," I said remotely. "Fletch's cabin. We've left Fletch pretty much to his own devices. According to Tam here, Nyra turned out to be one of his devices. I'm surprised I didn't think of it before."

Tam snapped his fingers. "So am I. Ingres, take a run up to Fletch's cabin and check. But go easy—just take a listen at his door, maybe a peek. Fletch is in bad shape. No need to turn him upside down, if they're there—"

Ingres nodded and went out without looking at Stone.

"But Fletch isn't *really*—" I started to say, dully.

"In the meantime, Mr. Stone," Tam broke in briskly, "one more question. Your arm is bare. Where's your slamband?"

That got to me. I jumped. I hadn't noticed. But Tam, of course, was one of the world's most expert noticers.

It got to Larry, too. He screamed, a high, pure note like the E above high C of a *cestraio*. He was up in a flash and clawing at the drawer of the wall-cabinet at the head of the bed.

Tam shot both knobs off the drawer so fast that they seemed to explode simultaneously. Larry snatched his hand back and looked at it as if to make sure he still had it.

"The next one's for you," Tam said flatly. "Blurt it out, sonny. Did you fix that slamband?"

"Fix it?" Larry moaned. "Fix it? My God, it was *my* slamband she was wearing! I didn't touch it. I didn't know it had failed until I—"

He staggered suddenly into the bathroom and lost his breakfast. Tam let him go, naturally, but not out of sight. After a while he came out again, talking in a slow, sick voice even before he sat down:

"When I came out of the *inertite* I went looking for her. We'd had a quarrel before the needles hit us. She walked out—said she was going to Miss Gale's cabin to borrow something to read. So I went there. And I found—"

His mouth jerked shut; his arms corded as he balled his fists and drummed them on his knees. He needed a doctor. I didn't volunteer. "I found what you found," he gasped. "Christ, you *saw* it—blood and bone and hair—you *saw* Nyra—"

"*Nyra!*" I echoed, amazed and, for some reason, furious. "What makes you think it was your wife? It was—" And I stopped short. My heart seemed to charge up and explode behind my eyes. And suddenly I remembered—I *knew!*

Among the blood, the shredded flesh—*there had been hair on that slamband!*

Glory burst in my brain. "Merlin!" I cried. "Damn you, Stone—*where is Merlin?*"

Tam's eyes flew to me, sharp and sad—then suddenly wide with utter blank astonishment.

"In there," Stone choked, and pointed to his wardrobe closet. "She's in there—"

I took a swing at him, missed, bent head and shoulders into the closet and started to cry again.

ONLY when I had Merlin's rigid body in my arms did I think again. "Cap!" I said hoarsely. "Ingres—we sent him to Fletch's cabin—Fletch'll kill him—for God's sake, move—it was Fletch who fixed Stone's slamband—"

Tam and Stanard turned white and vanished. Stone was weeping convulsively. A second later, the ship was ringing with Stand to Quarters. The Cap knew Fletch, all right.

I carried Merlin to my quarters.

She was still unconscious, of course. *Inertite* keeps you under indefinitely. But the space-fixing effect—which makes *inertia* what it is in interstellar travel—wears off very rapidly, and after that the drug is simply an inferior inducer of suspended animation. I could only hope that she was still alive.

But I had to believe that. I measured the *restorite* and injected it.

She half rose to meet me, frightened by my grim face, the strange surroundings. But she was equal to it. What a wonder she was, wonder upon wonder!

"Peter dear," she said, grappling to my shoulder for support. "Have you gone and compromised me?"

The next half-hour is nobody's business. It happens that way; and we had a lifetime for explanations. If it was a girl, we would name it *Starling*...that was our whispered agreement.

But one impulse I could not resist, when we finally got around to talking with words. I stroked her soft, dark head, and said, "We had an accident and a woman was killed. I was crazy for a while, but at the last I knew she wasn't you."

She made a pretty frown, "Wasn't me, Peter?"

She didn't understand, of course. I smiled, took a wisp of hair between my thumb and forefinger, and tugged.

"Oh!" She said indignantly. Then, in a tiny voice: "Hell, you had to know sometime. As if you didn't already."

"I knew the moment I saw you. Any physician would. But it's so common, I just didn't think about it again—you Earth-bound people don't realize how normal it is among spacemen. It must have happened when your father was spacing, and took you along as a kid—"

She nodded and grabbed it back from me, put it expertly on again. "Think of my public," she murmured.

141

"I'm your public," I said. I traced the smoothness of her leg with one finger.

Radiation. Space-baldness. An occupational hazard with early hyperspacers, before the perfection of the Sorenson shields. No head hair; no body hair.

No hair to find on a slamband had my Merlin.

And it had been right under my nose all the time.

AT the end, just before landing, I talked to Fletch. Not because I wanted to, but because he would talk to no one else. Me he trusted—why, I don't know.

I brought him a cup of coffee for an excuse. He was sitting in his cell, looking out at the black and silver and the nearing globe Goran III. It was a big Florida orange now, cloud-laced, sea-sparkled. We were blasting toward nightside. Fletch drank the coffee in silence, and at last looked at me.

"Nyra wasn't worth it, Fletch," I said.

"I know that," he said. "Larry Stone is okay after all—not that I like the bastard, but I'll admit he's okay. I was potty to credit what she told me about him. Beatings and so forth. But I was potty anyhow, sweetheart. Everybody agreed on that."

I shook my head. "Not everybody, I knew that breakdown of yours was a phony—but it was all the more reason to put you on the shelf, as far as I was concerned. It was the expert job on the slamband, and Tam's spotting you and Nyra in heat, that really did for you. Pretty clumsy, Fletch."

"Maybe so, lover boy. Ever since you told me that the future is just a series of cataclysms, I've been getting myself used to the notion. But what I want to know is—what the hell *happened*? I had Larry's slamband fixed but good, and Nyra had sent the Cap her letter to make it all look like a murder attempt that back-blasted. And then—" his face was white and loose—"then—"

"Let it lay, Fletch. I thought it was Merlin for a while. So must you have, and blasted in orbits trying to figure it out. Now you know it was Nyra. So I know how you feel."

"But *what the hell happened?*" Fletch repeated plaintively. "Nyra got Stone out of the cabin for a walk and I did exactly what we'd planned. Her slamband was supposed to be on the bed, with its strap lengthened for her leg. Stone's was the wrist-set band on the desk. I jimmied the wrist-set one on the desk. So *how*—"

"I'll tell you what happened, Fletch—" and I told him what Larry Stone had told me. "After Larry and Nyra came back from that walk, Nyra went in to take a shower. While she was in the bathroom, Larry decided to put on his band before going to sleep so he wouldn't have to get up when the on-bands alarm sounded. He put on Nyra's band because he was lying in bed and it was nearest at hand, and because he was as miserable as a kid cuckolded by his first love can be. Then, because he's a considerate kid, he reached over and got his own band from the desk and lengthened the strap and put it on the bed beside him, ready for Nyra when she came out. Then he went to sleep. He loved her, Fletch, and that's what happened."

Fletch stared out the port, face rigid.

"You loved her too, Fletch—maybe still do?"

"Like crazy—the beautiful bitch! All I was to her was a hot playmate and a perfect way to get rid of a used-up husband. I'd have been dropped soon enough, I know that now. And it doesn't help one God damned bit—"

I sighed, and went on: "Later, when the alarm went off, Nyra left the cabin so she wouldn't get messy—or killed—when Larry went splash. She woke him up to get in some last digs, and told him she was going to Merlin's cabin to borrow something to read; then she evidently decided she might just as well do that as stand around in the corridor, waiting for the needle. Merlin had barely opened the door and said hello when the needles hit and she dropped. A second later the HS drive cut out, and Nyra, with no shot of *inertite* in her, was in effect flung through the door and against the wall at twice times the speed of—"

Fletch groaned. "Let *that* lay, honey!"

"Okay, Fletch. For good. Well—then I made my rounds. I gave Larry his shots; and the first thing he did was go looking for Nyra. Somewhere along the line he passed me and the kid I had helping me, unnoticed; he found—Nyra—and he found Merlin, lying beside the door.

"His actions at that point need a little explaining. Before Nyra sent that letter to Stanard, she had herself a little fun reading it to Larry. She always did that kind of thing well—probably made quite a production of it—and it put Larry into a long, flat spin. Probably his first inkling that Nyra was—the person she was. As you said, he's a big, decent kid—wouldn't suspect a cannibal that was weighing him.

"Anyway, when he found Merlin, he knew that the—other—must be Nyra. That knowledge—and the sight itself—threw him out of gear. He was terrified that discovery of her death, along with the letter, would make him out a murderer. So he picked up Merlin and carried her back to his own cabin through the emergency corridor, just about the time I was sending the kid on ahead to her cabin. He put her in his closet—even tried to make her comfortable with pillows—and worked like the devil all night and morning making *restorite* for her."

"Cool," Fletch nodded, understanding.

"If a sort of psychic catatonia can be described as 'cool'—yes. He was planning, of course, to revive her before we landed and force her to walk off-ship with him as his wife, veiled probably. Then he'd let her go and he'd have vanished into the exile continent, or ridden the skins out to the Edge."

Fletch managed a smile. "He didn't have a chance. For

one thing, the Goran quarantine station would have looked under that veil...God! Like you say, catastrophe—one after another after another."

"A catastrophe is a surprise," I said. "Not all surprises are unpleasant. In the old days they'd have shot you. Now you'll just get a Class A conditioning. You'll forget this—every bit of it. Maybe you'll wind up a farmer. Does it sound good?"

He turned from the port and looked at me with eyes like twin gates to Hell. "I'll really forget?" he whispered.

"Yes, Fletch." I was gathering his personal, belongings. "We'll be landing in a moment. Ready?"

He stood up slowly, "Sure—friend," he said. "Let's go."

Tam was waiting outside the cell, hand in pocket. He took the hand out empty when he saw Fletch's face. We joined the group in Control. A very intent Ingres was juggling the *Starling* toward the quarantine station; Marlin was watching him, vastly interested. Beetsy was at the screen, chatting with the station master.

Fletch sank into the co-pilot's seat and stared hungrily at the bright surface of Goran III. Stanard looked at me, and then went over and sat down beside Fletch. They didn't speak much, but I learned something about Stanard then. He had loved Fletch, I could tell, because something he said made Fletch turn and smile.

And Stanard had said nothing, done nothing, from the moment Fletch had staged his breakdown until the end. That's why Stanard is captain of the *Starling*.

As Ingres goosed the ship to within yards of the graving dock, and tractors and space-suited men started toward us, Merlin walked to Fletch and touched his forehead lightly. She, too, understood.

That's why Merlin is my wife—and why our son is named for a murderer.

The Second Ship

"When you grow up, Danny, you're going to be a mighty important man on Mars." Danny couldn't know what the Prof meant by that remark now.

THE PROF—that's what I'd called him ever since I could remember—had rebuilt the radio set from what he could scrape together out of the wreckage of the *Mar's I*, and the reception wasn't very good. But we could get Earth.

He used to sit by the table, looking out the window at the sandy slope that led from our cabin down to the desert floor and the blue canal beyond, and listen to the broadcasts from New York and London and the U. N. The haywire set got them all—the parts had been designed for inter-planetary— but very dimly, and there was a lot of static sometimes.

It got the messages the Project Mars Foundation kept sending, too. Then his big hands would tighten on the edge of the table, and I knew he wished that somehow he could send a message back, telling them yes, the *Mars I* had crashed and that was why they'd never heard from it; and yes, there had been survivors...two survivors—the Prof and me. All the rest—colonists and scientists—killed, when the gyros failed in landing.

But our steam-turbine wouldn't generate enough power to let us transmit; attached to the ship's pile, it would have—but the Prof had dismounted it, heat transfer and all, with a wary Geiger on the pile...and anyway, we didn't have the radio working at that time.

"Sometime, Danny," the Prof would say, "they'll get around to sending another ship—if the Foundation can keep going, and get funds—the way the world is right now. Then we won't be all alone like this."

It was pretty terrible, the loneliness. The feeling of being

THE SECOND SHIP

By Jerome Bixby

"When you grow up, Danny, you're going to be a mighty important man on Mars." Danny couldn't know what the Prof meant by that remark now.

the only two people on a whole planet. We had everything we needed, though—the turbine, a short-wave cooker, the radio, books, furniture…oh, just about everything—and we had the cabin, built out of curved plates from the ship. It had a funny shape, but it was airtight and strong; it had to be, what with the sandstorms that came every sunset. And we had a greenhouse going out back—peas, carrots, stringbeans, potatoes—and every day the Prof would go down to the canal and carry up water for our needs. For a while we had a pipeline running up; but the Prof decided we'd better save the turbine for things that only it could do.

Mars was lonely, and harsh, and somehow beautiful. Days, we'd work in the greenhouse, or at building the laboratory-shack up on top of the hill. The sky was a deep blue-violet, and you could see the brighter stars overhead, even at noon. Sometimes we'd explore—we found a broken-down canal-pump station, its big valves sixty feet above water-level now, and an old town, stone buildings half buried in sand, way out in one of the little oases that lay scattered along the horizon.

Every night after supper there'd be the lessons. The Prof would sit in his big chair in front of the fireplace, and ask me what I'd like to study tonight. He left it all up to me, because every day I would find something out in the desert or in the red hills—a bug or a plant or a rock—that I wanted to know about. The books we had along one wall covered just about everything, and the Prof had a way of teaching that made me want to learn. Then there was the other reason for learning, that I came to understand: the Prof used to say, "Danny, you're practically a Martian, you know. It may be years before the other ship gets here, and by the time it does, I want you to know all you can about this planet. Its soil and its air; where what will grow and why; what can be made use of and what should be avoided. If I teach you geology and biology and chemistry now, you'll know more about Mars than anybody else— At least more than any one man could learn for a long time. Then, Danny, when they come, you'll be a mighty important man on Mars. A mighty important man."

SO I LEARNED. I learned about the plants and rocks, the fish-bugs from the banks of the canals, the bacteria in the water we drank. I learned about the weather of Mars and how to make it work for you, and about its soil properties, and what the seasons would kill and let live; and one day we cultivated a nine-inch beet in sand, lizard excrement and phosphates we fixed from the air. After that, our greenhouse vegetables weren't stunted any more.

Before, I mentioned two survivors—well, I should have said four, because two golden hamsters survived the crash. Mates. They are the Lord's dumbest creatures, but there's one thing they do well, and pretty soon we had more laboratory-animals than we could use (we turned some of them loose and they seemed to do all right); so I learned what animals were vectors for what diseases, Earthly and alien, and the life-cycles of the hosts, and how to deal with the diseases. Luckily, Mars didn't have many of its own to offer.

When we explored, it was usually with a purpose. Most of the water-movement on Mars is underground, so there were a lot of caves, particularly back in the hills. That made coal comparatively easy to find—we located several narrow seams within a mile of the cabin, and charted some rich mineral lies within a not much larger radius.

We finished the laboratory on the hill. It had a microscope, and a port-glass Newtonian that could see miles in every direction, and a lot of equipment we'd jury-rigged from the remains of the ship's lab; we worked there a lot, weighing, analyzing, dissecting. Against one wall were my specimen-cases, filled with stones, insects and animals both dead and alive, cultures, plants and microscope slides; I knew each item inside out—biology, chemistry, habits and uses— before it went in there.

So, through the years, I came to know the planet Mars. Of course, the Prof learned everything right along with me— learned it first, really, before he taught it to me. But that didn't matter much, he said.

"You see, Danny," he said one time, "I won't be around

forever. I'm glad to learn all this—Mars is Paradise, for a man like me—but it's far more important that *you* learn it, so when the other ship arrives you'll be able to help them get started. Then you'll be a mighty important man, Danny...because they'll need you."

One day the Prof was fixing lunch and listening to the radio. I was reading. The static was pretty bad, but we both heard the broken, far-away voice say: *"...second space-ship, the Mars II, left Earth today...the dangers of space in an attempt to...God smile on you..."*

By the time the Prof had stopped laughing and crying enough to listen again, the voice was saying: *"...fourth world war is...no compromise...Bomb..."*

Even that didn't sober the Prof, he was so happy. But the next night, while we were sitting out in the greenhouse looking at the blue-green star of Earth, it flickered and swelled into a shaking white flame.

WE WAITED for the second ship.

We knew, from the messages it constantly sent, that the people aboard were planning to land at the same point the *Mars I* had announced it would try for—the south point of Syrtis—and that they were hoping to find survivors.

The Prof hardly slept at all. He just sat in his big chair that he'd pulled over by the window, and looked at the sky. Once, when he did sleep, huddled in the chair with his chin on his chest, he talked; "Oh dear Lord, if there's only just one. Just one, Lord. That's enough—"

Two weeks passed, and the second ship landed right by the canal; the airlock opened and men came out. They looked at the desert and the evening sky and the white flare that had been Earth. One of them saw our cabin, up on the hill, and shouted...but by that time we were down to greet them. I sort of lagged behind in the shadows—this was the moment the Prof had always talked about, but I wasn't very used to people.

The Prof quietly shook hands with the leader. "I'm Professor Hale."

"Ernest Loring, Professor."

"That's a—a rather small ship; are there any colonists with you?"

"No." He was short and grey-haired, and his voice was very deep, with a bitter sound. "Five old men. Scientists...volunteers. Eight started out. The young were all fighting, when..." He looked up at the flame in the sky, brighter than Phobos, then down again with a sigh. "That's the first time we've seen it. But we caught it in on our instruments, and we knew. Professor, are you—all?"

The Prof moved a hand, including me where I stood back in the shadows. "Yes. All."

They talked about the *Mars I* and Earth, while I stood silently, looking up at the shining ship. Three more grey-haired men came out of the airlock. Then I heard the Prof's voice, "—sorriest for him—" and I saw him motion in my direction, and he looked very old and tired. The leader looked sharply toward the shadows where I stood, and I knew he hadn't read the Prof's gesture, that he hadn't seen me until now. I could see his face in the glow of the setting sun...first, there was surprise; then he closed his eyes tight, but that didn't stop two tears from rolling down his cheeks. He took the Prof by the shoulders and turned him around so that he faced the airlock.

Coming out of it were two people—maybe the last two, for there wasn't anybody behind them and the ship was dark now—a man and a little girl.

"His wife is dead," I heard the leader say, "and he didn't want to leave her behind in a world like that—"

"Like me," the Prof said, and his voice trembled so I

could hardly hear it. "Like me." I saw that he was crying, and I wondered why. He walked over to me and put his hand on my head, while the scientists suddenly stopped talking and looked on, and the man with the little girl came forward with her.

"This is Mary," he said to me. Awkwardly, I took her hand, and quickly dropped it. "Hello," I said.

"Hello," she said shyly.

The Prof said, his hand now on my shoulder as he looked around at the faces of the men, "It's like I said, Danny. When the second ship comes, they'll need you; we'll all need you. When you grow up, you're going to be a mighty important man on Mars, Danny. A mighty important man." *Now* I know what he meant, but I didn't then. I felt very thrilled and happy, though, as each man came up and shook my hand. And a little bit like crying—except that there was a girl there.

The Bad Life

There wasn't any middle ground on Limbo. Its people were Saints or Sinners…and both were doomed!

CHAPTER ONE

THEY MADE a sort of statue out of the spacesuit, just by not moving it, just by letting it stand there in the back of Turk's Repair Shop, right on the spot where it had gotten Thorens. Not that the rough men of Limbo were the type who'd have any qualms about handling an object with so eerie a history. Nor did they consider it any kind of hoodoo.

It appealed to their sense of humor.

New convicts came to stare at it, and soon it figured in certain colorful practices of initiation. It came to be the subject of a spacemen's ballad, a vulgar ditty intended not to be sung but roared:

> *Oh-h-h, Svenson's Spacesuit had a hell of a night—*
> *It caught three men, and it mucked 'em up right!*

Goldy Svenson absolutely refused to have anything ever to do with the suit again, and so the Patrol issued him another without complaint, knowing that a Swede in space is more trouble than an Irishman once his superstitions have been churned.

The story of that night is no story, for it has no plot. Rather, it is a few nasty incidents whose only connection is a three-hundred pound, mercury-steel, Space Patrolman's bulger. But, since you ask…

THE *MAESTRO* was old, vintage 2080 or so. The contralto whose voice swelled from it had died long before that,

around 1970. The song was a wiring of one of those antique modulated-groove "records" that gave their impulse to a "needle" and thence to a diaphragm-type speaker. Thorens could faintly hear the "surface-noise" behind the music…sweet and low, sweet and low:

Sometimes I feel like a motherless child—

Thorens' discolored, half-closed left eye ached. He held his drink to his lips, elbow on table, his head bent forward a little over the soiled cloth. This shielded his face from the lamp overhead and kept Turk and the others from seeing the tears that might trigger one of them—or all of them—into coming over and knocking his head off.

Far—far—from home…

Thorens' chin moved under its sandy beard as he tried to soften the lump that was hurting his throat. He took a quick unpleasing sip of the whiskey, winced as it knifed into his cut lips, set the glass on the table. Then he looked hesitantly at Turk, knowing somehow that the fat man was studying him.

Five months on Limbo had taught him that the best defense was a reasonable pretense. He cleared his throat and said falteringly, "Kind of gets you, doesn't it?"

Turk stared at him unwinkingly. Thorens' eyes sheered a-way, ran the length of the floor, up and along the dirty mirror that hung behind the bar—in it, his own reflection, dark shadows and smudgy faces, dingy chromium, the amber monotony of bottles, cigarette and marijuana smoke coiling, the spider-shaped bloodstain on the wall where the little Spaniard's high blood-pressure had geysered through his cut throat.

"It don't get me," Turk rumbled. He got up, wheezing, flat dark face glistening, carefully plucked eyebrows arched into the satanic shape that pleased him. "This is home. Don' you like Limbo? I like Limbo. Don' you? You make your friends feel bad!"

THORENS' HEAD lowered again. Turk chuckled and moved to the bar—big, slow man whose bulk had no solidity but instead ran to pouches and blobs that bulged sleekly in Limbo's .63 Earth gravity. He thumped for a refill and Potts turned and said sharply, "Keep your pants on, boy. I'll get to you *when*."

Watching them from shadowed eye-sockets, Thorens thought fiercely how stupid they were, with Turk a little more exquisitely so than Potts--and how he loathed them both, and feared them both, as he loathed and feared all the half-men here on Limbo.

Suddenly Thorens closed his eyes, making the shadowed eye-sockets darker...the old, old fear that somebody was reading his mind. Not really *reading* it, but detecting from visible signs what his thoughts were about. Covertly he brushed a hand across his forehead, up into his thin hair, down again, bringing with it a workable shield of hair from behind which his eyes flickered, searching for the clenched fist, the boot, the knife—

Nothing. Shadows. Men drinking.

He released his hate. It filled his mind and exploded against the far corners of his skull. *Turk—fat strong-arm artist, with glands for brains! Potts—wife carver! Of all on Limbo, I hate you most!* His eyes flickered again. They hadn't "heard." He sat there, hating. *Why do I hate you most? Because you have hurt me most...*

"I ain't a boy," Turk said. He leaned over the bar, his belly rolling onto it like a squeezed balloon. "I'm a man."

Potts spun a beer at him. Turk picked it up and turned around. His muddy eyes brushed Thorens, and he decided to sit elsewhere. He went over to the front window, where there was a booth that Potts kept a little neater and cleaner because business was still business, even on Limbo, and sat down, inching himself along until he sat almost pressing the window.

Thorens was reminded of a captive hippo, stinking and streaked, looking dully through bars at a world it hadn't the brains to realize was there and strange.

"I bet he's a liar," said one of the men at the bar. The man turned toward Turk, hand on knife. He was drunk and out to bury his steel—his left hand made the challenge-sign. "Tell us what you are."

TURK DIDN'T look at him. "No good, Sammy. Old Turk's too slow for knives." (He carried spring-knives up his sleeves, but the other was too far away. *Just a little closer, Sammy*, he chuckled silently to himself.)

"Y'ain't too slow to bleed."

Another man said, from the shadows, "Sammy, is it? Well, I'm a stranger here, Sammy, and I don't know you—but I'll tell you something. I'm not too slow."

Sammy's knife was out. "You know what else you are?"

"Not slow."

They moved toward each other, coming to a crouch. Potts leaned over the bar and broke a bottle of bourbon over Sammy's head. Sammy shrieked and dropped his knife. He fled for the door, blood and whiskey masking his face.

The stranger drew back his knife for the throw.

Potts said harshly, "Outside, damn it! I run a friendly place. Why do you think I bumped in?"

Sammy slammed through the door. The stranger cursed and followed. Footsteps faded.

Thorens allowed his gaze to fall beyond the specter of knives, out the window and across the glistening concrete roadway and the fog-shrouded fields of tobacco and marijuana to the spaceport. The gray shapes of its administration building and hangars were beaded with faint strings of window-lights. Its cradles slanted up like fingers pointed at the stars—giant fingers that could unleash the Jovian lightning of rocket-power to reach those stars.

Now a glow washed into Limbo's thin air. It widened and brightened, beating down from the night. The bottles on Potts' shelves behind the bar began to vibrate. The trembling grew, and Thorens shifted as the bench tickled his rear. Men looked up, listened. Potts came around from behind the bar and went to stand beside Turk's table, looking out through the metaglass.

Turk said, not looking at Thorens, "Patrol ship. Maybe the Hand got his transfer. Maybe he'll take off pretty soon. Maybe he wants a so-long present."

Thorens' belly twisted hotly into itself. He kept his face down, eyes in hiding. The whiskey in the bottom of his glass danced. His trembling hand forced the glass flat on the table, released it, fell limp. He sat and waited.

Outside, the glare was bright as day. High in the air a roaring pinpoint appeared, lowering, spitting out light like a fragment of the Sun. Fog boiled around it. Above it the sky was night. As the speck descended, night followed it down through the fog almost respectfully until, as the ship hovered over the pitted apron of the port, its rocket-glare had contracted to a blinding conical affair only a few hundred yards across.

Thorens dared to glance up.

It had been just talk. Turk's heavy features, disinterested in Thorens, were reflected in the window as he looked out.

ROCKET-SOUND thundered, slammed, snarled. The ship touched a cradle, rocked, and the magnetics took hold to fit it tight. The pilot boomed the tubes once, unnecessarily— maybe he was just glad he'd worlded his ship. The boom lit the scene like a flash-bulb, then there was blackness into which the distant dim windows of the port slowly faded as pupils dilated.

Potts was back at his bar, setting up bottles, opening new

ones and sticking spouts into them. Solar-system cash was good on Limbo. The wife carver would make money tonight.

A far, faint, dying bleat cut the night. Sammy's? Impossible to tell. Turk gazed dully out the window and Thorens wondered if the man could see in the dark. Nothing of the beast in Turk would surprise him. Turk had forcibly taken a girl, back on Earth—a very young girl—and while he might prefer to be elsewhere than on Limbo, the preference depended on no major discontent. Turk functioned. There were the monthly supply ships, and the frequent stopovers of ships making the Callisto freight-run. There would sometimes be, with so many ships worlding on Limbo, a young and curious passenger who, prepared by the dark lonely months of space, could be persuaded to new adventure. And Turk could be convincing, even likable, when he put his mind to it. He kept, Thorens knew, a small hoard of handkerchiefs, buttons, dog-tags, carefully worded notes, personal jewelry, clothing, souvenirs.

With a hand that was heavier for the ring it had lost, Thorens picked up his drink, mouth twisting bitterly at the rim of the glass. His eyes closed again. He began to assemble words in the darkness, slowly, carefully, picturing them in the cramped pencil strokes that would be realized later when he returned to his office and added them to this manuscript:

The always dubious coin of sensitivity and intellect amounts to less than ever when you are forty and undersized and alone in a cultural cesspool. Brutality it buys, without being tendered, and ridicule and violation, mixed to a poison whose taste is Fear—

No, no no, he thought—too flowery, too abstruse…

He opened his eyes slightly. In the space of a second they went from side to side, registering the murky room, the men.

Then they closed again in hopelessness.

If only I could join you, be one of you, just like you—without conscience or intelligence, as far from God as you are, as close to the slime. Then I would not be set apart—I would not be a target—the hare could run with the hounds. But I could never be like you, or anything like any part of you, you scum, you filth, you animals. I could not be like you in a million years...

CHAPTER TWO

SIXTY YEARS ago the Solar Council, during the tenure as Chairman of the shrewd Ghaz of Venus, had been persuaded to launch Limbo as a money-saving proposition—a prison asteroid, undisciplined and self-sustaining, whose only upkeep would amount to the salaries of a few rookie Patrolmen assigned to orbit their ships within scope range and keep a bored eye out...

Ah, God! Thorens thought. *Why* had the Helping Hand sent him *here*! Why not to Neptune, or Ganymede, or Callisto, or Tethys, for the frontier duties he had expected when he'd signed on!

Council Engineers had scouted the Trojan Asteroids, selecting at last a body with adequate size and soil—one of the few fragments of Planet X's outer surface that hadn't been blown clean out of the System in that eons-ago catastrophe. Altering the asteroid's core to create a decent gravity, at the same time hopping it up to function as a central heating system, they had atmospherized it, deloused it of inimical micro-organisms, installed a balanced ecology and two weeks later blasted off, leaving some two hundred thousand crates of essentials on its twitching surface. Within another month, every male lifer in the System had been transported to Limbo to fend for himself, each new group being abruptly depleted on arrival by the settling of countless black scores...

The Helping Hand! Thorens tore at the words with his mind, shredded them with hate. The great HH! Was he, John Thomas Thorens, on file in some drawer in some office on some level of one of HH's giant headquarters buildings in New Jersey, marked *Discontent—Refer to Transfer?* No, by all the nonexistent gods of Space—not even that! Not even a long wait to be endured, while the wheels of bureaucracy ground out his fate. The hated words boiled up out of memory: *Transfer denied. Transfer denied. Transfer denied.*

Within a year Limbo had sprouted landowners, six slap-dash towns, a caste system, interurban warfare, and a gang-rule throne whose cushions bore the dark stains of a dozen deposed. Within five, Limbo had shaken down. Gone was the throne, for none could hold it. Warfare had ceased (having been largely a matter of indecisive knife and hatchet forays anyway, no deadlier weapons being permitted). Famine and disease had at last brought the Limbos to the realization that pull together they'd damned well better, or die of perfectly natural causes. A Council of Limbo was formed, a Plan was drawn, some shaky, jury-rigged shops thrown together, some atrocious furniture and fair-to-middling ceramic were produced, and Limbo made an earnest bid for System trade. Sanctioned by the pleased Solar Council, a valid monetary exchange sprang into being, based on Solar dollars but subject to devaluation should Limbo need chastising. The spaceport was built, and a Patrol squadron moved in to sit casually on top of the new order. Limbo bought machinery, parlayed its gains, built factories, manufactured and exported mostly—of all things—toys.

The great HH!...which "Watched Over its Flock in Distress and Disaster" (*Our Hands Are on Venus, and They're Helping on Mars*), but which could not note the predicament of one lone, terror-bound field-worker, nor stretch red tape to free him, in its concentration on its main objective: Campaign and Collect (*And They'll Be Right There. When We Reach—the—Stars!*).

THORENS sought to assemble saliva in his dry mouth, wishing he could spit his hatred.

Helping along the frontiers, maybe, where the seed of publicity might be planted to bear plump financial fruit at home—but certain as death it was that no HH benevolence ever came this way, out across space to Thorens' rat-hole office on Limbo where he was a Beam of Light in the Outer Darkness.

Eventually, there being plenty of room, the life-term inmates of the Tycho Women's Penitentiary were removed to Limbo, there to live beside and among the males to the satisfaction of both.

Thus Limbo functioned—unpoliced, autonomous, even profitable. There was no slightest sign of moral or spiritual rehabilitation among its populace, however. If the Limbos applied themselves to the matter of collective survival, it was only that they might survive as happy hellhounds in the biggest, goriest padded cell in history. Limbo outdid in sheer social savagery any lawless frontier that had ever existed. Frontiers always attract a percentage of misfits, outcasts and crackpots; but here was saturation. Dog snapped, snarled, chewed and eagerly ate dog. Murder was the way of life. To hear a scream was to shrug at somebody's clumsiness, for it is simple to kill quietly. To step in blood was to curse, for it rots shoes.

The largest town was Damn Earth. It had seven sprawling square miles of sloppily paved streets, three hundred and forty-two saloons including Potts', four distilleries, ninety-four gambling palaces, three toy factories, a general warehouse-store, several thousand scattered huts and cabins, seventeen joy-houses (possibly the best living to be made on Limbo), a psychotic German who lived in a cave and collected skulls and the Patrol Spaceport, the latter being the only thing on the tiny planet that the Limbos had not themselves built. About the Spaceport was a network of tall silver towers—a crackling violet wall of death, if need be. But the Limbos displayed no tendency to storm the port, slay its personnel, blast off toward freedom in stolen ships—

They liked Limbo.

It was their oyster, their raw meat, their cup of bloody tea. It was as vicious, as mad, as loose and twisted as they. Paradoxically, it was their prison and the one place between Heaven and Earth where they could roam free, brawl, bay at the stars, kill, live the good life.

ANY NON-LIMBO could, for this reason, walk the streets unescorted in perfect safety. His Visitor's Armband was his shield and security. If he happened on a scene of battle, knives would cease flashing to allow him to pass. And anyone so thoughtless as to threaten him would be cut down by friend and foe alike. For Limbo wanted no reprisals, no curtailments, no kill-joy Patrol teams stalking its surface.

The word regarding visitors was: Leave them alone.

This did not apply to John Thorens—

Who had arrived five months ago, with some thirty books, a few games (checkers, Spacelanes, Guess-an-Element), a three months' salary advance (bait conceals the point on the hook) and a twelve-week course (Encompassing the Humanities) under his belt that made him a "constructive and rehabilitative force among the unfortunate."

He had busily cleaned the HH office, rousting vermin, painting over filth in cheerful colors. He had then thrown open the doors to the unfortunate, a few of whom took notice.

All the books had been lent out the first day, and were seen no more. The games had generated more interest, but the Limbos played rough. When at first he had sincerely tried to talk up the straight and narrow to these men, he was told that his predecessor had ended up in the quarry with his face torn off, because he'd had brown eyes and the Blue-Eyed Gang collected brown eyes.

(Not precisely so, other Limbos had told him later—the man had disrupted an orgy at the South Pole Arena, with loud complaints that these were Satan's activities. His more specific comments had angered female participants, so they'd dragged him back to Damesville, where, with luck, he eventually managed suicide. When the Patrol investigated, accompanied by an HH representative, they were permitted to discover evidence that the deceased had had a sideline involving a third H, with the catch that the stuff he peddled had been sugared down to substandard. Apparently a customer had complained. End of investigation.)

Thorens naturally had tried to get out. In reply to his first frightened space gram, HH had said: *Unfortunate demise of predecessor due to involvement in prison intrigue. In no way result of duties you are expected to perform. Patrol denies conditions you describe, Extend the Hand.* The essence of the reply to his second plea was that in view of the contract he had signed it was to be hoped that he might experience a change of sentiment. Extend the Hand.

OUTRAGED, Thorens had sought a more direct means of self-preservation. His HH card brought him to the desk of the secretary of the personal aide to the secretary of the Lieutenant Commander of the Spaceport—a bored-eyed man in neat civvies who had listened carefully to Thorens' story, managing at the same time to make Thorens feel like daddy's little boy, and then, glancing idly out the foot-thick, ray-proof, pellet-proof window at the twisting streets of Damn Earth, candidly admitted that Limbo was a bit rough at first, but, after all, *some* of the Limbos, at least, were struggling along the difficult path toward readjustment and certainly deserved a Hand, and all Thorens needed to do to insure his own well-being was to be friendly, mix with those who showed interest, and, above all, keep his nose clean.

To Thorens' last question, as he ushered the Hand out the anything-proof steelite door, the secretary had answered, No; Patrol regulations forbade any civilian communication over Patrol radio apparatus.

Thorens had next systematically buttonholed the captains of the freight ships that sat down every week or so—a simple matter of hanging around bars, since liquor was not permitted aboard ship. He would pay his fare—twice that—ten times that. But soon he came to anticipate their reply: No passage off Limbo without Patrol authorization, HH authorization, authorization, authorization...

They had seemed somewhat understanding, however—and one in particular had sympathized. Thorens had promptly tried to stowaway on that one's ship, believing he had detected in the man's manner tacit approval of the measure. He was caught and sympathetically turned over to the Patrol. Back in the bored-eyed man's office, he was told that that was scarcely the way to keep his nose clean...did he want to end up as a Limbo himself, charged as a stowaway?

"What am I *now*?" Thorens said dully. "They are your prisoners, and I am theirs. Give me sanctuary."

"Nothing will happen to you if you keep your head."

"Do you know what happened to my predecessor's head? Do you see these bruises? Help me!"

"Roughed up a little, eh? Well, I'll tell you, I personally don't think too much missionary zeal will payoff here. Better just sit it out."

"The worst torture is the threats."

"You've been threatened?"

"Every moment is a threat. Every look is a threat. Every-one I meet is a threat. It's not only the bruises…God, it's the *fear* of bruises!"

"Fear can do strange things to one's imagination, eh?"

"How often have you been outside these walls? And for how long?"

"I get out occasionally, I don't have much reason—"

"I've told you what is happening."

"Surely you've exaggerated."

USHERED OUT, Thorens cringed against the wall of a hangar, staring around through the ever-night at the vast, waiting, murmuring, neon-lit, death-shot psychopathy that was Limbo. Then he darted into the building, into depths cool with the presence of positives—discipline, order, repair, precaution, direction, rational quantities and qualities in rational degree. He veered this way and that through the darkened silver forest of Patrol steel—cranes, engine-pits, fuel storage tanks, machine-shops, great trolleys, giant vaulted ceilings cobwebbed with girders—and hid.

Next morning he was found and ejected.

Temporarily unbalanced, he got drunk. Three bars later, he was smashed. A grinning Limbo shoved a weed under his nose, and Thorens experienced his first flight, during which he challenged three men to a fistic duel and won hands-down when they all collapsed laughing. This was the first, vague, exciting glimpse of the unique "value" he might have to the Limbos. He grabbed at it frantically. He stayed drunk for three days, and bought drinks for the house in every dive from Damn Earth to Saintsville, in an effort to buy more good will as a dividend. He bought pack after pack of reefers from the machines, and distributed them lavishly. He bought six kits of Harrigan's Horse (powder, self-heating water capsule, disposable hardware) in the General Store in Virtue, and gave them to those whom he considered his closest buddies. By this time he had attracted quite a coterie. They wound up their blast by driving to Virgin Springs, down in the southern hemisphere.

The next six hours were quite unforgettable.

Thorens knew this to be true. He tried to forget them—and failed.

CHAPTER THREE

THE HH records—*all* of them; the records of nineteen years of HH activity on Limbo; quite irreplaceable, if hardly of any significant worth—made quite a fire in the potbelly stove in Thorens' office. Until the wee hours, he tore the contents of six filing-cabinets and his desk into thumbnail-size pieces and fed them to the flames. He crouched before the pot-belly, face contorted, eyes glazed to a mica finish, mouth busy (pursed, stretched to gargoyle width, pursed again), like some alchemist working a miracle of hate. Then he danced around the room, laying about him with a poker, creating dents and splinters in the woodwork and breaking every pane of glass in the place.

He then set fire to the desk and lay down to die.

When the smoke became too much to bear, he got up and doused the fire with water from the sink. Death might be a welcome end—but too much discomfort preceded it.

At that moment, and in the days that followed, he set himself to survive. The nightmares of that task refuted Darwin.

He must polish dirty apples, lick boots, take every kind of filth and violence the diseased minds of Limbo could dish out. He must be the mascot of maniacs, the whipping-boy of a collective Id, the creature around explicitly to be hurt, bullied, tormented, used; for this gave him a functional value not easily duplicated on this little world of paranoid sadists. He was the goat among the Judas wolves; he gave them something they needed, the sight of abject fear, and it bought his life from day to day, for the Limbos held everything but themselves in hate and contempt, and "everything" was so far away—except John Thorens.

He won scars, hideous memories and the continuation of life. His first serious beating was at the hands of Turk. Thorens was bedridden for three days, with hot pads on his abdomen and groin. Turk came around on the second night for some more of the same, took one look at Thorens' haunted eyes and went away muttering something about "necrophilia"—possibly the only five-syllable word the man knew; certainly in a predictable category.

His value as patsy begot Thorens champions: it was circulated that the man who killed him would be buried all around him as a garnish; and when one day a visitor from the nearby town of Freedom had thumbed his knife and advanced to whittle Thorens for the sin of stumbling against him, another knife, flipped expertly from sheath and halfway across the street into the back of the visitor's skull, had ended that. Two days later Thorens' rescuer got whopped at blackjack and worked off his annoyance by beating Thorens into a state of gibbering half-consciousness and throwing him at the mirror behind Potts' bar. Potts, in order to save the mirror, had hastily interposed his own body. Staggered by the impact, he had missed his first knife-throw at the offender. Not so the second. Then, upset by the entire episode, he had himself completed the job on Thorens and thrown him out.

OF COURSE, not all the Limbos were as totally vicious

and depraved as Turk, Potts, and their crowd. Some were scarcely more than brutally playful. Others were as often as not oblivious of Thorens' existence, unless he made the mistake of attracting their attention. In all, however, was the corrupt vein of cruelty, whether manifested by sins of commission or omission...a cruelty born of not-caring, of detachment from things human, of ruthless self-interest. They had stepped out of society and out of history to live their lives as a whim. They could not be predicted.

So he couldn't count on protectors—except on an unpredictable basis, where a wrong guess might be fatal. Nor, failing human bulwarks, could he find shelter, haven, sanctuary—for there was no place on Limbo to hide.

On a few occasions, Thorens thought he had made friends—especially among the newcomers who arrived in batches now and then. There was even camaraderie. But always came betrayal. At last he grew to understand the contamination factor in this world where the floodgates were down and the newcomer quickly inundated. He developed an instinct that told him that now was the time to step out of the path of one he had befriended, for another superego had gasped its last and another brawling madman been born.

Unlike his predecessor, Thorens had no devout religious convictions to sustain him (or, for that matter, to cause his immediate downfall).

No protectors. No physical escape. No mystical source of courage and strength...

Naturally, then, Thorens had a project underway, as sensitive men will have when forced to exist under conditions which they cannot bear but must. To it he devoted the predictable amount of fanatic concentration. Its title was LIMBO—*Hell in Space*, and some forty thousand words were completed in first draft. Thorens had a knack for literary expression. But the book, growing as it did from daily torment and indignation, was jumbled, incoherent, chaotic. Into it he poured his boundless hatred, his piteous cries, his curses and protests all unuttered in actuality. In it were masses of words bundled into sobs; scalding portraits of his individual tormentors, and descriptions in vivid and ana- tomical detail of the punishments he wished he could visit upon them; lengthy, sprawling psychosocial analyses that would not have satisfied a more objective eye. The book was a monstrous panorama which, drawn in the convulsive strokes of his agony, had even a certain power. With words as weapons, he slew his tormentors; and without that outlet he might have gone mad.

Or perhaps the book was itself his madness, externalized.

So far—so far—from home...

Three hundred million miles.

Turk shifted heavily (the hippopotamus responding to what?) His eyes turned to stare back into the room, seeking Thorens. "Patrol ship," he said sourly, disappointedly. "Tough guys." (That was what.) Then he kept his eyes on Thorens. Savoring melodrama, he grinned a slow grin.

At the bar, Potts cackled like a hen and said, "Hooray— those babies drink hard!"

Thorens got up stiffly and went toward the rear of the bar. He heard Turk wheeze behind him, the scrape of the fat man's boots on the floor—trying to get up—and he walked faster. He reached the washroom and locked the door behind him, leaned against the wall. He stood that way for a few minutes, face wet, throat tight, stomach churning. Still nailed to the wall was the pageless binding of his copy of *Paradise Lost*. He put his hand on it. Milton had lived and written (and had written *Regained!*) –there was an Earth, somewhere—there was a human spirit...

Finally the nausea passed.

Turk, chuckling, had gone away too.

THEY trooped in, the tough young men in Patrol uniforms. As usual, they sat around the front end of the bar, laughing, raising a hubbub, ignoring the scowling Limbos. One reached up to the shelf and turned off the *maestro*...

—feel like a motherless—

...and turned on the trivision. Hot, atonal music. A painted girl (gold, orange and green) dancing against a swirling, color-organ background. Whistles, laughter. Hands uplifted in the "I've-been-in-Space-and-I-need-it!" sign.

Back at his table, Thorens' head bowed to his hands. Then it proceeded to the table—a terrible bereavement welling up to add mass to his present misery. He remembered a voice singing *London Bridge is Falling Down*, remembered clearly from childhood (or thought he did) warmth and loving caresses; a smile from close above, and sweet breath—

Strong, soft arms that now were husks, and the only truly understanding eyes in the Universe were closed and desiccated, and the last sound-wave of her voice had dispersed to become only air molecules, and the in credible goddess of every man vanishes, vanishes, save from her castle—the tortured subconscious of her son. In compound gear, where Oedipus engages Death, Thorens had wandered that night a month ago, the space-gram from his father crumpled in his hand, and for some reason—perhaps it was his eyes—the Limbos had let him alone. The next night he had been beaten twice, and started his book.

"Thorens!"

Thorens flinched and slowly raised his head. One of the

Patrolmen had spotted him and got up—now came around the end of the bar lithely, one hand braced on the shoulder of a comrade. Thorens watched him come, struggling up out of his welter of tangled, miserable introspection.

"Hi!" The Patrolman dropped into a seat and in the same motion poured a little of his drink into Thorens' empty glass. "Still alive, I see, eh?"

"Still alive, Lieutenant."

"Not as bad as you thought at first, eh?"

"Not as bad."

LIEUTENANT Mike Burman was blocky and space-burned; head well shaped, mouth wide, eyes just a little too closely set; about 26; less than a year out of the Space Academy at Gagaringrad. This was his sixth stop-over on Limbo. He had met Thorens on his first, four months ago, and each time since. In him seemed to stir a vague sympathy for the little man—as vague and unformed as his comprehension of Thorens' true predicament on Limbo. Over any comprehension rode a Boston-bred suspicion that all such phenomena as Limbo and its gutter-bums weren't quite real, or at least shouldn't be. But he admired the Helping Hand. His family contributed regularly. He supposed things *were* fairly disordered on Limbo, poor devils. It was good to see a Hand out here, on the job. When you came right down to it, it all had rather a touch of romance. Thorens' tales of woe he chose, for the most part, to discredit. After all, there was a limit. Space, he knew, bred strange types—strong men, eccentric men—men possessed of some personal Hell. Like Thorens.

Looking at the young idiot, Thorens managed a smile. "It's good to see you. How's Earth?"

"Oh...still there, the last time I looked!" Burman laughed at his wit, and Thorens moved his lips to join in.

"Y'know, I've asked around a little," Burman said. "None of the Patrolmen stationed here has ever seen anyone lay a finger on you!" He grinned, his expression somehow sly. "You were putting it on a little, eh?"

"Maybe a little." You fool! ...of course they leave me alone when the Patrol is around!

Now Mike Burman frowned suddenly, exaggeratedly, as if he had just remembered something. "Hey, that reminds me, Thorens. I've got a message for you. You're supposed to go in and see the Lieutenant-Com."

A burst of laughter from the bar had drowned out his last few words. Thorens was blinking in that direction. Burman repeated the message: "You're supposed to go in and see the 2nd C. O."

THORENS looked at him. "What for?"

"I don't know," Mike Burman lied. You're shipping out, Thorens. Earthside. I know, because you're going back on my ship. That's what the Old Man wants to tell you.

"You didn't get the message at your office," Burman explained, "so they told me to look you up."

"I haven't been there for three days." In the dark universe behind John Thorens' eyes there appeared the tiniest, most hesitant flicker of animation—the stirring of some minute, slumbering particle; a particle that might become a flame...a light...a sun. The creation of suns from empty nothingness is mysterious; the creation of Hope is mystery itself. But the stirring primal particle in John Thorens' Universe darkened to nothingness again.

Your mother's last wish, Thorens—and then your father got to some softie in the HH. So back you go, for the atomicremation. Frankly, though, don't you think you're kind of running out on the job?

Thorens had lived with the "message" for about ten

seconds now. The particle of sub-Hope dared to stir again, since no inimical forces had put in an appearance.

"Why should the Old Man want to see me?" he whispered.

"Your packet," Burman said. "I think that's what it's about." He winked at himself in the mirror. Tomorrow, after all, was soon enough for Thorens to know the facts. Besides, Burman had no authorization to pass the real dope along. The packet—clever.

"My packet?" Thorens said, still whispering. "My packet? What about it?"

(The packet was the monthly HH mailing to all its Hands, containing: Instructions (if any); pay-check; report forms; requisition-slips for needed supplies (if any); and the monthly news-bulletin, BROTHERLY LOVE.)

"It came open, during shipping," Burman said casually. "You're supposed to check it over, see that it's all in order. Regulations."

No icy, rushing, negative forces were required to extinguish the particle. It simply went out. "That's funny," Thorens whispered.

Burman milked it. "Speaking of Earth, it's spring now in New York."

"Lord," said Thorens, after a moment, in a starving voice, "the heat'll be coming along…"

"Bad winter. Twenty-eight inches of snow one time. You couldn't drive a bug."

"I know. You told me last time. How are the new model bugs?"

"Chrysler's finally bringing out that one-wheel job."

Thorens shook his head. "I wouldn't trust it. You hit two hundred and the gyro goes out and you start turning thirty-foot cartwheels."

Tears gleamed on his cheeks. Burman shot him a look and pursed his lips, feeling a slight twinge.

THE trivision began to chant out a spaceman's song, describing the average space hand's affection for his superior officers. The Patrolmen at the bar set up a roar, and one shouted to Mike Burman, "Hey, loot! This one's dedicated to you!" Then they took up the song:

> *"Just tell him for me, he's an essuvabee,*
> *"And his mother's a Martian monstros-s-sity!"*

Thorens blinked—(*Sometimes I feel...*)—and shifted in his seat, feeling the comfortable if temporary security provided by the presence of these men.

A woman came in. Tall, hardfaced, green-eyed, with clipped dark hair. She wore two knives, handles forward. Her leather breastplates were neither new nor badly scarred, which meant her steel was fast. Eyes of Limbos brushed her up and dawn appreciatively, but no one made the sign. The tough ones were unpredictable. She got her drink, moved to a corner table.

At the bar a big young Patrolman new to Limbo, singing, had not taken his eyes off her ample curves. His chest had swelled. Now her eyes caught his gaze and became icy green flames. He looked away hastily, remembering a briefing.

Thoren's lips curled in loathing, hatred, contempt. The women of Limbo were even more repellent than the men. Especially the swaggering, strutting, leather-garbed alleycats of Damesville, with their cruel eyes and filthy mouths. That *they* should continue to live—

Mike Burman had been smiling at the song, and at his men's loud endorsement of the fact that he was a essuvabee. "Speaking of S.O.B.'s," he grinned, "two real beauts are heading Earthside!" He almost added: "—with you, on my ship—" but fortunately he caught himself.

Thorens still glared at the woman, head down, eyes up. "Paroles?" he asked, not caring.

"In one case," Burman nodded. "For him." He pointed to Potts. "The other one's going back so the shrinkers can have another look. Him." He pointed to Turk.

IT TOOK a moment to sink in—a process of appalled disbelief to furious rejection of fact to bitter acceptance that shriveled to numbness. Music blared from the trivision as the song ended. Applause, more laughter. Thorens' face sagged off the front of his skull—his voice seemed wrenched out of him— *"Those two?"*

Burman stared at Thorens, not realizing (*hate*) what he had done. The trivision started (*hate*) a new wham 'n bam song hit, and the two singers (*hate*) began to fake their blows at each other.

It canceled John Thorens' mind, shuddered down through his body to explode at his extremities. It was stronger than any other emotion he had ever known. He contracted in his chair, elbows and knees doubling. Half-huddled thus, he trembled violently. *Hate Turk, hate Potts, bite lips, taste blood, fight, hate, hate—*

Those two. Flying up out of Hell to the distant blue-green world that was Heaven. *No—no!*

Mike Burman searched the distorted features of the little, sandy-bearded man who sat opposite him. He talked, feeling uncomfortably that there seemed little else to do: "Potts— lack of conclusive evidence of premeditation. Changed to second degree, sentence commuted to what he's already served. And Turk—recalled for psychiatric—"

He said a few more words, hesitantly, barely audible under the general din, while he studied Thorens' face.

Thorens seemed to catch fire. He thrust up out of his chair, overturning it. *"Damn you!"* he gasped. *"No...not*

them...get me a transfer...get *me* a parole...*me*....*me—me—*"
His eyes bulged. He leaned far over the table, his breath
causing strands of Burman's hair to move, and shrieked at the
top of his lungs: "Take me to Earth—not them!"

An interested silence fell over the bar, save for the
trivision's wham 'n bam. Hands of Limbos went to knives,
anticipating action. The Patrolmen instantly, but casually,
grouped to leave, as protocol required.

But this was an unusual situation. Little Thorens, the
Hand, was blowing his stack at the Patrol loot. Expressions
became uncertain.

Mike Burman was rearing back in dismay, as if Thorens'
cry had boosted him under the chin. "What? *What?* Why, I
don't—Thorens, I really—"

Thorens swayed there, shoulders forward, hands working.
His half-closed, watering eyes caught a flicker of movement
outside the window—and even in his extreme agony he could
chill at a strange sight.

Two giants.

Then details registered and became not strange. He heard,
from far away, someone at the door say, "Somebody bringing
a spacesuit in here."

EYES, turning from the tableau at the table to the door,
saw a gigantic spacesuit float from the darkness. Gleaming,
shining, towering, it resembled a deepsea diving suit with its
great windowed helmet, its claw gloves, its massive body
three feet across, seven and one half feet high. A big man
carried the suit, his right arm about its waist, his left arm
grasping its left arm.

In this manner, holding it erect like a dancing-partner or
more like someone getting a gentle bum's-rush, he walked the
suit across the fog-shrouded concrete roadway, up onto the
curb toward Potts' bar. With one hand he opened the door.

With the other he easily jumped the suit across the sill. The suit weighed three hundred pounds.

The voice said, "Fixin' job, Turk." Turk nodded, his small admiring eyes fastened on the huge figures in the door.

Handsome, golden-haired, the newcomer; six feet nine inches tall and grinning. He stood there, balancing his specially built suit with its sprung demand-valve. "Where fat man?" he rumbled.

Thorens was stumbling toward the door. Mike Burman looked after him, eyes bright with bewilderment, pique, vague sympathy. Then, whistling tunelessly between his teeth, he started back for his fellows at the end of the bar. He called to 1st Engineer's Mate "Goldy" Svenson to join them as soon as he got rid of the suit.

Thorens scooped a bottle off the bar, evading its owner's indignant grab, and in perfect silence threw it at the head of the Damesville woman with all his might. It smashed against the wall by her head—or rather where her head had been, for she was on her feet, screaming and pulling her steel. Glass from the bottle still skittered and tinkled as she drew back full-arm for the throw that would skewer Thorens. A roar and a whoop had gone up from the bar. Men doorwise from the woman scattered from the line of fire. Men behind her watched, heads turned and wary.

Mike Burman shouted an order in single-syllable Patrol Code. Three Patrolmen sprang to positions between Thorens and the woman. They didn't draw their guns—they didn't have to. The woman's throw was already started. She couldn't hold it back; so she clung to the blade in a balk-throw and sank its point two inches into the floor at her feet. Instantly she snatched her second knife from sheath, on guard against the Limbo men. Glaring around, she cursed the grinning, Patrolmen.

"Where fat man?" rumbled "Goldy" Svenson again. He

had not moved.

Turk said, "Right here, cop." As he began to wheeze, preparatory to getting up, his eyes clamped on the giants at the door, a third figure, small and furtive, dodged around them into the night.

Watching Thorens go, Mike Burman thought: "I almost wish I'd told him…"

CHAPTER FOUR

ACROSS the roadway from Potts' bar was a steep rocky slope that led down to darkened fields some thirty feet below, and the flat gray expanse of the Spaceport beyond. A barbed-wire fence ran along the edge of the road, to discourage drunken Limbos from brawling through the fields and trampling the crops. Thorens bent down the top strand, tearing his forefinger to the bone.

He stepped over. He took two blind steps, put a foot over the incline to encounter nothingness and spilled, rolled, flopped to the bottom. He lay on his back in the rain-ditch, face barely out of the filthy water, and cried.

The seconds and minutes of his grief wore on. An occasional star winked down through the chill, slow-moving fog.

Thorens squinted up at each and sobbed the louder, wishing that mysterious forces could mesh to make him a vanished man, could transport him to each speck's vast flaming surface, push or pull him into the nuclear inferno of its interior, plunge him into the sweet methane or ammonia or formaldehyde of the atmosphere of its planets, if it had planets, or send him hurtling onto the bitter, airless surface of any of its planets' satellites—or rush him away to a point midway between the two suns that were Mira (which he recognized), there to hang suspended as a mote that once had lived but now took its motion, its vectors, its orbit, its course through Infinity and Eternity, as the product of forces that were not consciously cruel.

Footsteps above Thorens choked a sob into utter silence. His hands, under water, clenched at mud. His legs tightened in terror, and developed a cramp.

"Hear it?" a voice said, from the road.

"Yeah."

"See anything?"

"Too dark. Sounded like crying."

"Let's look."

Thorens heard the wire creak as it was stretched down, and, clearly, the whisper of a long knife from sheath. He gulped in air and sank his face under the water—it murmured in his eardrums, transmitting his own tiny movements.

When his lungs could stand it no longer, he bobbed his head up and gasped through his burning throat, "Kill me! Why am I hiding? Please, oh, my God, please, *kill me*!"

He lay with wide eyes staring up; he saw Mira appear, then disappear again into the fog. He saw the suns, the worlds, the moons, the vacuums and infernos that filled the reaches of space, but could not notice him nor help him to die. He waited, with a mixture of mud and gastric juices in his mouth, for the fist, the boot, the knife.

The fog around him was empty. Footsteps faded far down the road. They had not been curious enough to come down—or perhaps they had thought it was a muggers' trap.

If the latter, Thorens thought frantically, they might be going to get some friends together, so they could come back and fight. His arms and legs grasped, pumped, scrambled, flailed.

He crawled up the slope. He did not want to die.

TURK'S Repair Shop was located in a shack behind Potts'

bar. In it were a tool bench, some metal-working machinery and a cot on which Turk slept when he was too tired or too drunk to make his way home.

While the Patrol naturally maintained its own repair facilities for spacesuits and all other equipment, still Turk was expert and dependable. And he would work at night, when the Patrol machine-shops were closed. Also, when Patrolmen patronized Turk, they received a bonus in addition to good workmanship, i. e., tips on what bars were or were not watering their liquor that week, and where the cleanest girls were to be found, and at what gambling-dive the tables were running against the house. So Turk prospered. And no Limbo objected. What Turk did was, in the long run, good public relations.

Now, in the light of overhead 'tomics, Turk labored to repair "Goldy" Svenson's spacesuit—but he was thinking about John Thorens.

What a funny little jerk the Hand was! Sure, he got clobbered, day after day. But he asked for it! The crummy little milksop *asked* for it. He never talked to you straight from the shoulder. He hid in the back of his skull and played angles. He looked at you with rubbery little face, and you knew he expected you to murder him, so you got mad and did it. All he cared about was *out*. He ran around Limbo like a turpentined pup, squawking to life-termers about *out*. It was a drag. He'd make it off Limbo sooner or later, and good riddance. Right now he was just exactly where everybody else was, except for one thing—he looked at you that way and you had to cream him.

Then Turk started thinking about "Goldy" Svenson, all six feet nine inches of him, and that was Turk's mistake.

He undid eight screws and lifted a curved plate away from the back of the suit...

Thorens turned the last corner. His office was burning.

"We read your book," a voice said from the shadows, "It started a good fire."

That's Joe Moore's voice, Thorens thought. Joe. Joe. I bought you a drink on your second night on Limbo, and you said you were sorry for me. You said you were innocent of any crime. You hated the place as I do. What made you run with the pack?

"When you start yelling at the law," another voice said, "that's bad. Creates a scene. Draws attention. You need a lesson."

"But we won't kill you, you little bastard," another voice said. "You're too much fun to have around."

Thorens screamed, and for the second time since his arrival on Limbo dared to run. This time, he thought agonizedly, he must get away.

But that was before a beltbuckle, aimed low, lashed out of the darkness *ahead* of him.

THEY gathered around in Turk's Repair Shop and looked down at the large, sprawled, melted-looking, half-boiled, red and gray thing with staring, milky eyes that had been Turk.

Here and there white showed, where flesh had sagged in blobs away from bone. The cracked skin glistened with oil, cooked up out of Turk's enormous supply of fat.

"Christ!" said one. "Did you hear him *scream!*"

The spacesuit stood where it had killed Turk. But now it was harmless. Potts' frantic call to the Spaceport had brought a Radiation Squad on the double. (Wild radiation was one of the very few things on Limbo that the Patrol would tend to, mainly to insure the safety of their own men stationed there.) An officer in protective clothing had gone into Turk's shack and closed the small plate that covered the spacesuit's atomic-power-pack. The radiation, though it had killed Turk quickly and then cooked him through prolonged exposure, counted its half-life in mere minutes; so now the room was safe to enter.

The officer was removing the radiation suit. His companion said casually, "You know how it happened, anybody?"

Heads shook *no*. One man snickered and the officer looked at him: "What's funny?"

"What isn't?"

"Do you know what happened?" (Ordinarily, the officers wouldn't have given a damn what happened; but since Patrol equipment was involved, they had to shape up a report.)

The man shrugged, "Those plates are close together...the one on the power, and the one to the oxy-system. I guess he got careless."

"What's funny?"

"I owed him eighty bucks on blackjack," the man smirked. "He was gravving me for it. I was going to kill him myself, and he saves me the trouble!"

The officers looked around, mouths curled in wry distaste. The Limbos grinned back, disliking them, wishing they could kill them—but no one could be safer anywhere than a Patrolman on Limbo.

Without another word the Patrolmen left. Over the motor-noise of their bug fading down the street, Potts cursed as he looked at the mess on the floor: "How do I clean *this* up?"

"Bring in stray dogs," one man said.

Potts nodded appreciatively. "That's sharp." He kicked the mess in the ribs and went over to the spacesuit. "Somebody help me get this damn thing outa the way!"

Two men joined him, and they inched the heavy bulger toward a wall.

Lieutenant Mike Burman was among the watchers, with some of his buddies. He stared down at the mess, thinking.

He never even knew he was going back.

Potts wrestled with the spacesuit. Another step, and his foot slipped on the wrench that Turk had dropped in dying, and he lurched sideways. He made the error of hanging onto the suit, trying to right himself, and his added weight overbalanced it and took it out of the hands of the other two helping him. For a second they made an effort to hold it back, but the mass was great and slippery, and so they let go, with the suggestion of shrugs.

In mid-air, falling, Potts began to scream.

The suit followed him down in the same arc, not very quickly, it seemed, stiffly, like an inexperienced lover bending to the loved. The heavy angle of a shoulder-plate shoved into Potts' mouth as the back of his head hit the floor, and his scream cut off with a crackling of bone.

They watched his hands twitch until finally every part of him was dead. The big young Patrolman who had looked at the woman was in a corner, holding his stomach with folded arms and swallowing excess saliva. Mike Burman was standing in front of him, thoughtful-eyed, as if not wanting the Limbos to see that Patrolmen had nerves.

He had another reason for being thoughtful. Tonight Mike Burman was very near to believing in Fate.

The Limbos looked at the spacesuit. One whistled.

THORENS takes a step, and somewhere in the cauldron of pain, humiliation and fear that is melting down his mind and nervous system to basic animal responses, float fragmentary memories of this last half-hour he has endured...

Another step.

Let him go. A shape moves aside. *He's had it.*

One more.

A blow—somewhere in his back.

Layoff the kidneys. We don't want to kill him.

Please kill me.

Poker game at Charlie's...how about it?

Thought you were looking for Cat Redfield, to slice him.

Ah...I don't feel like it Come on—let's go.

A nudge in Thorens' back, and he falls down. Drooling blood he gets up, takes a step.

Voices fade.

Another step...

Walk through darkness, walk through pain, walk through fog past shadows that are things half-known, down winding, wet-gleaming streets, past lighted doors and windows, past jags and whirls and bursts of rainbow neon, under humming power lines, past toy factories whose tall smokestacks flicker at the tops with red-shot smoke (and through the walls a Teddy-bear grins; a shiny fire-engine blinks its headlight eyes and sirens a hello; an electric monorail whirs on its figure-8 to nowhere; a sleek rocketship charts a course for a far-off, better world; a hundred, harmless, joyous games play noisily all by themselves; a ChemCraft Set percolates a panacea, while an Erector Set places the last shining girder in its bridge to Elsewhere; a Limbo night-watchman sprawls, bottle in hand, surrounded by the Answer apparent to any boy—and through the walls a wistful touch, a loving recollection)—and now along a fence, over dirt, across sand, past stunted plants that never have seen day, past looming dark hills and silent mineral diggings with gaunt machinery like poised skeletons, past a silver Spaceport that is a door to Heaven that has no key, past men who stare and squint through foggy darkness and nudge each other and laugh, past sight and sound of men talking, laughing, breathing, and their hearts pumping blood that rushes noisily through tiny tubes surrounded by muscles that whisper against one another as they gather to give pain...walk past life, or around it, or over it, or any way but through it, to some other place.

Walk crying, walk bleeding, walk hurting, through and

then beyond the veil of thoughts that govern thought to keep the Universe real.

AN ALLEY. Muddy water cool around ankles. An alley, somewhere off behind the world, containing its refuse, its secrets, its littered history. An alley, closer to the past than a street...on the dark other side of Now. A building gray-crouched in the fog—a dirt-encrusted back window—a searching...

Her.

Thorens stopped, swayed, stared.

Her.

Giant shape waiting against the wall inside, outlined in re-flected flickerings from the Spaceport across the way as a ship prepared to take devils to Heaven; and now it could go, and nobody cared, for an Angel had walked with love across the stars, and the Universe had heard, and now a giant shape, strong, exuding warmth, concern, a solidity—

Thorens' mind squirted out through the sutures of his skull.

Smash of window-glass—cut hands— Has darling hurt himself? Let's see! Toward the huge, longed-for shape, and that smile like the birth of a Sun: Did you think Mummy was lost?

Thorens was murmuring. His fists hurt from clenching. He lay down beside her. His head rested on the wide shoulder, his nose in the socket of the great neck. Outside, the rocket blared, took off, yellow flash, up fast, faster, dying, echoes.

Mom, a big noise!

It's all right, dear.

Rubbing his cheek against the shining right arm, his left arm behind her back—close to the cool, sure strength.

Close doors, slam hatches, lock windows, pull shades, dig moats, build dikes, fasten gates—eyelids shut and everything's outside. Pictures through a killiedescape—white mountains with pink-candy tops—checkerboard fields and green, fragrant trees and little animals that stare with bright friendly eyes. Childhood was a wonderful place, even with the dead bird—so fun, so safe, so hurt to remember. Blanket tucked in warm, and the Sandman is coming; the sky rips down the middle, falls shining, and the world is sliced into (*Happy*) birthday (*to you!*) cake with roast turkey; the songvoice rises, and London Bridge topples finally and forever across the *Thems*, amid waves and enveloping splashes of want-her—

Warm. Little legs drawn up against round little belly. Finger poked into limp little mouth. *He's the living image of his mother. Oh, look. He's smiling!*

"WHAT THE hell is *that* racket?"

"It's coming from over here. The suit...."

"You're crazy."

"*Listen.*"

"Open the belly-clamps."

"*You* open them."

"They already are." (Grunt.) "What the hell? Something's holding it shut from inside." (Louder grunt.)

"What's *he* doing in there?"

"Look at his *face!*"

"Hey—come on out, stupid! Come *outa* there—" (Pause.) "He *bit* me!" (Slug!) "Somebody call the Patrol..." (Slap!)

"Wa-aa-a-a-aa-a-a-a!"

Two Patrol bugs through the dawn-light on a howling Code Three. Laughing, chatting Limbos evicted for the steel Caesarean. A half-hour battle—sick tenderness, and flaring tempers too.

Lieutenant Mike Burman never in his life stopped dreaming of the wailing, flailing, sweating, oversized foetus born of Svenson's spacesuit.

Zen

Because they were so likable and intelligent and adaptable—they were vastly dangerous!

IT'S difficult, when you're on one of the asteroids, to keep from tripping, because it's almost impossible to keep your eyes on the ground. They never got around to putting portholes in spaceships, you know—unnecessary when you're flying by GB, and psychologically inadvisable, besides—so an asteroid is about the only place, apart from Luna, where you can really see the stars.

There are so many stars in an asteroid sky that they look like clouds; like massive, heaped-up silver clouds floating slowly around the inner surface of the vast ebony sphere that surrounds you and your tiny foothold. They are near enough to touch, and you want to touch them, but they are so frighteningly far away...and so beautiful: there's nothing in creation half so beautiful as an asteroid sky.

You don't want to look down, naturally.

I HAD left the *Lucky Pierre* to search for fossils (I'm David Koontz, the *Lucky Pierre's* paleontologist). Somewhere off in the darkness on either side of me were Joe Hargraves, gadgeting for mineral deposits, and Ed Reiss, hopefully on the lookout for anything alive. The *Lucky Pierre* was back of us, her body out of sight behind a low black ridge, only her gleaming nose poking above like a porpoise coming up for air. When I looked back, I could see, along the jagged rim of the ridge, the busy reflected flickerings of the bubble-camp the techs were throwing together. Otherwise all was black, except for our blue-white torch beams that darted here and there over the gritty, rocky surface.

The twenty-nine of us were E. T. I. Team 17, whose

assignment was the asteroids. We were four years and three months out of Terra, and we'd reached Vesta right on schedule. Ten minutes after landing, we had known that the clod was part of the crust of Planet X—or Sorn, to give it its right name—one of the few such parts that hadn't been blown clean out of the Solar System.

That made Vesta extra-special. It meant settling down for a while. It meant a careful, months-long scrutiny of Vesta's every square inch and a lot of her cubic ones, especially by the life-scientists. Fossils, artifacts, animate life...a surface chunk of Sorn might harbor any of these, or all. Some we'd tackled already had a few.

In a day or so, of course, we'd have the one-man beetles and crewboats out, and the floodlights orbiting overhead, and Vesta would be as exposed to us as a molecule on a microscreen. Then work would start in earnest. But in the meantime—and as usual—Hargraves, Reiss and I were out prowling, our weighted boots clomping along in darkness. Captain Feldman had long ago given up trying to keep his science-minded charges from galloping off alone like this. In spite of being a military man, Feld's a nice guy; he just shrugs and says, "Scientists!" when we appear brightly at the airlock, waiting to be let out.

SO the three of us went our separate ways, and soon were out of sight of one another. Ed Reiss, the biologist, was looking hardest for animate life, naturally.

But I found it.

I HAD crossed a long, rounded expanse of rock—lava, wonderfully colored—and was descending into a boulder-cluttered pocket. I was nearing the "bottom" of the chunk, the part that had been the deepest beneath Sorn's surface before the blow-up. It was the likeliest place to look for fossils.

But instead of looking for fossils, my eyes kept rising to those incredible stars. You get that way particularly after several weeks of living in steel; and it was lucky that I got that way this time, or I might have missed the Zen.

My feet tangled with a rock. I started a slow, light-gravity fall, and looked down to catch my balance. My torch beam flickered across a small, red-furred teddybear shape. The light passed on. I brought it sharply back to target.

My hair did *not* stand on end, regardless of what you've heard me quoted as saying. Why should it have, when I already knew Yurt so well—considered him, in fact, one of my closest friends?

The Zen was standing by a rock, one paw resting on it, ears cocked forward, its stubby hind legs braced, ready to launch it into flight. Big yellow eyes blinked unemotionally at the glare of the torch, and I cut down its brilliance with a twist of the polarizer lens.

The creature stared at me, looking ready to jump halfway to Mars or straight at me if I made a wrong move.

I addressed it in its own language, clucking my tongue and whistling through my teeth: "Suh, Zen—"

In the blue-white light of the torch, the Zen shivered. It

didn't say anything. I thought I knew why. Three thousand years of darkness and silence...

I said, "I won't hurt you," again speaking in its own language.

The Zen moved away from the rock, but not away from me. It came a little closer, actually, and peered up at my helmeted, mirror-glassed head—unmistakably the seat of intelligence, it appears, of any race anywhere. Its mouth, almost human-shaped, worked; finally words came. It hadn't spoken, except to itself for three thousand years.

"You...are not Zen," it said. "Why—how do you speak Zennacai?"

It took me a couple of seconds to untangle the squeaking syllables and get any sense out of them. What I had already said to it were stock phrases that Yurt had taught me; I knew still more, but I couldn't speak Zennacai fluently by any means. Keep this in mind, by the way: I barely knew the language, and the Zen could barely remember it. To save space, the following dialogue is reproduced without bumblings, blank stares and *What-did-you-says*? In reality, our talk lasted over an hour.

"I am an Earthman," I said. Through my earphones, when I spoke, I could faintly hear my own voice as the Zen must have heard it in Vesta's all but nonexistent atmosphere: tiny, metallic, cricketlike.

"Eert...mn?"

I pointed at the sky, the incredible sky. "From out there. From another world."

It thought about that for a while. I waited. We already knew that the Zens had been better astronomers at their peak than we were right now, even though they'd never mastered space travel; so I didn't expect this one to boggle at the notion of creatures from another world. It didn't. Finally it nodded, and I thought, as I had often before, how curious it was that this gesture should be common to Earthmen and Zen.

"So. Eert-mn," it said. "And you know what I am?"

When I understood, I nodded. Then I said, "Yes," realizing that the nod wasn't visible through the one-way glass of my helmet.

"I am—last of Zen," it said.

I said nothing. I was studying it closely, looking for the features which Yurt had described to us: the lighter red fur of arms and neck, the peculiar formation of flesh and horn on the lower abdomen. They were there. From the coloring, I knew this Zen was female.

The mouth worked again—not with emotion, I knew, but with the unfamiliar act of speaking. "I have been here for—for—" she hesitated— "I don't know. For five hundred of my years."

"For about three thousand of mine," I told her.

AND then blank astonishment sank home in me—astonishment at the last two words of her remark. I was already familiar with the Zens' enormous intelligence, knowing Yurt as I did…but imagine thinking to qualify *years* with *my* when just out of nowhere a visitor from another planetary orbit pops up! And there had been no special stress given the distinction, just clear precise thinking, like Yurt's.

I added, still a little awed: "We know how long ago your world died."

"I was child then," she said. "I don't know—what happened. I have wondered." She looked up at my steel-and-glass face; I must have seemed like a giant. Well, I suppose I was. "This—what we are on—was part of Sorn, I know. Was it—" She fumbled for a word –"was it atom explosion?"

I told her how Sorn had gotten careless with its hydrogen

atoms and had blown itself over half of creation. (This the E. T. I. Teams had surmised from scientific records found on Eros, as well as from geophysical evidence scattered throughout the other bodies.)

"I was child," she said again after a moment "But I remember—I remember things *different* from this. Air...heat...light...how do I live here?"

Again I felt amazement at its intelligence; (and it suddenly occurred to me that astronomy and nuclear physics must have been taught in Sorn's "elementary schools"—else that *my years* and *atom explosion* would have been all but impossible). And now this old, old creature, remembering back three thousand years to childhood—probably to those "elementary schools"—remembering, and defining the differences in environment between *then* and *now*, and more, wondering at its existence in the different *now*—

And then I got my own thinking straightened out. I recalled some of the things we had learned about the Zen.

Their average lifespan had been 12,000 years or a little over. So the Zen before me was, by our standards, about twenty-five years old. Nothing at all strange about remembering, when you are twenty-five, the things that happened to you when you were seven...

But the Zen's question, even my rationalization of my reaction to it, had given me a chill. Here was no cuddly teddy bear.

This creature had been born before Christ!

She had been alone for three thousand years, on a chip of bone from her dead world beneath a sepulchre of stars. The last and greatest Martian civilization, the *L'hrai*, had risen and fallen in her lifetime. And she was twenty-five years old.

"How do I live here?" she asked again.

I got back into my own framework of temporal reference, so to speak, and began explaining to a Zen what a Zen was.

(I found out later from Yurt that biology, for the reasons, which follow, was one of the most difficult studies; so difficult that nuclear physics actually *preceded* it!) I told her that the Zen had been, all evidence indicated, the toughest, hardest, longest-lived creatures God had ever cooked up: practically independent of their environment, no special ecological niche; just raw, stubborn, tenacious life, developed to a fantastic extreme—a greater force of life than any other known, one that could exist almost anywhere under practically any conditions—even floating in midspace, which, asteroid or no, this Zen was doing right now.

The Zens breathed, all right, but it was nothing they'd had to do in order to live. It gave them nothing their incredible metabolism couldn't scrounge up out of rock or cosmic rays or interstellar gas or simply do without for a few thousand years. If the human body is a furnace, then the Zen body is a feeder pile. Maybe that, I thought, was what evolution always worked toward.

"Please, will you kill me?" the Zen said.

I'D been expecting that. Two years ago, on the bleak surface of Eros, Yurt had asked Engstrom to do the same thing. But I asked, "Why?" although I knew what the answer would be too.

The Zen looked up at me. She was exhibiting every ounce of emotion a Zen is capable of, which is a lot; and I could recognize it, but not in any familiar terms. A tiny motion here, a quiver there, but very quiet and still for the most part. And *that* was the violent expression: restraint. Yurt, after two years of living with us, still couldn't understand why we found this confusing.

Difficult, aliens—or being alien.

"I've tried so often to do it myself," the Zen said softly. "But I can't, I can't even hurt myself. Why do I want you to kill me?" She was even quieter. Maybe she was crying. "I'm alone. Five hundred years, Eert-mn—not too long. I'm still young. But what good is it—life—when there are no other Zen?"

"How do you know there are no other Zen?"

"There are no others," she said almost inaudibly. I suppose a human girl might have shrieked it.

A child, I thought, *when your world blew up. Now you're a young three-thousand-year-old woman...uneducated, afraid, probably crawling with neuroses: Even so, in your thousand-year terms, young lady, you're not too old to change.*

"Will you kill me?" she asked again.

And suddenly I was having one of those eye-popping third-row-center views of the whole scene: the enormous, beautiful sky; the dead clod, Vesta; the little creature who stood there staring at me—the brilliant-ignorant, human-like-alien, old-young creature who was asking me to kill her.

For a moment the human quality of her thinking terrified me...the feeling you might have waking up some night and finding your pet puppy sitting on your chest, looking at you with wise eyes and white fangs gleaming...

Then I thought of Yurt—smart, friendly Yurt, who had learned to laugh and wisecrack—and I came out of the jeebies. I realized that here was only a sick girl, no tiny monster. And if she were as resilient as Yurt...well, it was his problem. He'd probably pull her through.

But I didn't pick her up. I made no attempt to take her back to the ship. Her tiny white teeth and tiny yellow claws were harder than steel; and she was, I knew, unbelievably strong for her size. If she got suspicious or decided to throw a phobic tizzy, she could scatter shreds of me over a square acre of Vesta in less time than it would take me to yelp.

"Will you—" she began again.

I tried shakily, "Hell, no. Wait here." Then I had to translate it.

I WENT back to the *Lucky Pierre* and got Yurt. We could do without him, even though he had been a big help. We'd taught him a lot—he'd been a child at the blow-up, too—and he'd taught us a lot. But this was more important, of course.

When I told him what had happened, he was very quiet; crying, perhaps, just like a human being, with happiness.

Cap Feldman asked me what was up, and I told him, and he said, "Well, I'll be blessed!"

I said, "Yurt, are you sure you want us to keep hands off...just go off and leave you?"

"Yes, please."

Feldman said, "Well, I'll be blessed."

Yurt, who spoke excellent English, said, "Bless you all."

I took him back to where the female waited. From the ridge, I knew, the entire crew was watching through binocs. I set him down, and he fell to studying her intently.

"I am not a Zen," I told her, giving my torch full brilliance for the crew's sake, "but Yurt here is. Do you see...I mean, do you know what you look like?"

She said, "I can see enough of my own body to—and—yes..."

"Yurt," I said, "here's the female we thought we might find. Take over."

Yurt's eyes were fastened on the girl.

"What—do I do now?" she whispered worriedly.

"I'm afraid that's something only a Zen would know," I told her, smiling inside my helmet. I'm not a Zen. Yurt is."

She turned to him. "You will tell me?"

"If it becomes necessary." He moved closer to her, not even looking back to talk to me. "Give us some time to get acquainted, will you, Dave? And you might leave some supplies and a bubble at the camp when you move on, just to make things pleasanter."

By this time he'd reached the female. They were as still as

space, not a sound, not a motion. I wanted to hang around, but I knew how I'd feel if a Zen, say, wouldn't go away if I were the last man alive and had just met the last woman.

I moved my torch off them and headed back for the *Lucky Pierre*. We all had a drink to the saving of a great race that might have become extinct. Ed Reiss, though, had to do some worrying before he could down his drink.

"What if they don't like each other?" he asked anxiously.

"They don't have much choice," Captain Feldman said, always the realist. "Why do homely women fight for jobs on the most isolated space outposts?"

Reiss grinned. "That's right. They look awful good after a year or two in space."

"Make that twenty-five by Zen standards or three thousand by ours," said Joe Hargraves, "and I'll bet they look beautiful to each other."

We decided to drop our investigation of Vesta for the time being, and come back to it after the honeymoon.

Six months later, when we returned, there were twelve hundred Zen on Vesta!

Captain Feldman was a realist but he was also a deeply moral man. He went to Yurt and said, "It's indecent! Couldn't the two of you control yourselves at least a little? *Twelve hundred kids!*"

"We were rather surprised ourselves," Yurt said complacently. "But this seems to be how Zen reproduce. Can you have only half a child?"

Naturally, Feld got the authorities to quarantine Vesta. Good God, the Zen could push us clear out of the Solar System in a couple of generations!

I don't think they would, but you can't take such chances, can you?

Mirror, Mirror

The native custom was harmless to Earthmen and their aims for exploitation of this world. But the facts about purnya brought a sickness to the Colonel—a sickness for which there was only one remedy, which could alleviate, but not heal.

LIEUTENANT-COLONEL Robert B. Corcoran stood in front of the mirror in his quarters, brushing his hair. His military brushes moved through his short grey hair with the precision of two tanks strafing an occupied hill. The front-to-back path they followed had begun just above his left ear; now it was working its way across the crown toward the right ear.

When his scalp was tingling pleasantly he put the brushes on the dresser, examining them briefly as they passed eye-level and noting with satisfaction that few hairs clung to the scrupulously-clean bristles and that there was no slightest sign of dandruff. At sixty-seven Corcoran had all his hair. Black had long ago conceded to iron-grey—but not an inch at the temples had he lost. And greying was to be expected. Abhorred, but expected.

Now he examined his uniformed figure in the mirror, having to move back a step in order to see anything more than head and chest. He turned a little to one side, eyeing his midsection. It was—or at least looked—as flat as an athlete's. Once conscious control had been necessary for that, when the muscles had first begun to loosen; but exercise and constant pulling-in had done the trick, and the maintenance of the silhouette he desired had at last been entrusted to habit. For a man of sixty-seven it was a good figure, almost a youthful one…if one chose to ignore that sheathing it was a sixty-seven year old skin. This, Corcoran could—of course—do nothing about: the skin was browned from soldierly exposure and officerial sunlamping, and the muscles underneath were in fair shape, but still the skin told its story: soft, with multitudes of tiny, tiny wrinkles—no, not quite wrinkles, just infinitesimal soft crinklings about navel and pelvis and below the settling breast muscles, like a crinkle-finish on metal; and the skin of the nipples was hardening, and the skin about the neck and collarbone was disposed to brittleness and easy discoloration.

Now Corcoran's impeccable uniform covered these tragic evidences, of course: olive-drab jacket; pearl trousers; shiny belt; polished buttons; the three Sol-bursts on each shoulder denoting his Lieutenant-Colonelship. Bob Corcoran was a tall, wide man, and had always worn the uniform of his planet well. Standing before the mirror, he went after imperfections: the belt was straightened—it had crept up slightly on the left side. A tug at the bottom of the jacket put several wrinkles to flight and made of his large chest a satisfyingly smooth and powerful-looking expanse. He touched the tie, straightened the collar insignia which told that he was attached to the Terran Occupational forces on the planet Nurra of the double sun Mira. Lastly he straightened his shoulders and raised his eyes.

His face...he had often thought sourly that the only fault with his uniform was that his face stuck out the top of it. Yon cannot conceal a face, and what it reveals.

A MASSIVE face—once it had been handsome in a hawkish sort of way. Big jaw, strong nose, a good brow, a wide mouth that seldom really smiled. Bristling brows which ten years ago had suddenly started to grow at a furious rate and which gave him, when he put his head down and looked up from beneath them, a singularly formidable appearance. Blue eyes, which behind glasses were sharp, and without them were squinty.

Corcoran put out his jaw, stretching the skin under it to lessen its sagging. There was absolutely nothing he could do about the two large wrinkles that creased downward from his nose to form inverted question-marks on either side of his mouth, and the many smaller tributary wrinkles that webbed from them across cheeks and chin. If he relaxed his face, the flesh sagged. If he tightened his mouth, the wrinkles deepened. It was the same way with his forehead: if he frowned slightly to smooth its skin, the frown created other wrinkles where his brows met, and moreover brought into prominence the crinkles and crowsfeet about and under his eyes.

He sighed. Keeping his jaw thrust out and his head slightly back, he put on his cap. He took a deep breath. He had a commanding appearance, he thought. An alert appearance. A commanding, alert, old appearance.

One last look, with a twist of mouth that had something of fury in it...then he turned and walked to the door of his quarters.

Outside, the vast, red, fuzzy-edged half disc of Mira was settling toward the black hills to the north. The giant sun's tiny white companion was riding high farther west, and Nurra's curious shadow effect was everywhere in evidence: where a building or a tree or a blade of grass obstructed the white light of the companion, casting a shadow, Mira's great bulk, looming above the horizon like the shoulder of a sunburned god, was able to cast its red light down into that shadow area. Thus the shadows on Nurra, when both suns were risen, were a dusky, dusty red.

The chill of oncoming evening was in the air as Corcoran went down the wooden steps that led to the walk. A breeze whipped down Avenue B-11 of the Terran camp, rustling the stiff blackish grass-like vegetation that grew between the rows of pre-fab buildings. The camp looked almost deserted—but that was only because it was chow-time. Officer's mess must be about on, and Corcoran could have used a meal. But there was another hunger in him. He walked down the street, shoulders stiff, head up, casting his red shadow like blood.

IN HIS OFFICE his orderly rose and saluted. He had been arranging tomorrow's paper work on Corcoran's desk. Corcoran snapped off a salute in return and said, "Tell Sergeant Howard to bring the prisoner over, then take chow, I won't need you until tomorrow."

The orderly departed, going off across the street toward the guardhouse a few buildings down. Corcoran racked his cap and sat down at his desk. He picked up a few papers and glanced through them disinterestedly. There was nothing that couldn't wait—things to be okayed, to be counter-signed, to be considered. Only the top paper counted tonight; he separated it from the rest and held it almost lovingly.

He waited. Through the window across the room he could see giant Mira, a little more sunken below the horizon than it had been before. From where he sat, the white companion was not visible. He leaned back in his big chair and lit a cigarette; the smoke was rosy in Mira's light. He snapped on the desklamp. Red light retreated to lurk about the walls of the room.

There were steps outside. Sergeant Howard appeared at the door. He saluted. "The prisoner, sir."

"Bring him in," Corcoran said. "Then wait outside." He jabbed the cigarette at the ashtray until it was shredded. His hand was trembling slightly.

When he looked up again the Nurran had appeared before his desk on soundless feet, white robe wrapped loosely around slender body.

"Sit down," Corcoran said, making his voice kindly. "Here, beside the desk."

The Nurran sat down.

Corcoran pretended to study the paper he held. Finally he

looked up. This was an old Nurran: he had tried to go *purnya*, and only old Nurrans did that. Yet it would have been impossible to tell from the creature's appearance that he was old. The skin of his humanoid face was smooth, slightly golden-colored. The large, dark eyes were clear and sparkling, despite the fear that clouded them now. The hands folded on the robed lap were slim, tapering, smooth. The Nurran sat straight as an arrow in his chair. Unconsciously Corcoran straightened his own back. It was not as easy to sit that way for any length of time as it had once been.

The Earth forces had been on Nurra for a year and a half. Corcoran spoke fluent Nurran: "You were caught," he said, tapping with paper, "trying to escape your village."

The Nurran nodded.

"You know there is a maximum penalty of death for that; why did you do it?"

"I have already told you why I did it," the Nurran said softly.

"You have told others; you have not told me. I want you to tell me now. Perhaps I can help you."

The Nurran looked at Corcoran with a faint smile. He opened his hands on his lap in a little gesture.

"There may be mitigating circumstances," Corcoran said.

"I would like that to be true, but I am afraid it is not. I tried to leave my village; I was caught; that is all."

Corcoran lit another cigarette and studied the flame of the lighter a second before releasing it. "You don't seem to want to live. Why did you try to leave?"

"To go *purnya*. I have already said that; it was noted on the paper you are holding."

CORCORAN leaned back in his chair. He puffed on the cigarette, his blue eyes intent on the Nurran behind his glasses. "All right. Tell me about it; tell me about *purnya*."

"You know about *purnya*."

"I want to hear you tell it."

"Why?"

With an effort Corcoran kept his voice kindly: "Because I am an Earthman. Because there must be things I don't know about *purnya*; I have no desire to punish you too severely."

Again the faint smile, this time a little puzzled, and a shake of the head. "Forgive me, Earthman, if I doubt that your intentions are to help me. You know what *purnya* is—it is simply defined, if not so easily understood. You have specifically forbidden it, on the supposition that those of us who wander on *purnya* might take with us information of value to the resistance movement, which you fear so much. You have isolated our villages and have imposed the death penalty on *purnya*. Always when you've caught one of us, he has died. It will do me no good to assure you that no one on his *purnya* is a spy—that they were not, and I am not. At any rate, the question is hardly that of your understanding *purnya* or not; I confess that I do not see why you ask me about it."

Corcoran made an impatient movement: the creature was more cold-bloodedly logical than most of them—and that was saying a great deal. "Aren't you willing to risk that I might be sincere? That I'm trying to help you? If you don't cooperate, I'll have no recourse but to sentence you to death as regulations require. But if you do, I might find something in your case that would bring you a lighter sentence—at least get you off alive; after all, we're not butchers, you know."

The Nurran seemed to be thinking. "No," he said after a moment. "You have taken our planet from us, and would destroy us forever as a people with a destiny of its own, simply for our mineral wealth—but it is true, you do not seem to kill without reason. Perhaps you speak truth, then...perhaps you would prefer not to—"

For the first time animation had come to the fragile golden

face. Something of hope, of belief, had replaced the quiet expectation of death. Then, even as Corcoran thrilled to the sight, the hope faded: "But I do not know what I can tell you that will help me. I was caught; all who are caught, die. I knew this danger when I began my *purnya*... I simply hoped I would not be caught. Or perhaps I was unable to help myself. The need to go *purnya*, when the time comes, is a consuming, an all-excluding purpose...almost an instinct. You would not understand, Earthman."

"I might," Corcoran said; "it can't hurt you to tell me about it."

THE NURRAN said nothing. After a moment Corcoran opened his center desk drawer and brought out some small objects—a red wooden ball about an inch in diameter; an intricately-worked miniature sceptre of a reddish metal; several startlingly Earthlike books; a jar of small greenish crystals that were probably candy; a tiny telescope almost unbelievably powerful for its size. He put them on the desk.

The Nurran's eyes had widened. Corcoran waited. He had done this before—all of it. Had seen hope and despair, skepticism and longing flicker on golden faces, and played on them lovingly as if every nuance of changing expression were fuel to the bitter flame in him. Through the window he could see the vast red shoulder of Mira sinking with visible motion below the dark hills: the flame in him, he thought, must be as big and as red as that sun.

The Nurran had been sitting very still. Now he stirred, the barest rustle of robe. Watching him, Corcoran knew that the articles he'd placed on the desk—the things found in the little knapsack affair the Nurran had worn when they picked him up—would do the trick. Sight of his treasures, and the feeling that a chance of escape existed, would make the Nurran talk.

The Nurran stirred again in his chair. He picked up the

red wooden ball; his slim fingers caressed it as he talked: "It was two nights ago that I knew my time had come to *purnya*. I knew that my death was near. Perhaps in one hundred years, two hundred, who knows? It was near—"

The paper in Corcoran's hand rustled as his fingers tightened. He sucked on his cigarette, narrowed his eyes behind the smoke. "Go on."

"Next morning I informed the Village Council that my time had come. A feast was held that night, as is the custom. I received gifts, which in turn I gave back to the givers, each of them receiving another's, for a man carries nothing on *purnya* but his pack containing objects symbolizing the life he has lived."

He put down the red ball and picked up one of the books, balancing it between his two hands: "When the feast was over I would commence my *purnya*. Until my death I should wander, having not, owing not, needing not. Wheresoever I might stop I should be led and given a place to rest and, if necessary, clothed. In my last few hundred-years of life only nature should know me well—the mountains and valleys and rivers and skies should be my friends.

"I should see places I had never seen before. I should visit, if time allowed, every village on the planet; and everywhere I should be welcomed and cared for and entertained. I should visit every region noted for its beauty. I should venture where none had gone before, to explore, perhaps to find something of value or interest to my people. I should adventure with no thought of injury or death, for the urge to come hard to grips with nature lies in all of us, and I must soon die, anyway. Without fears, responsibilities, needs, I should know the peace, the solitude, the beauty, the wonder of new places; where none might lay a claim on me; where all I encountered might help me on my way; where no purpose save that of living till I died might be in me. I should become pure. I should be made happy. In *purnya* a man is given the world before he dies."

THE PAPER in Corcoran's hand was a tight sweaty ball. "What would you seek?" he said harshly.

"Seek? Why...nothing, except to live, then die. Or in a metaphysical sense perhaps I would seek what it is I truly want: but would I have use for it if I found it? I had lived. I had worked. I had raised many families. I had—he put down the book and picked up the tiny sceptre— "served my people, when my turn came, in governing capacities. Now death was upon me. In a few hundred short years I should die. There was left only my *purnya*—my time of wandering, of release, of communion with—"

"*How old are you?*" Corcoran said. His eyes behind the glasses, were points of blue flame. He was trembling almost as if in eagerness. This was the moment.

"I am—" the Nurran thought a moment— "about eleven thousand years old. We do not keep careful track."

Every muscle in Corcoran's body urged to explode in the direction of the Nurran. The bitter flame surged in him. He shivered to it; it thinned his lips to a grey line. It was an orgasm in a dream—agonizing, exquisite, useless, awful. He said in a low, haling voice, "You don't keep track. You don't keep track. Eleven thousand of your years...nearly thirty thousand of ours. Oh, sweet God—" his voice sank almost to a whisper—"*thirty thousand years.*"

The Nurran stared at him for a long moment with his big, dark eyes.

"Finish your story," Corcoran whispered. "Finish it. Tell it to me.

The Nurran said softly, "The night I started on my *purnya* I was caught by your soldiers as I entered the hills; that is all." He closed his mouth. It was evident that he would say nothing more. His eyes, on Corcoran, were filled with quiet understanding.

Corcoran swept the objects on his desk back into the drawer and closed the drawer, returning the Nurran's gaze brightly and triumphantly.

The Nurran shook his head. "You have given me hope, then taken it. But I am not afraid to die. I regret only that I shall not *purnya*. It is you, not I, who are in torment—"

Corcoran said loudly, "*Howard!*"

Sergeant Howard stepped in, his proton-rifle half unslung at the abruptness of the summons.

Corcoran said, "Remove the prisoner. Tomorrow at dawn he is to be shot; you'll have the proper papers by then."

The Nurran rose from his chair. "I am sorry for you, Earthman."

ADJUTANT-COLONEL Wingate came up the wooden steps and into the office just in time to move aside for the silent-stepping Nurran and the alert Sergeant a pace behind. He watched them out the door, his thirty-five year old face a little troubled. "So that's why you didn't show up at mess."

Corcoran said with an insane calm, "Thought I'd get it over with." He looked at his hands. As he watched, their trembling stopped.

"Death sentence?"

Corcoran nodded.

"Honestly, sir, do you feel it's necessary to stand all of them to the squad? I can see how it affects you. After all, you don't *have* to give them the maximum penalty—"

"Discipline's got to be maintained." Corcoran wheeled and walked to the window, putting his back to that concerned young face. "You're too young—too damned young to understand, Wingate. I've been on a dozen occupied worlds. Discipline has to be kept up; you never know how trouble's going to start."

"Well, there was some talk at mess," came Wingate's voice, "about dropping the death penalty anyway. The Sociology gang is pressuring the General about it—and Intelligence seems satisfied that the *purnya* custom doesn't tie in at all with the resistance—"

"Good," said Corcoran. "Good."

Through the window he saw the last fuzzy red remnants of Mira just above the black horizon. Far to the left was the white diamond of Mira's companion, still above the hills but setting. In the window-glass Corcoran could see his face reflected in the light from both suns—red and white, every shadowed wrinkle standing out a blood red, old and afraid, eyes hidden behind glasses that were roundish gleams, stiff grey hair touched with red. Into his view moved Sergeant Howard and the Nurran, going toward the guardhouse down the street.

Corcoran watched them. Howard opened the guardhouse door. The Nurran walked gracefully through. Howard followed. At the same time the last glowing shreds of Mira vanished below the horizon, the red light faded, only the white companion remained, its pure white light burning into the window and making of Corcoran's reflected face, as he turned it to the sun, an almost young looking thing, getting down into the wrinkles, flattening them, smoothing the sixty-seven year old skin.

Corcoran straightened his shoulders, lifted his head. Tomorrow rifles would sound—and an idiot voice in Corcoran told him that in the moment when the rifles sounded, just as in all such moments when rifles had sounded, he would not feel so helpless, so baffled, so frustrated—that on rising he might, despite his tired flesh, feel by the sum of one soul, or by the assassination of a god, not quite so hateful of the dawn.

Halfway to Hell

*With a spirited forger on his side on the Other Side, why should
Morehead give a damn about the Letter of the Law?*

ON my twenty-first birthday, I decided that the best life
was the hell-raising life, and I'd live it. Wine, women, song
and ill-gotten gain. I wasn't religious; at the same time, I was
cautious. If there was an afterlife, I didn't want to chisel
myself out of my share of Heaven. Eternity's a long time,
and twice as long in Hell.

So I called up a demon. No common demon. An extra-
special demon. It took me four years to learn how, during
which I lived an exemplary life. I didn't drink, I didn't swear,
I didn't wench, I didn't even smoke.

Instead, I studied. I advertised—in cloaked terms, of
course. I traveled to some of the damnedest—literally—
places. And finally I found someone with the information I
wanted, and paid a small fortune for it: all the money my
parents had sent me, thinking I was very soberly and intently
studying abroad.

And so, as I've said, I learned how to summon a demon.

MY demon's name was Zurp.

After I'd concluded the ritual in my Istanbul hotel room,
he appeared in the pentagon I'd chalked on the rug with a
flash of nameless-colored light and a puff of putrid
smoke...except that he didn't really appear. He was invisible.

"Where are you?" I demanded peevishly. "I want to see
who I'm doing business with."

"Sight of me," came his voice from the empty pentagon,
"would drive you mad. Only damned souls are permitted to
see us, because they deserve it. Sorry I can't oblige."

I let it go. Relaxed in an easy chair in front of the

pentagon, I told Zurp why I'd called him.

"I took pains, my friend," I said, "to call up a demon who worked as a file clerk in Purgatory. One of those sadistic morons who work in Hell would be of no use to me."

"Okay," replied the voice, sounding a little flattered. "First time it ever happened to me, but I'm just like any other demon, except I got brains. You call me up, I gotta do what you want. What is it?"

"I'm going to sin my head off from now on. For the rest of my life, I intend to bust rules all over the place."

"We'll keep a spot warmed up for you," Zurp promised happily.

"That," I said, "is precisely what I want to avoid. That's where you come in."

"Huh?"

"You're going to juggle the records, pal. Every time an Observing Imp sends a nasty little memo on me to Purgatory, you're going to intercept it. When I die, I want my dossier to read: Faithful Little Lamb."

"How come you know so much about Purgatorial procedure?" he asked suspiciously.

"None of your business." The old man who'd sold me the formula for calling up a Purgatory file clerk had looked about a thousand years old, though he'd claimed to be only three hundred. He'd balked at telling me how he'd achieved his immortality, but I knew he'd come across if I blackmailed him with the threat of betraying his shenanigans to the proper demoniacal authorities.

"So," I told Zurp, "give me your Solemn Satanic Oath that you'll do it."

"You even know about that, eh?" the voice said uncomfortably, "Well, I don't know. Kill the memos on you before they get to the files, eh? Bless me, you could commit every sin in the Universe and get by with it, if I did that!"

"I intend to."

"Well, I don't know. It's never been done—"

"You'll do it, chum, or else."

"Or else what?"

"Or else I'll pour holy water all over you. I have a glass of it right here. Want a sample?"

I STUCK a finger in the glass and shook several drops into the pentagon. They struck something. Scalding hisses. Zurp squawled.

"Want more?"

"No, no! I'll do what you want! Bless me, where did you learn *that?*"

"You ask too many questions," I said, and shook more drops at him.

After he'd finished swearing, we got down to business. I made sure there was no opening whereby he could trick me. An agreement with a demon is as good as a contract: he's bound to it right down to the last letter, once he's agreed. But you have to be careful; you have to choose your words.

At last it was agreed. No loopholes. Zurp, in his capacity as clerk in the Purgatory Central File Room, would destroy every memo, every communique, every last line that related to my sins. He would do this the moment they reached his hands—if he had hands. He would double-check every Friday to make sure none had escaped him. He would do this with utmost energy right to the very second I died.

"It'll keep me up after hours," he grumbled.

I raised the glass of holy water.

"All *right!*" he yelped. "I'll do the job. You have my Solemn Satanic Oath I'll do it! What more do you want? I have to *like* it, too?"

So that was that. The demon would have to keep his Oath. When I died, the routine check of the Files would whitewash me and I'd head for Heaven. Period.

I dismissed Zurp. He gave me another cussing. I raised the glass of holy water. His nothingness vanished with another puff of foul smoke.

I poured myself the first drink I'd allowed myself in four years—since the age of twenty-one, when I'd become a man and accountable to the Powers for my acts. I killed half the bottle. Then I went out to get me a woman. Maybe two women.

It was good Scotch.

WELL, I swindled. I lied. I seduced. I cheated. I black-mailed. Pretty soon I owned a factory—I'd decided long ago that making for a nickel and selling for a buck was the safest way to steal money. Only fool luck had kept the law off my neck on the way up. I discovered that with the sure knowledge of Heaven awaiting me, sin as I might, I could happily take chances the ordinary person would never dream of—even the ordinary unscrupulous person.

Though I'd made no arrangement with Zurp for Earthly riches or impunity from the consequences of my Earthly acts, I climbed and climbed until I was set for life. There I stopped. I had no lust for power. Better not to push my luck too far.

Eventually, I wasn't as young as I'd been. I slowed to a fast run, because I couldn't gallop any more. Soon I was due for a burn-out. I didn't mind dying at around fifty, though: Heaven was waiting.

I'd never been able to locate the old guy who sold me the demon formula, in case you're wondering. I couldn't even remember his name. He must have known at the time what I'd probably try to pull in the future, and hypnotized me or something.

It was a gray November day when I was buried—the sort

of day that always depresses me anyway. It had snowed the night before. The poison my wife had put in my hot chocolate nightcap was as slow working and painless as (knowing my wife's efficiency) it must be indetectable. So I was able to distract myself during my last mortal hours, as I lay there expiring *a la carte*, so to speak, by estimating the number of big flakes that drifted silently, whitely past my bedroom window.

I was irritated at the whole affair, naturally. There were still a few things I wanted to kick around, but what could I do?

Toward morning, I died.

At eight o'clock, the maid, unable to rouse me by tapping at my door, roused my lovely young wife instead—the first time in years that Marianne hadn't sprawled around till noon. There were no angry yells. Obviously a lot of rousing hadn't been necessary. Marianne must have lain awake drooling all night for this moment.

She came in from her bedroom across the hall. We hadn't shared a bed for a decade. It was that kind of marriage: first a swap—she'd wanted money, I'd wanted her—and now a bad odor. Recently we'd just kept out of each other's way. Now she'd handed me the knife.

She wailed convincingly at sight of me and sent the maid hopping to call the doctor. After the door had closed, she bent over to tweak my ice-cold nose, and said, "Well, that takes care of *you*!"

Then she went to the window and fluttered a white handkerchief.

A FEW minutes later, my next-door neighbor, Harry Cramm, was let upstairs by the maid, who said the doctor was on his way, and departed looking sorrowful. I would miss her, too; in another week, I'd have scored.

Harry said eagerly, "Is he dead, sugar-skin?"

"It's hard to tell, sweetums," Marianne said with a happy smile. "With him, it's always been hard to tell. But I'm pretty

sure he is."

"C'mere, you gorgeous wonderful you," said Harry, and grabbed her close. Kissed her. Indulged still more of my husbandly provinces, though minor ones, before my glazed eyes. I wished for my flesh again—I'd have kicked them until they bled. But I could only watch.

Curious sensation. I lay there dead as last week's meatloaf, yet I could see and hear as plainly as ever. Minutes dragged by. The doctor came.

I was beginning to worry a little—when the hell would I start for Heaven?

As the doctor examined me, I reviewed my abundantly sinful life. As the damn fool pronounced me dead of heart failure, I decided that Zurp must have somehow doublecrossed me, in spite of all my precautions. As my weeping wife made arrangements for an immediate funeral, assisted by my sympathetic next-door neighbor—both of them giving Academy performances—I was one big bundle of frustration, fury and fear.

I prefer not to go into detail about the embalming process. Emptied out like a valise! The most outrageous experience of my life!

Marianne had the decency to pick out a good coffin— mahogany, silver, an excellent Danish satin. I wasn't impressed. With my bankroll, she could have bought a solid gold one.

I found, after they closed the lid, that I could see right up through it and, indeed, through the top of the hearse that carried me to my final resting-place.

As I've said, it was a depressing gray November day. I rolled slightly this way and that in my coffin, and watched treetops and telephone wires whisk by, and watched a large cloud float sedately from my left to my right and then execute an abrupt about-face as we turned into the Happy Eternity

Cemetery.

A few relatives were there—those that had lived within reaching distance of my wallet. I'd kept the terms of my will no secret and they all knew pretty much what their cut was. They cried because I hadn't left them more, and Marianne cried because she had to give them anything at all, and I felt like crying because I couldn't climb out and take care of her and them personally.

I WAS lowered into my grave.

A snatch of overheard conversation informed me that they'd had a hard time opening up the frozen ground to receive me. I'd have laughed if I could. *Thump* at the bottom. Faint voices from above, then a handful of dirt rattling down on my coffin like hail. They started to fill in the grave. It grew darker and darker until at last one lone dot of gray light found its way downward. Then a clod fell on that. Pitch darkness. The faraway thumping of spades, flat on dirt.

Silence. *What now?* I wondered.

The bottom of my coffin seemed to drop away from under me, and I seemed to fall endlessly, and it seemed to grow warmer. *So it's to be Hell after all*, I thought sourly: *that dirty little doublecrossing bastard Zurp.*

My fall slowed. I lit on my feet, light as a leaf, on an unimaginably high, unimaginably long bridge—a ribbon of a bridge. About six feet wide, composed of some black shiny substance—obsidian, probably—it ran far, far off into the hazy distance before me, arching slowly downward from where I stood and dwindling to thread-thinness before vanishing.

From below came vast red flickerings, like heat lightning, and gusts of pungent yellow smoke.

I walked a little closer to the edge and shuddered when I peered over. Deep smoky nothingness, nothingness upon nothingness, nothingness without end—mile after cubic mile of boiling yellow smoke, shot with ragged flames that licked through the yellow abyss like serpents' tongues.

As I watched, there came a lull in the smoke directly beneath me. A channel opened. It was like looking down a vast well, or through the wrong end of a telescope. I saw that the nothingness had a bottom: a black, jagged surface, incredibly far down, dotted with ugly cliffs and sluggish streams of lava and fuming lakes of molten metal. I thought I could see tiny figures leaping about, and even fancied I heard anguished wails.

I stepped back. So there was Hell.

So what was I doing up on this bridge?

The shiny black stuff was uncomfortably warm to my ghostly feet. Sulphur and brimstone were acrid in the air. The bridge was not the pleasantest place to be. Still, it was a long throw from what I'd imagined eternal damnation to be like.

Well, I thought, a bridge is to walk someplace on.

LOOKING around, I wondered which direction to take, and for the first time saw the sign—one of those metal things in the shape of a hand, finger pointing. It was riveted to a rod set into the bridge about thirty feet away. In large, heat-crackled black letters, it said:

TO PURGATORY:

I could have kissed the thing, I was so relieved. Purgatory was better than Hell any old day! A thousand times better! Evidently I was only partially damned. Now I had a chance coming to expiate my sins—a chance to head for the Pearly Gates instead of down into that stinking flame-shot yellowness. Maybe Zurp *hadn't* crossed me; maybe he'd just slipped up and let one or two of the less hair-raising memos on me get through.

Hopefully, I started walking. I'd gotten only a few feet when I heard a shrill whistling sound overhead. All my money hadn't kept me out of the last war—I'd ducked bombs in Normandy. My first instinct was to hit the dirt now. But there wasn't any.

I looked up. A thin middle-aged man, wearing a burial tux and an expression of utter disbelief, came spinning down through the smoky darkness.

I waited for him to light, being only too glad at the prospect of company on the long walk to Purgatory. But the middle-aged man's velocity didn't slow, as mine had. Turning and twisting like a hooked trout, he descended to the bridge...and *through* it!

I peered over the edge. He was still falling, still spinning, dwindling, now hidden by the boiling smoke, now revealed again, smaller and smaller. As he approached the floor of Hell, he began to wail. The wail rose to a blood-curdling yowl. His tuxedo burst into flame and vanished from him in a puff of smoke, as did his hair. He landed flat on his back, bounced, scrambled to his feet and started to dance around.

His rapid passage had created another of those channels down through the smoke. I got a good look at the demon who came bounding across the black rocks to take charge of the newcomer. I shuddered again. Four feet tall, it was, and muscled like a gorilla. Bright red skin, and a white-hot pitchfork.

Squish went the pitchfork into the middle-aged man's—or soul's—stern sheets. A piping scream. The soul leaped six feet into the air, every limb rigid. The pitchfork thrust out again.

The smoke closed in.

I WALKED on. And on and on.

And on. The bridge showed no sign of ending. For every mile I put behind me, another emerged from the mysterious haze ahead.

At last I came to another sign:

> 5 MILES TO PURGATORY
> Prepare Yourself
> Are You Ready to Repent?

I wasn't—but I would if necessary.

I walked on. Three more souls came spinning down to swish through the bridge and on down to Hell. I sneered after them. Jerks. If they'd had any imagination, they'd be up on this bridge instead of down there getting the white-hot prod.

Another sign: ONE MILE TO PURGATORY

Another: 1/2 MILE TO PURGATORY

Then five signs in a row:

> NOW THAT YOU'RE
> TO THIS PLACE SENT,
> PREPARE YOURSELF
> YOU MUST REPENT
> PURGATORY IS FOR *YOU*!

Ahead I could see the end of the bridge, at last. It brought up smack against a reddish stone wall that extended up and down and to either side as far as I could see. A huge, smoke-shrouded, perfectly blank wall—no windows, turrets, nothing. Just two small bronze doors, where bridge and wall met, and beside them a sort of low stone blockhouse.

As I came closer, I saw that the blockhouse was actually separated from the great wall by a gap of ten or twelve feet.

The bridge just ended with the building, and beyond, across that formidable smoky space, were the doors shining dully in the red flickerings from below.

I reached the blockhouse dead-tired—and if you don't like puns, you should feel the way *I* felt. And there I got my first close-up look at a demon.

Except that this one wasn't entirely a demon.

HE came out of the blockhouse, scowling. Four feet tall, muscles on his muscles, bright-red skin, barbed tail, two pointed horns like a bull yearling's—all that was okay.

But the horns supported a *halo*...a lovely, shining faintly bluish halo!

He looked at me indifferently as I stopped before him. "A rich one, eh?" he grunted.

Looking down, I realized for the first time that I still wore my burial tux.

The demon extended a hand with three-inch claws and fingered the material of my sleeve. "Not bad. I'll put in a bid for it—you won't need it no longer. Okay, mac, what's your name?"

"C-ch-ch...Charles Morehead."

"Um." He opened the book he'd brought out and clawed over pages, ran down a list of names. "—Moreby, Morecik, Morefingle...ah, Morehead. Charles B. Morehead. Murdered by your wife on December 17, 1953. Time of death, 5:11 P. M. Age 44. Occupation, manufacturer. Reported Sins—" His eyes widened. He looked up at me in surprise. "Well, I'll be blessed! You're the first Interim Sinner we've had for a *long* time!"

"I—Interim Sinner?"

"Yeah. You got only a couple small sins on you. Heck, they're not even sins—just sinful *thoughts* you had, after you died and before your soul was picked up by the Soul Squad.

That's what Interim Sinning means." He spat a stream of vitriol over the edge of the bridge. "Stupid thing to do. Live a peachy-pure life, and then get the boot to Purgatory on an I. S. rap." He studied the book again. He leered. "Was she really such a hot looker?"

"Who?"

"The maid. Who else? Says here you lusted carnally for her three hours after you died. Man, don't you *ever* give up? Also says you harbored homicidal desires, same time, same place. You wanted to kill—" he squinted to read—"Mari-anne Morehead—your wife, huh? —and Larry Cr—"

"Harry," I said bitterly. "Harry Cramm."

SO Zurp *had* doubledealed me, after all, by not warning me about Interim Sinning. If I ever got my hands on him, I'd freeze his—

"H'm," said the demon, blinking. "New entry. Homicidal intentions toward one Yurp…no, it's Zurp. Hey, what's the guy's last name? We got a demon here by that—"

"Jones," I said hastily. "Zurp Jones." I'd have to be careful what I thought, evidently, or I'd have a record of Interim Sins as long as my arm.

"What now?" I asked warily.

"Oh, just go on across. Take the door marked REDEMPTION OF CLASS B SINS—"

"Go on across *what?*"

He grinned as he saw me eyeing the twelve-foot gap of smoky nothing between the end of the bridge and the door he'd indicated. The grin revealed two-inch tusks.

"You can walk right across, chum. You see, every so often something louses up and the bridge catches a damned soul instead of letting it slip through. So I check on every soul that gets here, and if down below is where it belongs—" he made a pushing motion with his thick arms—"that's where it goes! You oughta hear them holler when they realize they're not going to get into Purgatory. Man, it's *crazy*!"

"But—but I can just walk across?"

"Sure. Go ahead."

I didn't like that tusky grin. I thought, What if I'm one of those accidentally caught damned souls, and he's just been waiting for me to go near that edge so he could push me off...

Then I thought, Well, I can't hang around *here* for the rest of eternity.

So here goes.

Grimly I strode forward and stepped off the end of the bridge. I didn't fall. Though there was nothing under my feet except space and smoke, I was able to walk right across the gap to the door marked: REDEMPTION OF CLASS B SINS.

I turned to give the demon a shaky wave, standing on nothingness by the door, but he'd vanished back into the blockhouse. He'd be out soon enough, though. Far, far back along the bridge, I could see another tiny figure walking toward the gates of Purgatory.

I pushed open the door by its huge bronze handle, and stepped through.

THE change in atmosphere was spectacular. Outside, the scene had squared more or less with the conventional pictures of Hell and damnation and so forth. But inside was a clean cool corridor, indirectly lit, softly carpeted, decidedly pleasant. The only jarring note was the paintings—or were they photographs?—that lined the walls in modern frames: blood-chilling scenes of Hell and Hellish torment, done with an authority and craftsmanship that would have turned Dore green. Also, there was the faintest tang of sulphur and brimstone in the air. I supposed no amount of air-conditioning could keep that out.

Suddenly I wondered if the whole approach to Purgatory—the bridge with its terrifying vista below, and the damned souls screeching as they fell, even this hall with its hair-raising pictures and tang of Hellish odor—I wondered if it all wasn't designed to scare the pants off halfway-souls like me and promote our repentance.

I straightened my ghostly shoulders and walked down the corridor to the door at the far end. I opened it and, ready for the worst, hoping for the best, went inside.

A neat, modern reception room. Several comfortable-looking chairs and a divan, a glass-topped table with magazines and newspapers on it; and across the room an enormous metal desk at which sat another of the demons with horns supporting halo. This one was taller and slimmer, though, and had white hide instead of red. And no three-inch claws.

"Please take a seat," he said in a mild voice. "I'll be with you in a moment." He turned again to the old lady soul who sat in the chair beside his desk.

I sat on the divan and picked up a copy of *The Wall Street Journal* and pretended to read. An item on Ansel Copper caught my eye. I blinked and looked again.

Ansel Copper up six points? Since *when*? I thought unbelievingly. That stock was a dog from way back.

I turned to the cover of the *Journal* to see the date, and my eyes practically came out on stalks.

The thing was dated June, 1954!

Naturally Hell and its surrounding regions would be the first to receive advance copies of the *Journal*, I thought a moment later—but this was really an advance copy! Lord, what it would be worth up on Earth. Why, with it you could—

Whup!

I clamped a curtain over my inner eye and put the magazine aside. I wanted no dreams of avarice and dishonest gain added to my record. Things were risky enough at present.

AFTER a minute or two, the old lady soul departed. The receiving demon beckoned me over to the chair she had vacated.

"Now, then," he said, picking up a sheaf of papers from a tray and glancing at the top sheet. "Mr. Morehead, isn't it?"

"Y—yes, sir."

"My name is Alfad." He riffled the papers in his hand and gave me a pleasant smile. No tusks. "Nothing to be afraid of, Mr. Morehead. You're in no danger. Purgatory is at your service. Here we offer you a chance to redeem certain sins which, though not sufficient to condemn you to Hell, are enough to bar you from Heaven, at least for the present."

"I—I understand," I said nervously.

"You won't enjoy your stay here," he went on a little grimly. "You're going to suffer, Mr. Morehead. Facing up to your past sins is not a pleasant thing. But it must be done, if you are to enter Heaven." He looked at me sharply. "You do want to enter Heaven, don't you, Mr. Morehead?"

"Oh, yes—yes, I do!"

"Very good, then." He studied the top sheet briefly. "H'm. You're not badly off, really. A few Class B Sins and one Class C. You know, sir, it's hardly proper to lust for a member of the opposite sex after you're dead."

"I know," I said humbly. "I'm sorry."

"I wouldn't worry, however. If your repentance proceeds as it should, you'll be in Heaven within a month."

"A *month?*"

"Perhaps even sooner. We've speeded the process quite remarkably in recent centuries by employing modern psychiatric techniques. You will suffer enough for each sin in a few days to cleanse your soul of it entirely and forever. As I say, it's not pleasant, but you'll thank us afterward. We receive many testimonial letters from Heaven. Would you care to see a few?"

"Oh, no. No, thanks. I'll take your word for it. And I'll do my best."

"I'm sure you will, I just thought you might need a little encouragement. I realize how disturbing this is to you."

LIKE blazes you do, I thought, my ghostly spine cold as ice. I'm walking the tightrope to end all tightropes... Heaven on one side, Hell on the other!

"Just remember, Mr. Morehead," Alfad was saying. "The pain you'll feel is like any other pain—mere agony, soon over—though, in this case, never to be forgotten. Now, if you'll just go through that door marked IDEN-TIFICATION—"

"I—yes, sir," I said, getting up. "Excuse me. I wonder if I might ask a question?"

"Anything at all."

"How is it that you dem—I mean, you—er—people all wear both horns and haloes? Are you demons or angels?"

He sighed, ran a hand over his horns, on up through his blue-glowing halo. "It is confusing, isn't it? Actually we're both. That is, the officers and personnel of Purgatory comprise both demons and angels. Purgatory is a two-power zone, you see, under the joint administration of Heaven and Hell. So we who work here wear the emblems of both. We don't like it, but orders are orders. While on duty, we're called Demels."

"Are you—are you—?"

He smiled. "I'm an angel, Mr. Morehead. The halo is real; the horns are plastic."

"I see. Well, I certainly want to thank you for your trouble."

"Not at all. Simply my job. I think I should warn you in advance that you may not find the demons among us quite so cooperative. Or perhaps you'll find them *too* cooperative. Our work here is—or should be—an objective examination of halfway-souls to determine their qualifications for Heaven or Hell. But I'm afraid that the demon Demels often try to corrupt souls during the process and thus doom them to Hell. Better watch your step."

"I—I will."

Alfad handed me my dossier, and I walked toward the door marked IDENTIFICATION.

"Good luck, Mr. Morehead." He ran a hand over his horns, and sighed again.

IN IDENTIFICATION, a barrel-chested, sullen character whom I pegged immediately as a demon—horns and halo, naturally, but also claws, tusks and a scowl—sat me down before a huge camera and mugged me, front and side and from another angle I couldn't quite grasp. Then I was finger-printed. Each of my ghostly fingers was stuck in a little thimble gizmo filled with greenish gas and, after removal, left a print floating there.

The demon Demel tore open a cellophane packet with his tusks, and flung a folded white robe at me. It smelled of recent laundering and a mild disinfectant.

"Get outa the monkey suit and inta that robe," he growled.

I did so.

The demon said, "Go through that door for your physical," and sat down with his back to me.

I resisted the impulse to kick him through the ceiling, and opened the door.

The doctor was an angel Demel. It was a relief. I was beginning to have my fill of the demons—they looked at you as though they'd like to tear you apart and put you back together wrong. Also, there was the warning Alfad had given me that the demons often tried to corrupt Heavenbound souls. I decided to keep my guard way up until I got out of Purgatory and was tuning a harp; the stakes were far too high to gamble with.

The physical was short and simple. The doctor measured the density of my shade by taking a sample from an earlobe; then he measured my cohesiveness by standing me in a sort of wind tunnel in which I flipped and flapped and stretched into quivering streamers. And that was all.

"You're in fine shape," he said, stamping my dossier. "You'll survive your redemption easily."

That was both encouraging and a little blood-chilling—if I'd had blood. Evidently you went through Hell, or a large fraction of it, before you repented.

Thank God, I thought (as if He'd had anything to do with it), I don't have to redeem all my *real sins*—the ones they don't know about! They'd keep Hell hustling for half an eon!

The doctor sent me through a door.

It began.

YOU'LL have to forgive me—or *don't*, for all I care—if I brush over the details. I find them agonizing to recall, much less write about.

There was no physical torture involved. It was all mental.

Give me plucked fingernails any day!

I *faced* myself.

In small dark rooms, with Demels invisible beside me speaking in insistent tones, I writhed and groaned and screamed and perspired ghostly perspiration and was carried back to the moment of my Interim Sins.

I turned my face away in horror from the full sight of them—from the almost fourth-dimensional sight of them, as if I were somehow seeing around *around* each sinful thought, seeing it as a whole, cause and effect and my ugly little motivations and their terrible truancy from all that was Good, seeing how I'd wandered—poor little lost lamb now found.

I turned my head away. Always an unseen force turned it back and kept my eyes open. I wailed to be allowed to undo my sins. I was told implacably that I could not, that all I might do was cleanse my soul.

All this from my measly Interim Sins! Even in my agony, I could wonder what it would have been like if I'd been below in Hell repenting *all* my sins. It was a hideous thought.

Agony of the spirit increased.

I could think of nothing but the repentance at hand.

I screamed. I wept. Days passed. Weeks. Expertly the Demels guided me back again and again to my Interim Sins, magnified them, brought them to focus, left me with them.

I saw. I repented.

At last it was over.

The Demel in the last small dark room, where I had been for nine days, reached over and switched on the desk lamp. He regarded me critically as he made notes in my dossier. "All done, Mr. Morehead."

Trembling, almost unbelieving, I rose to one elbow on the couch. "It's—over?"

"Yes. You've repented admirably. You are genuinely sorry for the sins we've worked with."

And, by Heaven, I was! It was incredible. Not sorry for all my other sins, mind you, but the Purgatorial techniques had filled me with a vast and sincere repentance for the Interim Sins!

How had they made me repent wanting the maid and to kill Marianne and Harry? Damned if I knew. Damned if I wanted to think about it. But they had. I might feel foolish about it, but I was sorry for the sinful thoughts I'd had.

It felt strange, being sorry about something.

AN escalator took me to the top floor of Purgatory. A two-foot imp, the first I'd seen, conducted me into the Waiting Room and told me that Heaven could accommodate only two hundred souls per hour from this station, and that I might have a long wait ahead of me.

I was happy to wait. The ordeal was over. I was in! I'd expiated my sins and was headed for Heaven!

I found a seat and looked around at all the other shining, smiling faces. In me was all the vast and indescribable relief they must be feeling—and a deep-down smug satisfaction at having pulled off an all-time dilly.

Man, if those half-witted Examiners only knew what a galloping sinner they were passing out of this place!

The enormous golden door at the far end of the room folded up and back and two Demels beckoned the foremost row of souls to rise and follow them. They filed through the door. As they crossed the threshold, one by one, they shot up out of sight at tremendous speed. I thought I heard faraway laughter and the strains of a distant harp. The door folded down again.

Now there'd be another hour's wait before the next lot. I counted the rows in front of me: three of them.

In three hours I'd be in Heaven!

I closed my eyes contentedly.

"Hey, mac. Pssst!"

I opened my eyes again and looked around. A small, furtive-looking Demel—demon type—had seated himself beside me and was whispering to me, hand over his mouth.

"What do you want?" I demanded, instantly wary, remembering Alfad's warning.

"You're Morehead, ain'tcha?"

"So what?"

"Thought I recognized you, I'm Zurp."

"*Zurp!*" I half-rose off the bench. "You lousy double crossing little damned—"

I stopped in utter horror. What had I *done?*

ZURP cackled. "Don't worry, pal. Use His name in vain all you want. I figured you might blow your lid, so I clamped a temporal warp around us. This is all happening in a split-second. Don't even show on your record. For all anybody knows, you're just sitting there."

I clenched my fists and stalked him, getting my first good look at him as he circled me just beyond reach. He was a runt of a demon, with a sly face and a broken tusk; otherwise, he looked about like any other demon Demel.

"I'll break your neck," I growled.

"Now, now," he said, ducking a roundhouse, "I'm sorry about what happened."

"You're sorry!" I exploded. "I've just been through Hell and you say you're *sorry!*"

"You call *that* Hell?" Zurp cackled again. "Listen, in comparison to Hell, you were livin', man, livin'!"

He dodged a left hook.

"Look, take it easy, will you? I said I was sorry. I just forgot to tell you about Interim Sins—"

I measured him for a right to the kisser. "I just bet you're sorry. In a second, you'll have *two* broken tusks—"

"You'll break your hand," he warned me. "C'mon, will you? Cool down and listen, I got a proposition to offer—"

I cooled down, all right. Fast. It had suddenly occurred to me that I had only his word that all this wasn't going on my record.

"Not interested," I said. "Go away."

"You *will* be, if you'll just—"

"Scram. I don't want to hear it."

I sat down and closed my eyes, hoping he'd go away.

His voice was a little hurt. "Well, okay, Morehead…no offense. I just thought you might wanta get a crack at your wife and that guy Cramm before you get shipped Upstairs."

MY eyes flew open. He was standing in front of me, switching his tail disconsolately.

"Marianne?" I snapped. "And Cramm? You're damn right I'd like to—" I stopped short in mid-sentence. "Oh, no, you don't! I don't know what you're trying to pull, but you're not going to get my soul!"

He looked surprised. "Who wants your soul?"

"You do, you little stinker! You're a God damned lousy treacherous little demon, aren't you?"

He blinked. "Sure. Just calling me demon covers it. But that don't mean I'm after your soul, does it?"

"I think it does. I don't trust you. Get lost."

"Look." He edged a little closer. "Listen to my proposition. That can't hurt you none, can it?"

"I don't know. Beat it!"

"It goes like this," he went on, squatting in front of me. "I got no desire to mess up your soul, see? We have more souls in Hell than we can torture right now. Long hours, no overtime—I should make it worse? Nope, it's just that I figure I owe you a favor, for forgetting to tip you off about Interim Sins. And there's another angle. The Big Boss—*my* Big Boss, I mean—figures that anybody who gets bumped off deserves a break and whoever done the job deserves a little Hell on Earth."

"*Will* you beat it?" I said, finding to my dismay that he had me interested.

"Just a second. Listen. You can ask any Demel here. Not

only the demon Demels—ask an *angel*. Ask *ten* angels. *They'll* tell you my proposition won't hurt your soul none. Look, I'm trying to do you a *favor*—"

That did it. "Okay," I said grimly. "Make your pitch. I'll listen. Then I'll check on you so fast, it'll curl your tail!"

"Well, your wife and your neighbor bumped you, right? That's a sin. But maybe they don't die for a long time yet. So in the meantime the Big Boss likes to get in a lick or two, Hell being overcrowded like it is anyway. All you gotta do is say yes, and we'll shoot you Earthside for an hour or so, and you can scare the living daylights out of 'em, before you go on up to Heaven. Haunt 'em…know what I mean?"

I did. I liked the idea so much, my ghostly teeth grated. He saw it in my face.

"Well, you *can*. There ain't nothing in the Book—" he shuddered— "against scaring people. Like I say, ask any angel Demel. He'll tell you it's okay. Just harmless fun for you and the Big Boss gets in a little damnation ahead of time. Whaddya say?"

"Come on," I said, "I want to find out if you're leveling."

I walked toward the exit of the Waiting Room. Zurp trailed along, rubbing his hands. Somebody grabbed my seat on the bench. I didn't care. For a chance to put a bit of the fear of God into Marianne and Harry, Heaven could wait.

ALFAD said, "What this Demel says is perfectly true, Mr. Morehead. Such an arrangement has been made, by joint agreement—though mostly the souls who want to return Earthside have in mind a last glimpse of their loved ones or something on that order. But there's no technical objection to your making the trip in order to haunt your slayers, if you wish."

"How about that stuff about 'Vengeance is mine, saith the Lord'? I wouldn't be committing a sin, would I?"

"No. Frightening people can scarcely qualify as vengeance for their having murdered you, though a species of vengeance is undoubtedly your motive. I can't say that I approve, Mr. Morehead."

"You would if someone had fed you poisoned chocolate."

"I suppose so. I can, and do, sympathize. But I don't approve."

"It's absolutely not against any rule?" I said. "It can't stop me from going to Heaven?"

"Correct."

"Then there's no danger in my doing it!"

He shook his head. "I didn't say that, Mr. Morehead. There's no danger in only *haunting* your wife and Mr. Cramm...but there *is* danger in accepting this demon Demel's proposal. Frankly, I believe he's trying to corrupt your soul—"

"I am not!" snapped Zurp.

"—and is counting," Alfad went on calmly, "on hidden pitfalls and unexpected opportunities for Interim Sinning—and there'll be many of them in the haunting process—to achieve his end. Remember, you're not yet in Eternal Abode. Any sins you commit will be recorded against you. I can't stop you from going, but if you do, I'd advise you to be very careful of what you do and say. Very careful indeed."

"Oh, I won't sin," I assured him grimly. "I'll just whoop and holler and bare my teeth and scare hell out of them—"

I hesitated, suddenly cold. Had I *already* sinned?

"That's quite all right," Alfad sighed. "We've been trying to scare Hell out of people for two thousand years. Anything you can do will be appreciated, I suppose. Just don't scare anyone out of a tenth floor window or under a truck. That *would* be a sin."

I nodded, still a little chilled.

"Ready?" asked Zurp gleefully.

"Hell itself couldn't stop me," I said.

"Hell itself is starting you," Alfad commented somberly. "Remember that."

Zurp made a motion with his left hand and his tail. "I'll give you a moment when your wife and Cramm are together," he said. "Have fun!"

Swish.

I WAS in my bedroom, in my house in Connecticut. It was night.

Marianne was in bed with Harry Cramm.

I expanded my ghostly chest. I couldn't have hoped for a better situation. So *that* was what Zurp had meant by "together."

Marianne saw me first. She gulped wildly, and Harry said muffledly, "Oh, peachums," and then Marianne let out a shriek that must have deafened him for a week.

Harry reared up and saw me. "Oh, my God in Heaven!" he gasped, and, disengaging himself from vanished ecstasy, he disappeared under the covers.

I pranced toward the bed, waving my hands, fingers clawed, in front of me. I snarled. I chuckled.

I reached the edge of the bed and bent over, just as Harry's face emerged, as bleached as the sheet. My nose was about two inches from his. I snapped my teeth at his throat. He screamed and disappeared again.

Meanwhile, Marianne was threshing madly, trying to capture enough blankets to hide in. A tug of war developed between them.

I laughed hideously. They screeched. I clicked my teeth.

The bedroom door burst open. The maid rushed in, followed by the neighborhood cop—evidently they'd been enjoying themselves in the kitchen when the storm struck.

The maid took one look at me, gasped, "*Mon Dieu,*" and

fainted. The cop's eyes widened until they showed white all around the pupils; I've read that, but I'd never seen it before. He pulled his service revolver and blasted away. I paid particular attention and noticed that he had clenched his fist until the knuckle actually showed white.

"*Who killed me?*" I boomed.

"*Who murdered me?*"

"*Confess!*"

It was all too much for Harry.

"We did it," he squawled. "I mean *she* did it. She poisoned his chot hocolate...I mean his tot chocolush...*she* did it! I don't know a thing about it!"

OH, it was wonderful. I could see the cop taking it all in, even as he emptied his gun at me.

Blam, blam, click, click, click.

He threw the gun at me.

I yelled at him: "Look at them! Look at my wife and neighbor! Not only do they murder me! Open adultery yet! Already he's in my house and my bed! And my wife—my own dear sweet loving wife—" And I move toward the bed and feinted as if to enjoy those very privileges which Harry had enjoyed a month ago as I lay dead on the bed. I didn't touch her, of course. That might be a sin, for all I knew.

My cup was overflowing.

I'll send Zurp a thank-you note, I thought.

Now I had only to wait for a Heavenly Messenger to pick me up and—

Swish.

Two Demels stood beside me. Two very burly-looking Demels. On their sleeves was the legend: SIN SQUAD.

"You're under arrest," one intoned, "Breach of Commandments IX and X."

The other grabbed my arm. "It's Hell for you, mac.

Come along."

"Oh, no!" I yelled, "My God, it's impossible! I mean can't I *expiate* —"

"No second chance," said the first Demel. "If we did that, every soul in Hell would be hollering for a review. Come on!"

I was falling again. Far, far below, I could see the black bridge.

You just can't win, can you? My wife hadn't wasted any time burying me. And she hadn't wasted any time marrying Harry Cramm.

So I'd borne false witness against my neighbor. No adulterer, he—at least, at the time I'd accused him. And I'd coveted his wife.

ZURP was standing on the bridge, leaning against the sign that said: 5 MILES TO PURGATORY.

"Hiya, pal," he smirked as I approached, spinning. "Finally got back at you for tossing that holy water at me, didn't I!"

"Don't pal me, you two-bit Satan," I snarled, and zipped through the bridge and continued on down to what awaited below.

Angels in the Jets

If, as appears more and more likely, mankind intends to start gadding about the universe it's high time somebody points out that the dangers of Infinity's frontiers may go far beyond gunslinging bandits and Indians in war paint. Take, for example, the lushly beautiful planet where Captain Dodge and his spaceship crew landed. Lots of danger in the air; in fact, the air was danger! Before matters quieted down, the skipper knew one thing for certain: In a world gone mad padded cells are for the sane!

IT WAS chemically very similar to Earth, but much smaller. It circled a nameless Class K sun in Messier 13, showing its one Y-shaped continent to the morning every sixteen-odd hours. It had mile-high green flora, hungry fauna, a yellowish-red sky that often rained, grey rivers that wound smoothly to a tossing grey sea. It had a perfectly breathable atmosphere—except for one thing. Because of that one thing, Captain Murchison G. Dodge had named the planet "Deadly".

Interstellar Investigation Team 411 had been on one of the seacoasts of Deadly for three days when Mabel Guernsey tripped over a huge, half-buried clam-like shell. In falling, she struck her head on the point of a huge conch-like shell. Her oxy-mask was torn off, and Mabel Guernsey got the madness.

They locked her up. They walked her over to the *Lance* that stood like a shining three-hundred-foot trophy on its sloping base of brown-black obsidian, created from sand by landing-blasts. They took her inside and put her in an extra storage compartment, and stacked crates in front of the door, and put a twenty-four-hour guard on duty to see that she didn't get away. For it became swiftly apparent that the one thing in the world—or, rather, on Deadly—that Mabel wanted to do, wanted most terribly to do, was to take off

Illustrator: Paul Lundy

everybody else's mask so that they would all be like her.

Murchison Dodge, who was the *Lance's* physiologist-biologist as well as its captain, went off searching the surrounding ecology for some cure for the malady, which was in many ways similar to ergot poisoning. Like ergot, the condition was caused by the sclerotium of a fungus— airborne and inhaled, in this case, as a curious microscopic

BY JEROME BIXBY

ANGELS IN THE JETS

unit, which Murchison Dodge thought of as a sclerotioid spore. Like ergot, it brought itching and twitching and numbness at extremities; but these were short-lived symptoms, and there was no ergot-like effect upon the involuntary muscles, so the victims didn't die. They only went mad, and stayed mad. From Mabel Guernsey's behavior, Rupert, the psychologist, judged it to be an especially manic form of insanity. Mabel seemed very happy. She wished they could all be as happy as she. She was still trying to grab off oxy-masks when they closed the door on her.

So Dodge went searching for an antidote. He was gone for two days. And while he was gone, the night guard at Mabel's storage-room prison—a spacehand named Kraus, whom nobody liked, and who found himself stimulated by the proximity of a fairly attractive and provocatively irresponsible woman—pushed aside the crates, opened the door, and went in to do some tax-free tomcatting.

When Dodge returned, in the little one-man crewboat, the *Lance* was gone.

Far below, a patch of bright color—red, blue, yellow,

purple, with the tiniest glimmer of steel to one side—told Dodge that he had at last found his wayward spaceship.

So they hadn't gone interstellar, thank God, or suicidally run the *Lance* into the local sun. That had been his first terrified thought upon finding the note they'd left and realizing what must have happened.

The note had been formed by large shells in the sand. It had been a hundred feet long. It had said: YOU'RE CRAZY. WE'RE GOING. YOU'LL NEVER FIND US.

And beneath, in smaller shells carefully selected for size and color, the names of the sixty-three spacehands and Team-members of the *Lance*.

Dodge sighed and cut the jets. He pulled the crewboat up into a stall. Its airfoils whined in atmosphere that was like Earth's, but almost twice as heavy. The green horizon of Deadly slid smoothly from the round nose-port, to be replaced by copper sky and yellow clouds and a hazy orange glow that was the sun, and at the moment of immotion Dodge released the chute. It whipped out, obscuring sky, clouds, sun. It billowed and boomed open. Dodge's couch and its empty companion pistoned back deeply at the jar, slowly rose. Dodge half-sat, half-lay, his weight on his shoulders, looking straight up into the stiff white underside of the chute with eyes that were feathered with red and burning under dry lids. His hand went out to the button that would right the couch, but he pulled it back. The lying-down position was too comfortable after eighty foodless and sleepless hours at the controls.

The little boat drifted down, swaying on its lines, the apex of each swing allowing him a view around the edge of the chute. Copper sky. Yellow clouds. Hazy sun.

Back and forth, back and forth; and suddenly glimpses of green replaced glimpses of copper and yellow; the crewboat was among the giant trees. Each swing now revealed a wall of green and brown sliding evenly, silently, up past the port. Behind Dodge the cyclodrive hummed *mezzo piano*, out of circuit; Dodge's hand rested on the board, ready to drop the boat on its jets should the chute tangle or be torn.

He started the gyro, and the swinging stopped.

He switched on the rear-vision screen. He blinked in astonishment at what he saw, down among the giant roots of giant trees, though he had been prepared for just about anything. He commenced to push buttons that controlled slip-strings. The boat's downward course altered, drifting left toward the clearing in the forest.

A last-moment adjustment brought it to rest on its fins in the center of a village square.

Wearily, he heeled the pedal that would draw the chute back into its cubby, automatically repacking it as it came. Then he turned on the side-view screens, one after another, leaving them on to get a panorama.

They were all grouped around in a wide circle, looking up at the boat. They were smiling. They were carrying guns. Even little Jansen, the bacteriologist, who had often professed a hatred of guns, had a brace of handblasts on his pudgy hips. There had been dangerous animals howling along the seacoast; Dodge supposed there must be just as many back here in Deadly's vast forests. So the guns argued that the madmen were at least able to recognize that menace, and were ready to fight it for their lives.

The glimmer of steel to one side of the colors was no longer tiny; it was huge and high—and not complete. The proud *Lance* had been partially stripped of her skin. There were ragged, gaping holes the length of her, with skeletal framework showing through, where great curving plates had been removed. Most of them cut out, Dodge saw dully, with torches. The *Lance* would never leave Deadly.

And the bright colors themselves...

Dodge felt a cold prickling back of his ears. The colors were giant fifteen-by-fifteen pine crates from the *Lance's* hold, a dozen or so of them, and the tarnished plates from the *Lance's* hull along with some shining new ones from her repair stock—all broken-down, sawed-up, bent, buckled, leaned--together, bolted, welded, nailed, glued, painted and arranged in a mad travesty of a village.

Holes—windows and doors—had been sawn or battered in the crates; and judging by the array of bolts and stays visible on their outsides, some had two storeys. They sat on the thick green grass like giant children's blocks thrown helter-skelter on a lawn. All colors and crazy angles; frills and frippery; scallops and gingerbread, ju-jubes and toyland, polka-dots and peppermint stripes and bright checked patterns like gingham. Raggedy curtains in the windows, moving with the breeze, and a doormat, formerly a seat cushion in the *Lance's* main lounge, with WELCOME in drying orange. The walls of one crate-house were covered with purple and green and yellow murals whose jumbled, whirling ugliness could have meaning only to their mad creator.

The paint, Dodge thought, must be the petrolatum vehicle for the *Lance's* fuel, pigmented with vivid clays, which abounded on Deadly. It was splotchy, and most of it had run badly.

A little grey stream ran through the clearing—Dodge had found the *Lance* by following waterways methodically up and down the continent—and several slapdash garden plots were already under way. Beyond, at the edge of the clearing, was the heavy glass and metal heap of machinery that had been in the crates.

Dodge turned the gyro off, but left the slower-starting cyclodrive on as precaution; he might want to get away in a hurry. His trembling dirty hands found another control. The couch turned slowly vertical; the straps that had held him tight demagnetized, retreated into slots. He got up, swaying a moment on the spider platform beneath the couch, took a deep breath that had acrid jet-odor in it. Then he stepped over to the shaft, found the ladder with his feet. He descended to the airlock.

Through the transparent port he could look down fifteen feet to the ground and see them staring up at him...

Jansen, Goldberg, Chabot, de Silva, Mabel Guernsey, young Jones, Marian—his heart ached as he saw Marian's face in the crowd, lovely as ever and smiling vapidly—Strickland, the four wide-eyed children, all the others. Standing in a wide circle whose center was the boat, and whose radius was the sharp-nosed shadow of the boat. Some presentably clothed, others incongruously clothed—like de Silva, who wore women's silk stockings and bathing trunks beneath the dress coat he'd affected for social gatherings aboard ship—and many not clothed at all. Dodge saw old, dignified Rupert, who had evidently not elected to come watch the crewboat; Rupert stood nude some distance off in front of a crate-house, facing away from crowd and crewboat, posing motionless with wrists crossed over his head and back arched. There was a puddle at his feet. Rupert was being a fountain.

Dodge worked the airlock mechanism, let the lock open a few inches, stopped it there; he had little assurance that they wouldn't blow his head off if they got the chance. First, of course, he put on his oxy-mask.

Looking out through the partly open lock, his voice nasal through the mask, he said, "You poor, poor devils."

"It's Dodge, all right," said Chabot, the *Lance's* Chief Engineer. He stood on the grass with his head just out of the shadow the boat cast, his body in it.

"It's God!" cried Mabel Guernsey, and prostrated herself.

Several others did likewise.

"It is not!" said Chabot scornfully over his shoulder. "It's only the captain!"

Dodge looked at Marian. She had moved to the fore of the crowd where he could see her fully.

She wore a halter affair, probably because her breasts had begun to sunburn, and nothing else except the Mercury-diamond engagement ring Dodge had given her. It glinted in the saffron sunlight as she stirred. She was looking, eyes sleepy, at his masked face in the airlock. He wondered bleakly if she even knew who he was. Her hair, unlike the matted dirty mops of several of the other women, appeared well tended; but her body was filthy, streaked with perspiration. Marian had always taken pride in her hair.

Dodge lowered his gaze to the sparkling black eyes of Chabot, who had come forward from the crowd and stood directly beneath the airlock. The man, Dodge remembered, had been a bit of a glad-hander aboard ship, always organizing and taking command of trivial activities; it was likely that this bent had led him to a kind of *pro tem* mayoralty here, for he seemed to be without dispute the spokesman. Dodge began searching for something useful to say.

Mabel Guernsey lifted her face from the grass and peeped up at Dodge. Then she got to her feet, apparently having lost her awe of God. She began to walk around the boat, within the circle of the crowd, staring up at the sleek metal sides. Several of the children followed her, singing nonsense in small piping voices.

Dodge decided that formality might be best. He put his captain's crispness into his voice. "You remember me, then, Chabot?"

"Sure, I remember you," said Chabot, smiling up. His hair was curly and as black as his eyes, with large flakes of dandruff in it. "You're crazy. You're crazy as a coot! You were going to try to make us crazy too!"

Dodge made his eyes icy, trying to frown Chabot down; then he remembered he was wearing a mask, and it didn't show. The frown remained, as he again tried to think of something to say.

"I got loose," Mabel Guernsey said, moving in her inspection of the boat. "Kraus came in, and I ran out, and he chased me. I opened the main airlock and ran outside. Kraus didn't try to close the airlock, he just stood there. Everybody else was asleep with their masks off. They all woke up happy, like Kraus and me."

"And then we went away," Chabot said, "before you came back. We hoped you wouldn't find us. We were sorry, but after all you're crazy, you know.

"Now you can't come out," he added, still smiling, "unless you take off your mask too. We'll kill you if you do!"

Every gun in the crowd came to bear on the airlock.

Dodge moved back behind the airlock door where he could watch them through the metaglass port. The port would stop a blaster bolt long enough to permit him to throw himself back out of sight if any shooting actually started.

So they'd made plans to deal with the event of his arrival. They were on the defensive. This would have been the most frustrating moment of all, had Dodge actually been able to find the madness-remedy he had searched for. But he hadn't, of course. It might take months of research and experimentation to produce one.

He couldn't help them. He couldn't help himself.

So here he was.

And there they were.

He was hungry. He hadn't eaten since starting back for the *Lance* after hopelessly concluding his search—almost four days ago. When he'd left the *Lance* the crewboat had had its regular stock of food for two days, no more. Now his stomach was twisting into itself with hunger. And he was tired. God, so tired.

He looked out at the upturned faces, at the tall ruined *Lance* that would never leave this world, and thought that he must be one of the loneliest men in the Universe.

"In fact," said Chabot loudly, "you'd better take off your mask and come out now. Take off your mask and come out, or we'll push over the boat and come in and get you!"

He stood, smiling and waiting. Looking at him, Dodge thought that the madmen must be eating, at any rate; Chabot still had his waistline. He hoped, with a sudden chill, that they weren't eating each other.

Behind Chabot, Marian turned away, moving with the grace that had always stirred Dodge so. She walked over and stared at Rupert, who was still being a fountain. He stared back, his iron brows crawling up. She pushed him over. She lay down beside him...

Dodge closed his eyes. Marian, and old Rupert... So the woman's passion he had so often sensed in her had at last, but too soon, found its release. Slow, black moments passed. At last he forced himself to open his eyes and felt a dull, sour relief. Rupert, it appeared, was a little overage. He was back being a fountain, and Marian was sitting up, staring at the boat again.

The feeling of relief went away, as if it knew it was ridiculous, leaving only a black hole in his mind, and sick futility, and a small, feverish voice chattering that this was good tragicomedy. He leaned tiredly against the airlock door. Behind the mask his face felt hot, was suddenly running perspiration. He found himself trembling violently, tight and clotted inside, his clenched fist pressed hard against the mask, cutting its bit into his lips, and his face was running tears too.

"We'll give you three," said Chabot. "On-n-n-ne..."

Dodge could taste blood in his mouth.

The others took it up like a chant all smiling, surging forward : "Two-o-o-o..."

Dodge sagged against the airlock and cried like a baby.

"*Three!*" Explosive, like "*Three!*" always is.

They milled around the boat with Chabot, by furious shouting finally succeeding in getting the effort organized. They shoved and the boat rocked on its fins.

Wildly Dodge went up the ladder. He sprawled across the twin couches to slap the gyro control. The gyro whined into action and the rocking stopped abruptly. He heard laughter from outside. He went back down the ladder to the airlock, in time to stamp on dirty fingers that clutched the very rim of the lock trying for a solid grasp. The man fell back, hooting. Looking down through the transparent port, Dodge saw that it had been de Silva, boosted on the shoulders of several others.

De Silva lay on the grass and grinned up at him. "Damn you, Cap, I think you broke my hand."

A woman—Susan May Larkin, Kobel physicist—came around the corner of one of the houses. She didn't walk; she hopped. She had a bouquet of alien flowers in one hand and her face was buried in them, and she hopped. Both feet together—crouch—hop! Both feet together—crouch—hop! A big bearlike man, one of the jetmen, came around the corner after her, grinning. He took her roughly by the arm and led her back out of sight. Still she hopped.

Sounds—a soft tinny clatter that could only be pots and pans and other kitchenware from the *Lance's* galley, beaten upon and together—came from the darkness beyond a rough-hewn, curtained window nearby. A certain periodicity of pitch-change suggested that it was music. Across the village, out of sight behind the crewboat, a female voice began to *la-la-la* tunelessly, loudly, in the very uppermost register. The singing children stopped singing to listen.

Dodge said sharply, "Chabot, come up here."

Chabot shook his head. "And have you make me crazy? Uh-uh!"

"I don't want to make you crazy," Dodge said patiently. "Remember, Chabot, I'm still captain of the *Lance*. Come on up. I just want to…"

And his voice trailed off, with no place to go. Just wanted to what? He had no cure for the madness. Chabot down there thought he had and was afraid—but he had none. Use Chabot as hostage, then? Why? On threat of the man's death, he might force them to bring food to him. But even then the oxygen supply in the tank at his belt and in the boat's tank wouldn't last forever. Or even for another week. And they quite possibly might abandon Chabot or simply forget him, and Dodge's threats would not avail. And Chabot wasn't going to come up in the first place.

What *could* he do?

"All right," he said. "Stay there."

"I intend to," Chabot smiled.

So seemingly rational, thought Dodge. So well-spoken and logical within their framework of lunatic action.

Deadly's swift rotation had moved the point of the crewboats shadow along the perimeter of the circle-standing crowd, like a giant hand on a giant clock, marking off alien minutes on smiling, mad-eyed numerals.

His mind rebelled with sudden, almost physical impact. He must do something. Not anything constructive, anything aimed at brightening his incredible position for there was absolutely nothing of that sort to be done. Just something, something. His mind screamed for action.

"I'm going to shoot," he said in a dead voice, "your damned silly village to pieces. With this boat's proton-buster."

"Oh, no, you're not," said Chabot. "We were talking

about that." Without turning, he said curtly, "Jones—"

Ned Jones, steward and cook's apprentice, ran forward from the crowd. Lithe, slim, young, he sprang to the broad leading edge of the crewboat's right stabilizer. Poised there, he got a foothold on the radar blister a little higher up. Then, one foot braced on the blister, leaning forward a little against the sleek side of the boat, he leaped a short two feet upward, bringing his head about level with the large oval barrel of the proton-cannon. He would have fallen back then—but he speared one arm into the cannon's muzzle. His body sagged. The muzzle moved an inch downward on its bearings, stopped. The arm broke audibly. Jones dangled, laughing with pain.

"You see," said Chabot. "You're not going to do any blasting, Dodge."

Not so rational after all, thought Dodge. No, I'm not going to do any blasting. But not because that boy's being where he is would stop the charge. He'd just vanish—or at least his arm would—if I triggered. But I'm not going to shoot because I couldn't do that to him. And because there just isn't any reason to shoot and destroy. Nothing but a crying, tearing, clawing need to do *something*.

But what *could* he do?

So here he was.

And there they were.

Big lonely world, thought Dodge, and my oxygen won't last forever.

Marian was at the edge of the crowd again, staring up at the boat and at Dodge. Her halter had come off—he saw it back on the grass—and she was standing straight and tall and sunburned. She'd always been proud of her carriage, too.

The madness, Dodge thought, was like most others; it impaired value judgements, but not so much any logic built on the shaky basis resulting. Each person afflicted— Chabot,

Marian, Rupert whose evident desire to be a fountain might signify a great deal, gun-shy Jansen whose wearing two handblasts might mean as much, de Silva, with his silk stockings —each had become a caricature of himself. The floodgates were down, Dodge thought, and they were living out their unconsciouses, and so they were happy.

He still felt that he had to do something. A man should be able to *act*.

"I'm taking off," he said loudly to the upturned faces. "Stand back. The jets will burn you if you don't."

Chabot didn't move. He laughed. "You're not going anywhere either. If you try to take off the boat will explode and you'll die." He stood there, hands on his hips. "Because we put angels in the jets."

He laughed again, at the look he thought he saw on Dodge's oxy-mask. The laughter caught and ran through the crowd.

Marian spoke for the first time. "Angels in the jets," she echoed queerly.

And Dodge remembered Marian's knack with a pencil, her certain skill in doodling.

Angels. Always angels. Little chubby, winged angels—almost cherubs.

He watched her as, with that lithe walk and an expression of intense interest, she came forward to pass Chabot and vanish under the stern of the boat. Then he heard her crooning. She sees the angels, he thought. So the madness included a powerful susceptibility to suggestion.

He looked up. Copper sky, yellow clouds. Giant trees, and a village. And he, almost cowering here in the crewboat—to the villagers, possibly, a kind of village idiot. Big lonely world.

Take off? To go where on this big lonely world? And why?

He couched by the partly open airlock, knees bent, fingertips touching the cold steel. There was a wariness in him, like a beast's. Behind him the gyro's whine, the cyclodrive's hum, were suddenly the song of death.

What did a man live for? All Dodge's instincts jostled and shoved forward to point to one answer: that in the last analysis a man lived to live.

Maybe in ten years or so a rescue ship would come searching Messier 13 for them. But it would be an almost hopeless search. And it probably wouldn't even happen, for Investigation Teams were presumably self-sufficient, and when not heard from, presumably lost.

"Yes," he said. "I guess you're right, Chabot. If I take off, I die."

He pressed the airlock mechanism. The sliding-door whispered the rest of the way open. Dodge reached up and stripped off his oxy-mask—quickly, without giving himself time to think—and breathed deeply, once, twice, t hree-e-e-ee…

He moved numbly to the rim of the lock, teetered there a moment on the edge of the world. His burning eyes caught the small mirror set into the wall over the first-aid cabinet; he saw his own face, looked through its eyes into the eyes of the mind he knew, and said, "Good-bye…"

And even as he watched, they changed.

Soft tinkling melody from one of the houses touched his ears pleasantly. He turned, started down the metal rungs set into the side of the boat, thinking. *But I don't feel much different!* He stopped on the way to reach over and help Jones out of the proton-cannon. Together, they jumped the short distance to the ground.

The crowd, now that the problem of the lunatic in its midst had been solved, had lost interest. They walked away, singly and in groups, chattering and smiling. Jones smiled and walked away too, clutching his broken arm. Dodge noticed with a start that Jones had two other arms—the broken arm and two others with which he clutched it. It was Jones, without doubt. But it was very strange that Dodge had never noticed those three arms before. Well, no matter...

Marian came out from under the stern of the crewboat, her eyes shining. Dodge wondered again if she knew him. She started to walk past him, hips swaying provocatively. He reached out and took her shoulder, bruising the flesh hard. Suddenly she was in his arms, flowing up against him.

"I like you too," she was saying hoarsely, raggedly. "I like you too."

They joined hands and began to walk. Marian, probably remembering the hopping woman, began to hop too, and soon it turned into a dance. Dodge joined in, laughing happily.

He bent over once, walking on all fours, just as they were entering the forest, so he could look back under the crewboat and see the dancing, darting figures of the angels in the jets.

The Battle of the Bells

*Charley's practical joke was usually good for a laugh when a city feller
made a rest stop; but it also aroused heavenly concern and began—*

IT would happen maybe once or twice a week—never
much more. Because things had to be just right.

For example, it had to be daytime for it to work. At night,
nobody was likely to notice the chain hanging down with the
handle on the end of it.

And naturally the victims had to be city folk. Had to be
used to just reaching up and grabbing and pulling without a
thought. Because when you stop to think about it, a chain
like that in a place like that is about the most unlikely thing in
the world.

But it worked—it worked often enough to bring grins to
the faces of any men who were around at the time, and
enough to make the town women sometimes a little cool
toward Charley Mason when they went in to buy things at his
store. Because it was strictly a man's joke, and he was the
man.

OWENSVILLE is a small town in western Pennsylvania.
It sits low in one end of a green-sided valley, just a few frame
houses and stores strung along a main street...and that main
street is on the one and only road that leads through the
valley: a road that all the maps show to be a convenient and
dependable connection between the Penn Turnpike and
several other major routes, should you be heading south.

So a lot of people drive through Owensville every week—
upwards of two hundred or so. And there's always one or
two of them in the mood to spend a little time in a
restroom—the last Howard Johnson's is twenty miles back
along the Turnpike, and the road down into the valley is a

bumpy one besides, and you know what that does to your innards.

So they come driving around the bend under the trees and their car wheels thump across the old wooden bridge across

BATTLE OF
THE BELLS

By Jerome Bixby

Miller's Creek—and once in a while one of them would pull off the road into the yard beside Charley Mason's General Store because they'd spot his crescent-doored outhouse standing there. Charley always kept it painted up so it'd be easier to see—clean white with a red roof—and over the door he'd lettered, big enough to see from the bridge, PUBLIC RESTROOM.

Then somebody'd get out of the car and go in, and a few minutes later the chain that came up through: the roof would yank down as whoever was inside reached up and pulled the handle.

And then the big old cowbell on the roof—the biggest and noisiest Charley'd been able to find—would dance around in the mounting he'd made out of an angle-iron, and go *Blongle, blongle, blok!*

After a minute the door'd open and the city folk would come out, looking puzzled and kind of sneaky. They'd give a glance up at the roof and see the cowbell mounted there. Some of them might grin at the way they'd been had. But mostly they'd get into their car and drive off maybe a little faster'n they would've ordinarily.

If it was a woman, it was five times as funny. Because some of the older men were always sitting around on the porch of Charley's store playing pinochle, or lounging down by the bridge just talking, and when the woman would come out they'd all grin at her and those who had mustaches might twiddle them a bit, and she'd get redder'n a bushel of to-matoes.

Women drove off faster'n anybody, usually.

Some townspeople said it wasn't a very good way to advertise Owensville to passersby. But Charley said that a town of thirty-two people didn't have to worry about advertising one way or the other—it just needed diversion. And since it was on his property, the cowbell stayed up.

It was just a gag. It never really hurt anybody. Charley, who could incline to philosophy when it suited him, said that the only person it could hurt was somebody who was plain ashamed of being human. And, on the personal side, he admitted he got a kick out at seeing them all flustered up that way.

Probably the outhouse and the bell'd still be there, and Charley'd still be getting his laughs, if the fat lady in the green convertible hadn't decided to do some praying.

IT was a late July afternoon, and plenty hot. The sun was reflecting like yellow-green fire off the hills around, and everybody was sitting in the shade.

Charley Mason and Sam Knudson were sitting on the store porch playing gin, and Luke Yates was just coming up the steps, when they heard a car approaching.

Charley and Sam paused in their game and Luke turned his gray head to look.

"Maybe this time," Charley said.

Luke Yates studied the dust cloud moving toward town above the tops of the trees.

"Coming pretty fast," he said. "Bet they drive right on through."

"A dollar," said Charley. "You bounce harder when you drive fast."

"It's on," said Luke.

Waiting, Charley Mason leaned back in his chair and half-closed his eyes, a lean, bald man in shirtsleeves, the hand holding his cards relaxed in his lap. They could hear the murmur of the creek carrying away the runoff from last night's rain, and the air was sweet with the breath of the fields off down the valley.

"Rich man," said Charley, looking across the yard at his outhouse, "poor man, beggar man, thief. In there, you're all alike in the eyes of God, I guess."

Sam Knudson nodded thoughtfully. "In the eyes of *something*, at any rate."

"All alike," said Luke Yates.

"Can't see your wallet from *there*," Charley said.

"Your brains either," said Luke.

After a moment, Charley said, "Some people's brains, maybe."

They all nodded.

A green convertible driven by a fat woman came around the bend, trailing dust, and rattled across the bridge.

"New York license plates," Luke said, squinting.

"Yep," said Charley.

"Maybe she'll bite."

"If she stops," Charley said, "maybe she will."

THE green convertible swerved off the road and pulled to a halt beside the store. The fat lady got out and looked around for a moment, blinking in the sun. She saw the three old men up on the porch and seemed to hesitate. Then she went around the back of the car and headed for the outhouse, walking a little defiantly, head up, her steps steady and deliberate.

The men exchanged glances. Luke handed Charley a dollar bill.

"Do her some good, maybe," Charley said. "Shy type."

"Like we didn't know how it was," Sam said, shaking his head.

"Or maybe," Charley said, "because we do. Funny."

Luke sat down on the bottommost step and scuffed the dirt of the yard with a toe. They watched the cowbell atop the outhouse, and listened to the murmur of the creek, and heard a bird sing in the big elm out back of the store, and waited.

The chain that came up through the outhouse roof yanked down.

The cowbell went *Blongle, blongle, blok!*

Charley puffed his pipe in satisfaction. Luke and Sam grinned. They waited for the fat lady to emerge.

When she did, a moment later, it was looking puzzled as usual—but there was a difference. She stalked ten feet away from the outhouse, about-faced, and stared up at the cowbell. The men saw the back of her neck get red and redder still. Then she turned and came toward the porch. Her eyes were narrowed, her hands were clenched into fists, her mouth was a determined slash.

She marched across the yard and stood facing the three men on the porch. She put her fists on her hips and glared.

Luke and Sam stopped grinning. Charley's pipe drooped.

The sun beat down on the valley, the town, the yard, the outhouse, the fat woman. Her brow was shiny with perspiration. She stood there turned her cold blue glare on one man after another, like you'd sweep a gattling against enemy ranks.

Luke said uncomfortably, "Howdy, ma'am."

"You old lechers!" said the fat woman tightly.

Charley and Luke and Sam exchanged dismayed looks.

"Now, ma'am—" Charley began.

"Don't say anything, you old lechers," the fat woman spat. "I don't want to hear your gloating, oily voices! Of all the lecherous, salacious, lascivious things to do!"

"Why," Charley said doubtfully, "I guess we're a little old to be all those things—"

"You're never too old to be evil-minded!" she snapped. "Even if your bodies are too old for unGodliness!" Her positive and indicating gaze raked them up and down, and she saw the cards which Charley held in his lap.

"Playing cards, too!" she said, her lips curling. "Well, I

guess *that* follows!'"

"Follows what, ma'am?" Luke asked puzzledly.

She saw the brown beer bottle resting on the box beside Charley's chair.

"*Alcohol!*" she hissed.

SHE stood glaring up at them, her breath coming fast and shallow, in a half-crouch that led Charley Mason to wonder if she planned to climb right over the porch rail and lace into them physically.

Then, as they watched in wary silence, her anger seemed to abate a little; over a period of five seconds her fists slowly unclenched, her breath slowed, she straightened.

She said in a low voice, "It's the work of the Devil. Anger is not the answer."

"The Devil, ma'am?" Charley asked.

"*He* has made you do this—it is a device to keep lewd and licentious thoughts uppermost in your minds and corrupt your immortal souls, I suppose I shouldn't blame you for listening to him...so *few* of us *are* able to resist his honeyed mouthings."

"Ma'am," Luke said, "I don't think you should get so excited on a hot day like this. Maybe a cold coke—"

"I'll pray," the fat lady said. "I'll pray for the Lord to undo this Devil's work. I'll pray that your souls be cleansed of the evil thoughts the Dark One has put there." Her pale blue eyes seemed a trifle fixed, and now she smiled, looking through the men who watched her worriedly. "I—I'm almost proud that I should have suffered this humiliation in order to help Him in His work—it is a small price to pay, to have been the object of your lustful thoughts, if I can save your souls by telling the Lord what you are doing and seeing to it that He stops you!"

She gave them a pitying, sympathetic look. "You hate me

now," she said, "but when you are pure you will thank me."

She turned away and walked toward her car, head bowed.

After a moment Luke got up from the steps and sank into a chair on the porch. "Does lust mean what I think it means?" he asked.

"Guess it does," Charley said.

"Well, back when I *could* lust, I wouldn't ever have lusted *her.*"

They watched her get in and drive off, head still down in an attitude of prayer, eyes up so she could drive. The car reached the other end of the main street, followed the road into the trees, and vanished.

Charley stared contemplatively across the yard at his outhouse.

"Work of the Devil, huh?" he mused. "Well, now doesn't that beat all! I bet Heaven would kick that prayer right out of court!"

"No," said a firm voice, "It was heard."

THE three old men turned and saw a tall, handsome, blond young man, dressed in a neat and utterly clean white suit, standing in the center of the yard. His face wore an expression of perfect peace and abounding love.

Actually, he wasn't *quite* standing in the yard yet. When they turned, his feet were about four feet above the ground. As they watched, he floated slowly down until he was standing straight, and tall and smiling a little.

At that moment, *timelessness* descended upon the scene—upon Charley Mason's store, the yard, the outhouse. *Timelessness* bounded the area from one edge of Charley's yard to the other, and from the road clear to the woods out back; and that *timelessness* extended downward to a perfect point at the very center of the Earth, and extended upward in a perfect cone to Heaven; and within its boundaries nothing that happened was visible to the outside world, or indeed even "happened" so far as the outside world was concerned: for it all happened in *timelessness*...in one of those particles of time-substance which exists *between* microseconds on Earth's time continuum: particles so small that they are of use only to angels, who in their work must often get between people and their intended deeds faster than seems possible.

The young man's calm eyes looked into the minds of the three old men on the porch, and saw no evidence there of lewd or lascivious thoughts of the magnitude reported by the fat lady in her prayer. This did not surprise him, for exaggeration is the backbone of prayer, and the Heavenly Workers are used to it. In particular are they used to nuisances like the fat lady, who continually turn in false alarms.

Closing his eyes, the young man contacted his secretary-cherubim in his office in Heaven. The cherubim immediately returned the dossiers of Luke and Sam and Charley Mason to the Heavenly Files, with no additional notations on the debit side.

That done—for nothing is so urgent in the eyes of Heaven as the latest data on souls—the young man turned his attention to the outhouse.

He saw the cowbell, and his lips pursed.

He left the porch, walking lightly, and crossed the yard to the outhouse. The three old men watched him dreamily, unmoving, comprehending, gripped by *timelessness* and a sense of wonder.

The young man opened the crescented door and went in. The chain yanked. The cowbell went *Blongle, blongle, blok!*

The young man reappeared in the door and looked at the old men on the porch. He pursed his lips again and shook his head reprimandingly. He disappeared again.

A second later, the cowbell and chain and angle-iron

disappeared too.

THE young man came out, dusting his hands with a white handkerchief. He came back across the yard and mounted the steps. He seated himself on the porch railing, where he could face the three old men.

"Shame on you," he said.

The men cast their eyes downward.

"The lady's accusations were somewhat excessive," the young man said. "Your motives seem not to have been primarily lascivious, and I have so informed Heaven. But still...don't you think you should be ashamed of yourselves?" He paused. "You may nod if you wish."

The men nodded, eyes dreamy.

"After all," the young man said, "isn't that rather a snide trick to play on tired travelers who seek your hospitality?"

Charley Mason's mouth worked; his Adam's apple bobbed.

"Speak," said the young man.

"Gosh," Charley said in a low voice, "it was just a little joke. We never had nothing else in mind—"

"I know," the young man said. "I have discounted that element. I am speaking of the unkindness of the prank—the discomfiture which you impose on its victims."

"Oh," said Charley. "I—gosh, it just embarrassed them a little bit, that's all. I mean...that's all, isn't it?"

"No," said the young man sternly, "there is more. Think a moment, humans, upon that common structure in the yard...think deeply, and you will realize that there is much more to it than meets the eye."

"Guess so," mumbled Charley.

"It is a haven...a place of wondrous solitude...a refuge for those who would contemplate without interruption, as many a weary traveler yearns for."

"Guess so."

"In what other situation can you be so completely alone...in a perfect isolation not only permitted but sanctioned by your society? Why, humans, I could tell you of the most extraordinary moments of piety, of philosophical reflection, of artistic conception which we have recorded as occurring under such circumstances..."

"I never thought of it that way, I guess," Charley said slowly. "I always did sort of think it leveled you off, though."

The young man eyed them soberly.

"In late afternoon," he said, "in the confines of the rustic outhouse, settled happily, hearing the quaint and natural sounds of the insects in the field, the flutterings of birds from branch to branch...do you know that in this day it is the only waking place where one may flee for the inner life?"

The old men looked down guiltily.

"It is ever a reminder of one's mortality," the young man said.

"It is Man in his true aristocratic state," he said.

"And yet at his most humble," he said.

"And now I will leave," he said. "I hope you have seen the light, and will no longer impose your crude, cruel joke on those who trust you for a moment's peace."

He stood up. "I hardly think that it was the work of the Devil, however, as the lady seemed to think—"

A cloud seemed to come over the sun—but there were no clouds, so perhaps the sun dimmed. The birds in the trees were suddenly silent. Even the rustling leaves seemed to pause. It grew still darker, and a chill breeze sprang up.

A head, whose face was dark and sharp and saturnine, appeared in the center of the yard.

AS the young man and the three old men watched, a tall, dark, gaunt man in a neatly tailored black suit rose from the ground and stood eyeing them mockingly.

"Wasn't it?" he said in a thin, dry voice, and laughed.

The young man's lips tightened. He said nothing. The three old men were shrunken back in their chairs, staring.

The Devil—or perhaps the man in black was only *part* of the Devil, for mysterious and complex are the ways he influences from his bronze throne in the exact center of mid-western Gehenna—turned and sauntered to the outhouse. He entered.

A moment later the cowbell and chain and angle-iron reappeared—though not quite as they had been. The chain seemed a little heavier, the cowbell a little larger and more shiny.

The chain was yanked. The cowbell went *Blongle, blongle, blok, blok!* –a metallic sound of triumph.

The man in black came out smirking. He made his way across the yard and mounted the porch steps. The young man frowned and lifted a shoulder so the fabrics of their clothing would not touch.

The man in black went to the opposite end of the porch and sat down in a chair there. He looked out over the bridge and the murmuring creek and the trees beyond and took a pipe from a pocket. From another pocket he took a live coal, which he dropped into the pipe. He puffed, and sulphur-smell filled the air.

The young man got up, sighing and bracing his hands on his knees. He stood for a moment regarding the man in black levelly. Then he went down the steps and across the yard and into the outhouse.

Chain, cowbell and mounting vanished.

The man in black rose, still smiling. He passed the three old men, trailing sulphur smoke from his pipe. They shrank back, eyes wide. He went down into the yard and toward the outhouse.

When he was halfway there, the young man emerged. They locked eyes, the young man's cool and determined, the other's hot and mocking and quite as determined.

They passed each other, saying not a word.

As the young man reached the porch steps, there came from the outhouse a loud *Blongle, blongle, blongle, blok, blok*, and he paused, one foot on the steps, lips thinned. He seated himself deliberately, and only then did he look around.

The new bell was twice as large as the former. The chain was heavier. It hung from a heavy cast-iron mounting.

The man in black came out. He sauntered back to the porch and seated himself.

HALF a non-existent hour passed—non-existent, because it passed in *timelessness*. The young man sat quietly, seeming to ponder; the man in black sat as quietly, smoking his sulphur; the three old men sat like mice, their eyes shuttling back and forth between the two antagonists.

At last the young man got up and walked slowly to the outhouse. The cowbell and its paraphernalia vanished. This time with a flash of white light.

The man in black dropped a new lump of smoking sulphur into his pipe and tamped it down with his thumb. He walked to the outhouse and replaced the bell with a still bigger one. He yanked at the chain, and raucous bellsound filled the yard.

He came back, and they sat around a while longer.

The young man went out. The new bell vanished with a flash like diamond-blue lightning.

The man in black sauntered out. In an enormous mounting atop the outhouse appeared a three-foot church bell.

Its chain yanked down.

Bong-g-g – bong-g-g – bong-g-g...

The young man hurried across the yard, shoulders stiff.

So quickly that the man in black, eyes mocking, was forced to stand aside at the very door of the outhouse to permit him to enter.

The church bell and mounting vanished. With a clap of indignant thunder.

The man in black resumed his chair on the porch. The young man came slowly back across the yard and sat on the steps.

After a few minutes the young man said, "That wasn't very funny."

"I hardly expected you to think so."

"This can go on for an awfully long time you know."

"I have," said the man in black, "an awfully long time. So do you."

"I think that it's rather a silly thing for you to be concerning yourself with," the young man said. "After all, it failed to incite these humans to any thoughts which could really be called sinful."

"Then it is an equally silly thing for *you* to concern yourself with, isn't it?"

"I do so because it disturbs humans at a time when they may be nearest to God."

"I concern myself for the same.

A NON-EXISTENT half hour passed. The young man sat on the steps, his white suit impeccable, face thoughtful. The man in black sat and smoked and smirked. The three old men waited.

Out in the yard the outhouse stood, a battleground of good and evil. Its coat of white paint gleamed in the sun, which still stood high as a result of *timelessness*. Its red roof was a challenge. To the young man, staring moodily, the crescent in the door seemed a mocking, lopsided smile.

On the roof stood a new and larger mounting, containing a

new and larger cowbell, from which hung a new and heavier chain.

Once the young man looked upward, as if for guidance.

Once he sighed and shook his head, as if discouraged.

"One of us must win," he said finally.

"Always," the man in black nodded.

"If I destroy that bell, you will replace it."

"With a bigger one."

"If you replace it, I shall destroy it."

"And then I shall replace it again."

"Do you really feel," asked the young man, "that so small a purpose is worth such an effort?"

"I might ask you the same question."

"Tiny building blocks may build a great edifice."

"The removal of one may contribute to its ruin."

The creek murmured. Out in back of the store, the bird in the elm sang a hesitant note, and then was silent.

Charley Mason cleared his throat.

The man in black turned his hot, mocking gaze on Charley. Charley closed his mouth so hard his teeth clicked.

The young man said, "You need not fear him, mortal—only his temptations. "

"Mister—" Charley said hesitantly.

"Yes?"

"Something sort of has me wondering."

"Yes?"

"Well—I've been watching you two go at it, and—well, it sort of looks to like like this other feller has the edge on you right down the line. I mean, like he was all confident, and you just don't know how to get around him—"

The young man nodded somberly. "I have been waiting for you to make that observation, human. It is true. Evil has only to be...has only to *exist* for its work to be half done. It is a pit; you have only to fall into it. While to be good, you must exert yourself to climb *out* of the pit." He looked sadly at the smirking man in black. "He walks confidently, for he requires no more than your acceptance of him, your tolerance, your passivity, your apathy. How can such a dynamic imbalance threaten him?...he must only *be* to be strong; you must *act* to make him weak."

The young man got up and stretched his arms. He looked upward at the sky again, and seemed to be listening. He shrugged a little.

"It has been pointed out to me," he said, "that I have demonstrated sufficiently—now there are other matters to be attended to. I will destroy the bell once again...but mark these words well, humans: the Dark One will create another—and it, like all his creations, will be a potential for evil. Not a large evil, perhaps, in this case, nor an evil in itself by the simple fact of its existence—rather his creations represent the potential of evil *within yourselves.* After he goes, I urge that you take down the bell and throw it away...destroy it...for as you have seen he is powerless to prevent that. If he creates another, cast it aside also. Keep doing so. The bell is but the symbol, the temptation: the conquest of evil can take place only in your own souls; you must *act* in the face of that temptation. The battleground is not this town, nor this yard, nor that structure, but in *yourselves.* In you is the pit; in you must be the strength and will to escape it. Do you understand?"

Three nods.

The young man looked into their minds for the last time, to assure himself of their purity.

And in Charley Mason's mind he saw a tiny, half-hidden thought that struck him so forcibly that he almost smiled. Deep in Charley's mind, beneath all his awe and wonder at the present situation, almost on a subconscious level, Charley's sense of humor was still working—the sense of humor that had come up with the cowbell joke in the first place.

Now, in Charley's mind, was a solution for the present difficulty. Not a solution, actually; for the realities of the problem were already solved—solved in the minds of the three old men and their firm resolve to do nothing ever again that would precipitate this kind of Heavenly and Satanic tug-of-war in the arena of their souls.

But it would end this business of bell/no bell very nicely. And not inappropriately, the young man thought. He would arrange the situation just as Charley was mentally picturing it. And seeing what Charley had in mind finally brought a smile to the young man's face.

He walked across the yard and entered the outhouse. The bell and chain and mounting vanished. This time the young man was gone from sight just a little longer than any time previously, and when he came out he looked just a tiny bit expectant.

He waved in friendly fashion at the three men on the porch and rose into the sky, faster and faster until he disappeared into the sun.

The man in black got up from his chair and knocked out his pipe on a heel—or rather, where a heel should have been, for it was now evident for the first time that he had black hooves instead of feet.

The wad of sulphur fell to the boards and smoked and stank.

"He was right, you know," he said. "The battle was in yourselves. And I suppose I've lost. I seem to be losing more and more these days...though I'm by no means through. I suppose if I put up another bell, you'll just take it down." He sighed and stretched his long black-clad arms wide, as the young man had done. "Well, it's been diverting. I think I *will* put up another bell—just for the Hell of it."

He went down the steps, across the yard, into the outhouse.

An enormous cowbell appeared on the roof—a prince of cowbells, a cowbell fit for the neck of Babe, the giant blue ox of Paul Bunyon. From it hung an inch-thick chain.

The chain yanked down, the cowbell went *BLONGLE, BLONGLE, BLOK, BLOK, BLOK!* —and Charley's plan which the young man had arranged before leaving the confines of the outhouse became evident.

There was a loud flushing sound, A herculean flush. The walls collapsed inward with a roar and an enormous swoosh and a gargantuan gurgle. A moment later there was only a deep hole in the ground where the outhouse had stood. And then the sides of the hole crumbled in to form a shallow pit.

Timelessness ended.

Luke scratched his head and stared from Sam over to Charley. "Did you two dream the same thing I did?" his voice was awed.

Sam pointed over to where the pit made a raw scar in the ground, "Weren't no dream. Or if it was, we're still asleep."

Charley had a laughing glint in his eye. "We're not asleep, and it wasn't any dream. 'Specially the ending."

Luke and Sam looked at him puzzled for a moment. Then they both laughed and Charley joined them.

"Bet that flush was the damndest joke Satan ever had played on him! " Luke gasped, holding his sides.

"One *hell* of a joke, Charley." Sam choked. "What I wouldn't give to have seen his face!"

Charley agreed. He began to laugh even harder as he wondered if there was any soap and water down in Gehenna. He had an idea Satan might be praying for some.

One Way Street

The multiple-worlds theme is quite a common one in science fiction. It extrapolates some scientific theory—heaven knows which one—into the premise that you're really a limitless number of people in many worlds doing any number of things at the same time. Confused? Maybe this story will clarify it for you—and maybe not.

PETE INNES skidded his '49 Dodge coupe into a tree at fifty-five per, out along Northern Boulevard, one Monday morning. He was on his way to work in Manhattan from Greenhill, Long Island, where he had a ranch-type house, a wife, a dog named Prince, an eleven-year-old son...a life.

He started swearing as the car turned over. As the top crunched in, he was thinking, *Now why in hell should I black out for a second and sideswipe a tree? Going to die, damn it.*

A little academic—but you get that way when you unexpectedly see the scythe coming. Your brain works faster than your glands: you don't have time to feel much, you only think: your first impulse is a kind of interest.

Luckily the impact of the sideswipe flung Pete over on his face across the front seat: the car flipped, and the top mashed down, but Pete didn't get his head broken—it wasn't there.

The car turned over again: Pete rattled back and forth between the seat-cushions and the crumpled top only a few inches away from his back. Metal howled; glass shattered, dispersing like water; a tire went *whop!* and then another. Pete's muscles wrenched agonizingly, particularly those in his back and neck.

The car lit upright and settled, rocking. Thousands of tiny squeakings for a few seconds. Silence.

Pete kept hearing all the noises, retaining them. He kicked until the left-hand door flew open. He inched himself backward toward it, and did all right until his shoulders reached

271

Illustrator: Augusto Marin

the steering wheel, which had been shoved back a foot nearer the seat. He tried to turn and crawl past on his side; he couldn't turn; the squashed roof was too tight overhead. All he could do was let out his breath, pull in his shoulders, and squirm.

His legs emerged, waved in air; he bruised a shin on the running-board. He screwed up his arms and shoved against

ONE WAY STREET

BY JEROME BIXBY

the steering wheel, which was now about even with his chin. He went out the door, his coat up over his head. His feet found ground, then his knees. He was kneeling, his cheek against the cold metal of the sprung door. Hating the car, he shoved himself away from it, hard, with both hands. He went over backwards on grass and dirt. He lay on his back, and brought his hands up to his face and started to cry.

A screech of brakes; footsteps running. Someone knelt beside him. Two hands touched his wrists lightly, as if they wanted to draw his own hands away from his face but were afraid to.

"Are you okay, mister?" a voice said.

The hands got rough. Pete's hands were dragged away from his face. Then the voice sighed; Pete felt a breath of tobacco across his face: "Lord, I thought your eyes were cut up."

Now Pete was shuddering—long shudders that started in his abdomen and ran up to shake his shoulders.

Another screech of brakes. More footsteps. A new voice

said, "Man, how'd he get out of *that* one! He okay?"

The first voice said, "I think so. He's half nuts. Shaken up. Got the hell scared outa him...oh, I'm sorry, lady—I didn't see you there."

"I've had first aid," she said. "Move over. I'll feel him."

Pete found it funny. He began to laugh. Stopped. Hell with it.

There was a studying pause. A light woman's touch ran over his head, his jaw, his neck. Down along his chest. Ran over again, a little harder. It tickled. Pete laughed.

He got a slap on the left cheek that rocked his head; a slap to bring him out of it.

Shock to hysteria to rage. He said ten filthy words, most of them present participles.

The woman said, "I think he's all right. Some ribs broken—bad to laugh."

Pete tried to sit up. He said another few words—gasped them, rather, clapping one hand to his side.

The woman said, "Get down."

She helped him do it. He felt a crunching in his side. Pain was starting. He took a look around at the faces, saw nothing, closed his eyes again and waited for things to happen. He wasn't his own problem, right now: he was theirs. Social action was underway: policemen would come, and an ambulance, and he would be taken care of. People were focussed on him: it often takes disaster to do it, but that's when you're loneliest.

Sound of a motorcycle. Footsteps coming up, then going away at a run; the motorcycle blurted off. About that time Pete slipped into a pain-shot night.

The first thing that was wrong was the telephone in the hospital where he woke up about noon, the same day.

The nurse who was straightening his blanket said, "How are you feeling, Mr. Innes?"

He winced up at her, "Alive."

"Aches and pains?"

"They're lovely."

"It was a bad crash. The officers said the only thing that saved you was that you were pinned between the crumpled roof and the seat—you couldn't bounce around a lot. Except the steering wheel caught your ribs."

"Has my family been notified?"

"I came in to see if you were awake. Your wife's waiting outside."

Pete sighed. "It'll be nice to stay off the job for a while and romp with my kid...as if I could romp!"

The nurse paused at the door, smiling a little severely. "You know, it's no help to put your identification in code, or whatever it was."

Pete blinked.

"Your wallet told us your name, of course—but you have your address and telephone number wrong."

"I don't get you."

"The phone especially—the address was almost right; 1801 instead of 1811. But the thing you have down for your phone number doesn't make any sense. There's no such exchange. We had to check with Information before we could locate your family."

"You're very pretty," Pete said slowly, "and evidently nuts."

"Thank you, and I'm not," she smiled. "You'd better get that straightened out."

"My identification," Pete said, "is in perfect order—"

But she was gone.

He lay there frowning.

The stuff he'd had in his pockets at the time of the crash was piled neatly on the table beside the bed. He reached over and picked up his wallet and leafed it open to his celluloid-covered card:

Peter M. Innes
1801 South Oak Street
Greenhill, Long Island
New York
Highview 6-4509J

It was absolutely correct.

The nurse had said it was wrong. Hadn't they *tried* it? The phone? She'd said there was no such exchange. There was a telephone on the table. He gave it a sour look as he put the wallet back beside it. Ordinary black French phone. Maybe a little more streamlined than most—

With a dial that went like this: A-123—B-234—C-345—D-456—E-567—and so on to J-000…whatever that was.

He was staring at the phone and shaking his head when Mary came in.

Tears, of course. "Oh, thank God, thank God, thank God," she kept saying against his shoulder. The pressure of her against his side hurt, but he pressed her closer, thinking the same thing: *thank God.*

Then she was saying, "Oh, darling, I'm sorry, I'm so sorry—"

"For what?" he said.

"The argument." She pressed against his side. "You wanted to die. I just know that's why you had the accident!" He couldn't help gasping at the pressure. She made a shocked sound and pulled back: "Oh, darling! I was hurting you—"

"Loved it," he said.

Her dark eyes were filled with tears, and she did something she hadn't done in years. She bent her head so her hair fell over her face and she brushed the hair across his face, lightly. He inhaled with satisfaction.

"You're not mad, then?" she asked through her soft hair.

"Mad about what?"

"The argument."

He thought a moment, hand on the back of her neck. "What argument?"

The hair swished across his face delightedly. Then her nose was pressed under his ear, and something else happened that hadn't happened in years: she caught a bit of skin between her teeth and worried it with her tongue. His hair lifted.

"Then you're *not* angry anymore?" she whispered softly.

"I—" He gulped, feeling many things. "No, honey, I'm not mad. I—I've even sort of forgotten what we argued about."

"Oh, you *sweet*," she said.

With gentle force he removed the source of the disturbance, getting her to sit up. "This bed's too small for two," he said. "Besides, people like doctors keep wandering in. Cut it out, honey."

She got out a tissue and wiped tears away. She wasn't crying any more—just dry-sobbing a little. She sat on the edge of the bed and held his hand. "You get well," she said.

"Not much to it. Just a couple of busted ribs and some bruises, they tell me. I can leave in a couple of days." He looked at her with a fondness he hadn't felt in some time: maybe the accident had been a good thing. Maybe it had struck away some unpleasantness—or indifference. Married for twelve years. Up and down. A kid. Getting on toward forty, both of them. She was still a darned attractive woman and he wore his years better than most. Lately they'd been— well, just apart. But now she seemed to have taken on flame, and it was welcome warmth. Let it burn. He could feel response in himself; and that old fondness. Flicker, flicker, flame—

"It was an awful quarrel, wasn't it?" she said. "I've felt awful for days. But it was my damned old pride...if you thought I was fooling around with Phil Tarrant, I wasn't going to try to change your mind."

"Phil Tarrant," he said vaguely. "Phil Tarrant...do you mean Phil Terrance?"

She frowned. "Phil Tarrant. Our next-door neighbor." Then she smiled. "Our big, bald neighbor, who's just about as attractive to me as a water-buffalo! Oh, Pete, how could you ever think I was having an affair with him? And I'm sorry I threw the picture at you—"

Pete Innes closed his eyes. His next-door neighbor was a big fellow named Phil Terrance. Phil Terrance had all his hair. He was a nice guy, happily married: Pete had never in his life said a word, or even thought a thought, about the possibility of an affair between Phil and Mary. *Never.* He knew damned well that Phil was the big, jovial type of guy that Mary found sexually unattractive. Besides, Mary wasn't the affairing kind: after twelve years he still had to employ the most delicate gambits or else meet a wall, and lately things had simply been *nicht.* Now, of course, Fate had struck a spark; the prognosis was good; maybe if he *had* suspected her of tramping, he would also have suspected that someone had done a fair job of velocitating her. But he didn't suspect anything of the sort, and he'd certainly never accused her of it.

It would all straighten out.

"What picture?" he asked cautiously.

"Oh!" She bent and kissed him. "You just want to pretend you've forgotten all about it! It's *sweet!* But don't. Let's admit honestly that it happened, and *then* forget it. Now—I'm sorry."

"I—I'm sorry too," he said.

Indirection was in order.

"Lucky you didn't hit me," he said.

"Well—" she grinned a little shamefacedly. "I really didn't throw it to hit. But it certainly wrecked the finish on the piano!"

Piano...

He *had* no piano. They'd been planning to buy one, for Pete Jr., but they hadn't yet.

It was too much.

"*What* piano?" he said, half-rising against pain. "We don't *have* one. Mary, what in blazes is going on? I don't remember you throwing any picture. I don't remember any argument. Phil Terrance is *not* bald. I've never accused you of fooling around with him. *What's going on?*"

The doctor said, "It's probably only temporary, Mr. Innes. Amnesia induced by shock."

Pete said patiently, "Doctor, I do not have amnesia. There is no blank spot in my memory, I remember everything right up to the moment of the crash."

"Well," said the doctor, smiling, "I wouldn't worry about it. Not exactly amnesia. You've just forgotten certain things, and gotten others a little mixed up."

Pete said, "Like hell I have."

"You wouldn't *know*, Mr. Innes. You wouldn't know if you had things mixed up. They would seem real to you, even if you were seeing pink dragons. But—well, after all—" he indicated the telephone dial—"you have described some other sort of telephone, for example. What can I say, Mr. Innes? I am fifty-seven years old. Since I was a child, telephone dials have been numbered in this manner. They're that way all over the United States, I believe, and very possibly all over the world."

"They're not."

The doctor sighed. "You're a little confused from shock, that's all. I wonder if you'd mind talking with one of our staff psychologists—"

"I would."

"I've already taken the liberty of calling him."

"I resent that," Pete said coldly.

"You shouldn't."

"I'm as sane as you are."

"I'm sure you are. But he will be able to do a more expert job of convincing you that the things you imagine to be true, and the things you imagine not to be true, are simply as they are and must be accepted as such—because you *are* sane."

Pete reached for the telephone. He let his fingers think for him. He could make no sense out of the number system anyway. He dialed his office—not the number, but the fingerhole-sequence.

A voice said, "Yes?"

Pete said, "Reilly, Forsythe and Sprague?"

Pause: "Sorry, buddy, wrong number."

Pete tried again, letting his fingers do the aiming. He dialed his mother's place in the Bronx:

"Mom?"

"Not that I know of," a man's voice said dryly.

Pete slammed the phone back on the carriage so hard the bell tinged. He lay back and closed his eyes.

Mary said—she was crying a little again—"Oh, Pete, darling..."

Pete compressed his lips.

"You'll be all right..."

"I *am* all right."

And the whole world's wrong.

"Of course you're all right," the psychologist said.

"You're not crazy."

"Don't use kid terms on me, doc," Pete said. "I took psych in college. I'm not afraid I'm 'crazy'. I can describe the condition you think I'm in just as resoundingly as you can. But I'm not *in* it."

"Then you didn't pay attention to a very important point in your psych course," the psychologist said. "It's the hardest thing in the world for even a trained person to apply to himself. You should know that a person who is illuded or hallucinated or subject to fantasies of any kind cannot be expected to—"

"So I'm—"

"—the validity of his beliefs—"

"—I'm not in a position to evaluate in terms of the real world," Pete said wearily. "*A priori* you're right, *ipso facto* I'm wrong."

"—needs outside assistance, don't you see?"

"*Caveat emptor.*"

The psychologist indicated the phone, as the doctor had done. "This is the real world. It exists. Evidence. As a lawyer you must appreciate evidence."

Pete Innes thought very deliberately and carefully for two, three, four, five minutes, while the psychologist waited, as psychologists do.

Then he said, "I suppose so. You *must* be right. I hope I sound sane. Phones have always been built that way. I have a piano. My wife threw a picture at me...what picture, honey?"

"The picture we took last summer of Pippy," Mary said.

Pete's lips tightened. "Pippy?"

"Our dog...our...don't you—remember?"

"I remember," he said. *Our dog Prince.*

"It should pass," said the psychologist. "Traumatic amnesia and fantasies. I would advise you strongly to see an analyst if it doesn't pass—you may not he able to recover all you've forgotten, but he should be able to—"

"Get out," Pete said.

"—and help you adjust." The psychologist rose. "I'll drop in later."

"Don't." Pete stiffened his body on the bed, wanting to leap and scream. "Get out, Mary."

"*Pete*—"

The psychologist said quietly, "Come, Mrs. Innes." He paused at the door. "You won't like this, Mr. Innes, but I'll naturally have to take precautions. In your state—"

"I understand," Pete said. "I accept. Have me watched. I don't care. I just don't want to talk any more."

The psychologist went out. Mary started after him, nose buried in tissue.

Pete felt two tears start down his own cheeks. Suddenly his eyes filled. He yearned. He was terrified and cold. His back teeth gritted together. "Stay, Mary," he said.

They were close on the bed for a few minutes, she lying on his broken ribs and hurting them, he hugging her fiercely so it would hurt more. Pain was real.

She was crying silently, eyes and nose running—the way she cried when she was really miserable, not just being feminine. After a while she got up and went over to the window. The venetian blinds were down and slanted shut. "Maybe some sun will cheer us up," she said.

Up went the blinds.

Pete knew he was in the New York Hospital. On the tenth floor. Looking out the window he could see the Chrysler building, downtown on 42nd Street, and beyond it, the Empire State building, with a slender spire atop it, like the Chrysler, instead of a never-used blimp mooring-mast and TV tower surmounting, good old Channel 4.

He screamed. It all came out. A large interne was in the door and at his side, looking wary, before he had exhausted the breath. Mary fainted.

Two months later they let him go home.

He objected at first to what was virtually imprisonment, but they said, "Citizens' Protection Law, you know."

He didn't know. And he was a lawyer.

The psychiatrists were good. They worked hard. He understood that their fees were paid by the Government—Citizens' Protection Law. Well, fine.

They made him socially acceptable. They showed him where and how he was wrong. They brought in proof by the armload—books, photographs, films, actual documents and records of his own life containing mention of three jobs he couldn't remember ever having held and numerous other interesting data, such as his former marriage to a girl named June Massey—

Once he had been engaged to a girl named Jane Mason.

They brought in the proof and talked to him about it.

They convinced him. They proved that the world he lived in was not the world he thought he knew. They proved that he was imagining. That he was occluded here, and was building dream-stuff of asynchronic data there. They proved that the Empire State building had always had a spire; that the U. N. had resolved the Korea conflict two months after hostilities had commenced; that Prokofieff—always a favorite of Pete's—had not died in 1953 but was still alive, though ailing; that television was not yet commercially perfected; that Shakespeare had written no *Hamlet*—

He quoted from the play. They were amazed. They said, My God, you should write!

There were times when he thought he'd go crazy. Other times he was certain that he already was. There were still other times when it was all a diabolic plot—Pete Innes vs. the World.

Heady conceit. For a madman.

Pete wasn't, of course...just a whim that delighted him, and concerned the psychiatrists, at one stage in his progress.

There had been no Shelley. He quoted Shelley.

Keats, they said.

He quoted Keats.

My God, you should write!

Still, they adjusted him. Physical facts talked.

But he never ceased to recall the world he'd imagined. It remained as clear in every "remembered" detail as this one, the real one, was in physical fact.

They adjusted him.

After all, he was an intelligent man. The theory of what had happened to him was clear: the actuality of it, once presented authoritatively to him, was equally as clear.

They adjusted him.

Now he knew what it must feel like to believe you are Napoleon. Long fall from the saddle.

Emotional acceptance came.

He believed.

Home was different. Well, he'd had to expect it to be.

Pippy was a cocker. *Prince had been a Collie.*

His house had five rooms. *Six.*

It was green. *Rust.*

There was a flower garden out back. *Vegetable garden.*

Pete Jr. was dark-haired. *Towhead.*

He wandered around, acquainting himself with his life. Some things were a lot different. There were shades of difference in others. Still others were identical, or so nearly so as to defy him.

His library...he went over it book by book, and came across his copy of Bertrand Russell's *HISTORY OF WESTERN PHILOSOPHY*—the one he'd taken to Russell when the philosopher was in New York on a lecture tour back in '45.

He sat there, hugged it, cradled it, loved it. It was a

remembered thing. Then he opened it.

He had *never* made marginal notes in that book.

But obviously he had.

Adjust.

That night Phil Terrance—Phil *Tarrant*—came over. Phil was bald. *Brown hair.* Pete found that he was evidently not quite so close to Phil as he'd been in his dream-world. He mentioned the golf games they had played together.

They hadn't.

Undressing for bed, Pete said, "Where do you suppose I *got* that world, honey? The dream one. It's so—complete."

Mary tossed aside her slip and swayed a little toward him, her dark eyes inviting, warm, soft.

"Forget your dream-world, Pete," she whispered. "This is real."

A much nicer, more open bit of enticing than he could remember Mary ever doing. He wondered what had triggered her, and thanked whatever it was. And she had a small mole on her stomach that he didn't remember.

They made the kind of vigorous, exhausting love they hadn't made in years…the years of his dream-world, at any rate. Now his still-mending ribs made it both a little difficult and delightful. They laughed at the necessary concessions, and had fun. This was a sweeter Mary than dream-Mary.

In the following days home from the office he spent a lot of time at the typewriter.

Doing?

He was writing a conspectus of the dream-world. He was looking for identities, similarities, antitheses in the real world, and noting them. He was pouring out his incredible fantasy before it should vanish in years.

He used a two-column system:

DREAM-WORLD/REAL WORLD
Jewish State: Israel/ Sholom
FDR died in 1945/ Same
Atomic power/ Not yet
Stalin dead /Alive
Lautrec a dwarf/ Normal

...and long pages of intense lawyer's analysis, drawing fine and significant distinctions, searching for historical bases for existing things and measuring them against "memories." The manuscript grew to several hundred pages. It could have gone on forever. It's perhaps easier to change a world than one's understanding of it.

Through this project, and the omniverous reading it involved, he became closer to the real world. His analyst—he had consulted one, and now visited him twice a week—was thoroughly in favor of it. He learned. At first it was often shocking. Then only exciting. At last enjoyable, nothing more.

Then it palled. Pete ceased writing. Six months had passed. He only read. More calmly, now. The need to discharge tension, and even a tiny lingering disbelief, had vanished.

There had been newspaper publicity, of course. At first just a little—then, as the sensational aspects of his case got out, a lot.

NEW YORK LAWYER HAS DREAM-WORLD
Sex, Science and Sociology on Another Earth

The *Times* did a dignified interview. *Life* gave him four pages, *Time* a column, *Scientific American* a squib.

Adjusted. And far happier than he'd ever been in his life.

Then they came and tore it all to shreds. Ripped it all to

pieces.

The dry voice on the phone said, "Mr. Innes, we've read about your case in the Scientific American."

"Yes?" said Pete, wondering what they were selling or buying—he'd already signed for several articles.

The voice hesitated. "I don't think this should be discussed over the phone. May we come and see you personally, at your convenience?"

"Who are you?"

"Forgive me—I—this is all rather extraordinary, Mr. Innes. Most extraordinary. My colleagues and I...allow me, I am Doctor Raymond van Husen. I—hello? Hello?"

Pete was staring across the room. At his bookcase. At the green-jacketed book entitled THE COMING CONQUEST OF THE ATOM, by Dr. Raymond van Husen, twice Nobel Prize winner, Van Husen, who in the dream-world had figured so importantly in the Manhattan Project and Oak Ridge.

"Yes, Doctor," he said, "I've heard of you. What can I do for you?"

"What is important," said van Husen, "is what *we* may already have done to *you*, and what we may be able to do about it."

Pete clutched the phone so hard his knuckles crackled in his ear, "*Done to me?*"

"I—well, actually, *we* didn't do it to you. If our theory is correct...Mr. Innes, I think we had better come and see you."

"Tonight," Pete said harshly, standing alone between wavering realities. "Tonight."

Van Husen's grey goatee bobbed as he said, "Parallel worlds, Mr. Innes. Coexisting worlds. We believe that you are on the wrong one, simply on the wrong one."

Pete was sprawled in the big chair by the fireplace.

Enrique Patino, physicist, sat on the piano bench. Doctor Hazel Burgess, an attractive woman of fifty or so, was on the couch, sitting beside Mary.

Pete said, "Simply on the wrong one."

Mary said, "Pete...Pete, what are they saying?"

"They're saying I'm on the wrong world. Don't listen."

Mary bit the back of her hand.

Pete took a belt at the straight Scotch he held. "So your machine got out of whack," he said. "Somebody forgot to tighten a bolt, you say. It flipped on its mounting, you say. Instead of shooting its tight beam at the pretty target, it went through the side of the building, across Flushing Meadows and walloped me before you got it under control. You say."

"Not *our* machine," said Hazel Burgess, "Our machine radiated at the real Peter Innes, you see."

"That's either stupid or insulting," Pete said. "I think it's both, in fact. *I'm* Peter Innes." He took another belt.

"I'm sorry," Hazel Burgess said. "I meant that our machine radiated at the Peter Innes who belongs on this Earth. The machine on your Earth radiated at you." She stopped and bit her lip. "I *am* sorry. When we read about you...it was quite a shock to finally realize what must have happened—"

Pete stood up quietly and, without a break in his motion, flung his glass into the fireplace with every ounce of his strength. Scotch hissed on the burning logs. "Damn you," he said. "Damn you, one and all."

"Two Earths," van Husen said, looking at the blue alcohol flames. "Almost identical. Two almost identical experiments, aligned on the time continuum. Two almost identical mishaps. A transposition of Peter Inneses. It must have happened that way. There is no other satisfactory explanation. Very likely identical results as well. The automobile accident—the hospitalization—the...m'm—" He looked at Mary, caught Pete's eyes full-blast and looked away, goatee bobbing.

"Don't be a damned old Dutchman, Raymond," Hazel Burgess said. "My God!"

"Please go," Pete whispered.

"Perhaps we can help you, Mr. Innes," Enrique Patino said softly. His wrinkled face turned toward Mary. The look he gave her was old and Latin. "If you wish us too, that is."

Pete swayed on his feet.

Mary got up and half-ran into his arms. "Peter, I *don't* understand—"

Mary? Was it *Mary?*

"Our experiment," said van Husen, "was an attempt to—"

"God damn your experiment. Get out and leave us alone!"

"But, Mr. Innes, we may be able to reverse the effect and return you—"

At last tears came. They rushed. Sometimes a man has to cry like a baby—when the world gets as fearsome as a baby's. Or when there isn't any world.

"He's been drinking since you called," Mary said, holding him fiercely.

The scientists left. And they left a card:

GRADEN RESEARCH INSTITUTE Flushing, N. Y. 27
F-E 395

He became a meaningless man. A wrongness. Earth beckoned. His own reality called: called in a giant voice that sounded his nature like a taut wire, now that he knew.

He couldn't doubt.

Men of van Husen's caliber didn't speak loosely. They'd all seemed pretty positive. And, of course, it explained everything.

Earth called.

At times he felt alone in the Universe. This Universe. Mary lay warm beside him, holding him with body and mouth, and this Universe was an icy microfilm between them that kept him alone.

He became aware of a force. A tension grew in him, became nearly intolerable. *He shouldn't be here.* Originating in the farthest slow galaxies, transmitted to nearer ones, gaining amplification with every angry star, transmitted again and again, strong with the hearts of novae and the rioting pulse of variables, a complex of forces seemed to be gathering— forces that were trying to push him out of this Universe: as if in some manner he were alien, a dissonance. Fact? Fancy? Had he added one atom too many to the sum of this Universe? If so, he might break the gears.

Pete Innes, Universe wrecker. Once or twice he watched red sunsets, wondering if this might be the night of his nova.

No longer alone.

Pressure.

This Universe was too much with him.

The little things closed in:

Eroica Napoleon Symphony

Democrats Jeffersons Trueorfalse? Trueorfalse?

This Universe hated him. Resisted him. Struck at him. Whether real or subjective, the sensation grew to a torment and a terror. It lashed at him from directions he could not defend against, or even define...

Unable to sleep, he would pace in darkness comparing his now-situation with his then-situation.

Earth *II*—he thought of this world that way—was preferable to him in many, many ways. He liked his job— he'd discovered that he was a partner in his firm—

But only one was important. The love and warmth at home...the new Mary...

He paced, and cringed, and thought, and cursed this Universe—and decided.

She cried when he said he must go back to his Earth.

He explained and explained. He wasn't her Pete. She wasn't his Mary. This wasn't his world. He could not remain here and stay sane.

"Oh, I love you," she wailed. "I won't let you do it."

"You'll get your own Pete back," he said heavily. "On my Earth he must be going through just about the same thing as I am here. The scientists will have contacted him. He'll be planning to return."

"I don't want any other Pete! I want *you!*"

That, he thought, *goes double*, and he went for a long and miserable walk. Nothing else to do.

He wondered if his counterpart, his *doppelganger*, was out walking too, feeling all the things he felt: the tearing need to get back to his own life-situation, but with specific regrets. Perhaps he'd even found in Mary *I* something comparable to the things Pete had found in Mary *II*. It was possible, in this intricate business of balances.

Also, he probably had a hating Universe on his back—

At any rate, there was no way out. Or rather, the *only* way was out.

And his double on Earth would be thinking the same thing, for whatever reasons. Identity. Or near identity.

He decided on one last week. Mary seemed reconciled. The reality of the situation, and its necessities, had at last become clear to her; or perhaps she had at last accepted it.

They spent that last week almost as lovers. They went out. Nightclubs, the theater. They had fun together. Their sexual encounters were spiced with a certain feeling of adventure, discovery. They had fallen in love for the second time, really, yet for the first time, really, and they made the most of it—

she perhaps unconsciously trying to hold him, he enjoying for the last time the woman Mary *I* was not.

The day they drove to the Graden Research Institute, he expected her to cry. But she didn't. She seemed to be thinking.

His tears?... They would come later, on lonely Earth. Best if she didn't know how much he cared.

The machine was bigger than he'd thought it would be. An enormous metal tube running off at a tangent from something very like a cyclotron. At the end of the tube was a metal ball about three feet in diameter, suspended on an equatorial axis. One round red glass eyelet peered out of the surface opposite the end of the tube—peered into a large, open-ended metal box, through which was strung an intricate webwork of wires.

"We wanted to send one atom—just one atom—into another dimension," Enrique Patino said. "So, I'm almost certain, did our counterparts on your Earth. But we sent our Peter Innes instead. And they sent you to us." He pointed at the two desks that stood back-to-back across the room. They were heaped high with papers. "We have computed. This has taught us interesting things. It would appear that one atom—and, believe me, our beam would scarcely touch more than one at a time—one atom will insist upon taking the organic whole of which it is a part with it on its trip between dimensions."

"I wonder if I crashed my car, then," Pete mused, "or his. Where's the thin red line? Molecules mixing, the vapor that is me mixed with the vapor that is the car—"

"His, we believe. It would be impossible to say for certain. It is our belief, however, that the phenomenon of transposition-of-the-whole applies only to living matter and all objects with the range, to certain degrees of distance and intensity, of its electromagnetic field—"

He talked on.

Pete looked at the machine.

Was another Pete Innes, on another Earth, looking at a machine right now?

He hoped so. And he hoped he was a good man. Mary *II* was a damned good woman.

"Where," he said, "do I get my ticket?"

"This way," called van Husen, from over by the metal ball. He'd been fussing with the round red eye.

"Shouldn't there be a fanfare?" Pete said sourly. "Reporters, cameras? Not that I'm in the mood."

"We—" Enrique Patino paused. "Understand, Mr. Innes, we would like to delay your departure, at least for a short while, and question you about your Earth. We might have questioned you before, but we had no wish to invade the privacy of your rather peculiar domestic situation. We wanted you to come to us. Now…well, I'm afraid we will have to be satisfied with the observations of *our* Peter Innes. Our recent work indicates that it may be very dangerous for you to remain here. Dangerous for you— and for us."

"I've felt it too," Pete said. "Out of tune. I don't jitter right."

"We made our decision this morning. We were preparing to invite you when you came of your own accord."

"And if you'd invited me, and I said no, you'd have called out the Marines."

Patino smiled an astonishingly young smile. "Oh, yes. Actually, we doubt that your introduction into our Universe will affect it for many millions of years. The disruption would have to proceed to fantastically high levels before it would make itself felt. But as scientists, we cannot take the chance of letting you stay any longer. Your influence is theoretically cubed every sixty-one point o-four-six-nine hours."

"I'm not the same as when I came," Pete said. "I've shed millions of molecules. I've incorporated others. I'm wearing different clothes."

"We must predict some sort of compensating mechanism, and hope we're right."

"Then maybe there's no problem…aside from the way I feel?"

Patino sighed. "Perhaps. But we know so *little* about such things…which accounts for the lack of fanfare. After you've gone we will dismantle the machine. The less anyone knows about this line of research, the better. Perhaps, right now, we are being foolish. But perhaps we should be terrified."

"Well," Pete said a little nervously. "When do we start?"

"Any time."

"When will *they* start?"

"When we do…or vice versa. I believe that identity on that level can be relied on: we seem to be expressions of Universal laws…"

"*Now*," snapped van Husen. "Let's not talk all day."

"If I could only take—a book or something," Pete said.

Patino shook his head. He took Pete by an arm and stood him in front of the globe. The red glass eye pointed at Pete's forehead.

Pete had said his good-byes to Mary. He didn't look at her now.

It happened very quickly.

Patino lifted a hand in farewell.

Van Husen pressed a button somewhere behind the metal ball.

Mary cried, "*Pete*—"

Machinery whined to instant high-pitch, drowning her cry.

Mary was in his arms.

The laboratory was about the same. So was the

machine. The round red eye lost its brilliancy. The whining stopped.

Everybody just stood and breathed.

Holding Mary, Pete looked around and smiled. He said, "I hardly recognize you without your beard, Dr. van Husen."

Then he said to Mary, "I'm glad you did that. I couldn't ask you to."

Now she was crying. "I—I thought that if *I* did, then *she* would…or maybe *she* thought of it first—"

"You'll like *my* Pete Junior," he said softly. "And the Mary who just left here will be a good mother to yours."

The scientists were coming alive. Ten minutes of gleaming-eyed inquiry followed, after which Pete said that he and Mary would like to get along.

Van Husen trailed them out into the corridor. The other two, an identical Patino and a somewhat less attractive Hazel Burgess, were busy dismantling the machine.

At the elevator door van Husen said, "You *will* cooperate with us, Mr. Innes?"

"With deepest gratitude," Pete said, and squeezed Mary's arm.

The elevator door opened. Inside was nothing but a steady blue light.

Van Husen said politely, "After you."

Pete said, after a moment, in a dead voice, "It's okay, darling—our elevators are different. Quite different."

Grimly he stepped off into empty blue space, five stories above the ground, Mary at his side. Van Husen followed.

They floated on blue light toward the ground floor.

Pete thought: *The only thing to do when you're going down a one-way street to nowhere is pull over to the side: I'll pull over here, I guess: I won't tell Mary: I'll keep quiet, and the others will too.*

His eyes opened wide: *How many others?*

Down.

The ground floor.

We'll just have to see if it's millions of years or tomorrow. Maybe this one won't hate me.

It wasn't tomorrow. And it didn't.

He was content.

The Slizzers

The main trouble is that you'd never suspect anything was wrong; you'd enjoy associating with slizzers, *so long as you didn't know...*

THEY'RE all around us. I'll call them the *slizzers,* because they *sliz* people. Lord only knows how long they've been on Earth, and how many of them there are...

They're all around us, living with us. We are hardly ever aware of their existence, because they can *make* themselves look like us, and do most of the time; and if they can look like us, there's really no need for them to think like us, is there? People think and behave in so many cockeyed ways, anyhow. Whenever a *slizzer* fumbles a little in his impersonation of a human being, and comes up with a puzzling response, I suppose we just shrug and think. *He could use a good psychiatrist.*

The Slizzers

by JEROME BIXBY

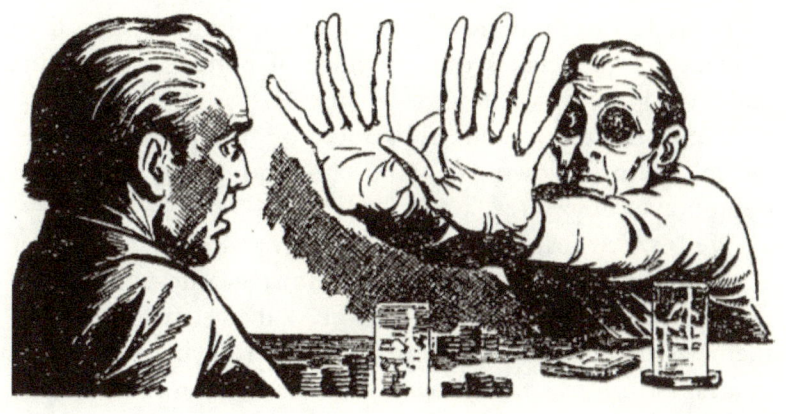

So...you might be one. Or your best friend, or your wife or husband, or that nice lady next door.

They aren't killers, or rampaging monsters; quite the contrary. They need us, something like the way we'd need maple trees if it came to the point where maple syrup was our only food. That's why we're in no comic-book danger of being destroyed, any more than maple trees would be, in the circumstances I just mentioned—or are, as things go. In a sense, we're rather well-treated and helped along a bit...the way we care for maple trees.

But, sometimes a man here and there will be careless, or ignorant, or greedy...and a maple tree will be hurt...

Think about that the next time someone is real nice to you. He may be a *slizzer*...and a careless one...

How long do we live?

Right. About sixty, seventy years.

You probably don't think much about that, because that's just the way things are. That's life. And what the hell, the doctors are increasing our lifespan every day with new drugs and things, aren't they?

Sure.

But perhaps we'd live to be about a *thousand*, if the *slizzers* left us alone.

Ever stop to think how little we know about why we live? ...what it is that takes our structure of bones and coldcuts and gives it the function we call "life?"

Some mysterious life-substance or force the doctors haven't pinned down yet, you say—and that's as good a definition as any.

Well, we're maple trees to the *slizzers*, and that life-stuff is the sap we supply them. They do it mostly when we're feeling good—feeling really terrific. It's easier to tap us that way, and there's more to be had. (Maybe that's what makes so-called manic-depressives...they attract *slizzers* when they feel tip-top; the *slizzers* feed; and *floo-o-m*...depressive.)

Like I say, think about all this next time someone treats you really ginger-peachy, and makes you feel all warm inside.

So see how long that feeling lasts...and who is hanging around you at the time. Experiment. See if it doesn't happen again and again with the same people, and if you don't usually end up wondering where in hell your nice warm feeling went off to...

I FOUND out about the *slizzers* when I went up to Joe Arnold's apartment last Friday night.

Joe opened the door and let me in. He flashed me his big junior-exec's grin and said, "Sit, Jerry. I'll mix you a gin and tonic. The others'll be along in awhile and we can get the action started."

I sat down in my usual chair, Joe had already fixed up the table...green felt top, ashtrays, coasters, cards, chips. I said, "If Mel—that's his name, isn't it, the new guy? —if he starts calling wild games again when it comes his deal, I'll walk out. I don't like 'em. I looked at the drink Joe was mixing, "More gin."

Joe crimped half a lime into the glass. "He won't call any crazy stuff tonight. I told him that if he did, we wouldn't invite him back. He nearly ruined the whole session, didn't he?"

I nodded and took the drink. Joe mixes them right—just the way I like them. They make me feel good inside. "How about a little blackjack while we're waiting?"

"Sure, They're late, anyway."

I got first ace, and dealt. We traded a few chips back and forth nothing exciting—and on the ninth deal Joe got blackjack.

He shuffled, buried a trey, and gave me an ace-down, duck-up.

"Hit me," I said contentedly.

Joe gave me another ace.

"Mama!...hit me again."

A four.

"Son," I told him, "you're in for a royal beating. Again."

A deuce.

Joe winced.

I turned up my hole ace and said, "Give me a sixth, you poor son. I can't lose."

A nine.

"Nineteen in six," I crowed. I counted up my bets: five dollars. "You owe me fifteen bucks!"

Then I looked up at him.

I'll repeat myself. You know that hot flush of pure delight, of high triumph, even of mild avarice that possesses you from tingling scalp to tingling toe when you've pulled off a doozy? If you play cards, you've been there. If you don't play cards, just think back to the last time someone complimented the pants off you, or the last time you clinched a big deal, or the last time a sweet kid you'd been hot after said, "Yes."

That's the feeling I mean...the feeling I had.

And Joe Arnold was eating it

I knew it, somehow, the moment I saw his eyes and hands. His eyes weren't Joe Arnold's blue eyes any longer. They were wet balls of shining black that took up half his face, and they looked hungry. His arms were straight out in front of him; his hands were splayed tensely about a foot from my face. The fingers were thinner and much longer than I could recall Joe's being, and they just *looked* like antennae or electrodes or something, stretched wide-open that way and quivering, and I just *knew* that they were picking up and draining off into Joe's body all the elation, the excitement, the warmth that I felt.

I looked at him and wondered why I couldn't scream or move a muscle.

"Guess I made, a boo-boo," he said. He blinked his big black globes of eyes. "No harm done, though."

His head had thinned down, just like his fingers, and now came to a peak on top.

He had practically no shoulders. He smiled at me, and I saw long black hair growing on the insides of his lips.

What are you? I screamed at him to myself.

Joe licked his hairy lips and folded those long inhuman hands in front of him.

"It hurts like hell," he said in a not-human voice, "to be *slizzing* you and then have you chill off on me that way, Jerry. But it's my own fault, I guess."

THE doorbell rang—two soft tones. Joe got up and let in the other members of our Friday night poker group. I tried to move and couldn't.

Fred raised his eyebrows when he saw Joe's face and hands. "Jerry isn't here yet? Relaxing a little?" Then he saw me sitting there and whistled. "Oh, you slipped up, eh?"

Joe nodded. "You were late, and I was hungry, so I thought I'd go ahead and take my share. I gave him a big kick, and he really poured it out...radiated like all hell. I took it in so fast that I *fluhped* and lost my plasmic control."

"We might as well eat now, then," Ray said, "before we get down to playing cards." He sat down across the table, his eyes—now suddenly enormous and black—eagerly on me. "I hate like hell waiting until you deal him a big pot—"

"*No*," Joe said sharply, "Too much at one time, and he'd wonder what hit him. We'll do it just like always...one of us at a time, and only a little at a time. Get him when he rakes in the loot. They never miss it when they feel like that."

"He's right," Fred said. "Take it easy, Ray." He went over to the sideboard and began mixing drinks.

Joe looked down at me with his black end-of-eggplant eyes.

"Now to fix things," he said.

...I blinked and shook my head. "You owe me fifteen bucks!" I said.

"Lord," Joe wailed, "did this gonif just take me!"

Ray groaned sympathetically from the chair across the table, where he'd been watching the slaughter. "And how!"

Joe pushed fifteen blue chips at me. I began stacking them. "Well, that's life," I grinned. Then I shook my head again. "It's the damnedest thing..."

"What?" Fred asked. He'd been over at the sideboard mixing drinks for the gang while I'd taken Joe over the bumps. Now he brought the tray over and shoved a tall one into Joe's hand. "Don't cry, Joe. What's the damnedest thing, Jerry?"

"You know...that funny feeling that you've been some place before—the same place, the same people, saying the same things—but you can't remember where the hell or when, for the life of you. Had it just a moment ago, when I told Joe he owed me fifteen bucks. What do they call it again?"

"*Deja vu*," said Allen, who's sort of the scholarly type. "Means 'seen before' in French, I think. Or something like that."

"That's right," I said. "*Deja vu*...it's the damnedest funniest feeling. I guess people have it all the time, don't they?"

"Yes," Allen said.

Then he paused. "People do."

"Wonder what causes it?"

Joe's blue eyes were twinkling. "Dunno. The psychologists have an explanation for it, but it's probably wrong."

"Wrong why?" Knowing Joe, I expected a gag. I got it.

"Well," Joe said. "Let me make up a theory. H'm...hoo, hah...well, it's like *this*: there are monsters all around us, see, but we don't know they're monsters except that every once in a while one of them slips up in his disguise and shows himself for what he really is. But this doesn't bother our monsters. They simply reach into our minds and twiddle around and—zoop!—you're right back where you were before the slip was—"

"Very funny," Fred said boredly. "Maybe losing fifteen bucks made you lose a little sense, Joe. You wouldn't want to lose more than fifteen bucks, would you? You need some caution in the games we play, no? So cut the nonsense and let's run 'em."

Ray licked his lips. "Yeah. Let's play, huh, fellows?"

Ray's always eager to get started.

WE PLAYED until 3:00 a.m. I won forty-six dollars. (I usually do win...I guess over a period of six months or so I'm about five hundred bucks ahead of the game. Which is why I like to play over at Joe's, even though I *am* always so damned tired when I leave. Guess I'm not as young as I was.)

Sometimes I wonder why the odds go my way, right down the line. I almost never lose. But, then, it *must* be an honest game...and if they're willing to go on losing to "Lucky" Bixby, I'm perfectly willing to go on winning.

After all, can you think of any reason that makes any sense for someone to rig a game week after week to let you *win*?

Frederik Boles, Author's Agent
2200 Fifth Avenue
New York, N. Y.
Oct. 20

Dear Fred,

Well, here's a new story. I've cleared it with Joe...he says it's okay to use his name; you know his sense of humor. I've used your name, too, but you can change it if you want to, being the shy retiring sort you are.

Frankly, I'm a little dubious about the yarn. It's the result of last Friday's poker-session...I actually did have the *deja vu* sensation, as you'll recall. On the way home I stopped in to pick up a chaser, feeling tired as all hell (like I always do— these long grinds are too much for me, I guess, just like the guy in the story) and the idea came to me to slap the old "we are fodder" angle into the thing as it happened and write it up.

But it's still an old plot. And one angle is left unexplained: how is the narrator able to know all about the *slizzers* and write about them after Joe gives him the *deja vu* treatment?

Well, maybe the readers won't mind. I've gotten away with bigger holes than that. Try it on Bob Lowndes...I still owe him on that advance. It's up his alley, hope-a-hope.

Jerry

Oct. 22, 1952
Jerome Bixby
862 Union Street
Brooklyn, N. Y.

Dear Jerry,

I don't go for "The Slizzers," It just ain't convincing. As you say, it's an old idea...and besides—again as you say— how does the narrator know what happened?

The manuscript looks good in my wastebasket. Forget about it.

> Sympathies,
> Fred

Oct. 23, 1952

Frederik Boles, Author's Agent
2200 Fifth Avenue
New York, N. Y.

Dear Wet Blanket (and aren't you a little old for that?)

Respectfully nuts to you. After proper browbeating I think I'll try the yarn on Lowndes...it's no masterpiece, but I think it's got a chance; he likes an off trail bit, now and then. I made a carbon, natch, so your ditching of the original comes to naught.

Funny thing...every time I read it over I get the doggonedest *deja vu* feeling. Real dynamic thing...almost lifts my hair. Hope it does the same for the readers, them as can read. Maybe Joe didn't quite do the job of making me forget what happened that night, ha, ha. Say! ...maybe that could explain the *narrator's* remembering what happened...or maybe—hey! A *real* idea!

Remember Joe's kidding us about monsters? —remember, you got a little sore because he was holding up the game, you money-hungry son? I think I'll rewrite the ending to include that! ...which oughta take care of the narrator's remembering: Joe can be sort of a dopey *slizzer*, a blat-mouth, and his screwy theory (which is *true* in the story, or will be when I write it in—say, isn't this involved!) can trigger our hero's memory just a bit, shake the block a mite, undiddle the synapses, Etc…and then I'll have you, platinum-butt, step in to head Joe off, under pretense of a poker itch.

You know, it's wonderful the way there are hot story ideas in plain old everyday things! S'long…gonna revise.

Jerry

Oct. 23, 1952
Mr. Robert W. Lowndes
COLUMBIA PUBLICATIONS, Inc.
241 Church Street,
New York 13, New York

MASTER,
Herewith a story, "The Slizzers," which Fred and I don't quite see eye to eye on. He thinks it stinks on ice. I'm sure you will disagree to the tune of nice money.

J.

ENCL: THE SLIZZERS

1952 OCT 24 AM 9 06
NB168 PD=NEW YORK NY 63 11OB=
JEROME BIXBY=
862 UNION ST APT 6H=
BKLYN=
JERRY=
URGE STRONGLY THAT YOU DON'T TRY TO SELL SLIZZERS STOP IT'S JUST NO DAMN GOOD STOP YOU'VE GOT YOUR REPUTATION TO THINK OF STOP WHY LOUSE UP YOUR GOOD NAME WITH A LEMON. AT THIS LATE DATE STOP KILL IT STOP I'VE TALKED IT OVER WITH JOE AND HE ISN'T FEELING HUMOROUS ANY

MORE STOP PREFERS NOT TO HAVE NAME
USED STOP REPEAT KILL THE THING FOR YOUR
OWN GOOD=
FRED

1952 OCT 24 AM 11 14
KL300 PD=NEW YORK NY 12 604B=
JEROME BIXBY=
862 UNION ST APT 6H=
BKLYN=
SON=
LIKE SLIZZERS STOP PREPOSTEROUS BUT CUTE
STOP DISAGREE WITH FRED TO THE TUNE OF
NICE MONEY BUT NICE MONEY STAYS IN MY
POCKET STOP YOU NOW OWE ME ONLY FIFTY
DOLLARS OF ADVANCE AUGUST 16 STOP DO I
HEAR A SCREAM POOR BOY=
BOB

Oct. 24, 1952
Frederik Boles, Author's Agent
2200 Fifth Avenue
New York, N. Y.

Dear Fred,

Your telegram came too late, and besides, the hell with it.
Sent the yarn to Bob yesterday (groceries and rent wait for no
man, you know) and he bought it, like the sensitive and
discerning editor he is. What're you and Joe getting your tails
in an uproar about? It's only a gag, so relax. Joe'll change his
mind when he sees his name in print.

Would like to have included another angle, by the way: if
the narrator's amnesia-job *had* been botched, wouldn't the
slizzers decide pretty damn quick that he was a menace to

them and get rid of him? Think I'll send Bob a line or two to stick on the end...you know, the old incompleted sentence deal...just as if, while the narrator was finishing the story, the *slizzers* came in and...

The Monsters

"Ya wanna know how to get along in this world, buster? Then I'll tell
ya. Be tough! Ya gotta be tough and don't let nobody soft-talk ya into
lettin' ya guard down. All they're tryin' to do is find an opening to lay
ya flat with a haymaker. I'm tellin' ya! Everybody's got a angle, see!
Ya take a guy what offers ya a piece o' cake and ya say thanks kindly
and bite into it and wham! Rocks in the cake! Busted molars! Big
laugh on ya! A guy comes along and says here's a juicy deal for ya, kid.
So ya sign up. Then the guy says, Oh, I forgot to tell ya—juicy for me,
not you. Then he walks away leavin' ya widout ya pants! I tell ya,
buster, everybody's out promotin' for a quiet buck and if ya give 'em an
inch they'll take everything but the sweatband out o' ya hat. Hey, kid!
Wait up!
"Cripes! Why ain't I more popular wit' my friends?"

THEY were sitting around in Packy's Bar-and-Grill on
Third Avenue, waiting for the historic television broadcast to
begin. The 26" colorvision at the end of the bar had been
blaring out spot announcements about it for the past couple
of hours. A big man in shirtsleeves came in and took a stool
halfway up the bar, signaling for a beer, just as the next spot
came up.

"Attention, please," the young man on the screen said.
"In exactly eight minutes—at two o'clock, Eastern Standard
Time—we will bring you a special news broadcast from
United Nations Headquarters in New York, where U. N.
Secretary Jacob Stern will officially greet the leader of the
aliens whose spaceship landed this morning on our planet!
We repeat: at two o'clock, on all networks, you will see
Secretary Stern officially greet the aliens who landed on Earth
this morning! We urge you to stay tuned for this historic
broadcast... See the first aliens ever to land on Earth! The
Interplanetary Age has begun, ladies and gentlemen! Beings

from another star—" here the announcer glanced down at a paper he held out of sight in his hand—"from the star," he went on carefully, "Beeta Centowri. They have traveled twelve years to reach our solar system—on a routine exploratory expedition, they say—and upon detecting signs of intelligent life on Earth, they proceeded directly here, landing at 7:32 this morning on a Kansas wheat field a few miles outside Wichita. Their skills enabled them to learn the English language almost in minutes, and U. N. authorities were swiftly persuaded that they meant no harm. I repeat, ladies and gentlemen: *the authorities are assured of the aliens' peaceful intentions*! There is *no* cause for alarm. The aliens are greatly advanced, and friendly. So stay tuned to this station to see the first alien ever to set foot on this planet! And now—"

A box of breakfast food walked onto the screen and began to sing.

"*I'm* not assured," the stocky man in the gray suit said sullenly. "How in hell can they tell in a few hours whether they're planning to attack us or not! I think we ought've thrown an aitch at them the minute they landed!" He stared up at the box of breakfast food, now dancing with a spoon and a pitcher of cream. "Wonder what the alien will say, anyway? Maybe it can't talk. Maybe it's a damn monster— can only grunt. *Gr-r-run-n-nk...oink, oink, oink*!" He laughed. He was a little drunk. His eyes were heavy-lidded and feathered with red. His girlfriend, sitting beside him, was the only one in the bar who laughed.

Packy, behind the bar, said, "Listen, Joe...anything that can build a rocketship and come across space from some other star can do a lot more than grunt. It's no dope, whatever it is!"

Joe said, "All right—I still don't like it. I don't like it, by Christ! I think maybe they come to take over Earth. To conquer us. Why else? They're just a bunch of damn monsters from some other star."

"Why else should they come?" The big man in shirtsleeves set down his beer, eyes amused. "You asked why else?

311

Curiosity's why. What's the universe all about? Same reason we've been trying to get out into space."

Joe turned on his stool to stare at the big man. "Who's been filling your ears with that crap? Only reason we ever tried to build a rocketship was to get the damn Russkies before they got us! That's the only reason, brother. I was in the army, and I know. And you can bet your life that these things from—whatever that star was—do things the same way. Costs a lotta scratch to build a rocketship. They build one and come all this way, you can bet there's a reason. Bet your life!"

"If you're right," the old man in the front booth said, "maybe our lives *will* be on the board."

Joe turned to look at him. "Go ahead, kid about it," he said nastily. "Wait'll you see the goddam monsters staring at you out of that screen there."

The old man said calmly, "Who's kidding?"

"Just wait and see," Joe muttered. "Monsters. You'll see!"

The breakfast food had vanished from the screen. A man in a white suit was leading a small orchestra. A customer got up and walked toward the rear.

The big man said, "Ever since nineteen-fifty or so, we've been trying to get out into space. Almost fifteen years. Back then maybe we *were* thinking mostly about military uses for rockets. But everything is pretty peaceful now. The U. N. is in pretty good shape." He signaled Packy for another beer. "And we're *still* trying to get out into space. Except now we're all pulling together. Why, do you suppose?"

Joe said nastily, "You know damn good and well that someday we'll have to lick the Russkies. Sure we're working together—swiping each other's ideas right and left. This is just a breather. One of these days we get the old knife in the—"

The big man said, "That's your opinion, chum. *I* think

we've got a lot of nice, quiet peace ahead. I think we've finally got a little sense about running a world. Things are working out just fine—"

"All you one-worlders spout the same line," Joe grunted. "Lotta crap. You got a finger in a U. N. pie, maybe, putting up buildings or something?"

The big man turned slowly to face Joe and said, "You mind your manners, mister, or I'll shove your head right through that mirror." He glanced at Packy. "Hey, Packy— where's that beer?"

Packy drew one, slid it down to the big man and said to Joe, "Now take it easy. They don't *have* to come here to Earth to conquer us, do they? Like he says, maybe it's just curiosity. Take a look around the universe, see what cooks. Man, this is the first time we ever met another intelligent race. It's gonna mean big things! I don't even *know* what it'll mean! Don't it mean something to you? Has it always gotta be war, war, war, Joe?"

Joe snarled like a lap-dog. "Just wait, like *I* said. Wait'll you see some goddam monster staring out at you. Then see if you think it's going to cuddle up next to us! Goddam monster from another star!"

"You keep calling them monsters," the big man said, looking up. "How do you know they're monsters? I haven't heard any descriptions."

"That's just why," Joe said, looking at him sourly in the mirror. "Why haven't we been told what they look like? Why keep it a secret, tarzan, if there's nothing to hide?"

Packy laughed nervously. "They ain't keeping it a secret, Joe. Jesus, they only landed this morning. The U. N. clamped down on the whole thing while they were making sure everything was okay. Now they're satisfied the aliens are leveling. If they're satisfied, why shouldn't you be?"

The big man said, from right behind Joe, "You call me just

one more name, Joe Shmoe, and I'll make a monster out of *you*! I'll turn you inside out and throw you away, piece by piece." He shoved Joe's shoulder, so that Joe spilled part of his drink in his lap. "Catch?" He shoved again, almost gently. "Catch?"

Joe didn't look around. He just stared down at the bar, his face ugly. His girlfriend glared at the big man as he went back to his stool and sat down. The big man sipped at his beer. The orchestra on the screen kept playing, the man in the white suit making jiggling motions with his baton and left hand.

Joe said, in a grating voice, "They'll be monsters anyway! Wait and see. Goddam ugly, slimy monsters. Come here to take over Earth!" He belched and shoved his drink away from him. The glass slid on the wet wood to the inside rim of the bar, teetered, fell over behind and broke. Joe began to curse in a thick monotone.

Packy said, "Joe, cut it out, will you?"

He paused. Joe had almost fallen off his stool.

"Ah, he's drunk as a bat," the old man in the booth said. "He's plain stupid to begin with, and now he's loaded to boot."

The big man said, "So because they're aliens, they're monsters, huh, Joe?"

Joe didn't look at him.

"And because they're monsters, they're going to wipe us all out and take over Earth," the big man pursued.

Joe's girlfriend said, "Why don't you all leave him alone?" She helped steady Joe on the stool.

The big man grinned. "Who should leave who alone, miss?"

The colorvision screen went gray-white for a moment, then lit up with a scene showing big white steps crowded with people. The picture suddenly pulled off to one side, stretching into rainbow lines. Packy grunted and turned the horizontal control. It was a very old set.

The picture came clear. It was a close-up of Secretary Stern of the United Nations. Behind him could be seen the shapes of other men in formal dress, and behind them was what looked like half the U. N. Army drawn up around the front of the building: tanks; soldiers with rifles and machine -guns; and beyond them, a crowd, filling the streets. A band struck up the United Nations anthem, "One World Forever."

"See?" Joe muttered. "Why all them guns, if the aliens are—"

"To protect them from halfwits like you," Packy said testily. "Keep quiet."

Reception wasn't very good, and Stern didn't speak very loudly. He never had been much of an orator. The watchers in Packy's Bar-and-Grill could make out only parts of his speech. His voice was trembling with some emotion.

"—this historic day—when the Almighty has in His wisdom seen fit to reveal to us the existence of another intel...in His universe...welcome—welcome to Earth, travelers of—"

Joe mistook the emotion in Stern's voice to be fear. "See," he began. "*He's* got sense enough to be scared—"

Packy said, "Will you *shut up!*"

The camera had turned on the alien.

There was silence in the bar-and-grill. Packy stared. The big man's eyes widened. The old man adjusted his glasses and peered. Joe's girlfriend gawped. Joe began to turn white.

The alien's face—two eyes, friendly-looking; a nose, straight-bridged with patrician nostrils; a mouth, firm and smiling; a strong column of neck; bronze skin overall—stared back at them. Below the face were broad shoulders that filled a gold-colored metallic cloak. The alien's arms were folded beneath the cloak. He stood motionless, a head taller than those around him.

"Human," the big man in shirtsleeves breathed.

"I am happy," the alien began, in a deep, pleasant voice, "to represent my people on this wonderful occasion—"

"Perfect," Packy gasped. "He speaks perfect!"

"—extend our heartfelt wishes for mutual understanding."

To one side of the alien, on the steps, could be seen a group of men rapidly speaking into microphones; translators, giving spot breakdowns in a dozen languages to waiting millions.

"I want to assure the peoples of Earth—"

Secretary Stern was smiling. General Alan Russell, who had taken charge of contacting and communicating with the aliens and finally transporting them, was smiling at his side.

"—that we of Beta Centauri –"

Joe glared up at General Russell. "Fine army man," he spat. "Disgrace to your stars!"

"—have no intention whatever of trying to invade your Earth." Suddenly the alien managed to be both smiling—and serious. "I thought I'd best be blunt about that. I could have put it more delicately, of course. Let me repeat: we have *no* intention of trying to harm you people of Earth or colonize your planet."

Cheering from the crowd started here and there; a moment later it thundered in the streets, drowning the alien out. The soldiers with the guns had them at dress salute. The cameras left the alien to move over the cheering crowd, then swung back to his handsome face. Finally he was able to continue.

"Your defense officials have already determined this to their own satisfaction. During our stay, we will happily submit to interrogation and psychometric—"

"Should have blasted that goddam ship to hellangone," Joe snarled. "Fine army man you are!"

"We are a peaceful people. We have colonized three

planets of our own solar system, and have absolutely no need or desire for further expansion. Believe what I say, people of Earth, and rejoice in our presence here as we rejoice in yours!" The alien was smiling broadly now. "We had no dream of such good fortune: to find a race so similar to our own! This is the beginning of a great age! Already we see many ways in which we may help you, and you us. We will work closely with your U. N. during our stay. When we leave, plans will have been made for mutual benefits that will endure down the centuries! And now...your United Nations Secretary, Mr. Stern, has more to say to you."

The alien saluted, hand to heart, and vanished as the cameras went back to Stern, who began paraphrasing the alien's promises of good faith. He was skillfully calm, reassuring.

But he did not manage to reassure Joe. Joe was suddenly on his feet.

"SMOOTH-TALKING lying sons a bitches," he bawled. "They *are* here to kill us! They *are*! I don't care *what* they look like. I'm telling you! We ought've killed them! When I was in the army—"

The big man got up, his face flushed. He strode down the bar and put his face within inches of Joe's. "When you were in the army you should've got killed instead of some other boys I can think of. Why don't you go crawl in a garbage pail where your kind of mind belongs? Way back in the dark ages, where anything different is *bad*. That kind of talk has started a hundred wars, you dumb bastard. Anything you can't understand, you hate. You were all ready to fight monsters. You were sure they were different from us, so they were bad! That's damnfool enough. But now the aliens turn out to be just like us, and you *still* can't give up your precious little hare-brained idea, can you! They're *still* bad, aren't they?—you Goddamned fool!"

Joe was retreating down the length of the bar, his face loose. The big man followed him.

"Maybe that's what took the U. N. so long to set in," the big man said savagely. "Too many people hang on to their precious ideas, even when they see them turning out wrong all over the place! They'll twist and squirm and fight like devils, just so nobody can prove *them* wrong. Well, listen, chump—those aliens are getting a chance to prove they're telling the truth—in *spite* of morons like you who judge somebody by shape or color or collar-size and let their crazy ideas get so important to them they'll blow up half of creation to prove they're right! Maybe the aliens *are* going to jump us. If they are, we'll know soon enough. And we won't be any worse off than we are right now when we believe what they say. I don't think we *are* bad off. I feel pretty damned good about the whole thing—"

Snarling, Joe turned and grabbed up a bottle and threw it at the big man with all his might. Joe's girl screamed. The big man ducked and hit Joe in the mouth. Joe slid to the floor.

The big man rubbed his knuckles. "I shouldn't've done that," he said. He let out a breath. "He's drunk. But he got me mad." He looked down at Joe. "Few years ago, down south, I could've been lynched for hitting a white man. This guy is the kind who always carried the rope."

"Don't worry about it," Packy said. He bent over Joe. "I think his jaw is broken," he said. "I'd better call an ambulance."

He went to the video booth. Joe's girl was crying. When Packy came back, Secretary Stern was concluding the ceremony. Smiling, he held out his hand right to the alien.

The camera moved back to show the alien up to his waist. The alien's gold-colored cloak stirred. His arms came out.

He took the Secretary's right hand in one of his right hands. With his other right hand, he shook hands with General Russell. One of his left hands still held the microphone he had used. His other left hand was hooked by its thumb into the belt of the jaunty tunic he wore.

"Well," the big man said finally. "Well, I'll be damned." He spread his own two hands. "I don't think we're any worse off now than we were half a minute ago, do you? I feel about the same. Don't you? What the hell. He's the same guy."

Packy was blinking. "How alien can you get? I sure could use four of them in *my* racket. Sure, he's the same guy. Makes you think."

Joe's girl said, "I kind of liked his smile."

Joe groaned on the floor.

If you've enjoyed this book, you will not want to miss these terrific titles…

ARMCHAIR SCI-FI, HORROR DOUBLE NOVELS, $12.95 each

D-1 **THE GALAXY RAIDERS** by William P. McGivern
SPACE STATION #1 by Frank Belknap Long

D-2 **THE PROGRAMMED PEOPLE** by Jack Sharkey
SLAVES OF THE CRYSTAL BRAIN by William Carter Sawtelle

D-3 **YOU'RE ALL ALONE** by Fritz Leiber
THE LIQUID MAN by Bernard C. Gilford

D-4 **CITADEL OF THE STAR LORDS** by Edmund Hamilton
VOYAGE TO ETERNITY by Milton Lesser

D-5 **IRON MEN OF VENUS** by Don Wilcox
THE MAN WITH ABSOLUTE MOTION by Noel Loomis

D-6 **WHO SOWS THE WIND…** by Rog Phillips
THE PUZZLE PLANET by Robert A. W. Lowndes

D-7 **PLANET OF DREAD** by Murray Leinster
TWICE UPON A TIME by Charles L. Fontenay

D-8 **THE TERROR OUT OF SPACE** by Dwight V. Swain
QUEST OF THE GOLDEN APE by Ivar Jorgensen and Adam Chase

D-9 **SECRET OF MARRACOTT DEEP** by Henry Slesar
PAWN OF THE BLACK FLEET by Mark Clifton.

D-10 **BEYOND THE RINGS OF SATURN** by Robert Moore Williams
A MAN OBSESSED by Alan E. Nourse

ARMCHAIR SCIENCE FICTION CLASSICS, $12.95 each

C-1 **THE GREEN MAN**
by Harold M. Sherman

C-2 **A TRACE OF MEMORY**
By Keith Laumer

ARMCHAIR MASTERS OF SCIENCE FICTION SERIES, $16.95 each

M-1 **MASTERS OF SCIENCE FICTION, Vol. One**
Bryce Walton—"Dark of the Moon" and other tales

M-2 **MASTERS OF SCIENCE FICTION, Vol. Two**
Jerome Bixby: "One Way Street" and other tales